The MIRACLE

After

The STORM

Qiana Rae

Beautiflaw Books

Beautiflaw Books

Cover Design:
SelfPubBookCovers.com/RLSather

ISBN: 978-1-7372696-6-3

Hey, my Sisters and Brothers in Christ!

I first want to say that I love you all so much! You all have shown me so much love and support over the years, and I'm so honored that you all can see God's anointing on my life. I'm here to tell you, it's not easy trying to always be obedient to God and do His will, so don't be too hard on yourself. Just make sure that you're doing your best, and that you're better than you were yesterday! Every day is a new opportunity that God has blessed you with.

With that being said, 2023 has been a very tumultuous year for me. I've been trying for so long to get this book completed, and every time that I would get into a good, solid routine, with my spirit on point, I would become distracted, and my spirit would become irritated. For all of you who don't know, if my spirit doesn't feel right, I refuse to write because I want to give you all the best of what God has given me.

God spoke loud and clear to me at the beginning of this year, telling me that this would be the best year of my life. Of course, it made me feel real good. I felt very confident about what was heading my way. The strange thing was, right after that, Satan began attacking me and my family like crazy, and it continued from January all the way to this point. I had to ask God, "I thought you said this would be the best year of my life, but it has so far been the worst that I can ever remember experiencing."

It has NEVER taken me so long to finish a book! Satan had been attacking me back to back this entire year, as I'm sure many of you have also experienced because we're all going through something. Once God would help me come out of one battle victoriously, shortly after, another would come. I still trusted God's word, *but some days were harder than others.*

He made me look at things from a different perspective. Just because things in your life aren't going great right now, doesn't mean the end result isn't going to be great. I actually found that throughout all of the struggles and pain that I went through this year, I got through each and every one of them victoriously, and in the midst of it all, I was delivered from many things that had me in bondage for many, many years. I consider that being the best thing that has happened in my life because those strongholds held me back from so many things, causing me sometimes to not be able to live the life that God wants me to live. I was once unable to feel that peace and joy that He has already instilled in each and every one of us, so, yes, God has done some great things in my life this year. It may have been uncomfortable and painful sometimes, but it was necessary, and those storms have definitely become miracles.

I also finally came to the conclusion that Satan did not want me to finish this book and release it. He obviously saw something that I could not see, but obviously, he couldn't see that no matter what, I wasn't going to give up. He just gave me that much more motivation and ammunition to finish my book because I felt like there were a whole lot of people in the world who needed to read it, be blessed by it, and be lead to God's kingdom. I will complete my assignment by any means necessary, no matter how hard Satan tries to destroy me and everything around me. He tried it, but God wasn't having it!

I say all of this just to say, no matter how much you're going through, remember that God is always with you, and He is in control. Keep your eyes on the things of Heaven and not of this world, and don't allow the traumas around you to become the traumas within you. Satan will try his best to continuously knock you down, but always remember, you have an assignment to complete and it's not over until God says it's over. Satan does not have the power to stop you from completing God's will for your life unless you give him that power. You may feel weak at times, and want to give up, but lean on God for His strength. If I made it through everything that has been thrown at me this year, then you can, too! You can do ALL things through Christ who strengthens you!

God bless you all, I love you, and God does, too! Keep praying!

Peace, love, and many blessings!

~Qiana Rae

Follow me on:
Facebook: Author Qiana Rae
Instagram: @iamqianarae
TikTok: @qianarae

Table of Contents

Ezekiel

Chapter One

"Thou shalt not commit adultery!" I said, with great intensity and very little inflection in my voice as I began my first Sunday morning sermon in my new church building. My congregation had grown so much that I had to move to a larger building, which, by the way, I wasn't complaining about.

My congregation and I had just experienced a very powerful praise and worship service, which had only been an appetizer to prepare them for what was yet to come. There was absolutely nothing better than following praise and worship with a spirit-filled message being the main course.

There was a sudden, uncomfortable silence in the sanctuary that I had never experienced during any of my sermons. The type of sermon that I had chosen, or I should say, was led to preach on this particular Sunday was very different from what my congregation and I were all used to. After not receiving the inviting reaction that I was hoping for from my congregation after my opening statement, I couldn't help but to be concerned that treading unfamiliar territory might not have been such a good idea after all.

Before today, I probably would've been considered the "traditional pastor" who preached traditional sermons that involved reading a few scriptures that I had thoroughly studied throughout the prior week so that I could teach the biblical meaning of those scriptures without stepping on anyone's toes when Sunday morning arrived. That's exactly what I had planned on doing this particular Sunday. I had worked hard attempting to prepare my sermon, which had already proven to be different for me. Normally, I never felt like I had to work hard to prepare my sermons because everything I had ever preached on was always felt deep within my spirit, therefore, it always seemed to come natural to me. The past week, while I prepared my sermon, no matter how much I prayed, I never felt the confidence that I would normally feel, knowing that I was doing what God wanted me to do. Saturday evening came, and I still felt quite a bit of uncertainty in my spirit, but I still planned to preach my original sermon titled, "When you feel like giving up."

As I did every Saturday evening, I went alone to my church building, going before God, praying over the sermon that I would deliver the next morning, and praying that my members would fully receive the message that He had given me to deliver. After I'd prayed for about an hour, I stood up, and felt a sudden uneasiness come over me. My stomach began to turn, and I felt dizzy, so I took a seat in one of the pews in the front row. As I sat there, I prayed for God to deliver me from whatever was trying to attack me. I then realized as I continued to pray that nothing was attacking me at all. What I was feeling was God's disapproval of my Sunday morning message. The message that he had actually given me, I had disapproved of, and refused to preach. Imagine that. I disapproved of something God had given me, telling me exactly what to do, but even as Christians, we do that each and every day.

God had made it very clear about what He wanted me to do, and before leaving the church that evening, I'd still made up in my own mind that I would have to sleep on it. After still refusing to listen to God, on my way home, I listened and sang along to William McDowell's "All I Want is You", attempting to convince God that I still needed and wanted Him even though I had just rejected Him. I had denied Him on three separate occasions by ignoring His insistence of what His people needed to hear, just as Peter had rejected Jesus on three occasions.

> [54] "So they arrested him and led him to the high priest's home. And Peter followed at a distance. [55] The guards lit a fire in the middle of the courtyard and sat around it, and Peter joined them there. [56] A servant girl noticed him in the firelight and began staring at him. Finally, she said, "This man was one of Jesus' followers!"
> [57] But Peter denied it. "Woman," he said, "I don't even know him!"
> [58] After a while someone else looked at him and said, "You must be one of them!"
> "No, man, I'm not!" Peter retorted.
> [59] About an hour later someone else insisted, "This must be one of them, because he is a Galilean, too."
> [60] But Peter said, "Man, I don't know what you are talking about." And immediately, while
> he was still speaking, the rooster crowed.
> [61] At that moment the Lord turned and looked at Peter. Suddenly, the Lord's words
> flashed through Peter's mind: "Before the rooster crows tomorrow morning, you will deny three times that you even know me." [62] And Peter left the courtyard, weeping bitterly."
> – Luke 22:54-62 NLT

I felt ashamed that I had been allowing myself to be conformed to the world, which was one of the things that the Bible clearly stated that we were never to do.

> [2] "Do not conform to the pattern of this world, but be transformed by the renewing of your mind. Then you will be able to test and approve what God's will is – his good,

pleasing and perfect will." – Romans 12:2 NIV

Thankfully, God never gives up on His children, and as soon as the song ended, my repentance came, just as Peter's did as he wept after his final denial of Jesus. I heard God clearer than I'd ever heard him before. It was as if He was sitting in the passenger seat right beside me.

He asked me, "Son, have I ever steered you wrong?"

As I thought about all of the things that He had brought me through, I knew that He hadn't, but God obviously didn't feel as though even that would be enough to really make me understand and convince me to listen to what He was trying to tell me. He then revealed exactly why He was giving me that particular word to preach. When He revealed the reason, He didn't allow me to be broken. If I hadn't had the relationship with Him in which I did, during the revelation that God had just presented to me, I probably would've felt as if my heart had shattered into a million pieces, and my entire life was over. Instead, I felt Him in my spirit, and He carried me along. After that very intimate moment with God, I was completely stripped of the arrogance that I'd just shown by acting as if I knew more than Him, and that my plan for Sunday morning was better than His. God will definitely show us what we need to see exactly when we need to see it, and after what He had just exposed to me, I not only knew that I needed to listen to God, but I also knew that I had to stop trying to please people, and instead, make pleasing God my top priority. At that moment, I didn't care how many members I might've lost due to the sermon that I was going to preach the next morning, or any of the future sermons that God would give me to preach. I needed to talk about things that were destroying the importance of trust, integrity, faith, and family values all over the world. Things that God had gifted pastors like myself to speak on to help bring his children to salvation.

Over the years, seeing other pastors preach, and then having the privilege of teaching God's word myself, I had learned that people preferred when pastors were "gentle" with them. They didn't like to hear their pastors preach about wickedness and sin, especially if they were involved in any of it. All they wanted to hear about were all the wonderful, glorious things that God had in store for them, and that was great, but even though I had avoided it, I knew it was also necessary to sometimes speak on the things that may have made some people feel uncomfortable. Those things consisted of what God expected of us in order to please Him. Yes, He had already prepared great things for us, but in order for them to be released, we first had to be prepared for them. Some people would ask, "But doesn't God love us without conditions?" I would simply answer, "Of course, He does, and as a father loves his children, He still expects them to be obedient. It doesn't mean that if we are disobedient that He won't still love us and bless us, but it should always be our desire to do His will.

I always believed that talking about God's expectations made people feel so uncomfortable because they knew that living according to what He expected of us involved eliminating things, habits, and sometimes people from our lives. Most people already know the things they should, and need to rid their lives of, but as long as they don't hear their pastor talk about it, or if they don't feel convicted by it, the necessity to get rid of it seems to be non-existent.

Although I knew for years that God had been trying to tell me that it was time to explore new territory and change some of my methods of teaching His word, I let fear keep me from doing it. I feared losing all of my members because I may have stepped on their toes one too many times. I also feared no longer being able to do what I loved, and what God had gifted me to do because no one would want to listen. Losing my credibility was one of the biggest fears that I had. The thing that I had failed to realize was that because my gift was, in fact, a gift from God, as long as I was using it in the way that He had intended for me to, I never had to worry about it failing me.

16 "A man's gift maketh room for him, and bringeth him before great men." – Proverbs 18: 16 KJV

When we're hardheaded and don't listen to God, He will always find a way to force us out of our comfort zone and do what it is that we need to do in order to fulfill our purpose in Him, and that was exactly what He had done to me that Saturday night. As soon as I got home that evening after having the most unforgettable, supernatural experience that I'd ever had with God, I prepared my new sermon on adultery, and there I stood before my congregation on Sunday morning, not knowing what to expect.

From the pulpit, as I looked out into the silent crowd that had almost completely depleted me of my confidence, I suddenly felt God move through my spirit. It was like a jolt of electricity traveling through my body, and I already knew what that meant.

"Keep going," I heard God say.

I continued, following God's direction.

"That's the seventh commandment of the ten commandments, but no matter what number commandment it's listed as in the Bible, it doesn't carry any less of importance than the others. We can find this particular commandment of God in the book of Exodus 20:14. I don't think it can get any clearer than what it states word for word."

All I could hear were the pages of Bibles shuffling as my sisters and brothers searched for the scripture I'd just cited.

Still, with some doubt, I continued, "Then again, it doesn't seem to be so clear by looking at the statistics that show such a large number of people who commit adultery. As a matter of fact, it is one of the most common causes of divorce. Adultery is mentioned in the King James Bible forty times, and it's included in thirty-three verses. Let's talk a little bit about the consequences of adultery in the Bible. Turn to Leviticus 20:10."

After I gave them a moment to find the scripture, I read, "If a man commits adultery with another man's wife – with the wife of his neighbor – both the adulterer and the adulteress are to be put to death."

I paused for a moment, allowing the Word of God to marinate in each and every one of their souls.

"What a severe punishment! That's what all of you are thinking, right?"

There was absolutely no acknowledgement of what I'd said. No "Amen", and not a nod of even one head. Not even from my wife, Stormie, who sat in the front row, filing her nails, not looking up, even for one second. Nevertheless, I went on with the task at hand.

"Under the Old Covenant Law, adultery was punishable by death! Just imagine what the world would be like if we still lived under those laws. We are all sinners! We've all done some wrong, but guess what? But God!!!! He is merciful! He is a forgiving God, and He has forgiven all of us!" I said, speaking forcefully into the mic with the strength and power God had given me.

It felt like the entire sanctuary shook. It was as if God himself had demanded his well-deserved respect right at that moment. The next thing I knew, everyone was up on their feet, some clapping, giving him all the praise and honor, and the others with their hands in the air, receiving everything God had to offer. That was, everyone except for Stormie. She remained in her seat, looking unaffected, but did manage to clap a few times. I knew that Stormie's antics and behavior were a trick of the devil to deter me from being fully focused on what I was there to do, so I chose to ignore it, and remain focused on the rest of my members.

After God had gotten almost everyone's full attention, and they took their seats, I looked over my congregation, and then realized that they had a different look in their eyes than they'd initially had before God had shaken the building and their spirits. The looks in their eyes now told me that they were ready and anxious to eat everything that I was about to serve. At that moment, my heart was filled with the confidence of God, and I became even more anxious to fill them up with the meal that God had helped me to prepare. Even under all of the unforeseen circumstances that had been comprised of God's revelation that I'd experienced the night before, I smiled inside, and continued my sermon with the zeal of God.

"Amen! I'm glad you all decided to join me," I said, with a little laughter to lighten the tone in the room a bit more.

"To continue where we left off, even though God has forgiven us, there are still consequences of our sin. Although adultery is no longer punishable by death, it still leads to spiritual death without repentance and change of behavior. God didn't send Jesus to condemn us for our sins, but to save us from them."

During my message, I felt total engagement from the crowd. I didn't just read scriptures to them and tell them what they meant. I taught from the Spirit. I was certain that someone in the room was able to relate in one way or another to the affair between David and Bathsheba in the second book of Samuel. They were also reminded of God's grace and mercy in the eighth chapter of John when the woman who was caught committing adultery was brought before Jesus by the Pharisees, but instead of allowing her to be stoned to death, He reminded the Pharisees that they were all sinners, and told the woman to leave her life of sin.

As I concluded, I came from behind the podium and candidly spoke to my family in Christ. As Stormie looked down at her cellphone, I cleared my throat, and when I seemed to have her attention, along with everyone else's, I began.

"Brothers and Sisters, we must understand that we are all sinners. Adultery is serious, but so is all sin. God doesn't look at one sin being worse than the other. With that being said, whatever sin you've committed, no matter how big or small, or even how many times you've committed them, it's not too late to change. If you woke up this morning, you were given another opportunity to get it right. Don't stay in the darkness because you feel as though you're no longer worthy to kneel before Him. Jesus laid down his life on the Cross of Calvary for us. Your sin is not a reason to turn away from God, my sister. God is bigger than your sins, my brother. He sacrificed His only begotten son so that we could have another chance! Your sin is a reason to grow closer to Him so that He can fill you up, making you more like Him. Again, God has already forgiven you, but I must stress, you still must repent, and you must forgive yourself."

After the final words of my sermon, I felt a sense of completeness come over me. I had progressed to a new level. It took for God to stop being "gentle" with me, and to be a little more direct. He had broken me, but He didn't break me in a way to hurt me. He had broken me in a way to make me better, and He did it with love. That's the kind of pastor He wanted me to be to the rest of his children. The things that I knew I would have to eventually face didn't even matter in that moment. All that mattered to me was that I was now able, without the fear of failure, to preach what God's children needed to hear, and not what they wanted to hear.

As I walked back to the podium to close my Bible and to pray the Benediction, I heard the sound of one person clapping. That might've been discouraging to some, but I'd accepted the fact that what I did wasn't really about pleasing other people. It was about being obedient and pleasing to God, and that would be my main focus for all of my sermons in the future. After I shut my Bible and closed my eyes to pray the Benediction, I suddenly heard the thunderous sound of every single person that God had entrusted me with to teach his Word to, clapping so loudly that it filled the room to the point that I could've sworn that the joyful noise was coming from the heavens above. When I opened my eyes, every member was on their feet, clapping, smiling, and praising the Lord. Even my beautiful wife, the first lady, Stormie. At that moment, my heart was filled with so much love that all I could do was throw my hands in the air and thank God for ordering my steps and doing His will in my life, no matter how uncomfortable it made me.

After the Benediction, I stepped out of the pulpit and walked towards Stormie, who stood alone in the nave of the church, as the other members socialized with one another. She wasn't the typical first lady, and I would be the first to admit that. She wasn't going to smile in everyone's face and tell them that she loved them, and she definitely wasn't going to try to pray for them. She was just . . . Stormie. Her personality wasn't very inviting, and she was definitely someone who had to grow on people.

Stormie didn't lead the Women's Ministry, teach Bible study, or participate in any community events that the other pastor's wives did. As much as I would've loved for her to do those things, that just wasn't in her nature, and I didn't know if it would ever be. Other women in the ministry volunteered to help out with a number of things, which was nice, but it placed a dim light on Stormie. I could tell that the members tolerated her because she was my wife and the first lady, but I also knew that they didn't respect her as the first lady should've been respected. They never disrespected her in any way, so I really couldn't be upset. I always wished that she would someday just come into her role and be at the spiritual level where I believed God wanted her. I prayed every day that God would do whatever His will was for her life. I had been praying that same prayer for years because I knew that I couldn't change her. Only God could do that.

As soon as I approached her, she stood directly in front of me. We were eye to eye as she stood to be over six feet tall with her five-inch Red Bottoms on.

She then squinted her almond-shaped eyes and said, "What was that, Zeke? You know you sounded crazy up there, right?"

My forehead wrinkled as I raised my eyebrows in a state of confusion. I wasn't confused by her reaction because that was Stormie. I was actually shocked that she had paid attention to any of it. There had been a time that I would ask her random questions about my sermons during Sunday dinner, and by her responses, I would be able to tell that she hadn't really listened to anything I'd said. It would hurt, so I stopped doing that to myself. I stopped asking her anything about the services, and she never said anything about them. She just did what she felt she was supposed to do, and that was sit in the front row and be pretty, but obviously this particular Sunday's sermon caught her attention and caused her to feel a certain type of way. I like to call that conviction.

"I did exactly what God told me to do," I calmly replied.

"That is not what God told you to do. You always make these decisions without talking to me, but at the same time want me to play the perfect first lady role. If that's the case, I should have some type of say so when it comes to your sermons, but that's not what you really want at all. That's exactly why you want to always put God in it, saying that He told you to do something. You figure, how can I argue with it if it came from God, right?" she said, folding her arms, eagerly waiting for me to respond.

Once she saw that I didn't even have the desire to entertain her ridiculous notions, she continued.

"I know your game, Zeke! You've been doing it for years to control me! You want to have all of the control, so I just sit back and let you. You'll end up kicking yourself one of these days."

Even through all of the harsh words Stormie was spewing out, I could still see her beauty. I stared at her, still seeing the young college girl I'd met and fallen in love with. She was perfect in my eyes, no matter what she said, or what she did. Anyone who knew me knew I loved my wife unconditionally, and I could've never imagined myself being with anyone else. Even though it was probably hard for other people to see it, or understand it, there was definitely a reason that God had put us together. Unbeknownst to her, I knew why she was so upset with my sermon. It was because of what God had revealed to me the night before. It had struck a nerve with her, and the conversation that we needed to have, I knew she definitely wasn't ready to have it.

I gently unfolded her arms, and held both of her hands in front of me as I said, "Storm, I'm not about to do this with you right now. This is a moment of breakthrough for me, and I just wish my wife could recognize that and celebrate it with me."

Stormie didn't say another word. I turned towards the crowd, still firmly holding one of her hands as she stood next to me, and I proudly watched the members of my congregation as they smiled, shook hands, and hugged one another. Suddenly, over all of the laughter and multiple conversations being held, I heard a loud, familiar voice getting closer and closer.

"Pastor Zeke, that was a great message you preached on today! You were all up in somebody's business! Probably a whole lot of somebodies! About time you got real with some of these so-called Christians! You know, the men and women of this younger generation just don't take marriage seriously. Well, I guess I can say, those of your generation, because you and the first lady are still pretty young. They just run around doing whatever with whoever, whenever they please!"

Ms. Geraldine Simmons was one of the first members who had joined my church when Stormie and I had first opened it almost five years ago. The five years prior to opening Path of Righteousness Worship Center, I had been Associate Pastor of Fountain of Renewal Christian Center, which was the church where my mom, dad, and I had been lifelong members. The pastor of that church, Pastor Drew Ervin, had taken me under his wing and helped change my life, for which I would be forever grateful to him.

Ms. Simmons was always very blunt when she spoke, and most times I would have to abruptly, but politely as possible, bring her conversation to an end, or at least tone it down quite a bit. There was no telling what would've come out of her mouth if I had just let her continue. I was sure that one day she would end up offending someone and I didn't need any fights in the house of the Lord.

"Sister Simmons, I understand the passion you have about people doing the right thing, and we want all of our members to have that same type of passion, so just continue to pray that we all continue to seek God for guidance, isn't that right Stormie?" I said, smiling at Stormie, as she looked extremely irritable.

"That's right," she said, without much credibility.

I always tried to respect Sister Simmon's opinions, but also attempted to stay in my lane at the same time.

She continued, "But Pastor, you know I'm right. These people just want to have a big, extravagant wedding, and when that's over, it's just all over! Just like Bathsheba! I'm sure she probably had one of those big ole weddings, but you see how easy it was for her to cheat with King David!"

Ms. Simmons suddenly looked as though a lightbulb went off in her head, and I had a really strong feeling that I didn't want to hear what she was about to say next, and I was right.

"You know what, Pastor? Now that I think about it, Bathsheba probably cheated on her husband because David was a king, which of course meant more money. Her husband was nothing but a soldier. She was just like these gold-digging skanks out here, going wherever the money is!"

Looking around, hoping no one had overheard her, I said, "Sister Simmons, we can assume a lot of things, but keep in mind what I just spoke about. Let him who is without sin cast the first stone," I said, as I gave her a hug and told her I'd see her next Sunday. I never wanted to seem as if I was being rude to her. I was thirty-five, and she was practically old enough to be my mother.

Just as Sister Simmons was about to continue our conversation, even after I had attempted to end it, she saw one of her friends walking by.

"Ok, Pastor. You always do this to me. I'm not about to let you talk my head off today! I'll see you next Sunday!" she said, as she quickly walked towards the other woman, who was also around her age.

"Delores, wait a minute! I have a bone to pick with you!" she yelled.

I sighed and then smiled as I looked over at Stormie. She remained quiet as she shook her head with a disgruntled look on her face.

"Is everything ok?" I asked Stormie.

She then did that thing that I had noticed her doing more and more often. She smiled through her apparent anger so that anyone who wasn't close enough to hear her would think that we were having a pleasant conversation, when, in fact, it would be the complete opposite.

"Why do you even entertain that ignorance? She comes up here every Sunday, talking all loud and ghetto, condemning other people! You want me to seem all perfect, but you let your members run around acting however they want to act, and saying whatever they want to say! And why did you choose to just put me on the spot like that? You never ask for my thoughts any other time!" she whispered harshly.

Quickly putting the conversation on pause before any of the other members walked over in the middle of their pastor and first lady having an argument, I smiled and said, "I never ask you because you never have a desire to be involved, but for some reason I thought you might've had an opinion on the topic. I guess you didn't, and I apologize, so Stormie, we'll talk about this later. This isn't the time nor place."

"There's nothing else to talk about. I've told you how I feel, so you just need to do something about it."

The tension in the air was so thick it could've been cut with a knife. As I greeted several of the other members on their way out, they expressed how much they had enjoyed the message and thought our new building was absolutely beautiful. I tried to remain positive, and not let what was going on with me and Stormie dim my light. She eventually left my side and disappeared. No one seemed to notice that there was definitely some tension between us, and it was probably only because Stormie had never been very personable anyway. To them, it seemed to be like any other Sunday, or whenever else they would happen to be in her presence. It was a shame, but that had been a glimpse of what my life with my wife consisted of. I was married to a woman who I completely adored, but the adoration I had for her was never reciprocated. I dealt with it because I loved her as Christ loved the church, and I would continue to love her for the rest of my life. Christ had sacrificial love for His church, and I vowed to maintain that same type of love for Stormie.

[25] "Husbands, love your wives, just as Christ loved the church and gave himself up for her [26] to make her holy, cleansing her by the washing with water through the word, [27] and to present her to himself as a radiant church, without stain or wrinkle or any other blemish, but holy and blameless. [28] In

this same way, husbands out to love their wives as their own bodies. He who loves his wife loves himself."
– Ephesians 5:25-28 NIV

I wasn't sure if Stormie was still in love with me, but I wasn't willing to give up on her. She had grown up differently than I had. She didn't grow up around a lot of love like I did, and because she had gone through so much, she never could bring herself to believe in God, which I wasn't proud of, and definitely didn't go around advertising. Even with that being the case after seventeen years of being together, I still believed that all of the praying that I had done for her over the years was not in vain, and I continued to have faith that God had a plan. I truly believed that one day she would come around. Once my mother found out that Stormie didn't believe in God, she refused to even be a part of my congregation. She continued to be a member of Pastor Ervin's church, and it hurt badly because I loved my mom so much, but I had to respect her decision.

After what God had revealed to me about my wife the previous night, I still wasn't ready to give up on my marriage. I wanted to give Stormie a chance to admit what she had done without me having to pull it out of her. As a believer, I'd already forgiven her, but as a non-believer, I didn't know if Stormie would even feel the need to apologize and even be forgiven. My marriage was nothing like what I had seen growing up in the house with my mom and dad, and I realized all marriages were different, but mine was beyond different, and I felt as though I was just winging it day by day, waiting for a miracle.

Ezra & Faith

Chapter Two

As a young boy growing up, I remember my mom and dad being a couple that everyone admired. My mom, Mrs. Faith Whitfield, always had a strong personality and never held back how she felt about anything, especially if she was passionate about it. My grandparents had named her appropriately because her faith was just as strong, if not stronger than, her personality. My dad, Mr. Ezra Whitfield, on the other hand, was meek and gentle, which was where he got his name, The Gentle Giant. He was a big guy who stood at six feet, five inches tall and weighed around two hundred fifty pounds, whereas my mom was only five foot two and probably didn't even weigh a hundred pounds. My dad loved everyone, especially my mom, and when I saw them together, I knew that someday I wanted to be able to love my wife just as much as he loved her. They complemented each other perfectly. When my mom would get riled up about something, my dad always knew how to calm her down, and when my dad didn't get riled up enough for my mom's liking, she was sure to step in and make it known that she may have been small and petite, but she was down for whatever!

I had heard the story at least a million times about how they had met their freshman year of high school. She didn't know anyone since she had just moved from North Carolina to New York. My grandfather was in the Army, so he was frequently relocated to different Army bases and my mom didn't get a chance to make many friends. The ones she did make, she ended up having to eventually leave and make new ones all over again.

My mom had been dealing with the girls at school picking on her because she didn't fit in. She had lived in so many different places over the years that she didn't have a specific thing about her that made her fit in with any group. She had basically developed her own persona based on what she had seen and learned while traveling the world with her mom and dad. Who she had become was very different from anyone else she would come to meet. The way she wore her hair, to her style of dress, and her overall forward and aggressive personality was different, and hard for most girls her age to relate to. She was her own person and never desired to be like anyone else, which would rub the other girls the wrong way. They felt as if she thought she was better than everyone, but she was just comfortable with being who she was, even though she was thought of as being different. She thought of it more so as being unique, and she was proud of that and everything she'd had the opportunity to experience over the years.

After about a month into her freshman year, the other girls at school had decided that they couldn't take anymore of Faith Ellison, so three of them approached her outside during lunch hour while she minded her business. They laughed at her, pointed their fingers in her face, and made derogatory comments about her and her family. She never backed down, and they continued to ridicule her, hoping that she would break. That was one thing they didn't know about her. She was not the type to be easily broken, and from as early as I could remember, I could never recall my mom ever allowing anything or anyone to break her.

As the crowd around them grew larger and larger, my mom became more and more amped up, having and showing absolutely no fear of the other girls. One of the girls became frustrated that they were unable to intimidate her, so she spat in my mom's face. That was the absolute wrong thing to do, and to this day my mom would say that was one of the worst forms of disrespect that existed. As small as my mother was, she picked up the girl who was probably double her size and body slammed her right there in front of the school. She wasn't done yet. As the other two girls ran, my mom jumped on top of the girl she'd body slammed and cocked back her fist. As soon as she was about to release a power-packed punch, she felt herself being lifted up off of the ground. Not knowing what was going on, she began wildly swinging her arms and legs.

"Calm down!" the boy who had just scooped her up with only one arm, said.

That boy who had just possibly saved someone's life was my dad, and from that day on, he had been the only one who was able to calm my mom down. They had never met each other before that day, but after that, they became very good friends. In fact, he became my mom's only friend for the two years that she and her family lived in New York. They were separated her junior year when her dad was relocated to Arizona. Although my mom never stayed in touch with any of her other friends each time she moved, she made it a priority to keep in touch with her "Gentle Giant". She always said that she knew they would eventually reconnect and get married, and that's what they did.

A few months after graduating from high school in Arizona, my mom made plans to visit my dad back in New York. She bought a round-trip plane ticket with the money she had saved from working part-time as a waitress, but only a one-way ticket was needed because against both of their parent's wishes, they went to the city court and got married. They didn't have much money, but they didn't care. They had love, and they were willing to sacrifice whatever they had to in order to be together. I knew that was where I got my determination to make things in my marriage work, even when things didn't seem to be going so well. I had enough love for Stormie to get past anything that was meant to break us, and I knew that she had enough love for me to do the same. The difference was, I believed that all the time, but sometimes I felt as though Stormie wasn't quite sure. We had already been through so much, and I knew that God hadn't brought us as far as we'd come to leave us.

⁶ "And I am certain that God, who began the good work within you, will continue his work until it is finally finished on the day when Christ Jesus returns." – Philippians 1:6 NLT

My mom and dad were determined to prove to everyone that the decision they had made was best for them. They rented a small, less than unacceptable apartment in one of the worst neighborhoods in Brooklyn, which was all they could afford with the money they had both saved while working their high-school jobs. My dad continued to work the part-time job that he'd previously been working as a car wash attendant, but he convinced the manager to let him move up to full-time so that he could take care of my mom. In the meantime, my mom waitressed at a restaurant not far from where they lived so that she was able to walk if necessary. She and my dad only had one car, which was the car my dad's parents had given him on his seventeenth birthday. My dad worked quite a distance away, so he had to use it on most occasions.

Even though they both had jobs, and didn't splurge on unnecessary things, they still struggled. My mom would bring home food from the restaurant so they didn't have to spend money to eat most days, but they knew that they couldn't continue to live that way. They were fresh out of high school and didn't have any real experience to do anything that would pay the type of money that they needed to live comfortably. One thing they refused to do was call and ask their parents for help, but they both grew up in church and began to pray together. They had faith that God would continue to provide and they never allowed their faith to waver. One day, unexpectedly, their prayers were finally answered.

"Hey, Ezra. Go pull the red BMW in," my dad's boss said before throwing him the keys to the brand-new BMW that was parked outside of the car wash bay.

As he walked outside with the keys in hand, he heard someone come out of the lobby. He turned around and saw a Black man in his mid-forties walking towards him.

"Hey, young man. Do you have the keys to my car?"

"Which one is yours?" my dad asked.

"The red BMW."

"Yes, Sir."

"I left something inside. I need to get it out before you take it."

My dad, very cautious when it came to his job and handling other people's property with care, looked around, confused about what he should do. He didn't know if the car really belonged to the man, but didn't want to seem rude in case it had been.

At that very moment, his boss came outside and said, "Ezra, is there a problem?"

My dad, relieved that his boss had shown up, said, "No, Sir. This gentleman just wanted to get something out of his car before we took it in."

"Ok, that's fine. Then bring it on back, and no joy-riding this time," he said, jokingly.

The owner of the car laughed and said, "Joyriding huh?"

Thinking that the man might've taken his boss seriously, my dad quickly defended himself, saying, "No, Sir. He was just joking. I would never . . ."

The man interrupted my dad, laughing. "I know he wasn't serious, but I like how serious you take your job. If you can treat a job like this as serious as you do, I can just imagine what an asset you would be doing something that really made a difference. I can tell you're young, too. How old are you? Nineteen? Twenty?"

"Eighteen, Sir."

"Great parents, too. I can tell they taught you good manners."

"Thank you, Sir," my dad said, smiling.

He opened the car door for the man so he could reach in to grab his wallet that he'd left inside.

"Ezra is your name, right?"

"Yes, Sir."

"I'm going to be honest with you because I feel so ashamed of myself, and feel that I owe you an apology. I left my wallet in here on purpose. I always do when I take my car to a carwash, but when I saw a young Black man walking towards my car, I felt the need to remove it."

The smile my dad had from the previous compliments that the man had given him completely diminished. He didn't know what to say in response to what he'd just said.

"I judged you by looking at you, knowing absolutely nothing about you, and that was wrong. We are judged every day by people who don't look like us. It's even worse when we're judged by people who do. I'm sorry, young man."

The man extended his hand out to my dad, looking remorseful, and my dad knew that he was being sincere.

My dad then smiled, shook the man's hand, and said, "I appreciate your honesty, but there was no need to apologize. I would've never even known why you did what you did if you hadn't told me."

"I know, but I would've known, and more importantly, God would've known."

"Ezra, enough small talk. Bring the car in. We're getting backed up!" my dad's boss yelled out the door.

"Yes, Sir," he turned around and yelled back.

"I guess I better let you do your job. Nice to meet you, Ezra. You're going to do great things."

"Nice to meet you, too, Sir."

As my dad quickly jumped in the car, the man said, "Mr. Myles Elliott.

"Thank you, Mr. Elliott."

"No need to thank me. Thank you!"

My dad nodded and carefully drove Mr. Elliott's car into the empty bay. When he got out of the car, he looked back to see that the man had walked back into the building where the lobby was located. He shook his head and smiled, not knowing what to really think of the encounter he'd just had. It had been a pleasant one, and he was appreciative for men like Mr. Elliott who were good role-models and set a good example for young Black men like himself. He didn't know anything about Mr. Elliott, but what he did know was that he had encouraged and inspired him to always be the best man that he could possibly be.

My dad didn't get to wash Mr. Elliott's car that day. His boss assigned him to detail the inside of another car that had just been brought in. Everyone knew that my dad was very particular and paid close attention to detail when it came to detailing, so his boss put him in charge of that whenever possible. My dad was actually looking forward to seeing Mr. Elliott again, but by the time he'd finished detailing the other car, he had already left.

That evening, when my dad's shift had ended, as he walked to the back of the parking lot where the employees were required to park their personal vehicles, he heard the sound of a horn. He then saw the red BMW parked a few spaces down from his rusted out blue Chevy.

"Ezra!" Mr. Elliott yelled out.

My dad walked over to the BMW as Mr. Elliott got out.

"I was afraid that I'd missed you, but if I had, I would've been back to try to catch you tomorrow," Mr. Elliott said.

Becoming worried, my dad said, "Is everything ok? Is something wrong with your car?"

Smiling, Mr. Elliott said, "No. It's perfect. I'm sure it would've been beyond perfect if you would've washed it, but it'll do."

My dad stood there silent, waiting on Mr. Elliott to tell him why he needed to see him so badly.

"I just wanted to give you this," Mr. Elliott said, as he handed my dad a card.

It was his business card. Mr. Elliott was the Fire Chief of the New York City Fire Department.

"I see great potential in you, Ezra. You really impressed me today with your entire demeanor. Upon meeting you, I could immediately tell that you have great work-ethic, and you genuinely care about people. I would love for you to come onboard as one of the city's newest firefighters."

Speechless, my dad just stared at Mr. Elliott.

"Ezra, are you ok?"

My dad snapped out of it and said, "You want me to be a firefighter? I have no idea how to do that."

"Yes, I want you to be a firefighter. We would get you trained first, of course, and I know you would be great at it. That's if you don't have other plans. You definitely have the size, and I'm pretty sure you have the strength."

"Wow! I prayed for a miracle, but I had no idea it would be something like this."

"I am so amazed by you, Ezra. Like I said earlier, you are going to do great things. So, is that a yes?"

"Yes!" Ezra replied excitedly. He then paused and said, "Wait, I have to talk to my wife."

Mr. Elliott was taken aback by what my dad had said.

"You're eighteen and married?"

"Yes, Sir," he said, smiling from just the thought of my mom.

"Man, you are already a wonderful man at such a young age. I can tell you really love her."

"Yes, indeed."

"Ok, Mr. . . . . What's your last name?"

"Whitfield, Sir."

"You're just as a man as I am, so I think you deserve to be called Mr. Whitfield, so Mr. Whitfield, you go home and talk to your wife, and give me a call."

"Yes, Sir. Thank you so much."

"No. Thank you. I'll be waiting for your call."

Mr. Elliott got in his car and waved goodbye. My dad stood there in shock with a million different emotions going through his mind. Hardly unable to wait to get home to tell my mom what had happened, he ran over to his beat-up car, and quickly jumped in.

He smiled the entire way home, and when he finally got there, he burst through the door.

"What's going on, Ezra?" my mom asked, as she ran out of the bathroom with toothpaste around her mouth and her toothbrush in her hand.

My dad picked her up and spun her around.

"Baby, it finally happened. Our miracle happened!"

He kissed my mom, transferring the toothpaste from her face onto his, and told her everything that had happened. Seeing how excited my dad was, she was excited for him. She knew that he had the desire to be able to take care of her, but firefighting sounded like a dangerous job and caused her to be a little concerned.

"I'm so happy for you! I'm happy for us, but are you afraid?" she asked.

"My dear Faith, where is your faith?" he asked.

My mom took a deep breath and grinned. That was what my dad would always say to her when she seemed to lose her faith just the tiniest bit, and it always made her blush and remember everything would be ok.

"That's what I'm talking about! Be happy! Be excited! God did this so you have to believe everything is going to work out!"

My mom jumped on my dad's lap and hugged him like the big teddy bear that he was. The next day he called Mr. Elliott from the car wash. That was his last week working there before he began firefighter training. Once he successfully completed training, my mom began her own journey as she enrolled in college and studied to become a schoolteacher.

Chapter Three

"Look at him. He's gorgeous!" my mom said, with tears in her eyes when the nurse placed me into her arms. My dad leaned in smiling, and said, "He gets his looks from his mom.

"You got that right!" my mom said, teasing.

They hadn't even decided on a name for me, but as soon as my mom saw me, she said that there was something special about me. She immediately felt it when she held me and looked into my eyes.

"Ezekiel," she said, looking at my dad.

"Who's Ezekiel?"

"Our son. It means "God's strength". He'll be strong in God. He has no choice with you and me as his parents."

My dad rubbed his chin and said, "Ezekiel Whitfield. That has a nice ring to it. What about a middle name?"

"That's not necessary. Ezekiel is strong enough to stand alone, and is to never be shortened. I want everyone to put respect on his name!"

My dad nodded and said, "I completely agree."

He then scooted his chair next to my mom's hospital bed and grabbed both of her hands as she laid me on her chest.

"Lord, my wife and I come boldly to your throne today to ask that you bless our new-born son, Ezekiel Whitfield. We ask that you watch over and protect him every day of his life. Destroy anything that tries to come against him and cause him any harm. Lord, we pray that our son grows to love you with all of his might, and has the desire to always be in your presence. Lord God, order his steps to be a mighty man of God who will love people as Christ loved the church, and help bring multitudes of your children closer to you, saving their lives. Allow everyone he comes in contact with to be able to see your light shining upon him and feel your presence within him. We pray that you give him the wisdom, strength, and all the tools necessary to serve the purpose you have for his life. Thank you, God, for blessing us with such a wonderful gift, and thank you for hearing and answering our prayers right now as we stand in agreement. In Jesus' name, we pray, Amen."

"Amen," my mom said, as she tightly squeezed my dad's hands.

My foundation had been firmly set at that moment, and it would crumble for absolutely no one or nothing. I was blessed to have praying parents who prayed for me from the time that I was only a pea-sized embryo, every single day of their lives.

When I was born, my dad had been a firefighter for seven years and my mom had only been teaching for a few years after finishing college. They both wanted what was best for me, so they agreed that my mom would stay home and take care of me and the house. My dad had been promoted to Fire Equipment Operator by passing a series of test, and receiving a recommendation from his fire chief, Mr. Elliott, who had become like a second father to him. With that promotion came more money. Enough money to financially support our family without the need of a second income from my mom. God always seemed to provide in one way or another exactly when we needed it.

[31] "So don't worry about these things, saying, 'What will we eat? What will we drink? What will we wear?' [32] These things dominate the thoughts of unbelievers, but your heavenly Father already knows all your needs. [33] Seek the Kingdom of God above all else, and live righteously, and he will give you everything you need." – Matthew 6:31-33 NLT

Life in my house was great. There was God, light, and a whole lot of love between those walls. My parents gave me a perfect balance of everything that I would need in every stage of my life. When I spent time alone with my mom, as early as I could remember, she would teach me to cook by letting me help prepare dinner. She always told me that I shouldn't have to depend on a woman to cook for me. When it came to conversations about girls, it seemed as though she never wanted me to depend on a woman for anything, or ever have a woman at all. During my cooking lessons, we would have deep discussions about what I wanted for the future, and of course, she was always curious as to where my mind was pertaining to girls. One thing she was always sure to remind me of was how important it was to always be strong in my faith.

My dad and I had some of the same types of conversations, but unlike my mom, who was extremely blunt about the way she spoke on things, he would bring things to me a little more subtly. Instead of asking me where my mind was regarding girls, since he already knew the answer to that, he would give me tips on how to deal with them, and how he managed to stay in a peaceful place with my mom. Everything he ever told me, I took it seriously because I knew he was a smart man, and I could rely on every word he said.

There was one conversation my dad and I had when I was ten years old that would always be at the forefront of my mind, and it resonated in my spirit to this very day. As I sat in my room, trying to hide that I was crying, my dad walked in. I quickly tried to wipe away my tears, but my parents always knew when something was bothering me.

My dad sat next to me on my bed, put his arm around me, and said, "What's wrong, Son?"

I shook my head.

"Now, are you going to really sit here and lie to me? You know I probably know you better than yourself, so what has you all upset?"

I slowly reached down and grabbed my bookbag off of the floor and unzipped it. I then pulled out my folder where I kept all my graded papers. Before opening it, I looked up at my dad with shame.

"Go ahead. Show me," my dad said.

I opened the folder and pulled out the paper that I had stuffed all the way in the back. I then handed the paper to him that had a huge red "C" at the top.

As he looked at the paper, he shook his head, which made me think he was upset, but then I saw him smile.

"Why are you smiling?" I asked. "This is unacceptable and I didn't work to my full potential."

"Is this what you're crying about?"

I quickly said, "I wasn't crying."

"Ok, sorry. Is this what you're so upset about?" my dad said, correcting himself to satisfy my pride.

"Yeah. Why wouldn't I be? I'm an "A" student. I never get "C's".

"Well, if you were talking to your mom right now, she would probably tell you, 'Well, never say never because you have a "C" now!'" he laughed. "But I'm not your mom, so I'll just say, none of us are perfect. It's ok to fall short sometimes. It happens, so to avoid being disappointed many times in your life because things aren't perfect, I'm here to tell you not to always expect perfection. Of course, we should always hope for the best, and do our best in everything we do, but we have to learn to accept when things don't turn out the way we want them to. Sometimes not so good things have to happen for better things to happen. We have to grow from the things that we go through, so we can have more knowledge and a better understanding of how to get through those types of situations the next time . . . or how to prevent them all together."

28 "And we know that all things work together for good to them that love God, to them who are called according to his purpose." – Romans 8:28 KJV

"But Dad, I want to be perfect like you. I want to be a great man when I grow up just like you," I said with passion in my voice, as it trembled.

"Ezekiel, I'm not perfect. I've made many mistakes in my life. Your mom, too. We all do, so never say you want to be perfect like me, but I do want you to be better than me. I know you will be!" my dad said with confidence.

He then held out the sheet of paper with the "C" on it and said, "Do you really think this one thing right here is going to stop you from being a great man?"

I sat there thinking about what he'd just said, and when he said it, I realized how stupid I was being. I shook my head.

"Absolutely not!" he continued. "You are going to be a great man, and you are going to do great things, Ezekiel. Keep believing that, and God will make sure of it. And guess what else."

"What?" I asked curiously.

"Standing by your side, you're going to have a great woman to accomplish all those great things with you."

"Like Mom?"

"Even better, but don't tell her I said that," he said, winking his eye.

My eyes lit up because I couldn't imagine a woman better than my mom.

"So, what did you learn from all of this?" my dad asked.

"No one is perfect, and there's still greatness without perfection."

"Absolutely!" my dad said as we both stood up and I gave him a great big hug.

Before he walked out of my room, he said, "It's ok to cry sometimes, too. You don't have to hide your tears and act all macho."

He smiled at me once more before walking out the door.

My dad had shown me that it was ok for a man to be emotional, but your emotions shouldn't be able to control you.

[28] "A person without self-control is like a city with broken-down walls." – Proverbs 25:28 NLT

While I watched him as I grew up, he expressed a range of different emotions based on how each day went in the life of a firefighter. He would see people lose everything, sometimes even their lives in a fire. The toughest ones for him to handle were when babies were involved. I saw him almost succumb to his emotions after seeing children die in some of those fires on several occasions, but he and my mom would hold hands, pray for the families, and do whatever they could think to do that would help the families in any way. Those were the types of people who raised me. They had instilled great values in me, and every one of those values helped me to become the man that I had become, and gave me the strength and knowledge to successfully maneuver through some of life's biggest tests and complicated challenges. Everyone who knew my parents knew what type of child they had raised, and I owed it to them to always represent them in the best way that I could. As early as I could remember, that was one thing that I always vowed to do.

Chapter Four

"**E**zra, it's Friday! You know Fridays belong to us!" my mom pouted, as I walked in the door from getting off of the school bus.

I heard her voice coming from the kitchen, so I headed that way. As I stood in the doorway, I watched my dad as he held my mom and kissed her on the top of her head.

"I'm so sorry, Baby. You know this is the last thing I wanted to happen. I love spending my Friday evenings with you."

"What's wrong?" I asked, startling the both of them.

My dad released my mom from his comforting embrace and said, "Hey, Ezekiel. I didn't realize you had come in."

"Hey, Baby. How was your day?" my mom asked, pretending as if she was no longer upset, but I knew nothing could've been further from the truth in that moment.

"My day was fine, but what is this I hear? The two of you won't be having your date night tonight?" I asked, sounding like a thirteen-year-old way beyond my years.

As long as I could remember, my mom and dad had always set aside a particular day to have date night, where it would just be the two of them going out to dinner, to a movie, or whatever else they felt like doing to enjoy one another. It had been harder for them to set specific days to have their date nights when my dad was a fireman, but became a little easier when he became a Fire Equipment Operator. He was now a chief, superseding his chief, Chief Elliott, who had retired, and he never worked on Fridays. That was why I was so shocked from what I'd heard when I had walked in on my parent's conversation.

My mom walked over to me and gave me a big hug, as she did every day when I got home from school.

Disappointingly, she said, "No, not tonight. Unfortunately, your dad has to work."

I looked at my dad and said, "I thought you would never have to work on Fridays?"

"Well, that's why I say never say never. Sometimes things happen that we have no control over, and this time one of the other captains who's supposed to work tonight has a wife who's in labor, so he needs to be by her side," my dad said, sounding proud to be able to help someone in their time of need, just as he always was.

On my parent's date nights, I would either stay over one of my friend's houses or invite one of them to come over to eat pizza and play video games. This particular night, I had planned to go over my friend, Kyle's, house. We had been friends since we were two years old when we met one day while we were at the park with our moms.

I refused to let my mom be alone, so I said, "Don't worry. I'll stay home with Mom tonight and keep her company."

My mom stood directly in front of me and put her hand on her hip.

"Oh no you won't. Just because my plans changed does not mean yours have to change," she said, demanding that I still go over to Kyle's house.

"I know, but I don't want you to be alone. We can even go out to dinner!" I said excitedly, with my eyes lighting up, looking as if a lightbulb had just gone off in my head.

My mom and dad both started laughing, and I didn't get the joke, so I stood there looking puzzled.

I guess by the look on my face, my dad realized that I hadn't found humor in anything I'd said, so he said, "Son, that's a nice gesture, but I have an even better idea."

My mom tilted her head in curiosity as she sat on one of the wooden barstools at the kitchen island.

"Well?" she said, waiting on my dad to finish.

"I still have all evening before I go to work tonight, so let's do something now! All three of us."

My mom looked at me, smiling, and said, "That's a great idea! Isn't it Ezekiel?"

"Yeah, but afterwards, I'm still staying home with you. You shouldn't be home alone overnight."

My mom leaned back and said, "Whoa! I didn't realize I was the child, and you were the parent. You are just so stubborn!" she said, giggling.

"I wonder where he gets that from," my dad interjected.

"Ok, don't get in trouble!" my mom said, playfully.

We ended up deciding to go to Lucky Strike, which was a bowling alley located on the other side of town. While my dad drove us there, from the backseat, I could remember smelling the scent of my mom's lightly fragranced, sweet smelling perfume that she would only wear when she and my dad went out. I listened to my mom and dad as they enjoyed each other's conversation. Their conversations were always entertaining to listen to, even if what they were talking about didn't interest me one bit. You never had to be interested in what they were saying in order to be entertained by them. My mom would frequently become overly excited and loud, while my dad would remain mellow, continuously using terms of endearment to calm her down. They showed their passion for things in completely differently ways, but they seemed to always be in sync. They definitely balanced each other out.

In the middle of their conversation, I suddenly heard a beat come on the radio that sounded very familiar. My mom and dad immediately stopped talking as my mom turned up the radio.

My mom then caressed the side of my dad's face as she sang, "All my love is all I have . . ."

My dad then glanced at her, smiling, and sang back, "And my dreams are very special . . ."

It was my mom and dad's all-time favorite song, and they sang it all the way through, sounding just like Debra and Ronnie Laws, themselves. I sat back and listened, as they took in every ounce of love that they offered to one another in that moment. Seeing how they loved on each other in so many different ways showed me how to love my wife when that time came around.

While bowling that evening, my family and I had the time of our lives. I actually felt privileged to be able to be a part of their time together. They had worked hard to raise me right, and deserved every moment alone to maintain their own relationship with one another. I never felt slighted when they did things without me, because by watching them, I'd learned that it was a necessary part of a marriage.

We bowled three games, with my mom, who was a pro, winning two of the games, and I believe she let me win one. She teased my dad, who could sometimes be a sore loser and make up some excuse as to why he lost, and this time was no different.

"They need to have bowling balls large enough for us big guys! The holes are too small, and the ball is way too small!" he said.

"Yeah, yeah, yeah. Just give your wife credit where credit is due," my mom laughed.

"I do have to give it to you. You're pretty good," he admitted.

"I know!" she said, snickering.

After bowling, we ate some of the bowling alley's famous pizza, and had root beer floats. We sat in a booth away from all the loud noise, with my mom and I sitting right across from my dad. My dad and I never did too much talking while we ate, but my mom still loved to ramble. As she continued to talk and laugh while she ate, seeming to have a conversation all by herself, my dad and I looked up from our food at each other, every so often, smiling, trying to hold in our laughter. I was sure we had the same thoughts going through our minds. We both then became distracted by the stretchy cheese hanging from my mom's bottom lip that stretched more and more as she continued to talk. Being the perfect gentleman, with his over-sized thumb, my dad took a moment and wiped the cheese from her lip. She stopped speaking just long enough to give him an air kiss, and for him to catch it.

I don't think she ever even realized that she was the only one talking, but it didn't matter because she was passionate as she spoke about how her childhood was traumatized because she never got to have Root Beer floats, and she didn't care who was or wasn't listening. Many would probably wonder how my mom could be so passionate about things that may have seemed so irrelevant to others, but that was part of her gift. She could make people feel just as passionate about something as she felt about it, no matter how small it seemed. She was just always able to engage people with the confidence, electricity, and fire that she exuded when she spoke. I'll just make it clear that most of the things that she was passionate about were a lot more important than not having Root Beer floats as a child.

I think I learned so much more about my parents in that one evening than I had learned in the entire thirteen years of my life. I knew they were awesome, and loved each other, but I didn't really understand the depth of it until that night. I couldn't imagine that any other thirteen-year-old boy in the world could've had as much of a good time with their parents as I'd had with mine that evening.

When we returned home that night, my dad had cut it close, and he only had a little time to relax before heading to work. I sat in the family room with him, watching television, while my mom was upstairs taking a bubble bath. Evidently, I had dozed off, because when I woke up, I was still lying on the sofa with a blanket thrown on top of me, and my dad was nowhere in sight. I jumped up and looked out the window and saw that his car was no longer parked in the driveway, so I wondered what time it was. I ran upstairs and peeked inside my parent's bedroom where I saw my mom sound asleep. I glanced at the clock on her dresser and saw that it was a quarter after midnight. I was no longer tired, so I decided to go back downstairs and find something to watch on television.

After flicking through the channels, failing to find anything I wanted to watch, I sat the remote control down and went to the kitchen to get something to drink. While I was in there, I suddenly heard whatever TV show I'd left the television on being interrupted by breaking news.

"I'm Kamryn Fletcher reporting for ABC News, and we are currently onsite at a home that has apparently caught fire. We don't have much information, but as you can see, the flames are blazing out of control and the fire department has just arrived," the Black, female news reporter stated.

As I ran out of the kitchen and looked at the TV, all I could see were flames engulfing almost the entire second floor of the two-story home. I then saw the most bizarre thing. A young girl who looked to be around my age ran into the burning home.

"Oh no! A little girl just ran inside! We don't know where she came from or why she ran inside, but this is a sad tragedy!" the news reporter said.

In shock, I continued to watch as several firefighters stretched the hose trying to get as close to the flames as possible. While they were doing that, I suddenly saw my dad running towards the home, moving everyone out of his way.

"Ma!" I yelled, not wanting to move from in front of the television, in fear of missing a crucial part of the current events.

"The Fire Chief just made an executive decision and ran in to save the little girl! Everyone watching, please pray for the safety of everyone involved right now. This has to be a nightmare, especially for the families of everyone involved," the news reporter said, updating the viewers.

My mom didn't come down, so I yelled out her name again, telling her to come downstairs. She finally came running down the stairs, looking panicked, as she tied her robe.

"What's going on?!" she asked, looking all around, with rollers half-way falling out of her hair.

I pointed at the television, and she said, "Oh my God! Is anyone in there?"

Sadly, I replied, "Dad."

"Your dad? Why is he in there? Why isn't anyone helping him?"

"He ran in after a young girl."

My mom, not able to keep her balance after I told her what was going on, balanced herself on the arm of the chair and slowly sat down, not taking her eyes off of the television.

The other firemen continued to try to hose down the fire, and they suddenly stopped.

"There's something happening," Kamryn, the news reporter said.

As everyone around watched in suspense, she continued.

"It looks like someone is coming out."

My mom stood up and walked closer to the television. We watched as the firemen surrounded the entrance of the home. We then saw my dad just lying there.

"No!" my mom began repeating over and over again. "He's going to be ok," she said.

From underneath my dad's lifeless body, the young girl came crawling out, crying, and coughing uncontrollably. The paramedics came running over with two stretchers, and the cameraman then quickly put the camera back on the news reporter.

"I've never seen anything like this. I pray that everyone is ok, especially the Fire Chief who risked his life to save another. He will be remembered for this moment for the rest of his life and beyond."

Unfortunately, my dad didn't make it. He had inhaled too much smoke and ended up suffering from cardiac arrest. We weren't the only ones who lost someone. Although my dad was able to save the little girl, she lost both of her parents in the fire. Even though my mom and I had been having a tough time coping, she still wanted to try to do something to help the little girl however she could, just like she and my dad would've done for anyone else who was in need after a tragedy. To be honest, I was so hurt by the loss of my dad, worrying about the girl that he'd saved was the furthest thing from my mind. Her name was never released to the public because of her age, and I wasn't really concerned with it. We did hear that her grandmother had taken her in, so with everything we were going through, knowing that much was enough for my mom to find peace with the girl's situation. I was sure if my mom hadn't been trying to deal with my dad's death, she would've put forth more effort to get more information, but she was satisfied with just knowing that the girl had someone to take care of her.

If it hadn't been for my mom's faith and everything my parents had instilled in me, we probably would've been completely broken, but God truly carried us through. Both of my parents were huge believers that everything happened for a reason. My dad wasn't even supposed to be working the night he died in the line of duty, but there was a reason that the wife of the other chief who was supposed to be working that night went into labor. My dad had been a great husband, and raised me to the best of his ability. He had given me thirteen years of his wisdom and great advice, and maybe that chief who was becoming a new dad, as my dad was being called home, needed to be there for his new-born baby and wife. He might've been the one to run into that fire that night, and his child would've never been able to know his or her dad. Every child should at least know their dad and have a relationship with them, if at all possible. I got to know mine and had a great relationship with him. I believed that God decided that my dad had completed his mission on Earth, and it was time for him to go live with his father in Heaven, while watching us from above. While he was watching, I wanted to make sure that I made him proud, every step of the way.

A huge memorial was held for my dad by the New York City Fire Department. It was so huge that the Brooklyn Expo Center was packed to the max. There were so many people who loved my dad, and so many of them who stood up to speak had some very beautiful words to say about him. The person who I could tell touched my mom the most was my dad's former Chief, Myles Elliott.

I had met Mr. Elliott on several occasions, and he'd always had a smile on his face. I could tell that he loved my dad, and was very proud of him. When I saw him get up to say a few words, it was the first time I'd ever seen him not smiling, but no one else in the room was either. It was a sad occasion, and every time someone got up to speak, although their words were so kind, there seemed to be a dark cloud over us that just wouldn't lift.

As Mr. Elliott stood at the podium, wearing dark sunglasses, he held his head down and took a deep breath. After about a minute, everyone stood to their feet and began clapping. Two other firemen who were good friends of my dad joined Mr. Elliott on stage to give him some support.

Mr. Elliott then cleared his throat, removed his sunglasses, and began.

"I apologize. This is a very hard one for me," he paused. "Where do I begin? I guess I'll begin when I first met Ezra. I met him when he was only eighteen years old. He was still a kid, but a man at the same time. When I saw how seriously he took his job at the carwash where I met him, I knew he had the potential to be one of the best firemen that New York City had ever seen, so I offered him a job. I just never thought it would've ended this way."

Mr. Elliott's voice shook as he struggled to get his words out. One of the firemen rubbed him on his back and told him to take his time.

"Ezra was so kind, and he loved his family more than anything! He would've done absolutely anything for them," he said, as he looked directly at me and my mom as we sat in the front row in the audience.

"Every time I saw Ezra, he always had a story to tell about an amazing thing his baby boy had done, and he continuously talked about how special he was. Listen to me, Ezekiel. To come from a man like Ezra, you have to be extremely special, because I've met no other like him."

My mom held me as I teared up.

"Faith, he loved you so much. For a man to marry a woman at such a young age, trust me, that man knew exactly what he wanted, and he saw all of those qualities in you. He adored you, and nothing would have ever changed that."

My mom held me even tighter, and kissed me on the forehead.

Mr. Elliott continued, "What he did to save that young girl, none of us should be surprised. I know I'm not. I just wish he would've lived to talk about it. Even if he would've lived to talk about it, he wouldn't have. He would've been so humble about it, as he was with everything. He would've acted as if risking his life for someone else was an ordinary, everyday thing for him. He would've said to me, 'Well, Chief, that's my job.'"

[10] **"Humble yourselves before the Lord, and he will lift you up in honor." – James 4:10 NLT**

There was finally some laughter coming from the crowd. Hearing Mr. Elliott talk about my dad changed the energy in the room. I could've sworn the lights even became brighter.

Mr. Elliott continued. "We had some wonderful years of working together, and he became more and more like a son to me every day. I honestly feel like I lost a son. I taught him as much as I could about the job, but he taught me so much more about real life. He was wise beyond his years, and anyone who knew him, knew that he was a genuine guy, and both he and his wife, Faith, would do anything in their power to help those who were in need of anything. They were a force to be reckoned with, but Faith, you will still be a force to be reckoned with because Ezra will forever be with you in your heart, and he will always be watching over you and your son. He'll probably be up there trying to watch over all of us because we all know he wanted to save each and every one of us while he was down here!"

Everyone began to laugh once again. I suddenly felt as though I could feel my dad in the room. He would've wanted everyone to be celebrating his life, not gathered together, sitting up in a venue all sad and teary-eyed, as we all had been only moments ago. Mr. Elliott had been the breath of fresh air that we needed, and he definitely lightened the mood.

Mr. Elliott concluded his speech by saying, "Long live our Gentle Giant!"

Everyone stood up clapping and cheering. There was absolutely no one in sight without a smile on their face. Not even me or my mom.

Ezekiel

Chapter Five

After the unexpected death of my father, I became extremely introverted. I no longer had a desire to hang out with my friends like normal teenage boys, and wasn't very much interested in having a girlfriend. The only friend that I remained somewhat open to was Kyle, and that was because he had been there for me through everything. We had been friends for so long, and he and his family treated me like I was part of the family. My mom and dad also always treated him as if he was also their own son. Whenever he was around, my dad dropped some gems on him that I was sure he'd always remember since he didn't have a dad who was around.

I started high school a year after my dad died, and that didn't start off very well. A girl who I'd blown off more than once started a rumor that I was homosexual because I wouldn't give her the time of day. Some believed it, some didn't. I wasn't really bothered by it because I was basically in my own little world and my mind was so far away from everything else. During that period in my life, unlike other kids my age, I wasn't concerned with what others thought of me. My mom was my world, and as long as I felt as though I was making her, my dad, and God proud, nothing else mattered.

Many days, I did feel as though my sense of self had been buried right along with my dad, but I knew I had to pull myself out of that pit and be the strong young man that he would've wanted me to be. Instead of allowing myself to die inside, I knew I had to use everything I had inside of me and lean on God's strength to keep living, and keep my dad's memory alive. In order to do that, one of the most important things I needed to do was to continue to represent him, and represent him well. With my dad no longer around, I didn't have a father figure to give me the daily advice that every boy needed from his dad. I had been blessed that he had given me so much good advice and knowledge during the time that we'd had together, and I would at least be able to later fall back on all of that whenever necessary. He had believed in me so much, and had so much faith that I would do great things that I had no choice except to do everything in my power to follow through and make him proud.

I always kept my head in the books so that I was sure to get a scholarship to whatever college I chose to go to after high school. From the day that my mom and dad found out that God had placed me in my mother's womb, they started a college fund for me, but I only wanted to have to use that if absolutely necessary. My dad always taught me to always have something for a rainy day, and that's what I expected to do, even if it was to help someone else's rainy day. I told my mom that I wanted her to keep the money if I got a scholarship, but she refused. She told me that my dad had worked hard for that money for me, and she wanted me to have it. Although I heard what she said, I still planned on sharing it with her.

Shortly after my dad died, she'd restarted the career that she had left once I was born, as a schoolteacher, but I knew that she didn't make anything close to what she deserved. I also knew she wasn't in it just for a salary. She needed something to keep her mind occupied and she genuinely loved teaching children. As her son, and seeing how much she put into her career, I still felt that she deserved so much more for the positive role that she played in so many children's lives. Especially for those who didn't have a positive role model at home. Her students loved her. Some of them probably loved her just as much as I did, and she would receive gifts from them and their parents on a regular basis. I desired for my mom to have everything that her heart desired. She didn't know, but I worried about her a lot. She always seemed to be doing well, but I knew she missed my dad terribly, even after five years. I knew it was in her nature to always try to put on a façade of being strong. She was definitely strong, but I knew it had to have been hard to lose her best friend who was also the love of her life.

I ended up applying to three of my top-choice schools, and received full scholarship offers to all three. I graduated as Valedictorian of my class, and I owed all the credit to God. The parents that He'd loaned me to had raised me to be the best man I could possibly be. Kyle was Salutatorian and also received several full scholarship offers. One of the schools in which he received an offer was the same as where I'd received mine. That Fall after graduating, I left the nest with all I'd learned in the eighteen years I'd been living. I arrived on the beautiful campus of Stanford University where I'd be spending at least the next four years of my life. I'd be experiencing those years with my best friend, Kyle.

"I can't believe my baby boy is leaving me," my mom said, sniffling, as she threw away the balled-up Kleenex in her hand, and pulled more out of her purse.

She was having a vulnerable moment, which were few, far, and in between for her. Kyle's mom, Ms. Morgan, was also having a fragile moment as we all stood in the middle of Kyle's and my new dorm room, however, they were both able to find a little solace in the fact that Kyle and I would be rocmmates and we could look out for one another. Kyle and I had to be strong for our mothers and let them know that we'd be all right. Since Kyle's dad had never been a part of his life, he had been like the man of the house. We still both knew that she would be ok because she was also a strong woman, just like my mom.

"I'll be ok, Ma. You raised me right, and I'm keeping all of that right here," I said, as I put my hand over my heart.

As she patted her eyes with the tissue to stop her makeup from running, she said, "I know, Baby, but the thought of you being almost three-thousand miles away is a little overwhelming for me."

I grabbed both of my mom's hands and smiled.

"My dear Faith, where is your faith?" I said, reminding her of exactly what my dad would've said at that moment.

We both began laughing, but then she suddenly broke down and began crying even harder.

I grabbed her and held her tight, trying my best to console her, as my dad would've done. I knew he was looking down on us at that moment, and I wanted him to know that I was making sure that his Faith was being well taken care of.

Kyle's mom, who had obviously released all the tears that she had, stood behind my mom, rubbing her back.

She then said, "Faith, we'll be just fine. Just think. Now we can go to the club all night and don't have to answer to these young men who think they're our fathers!"

Kyle and I looked at each other as our mouths almost hit the floor.

My mom and Kyle's mom both began laughing hysterically, but Kyle and I didn't think anything was funny. I stood there with one eyebrow raised and my arms folded as they gave each other a high-five. After they noticed the looks on our faces, they looked at each other and began laughing even harder. Funny thing was, I couldn't have ever imagined neither my mom nor Kyle's mom at anyone's club. They probably would've been in there taking cups out of people's hands, or standing at the door handing out church flyers. They were definitely not the clubbing type, and I didn't know why Kyle and I were even entertaining that thought because we both knew our moms better than that.

"Thank you so much for that laugh, Sonja," my mom said to Kyle's mom.

"Girl, you know I have your back just like you have mine," she replied with a wink.

My mom then looked at me and said, "I'm sorry for breaking down on you like that. I know you're not used to that, but please don't think I'm sad and let that keep you from enjoying your time here. I'm just so proud of you, and I wish your dad could be here with us."

I looked her directly in her eyes and said, "He is, and he'll continue to be with us until we meet again."

As my mom hugged me one last time before she and Ms. Morgan left us to begin our new journey, she said, "You two just make sure to keep on making us proud."

Making my mom the proudest mother in the world was definitely my plan, and I promised myself that I wouldn't allow anything to distract and deter me from doing just that.

Once Kyle and I were left alone, we both sat on our beds and stared at each other, having no idea what to do next. The day of finally being released out into the world all on our own was a young boy's dream. We were free to do what we wanted without our parent's being anywhere around, or having to be worried about any of their friends possibly seeing us, and telling them what they saw us doing. We were three-thousand miles away from home, so it would've been quite a coincidence for anyone who knew our moms to just so happen see us.

Even though we now had the freedom to do whatever we wanted, we still needed to remember that everything that we would do, and every decision that we would make, would still have consequences. My dad always told me, even if we are given the right to do something, it doesn't always make it right for us to do it.

[15] **"Now listen! Today I am giving you a choice between life and death, between prosperity and disaster. [16] For I command you this day to love the Lord your God and to**

keep his commands, decrees, and regulations by walking in his ways. If you do this, you will live and multiply, and the Lord your God will bless you and the land you are about to enter and occupy." – Deuteronomy 30:15-16 NLT

I had never been a problem child, and I can't even say it was primarily because of the way I was raised. Being brought up in church, I saw a lot of kids my age be raised the "right way", just as I was. Their parents were great, just as mine were, they were shown an abundance of love, they were sent to the best schools, and had an overall great life that any kid would've loved to have. Many of those same kids ended up in the streets, selling drugs, getting involved in gangs, or just losing all of their focus, motivation, and respect for their elders, even their parents, before graduating from high school.

I used to wonder how that could even be possible when you've been given everything, but I realized later in life that you could have everything in this world, but you really don't have anything if you don't have God. Parents could only instill the right values in their children in hopes of leading them onto the right path, but they couldn't make them receive and develop a close relationship with God. In fact, no one could be forced to receive Him. It didn't matter if a child was taken to church every single Sunday throughout their childhood. They had to open their hearts to God and invite Him to be the head of their life. No one else could do that for them. Any of us could be found in a church every Sunday, but that didn't necessarily make us a Christian. If a person is put in a garage, that doesn't make them a car. Just because a person grew up, or was placed in a particular environment, that doesn't define them, or make them a product of their environment. I was taught to always remember that God is in control, and even though a child may steer away from what their parents instilled in them, they will someday return to it, because those things that they were taught will always remain in their hearts. It may be after hitting their heads a million times, but they'll be back.

[6] "Train up a child in the way he should go: and when he is old, he will not depart from it." – Proverbs 22:6 KJV

"Why are we just sitting here? This is Welcome Week! We need to be out there exploring the campus, and meeting new people. I saw some real pretty girls walking around while we were unloading our stuff," Kyle said, as he stood up pulling his brush out of his back pocket and began brushing his hair.

"You know that's not where my mind is right now," I said, putting a damper on Kyle's burst of excitement.

"Bro, you can stop pretending like you're not thinking about these girls! Your mom is on her way back to New York! We're teenage boys that have just been given permission to do whatever!" Kyle said, trying his best to convince me to just have a good time and live.

Kyle was always more bold and outgoing than I ever was, even before my dad died. He had no problem approaching any girl that he found interest in, and was never afraid of rejection. I knew I wouldn't have had a problem either if that had been my main focus, but it wasn't. I knew that there were other things more important, and girls would always be there.

Kyle could see that none of what he was saying was enticing me the least bit, so he tried another route.

"Look, Man. You're like my brother. I know you're determined to be your best self, and trust me, you will be, but I won't let you have this college experience without enjoying some of it. You don't have to be crazy over girls to do that. I'll do enough of that for the both of us, but just enjoy the ride! You've worked hard for this."

I took a deep breath and exhaled after listening to what Kyle said. I then just sat there staring at him as he stood over me, waiting to see how I was going to respond.

"Well?", he said, as he threw his arms out to the side.

I hesitated before standing up and saying, "Ok. Let's do this."

Kyle always had a huge smile, but those words coming from my mouth seemed to make his smile ten times bigger than normal.

Chapter Six

As Kyle and I walked the campus of Stanford, there seemed to be a million and one different things going on throughout the quad. There was music playing throughout the entire courtyard, which was coming from a concert that was being held. The wonderful aroma of barbecue filled the air as we walked through the obvious picnic area. It was crowded with people of every ethnicity sitting on benches within groups, and others sitting around on blankets in the grass. There were at least five barbecue grills going near the tables where food was being served. Everyone seemed so comfortable with one another, and no one seemed new to the scene. Flyers promoting different on-campus events and festivities that would be taking place during the first week were being handed to us every few steps that we took. The first big event, which was a Kappa party, would be taking place that same evening. I quickly stuck that flyer in my pocket, hoping that Kyle didn't see it. I knew he would want to go, and I felt it was too soon to start going to parties. I needed to first get acclimated to my new environment, and preferred to socialize in small group settings before being introduced to the "wild side" of college life.

I was glad that Kyle had talked me into getting out of the dorm and going with him. I had closed myself off from other people for so long, I had forgotten how good it could feel when around the right group of people. Even though all of the faces were unfamiliar, they were all so friendly. California already seemed so much different from New York. Although I loved New York, there were a lot of rude people who lived there, and they would turn their noses up at you and make you feel like you were less than the dirt on the bottom of their shoes. I was sure that the people on campus were from all over the United States, and I definitely looked forward to meeting people from other places outside of New York.

Kyle smiled at almost every girl that walked by, and within five minutes I probably counted ten times that he had pulled his brush out of his back pocket and brushed his hair. Kyle had always been into his looks and girls. So much that I didn't know how he managed to keep up his grades, but he did. I could remember so clearly being in the third grade and Kyle's mom fussing at him for picking flowers out of her garden to give to his so-called girlfriend. She then called and vented to my mom, who only made matters worse by laughing and telling her that she had a real Casanova on her hands.

"Dude, how many times are you going to brush your hair? It's not going anywhere with all of that pomade you have in it!" I said, after not being able to bear even the thought of seeing Kyle pull that brush out one more time.

"Are you hating? That's really not a good look on you, Bro!" he said, jokingly.

"Not at all. There's no way I could possibly be so obsessed with myself."

"I wouldn't say that I'm obsessed with myself. I just like to look my best at all times!"

"I think we all want to look our best at all times, but you take it to the extreme! You love girls, but you want to look better than all of them! How's that going to work out for you when you finally find someone you really like? You'll both be competing for compliments," I said, laughing hysterically.

Kyle wanted so badly to be able to argue with what I'd just said, but he couldn't deny it, so he just shrugged his shoulders.

As we continued walking, looking around at all of what Stanford had to offer, we stopped where there was a table set up for the National Black Student Union and listened to the two representatives as they spoke to a large group of us about their mission and values. Kyle and I were both interested in learning more, and possibly being involved in an organization that celebrated Black culture, lifestyle, and history. Towards the end of the presentation, I noticed that the piquant aroma of barbecue that had been floating throughout the air the entire time had begun to dissipate, and was being replaced by the sweet tropical fragrance of pineapples and papaya.

As I began looking around, trying to find the source of the sweet aroma, Kyle looked at me and whispered, "What's wrong with you?"

"You smell that?" I whispered back.

Kyle put his nose in the air and then shrugged his shoulders. When he thought I was no longer looking, he lowered his head, inconspicuously sniffing his armpits to make sure it wasn't him that I was referring to. After we received all of our handouts and the presenters concluded their presentation, I slowly turned around and the sweet-smelling fragrance abruptly hit me directly in the face. Standing directly in front of me was one of God's beautiful creations who He'd definitely taken his time with. I could feel every muscle in my body tense up as I stared at this beautiful young lady who seemed to be perfect in every way. Her smooth brown skin was like silk. It had been perfectly kissed by the sun and her glow made her beauty surpass anything that I'd ever seen. Her thick, jet-black hair was tied back with a multi-colored floral bandana, and hung to the middle of her back. The being that stood before me had the shape of a goddess, and the white distressed shorts that exposed her long, lean legs took her height to another level.

While being caught up in my thoughts and trying to take in every single detail of her breathtaking beauty, I heard the voice that went along with the girl that I felt like I'd fallen in love with at first sight.

"Can you please move?" she said, standing in front of me with one hand on her hip, and rolling her almond-shaped brown eyes.

I failed to realize that I must've looked like a creep as I stood there in front of this complete stranger, staring at her as if I had never been in the presence of anyone of the opposite sex.

Nervously, I said, "Oh, yeah. Of course. I'm so sorry, but you're just so . . ."

Before I could completely get out of her way, and get out what I was trying to say to her, she pushed me out of the way and continued walking without looking back.

Sounding defeated, I said, "beautiful," finishing my sentence.

While regaining my composure after almost being knocked to the ground, I watched the young girl walk away, noticing a butterfly tattoo on the back of her left shoulder.

"Bro, are you serious?!" Kyle said, laughing uncontrollably, interrupting me as I watched her disappear into the crowd.

I looked at Kyle, with a confused look on my face, wondering what he meant by his statement.

"What do you mean by that?" I asked, as I started walking back towards the dorms.

Walking beside me, he said, "You go through the entire four years of high school without talking to any girls. Not even the ones who were throwing themselves at you, but you come here and want to try to talk to probably the finest girl on campus? Did you see her? I wouldn't even attempt to talk to her. That's just a rejection waiting to happen, although I don't mind a rejection here or there. Sometimes you just have to take your shot, but with a girl like that, you have to take baby steps, my brother! Start with an average girl and work your way up!"

After listening to Kyle, I was convinced that he had a completely different way of thinking than I did, and I was a little offended that he made it seem as if I wasn't good enough to talk to a beautiful girl if I had the desire to.

"I need to be asking you if you're serious in your thought process! I saw her very clearly, and yes, she is gorgeous. You act as if I couldn't have talked to any girl I wanted to in school. You're not the only one who can get girls. It was just that none of them ever caught my attention, but there's something different about her."

"Yeah, you're right! There is something different about her. She's beautiful! There were no beautiful girls in high school. Some were cute, but none were beautiful!"

I stared at Kyle, shaking my head, wondering where his mother had gone wrong. There had been several beautiful girls in high school, and he had probably dated them all at least once. I didn't know why we were going back and forth anyway. It was very apparent that the girl that we were carrying on a conversation about, whose name we didn't even know, wasn't interested in me. If she had been, I was sure she would've at least smiled at me instead of scowled as she pushed me out the way, and hurried off as she did.

Picking up my pace, due to my irritability towards Kyle's comments, I said, "Let's just stop talking about it. We saw an attractive girl. This is our first day here, and I'm sure there will be plenty more where she came from. I told you, that's not why I'm here anyway. I'm trying to focus on getting my degree, and everything else comes later."

I was trying to sound like I was cool, but Kyle picked up on the apparent animosity in my voice and said, "Man, I didn't mean to make you mad. I just know how those kinds of girls are. They know they can have any dude on this campus so they're disrespectful. I'm just trying to save you the heartbreak."

"It's all good. I'm just tired. It's been a long day," I said.

Kyle jumped in front of me and said, "Wait a minute! I know you're not tapping out for the day! What about the Frat party tonight? We have to go!"

I stopped walking, took a deep breath, and exhaled. I then pulled the flyer out that I had folded up and stuck deep down in my pocket after it was handed to me while we walked around campus.

"Let me see that," Kyle said, as he snatched the flyer out of my hand.

As he read it, his natural high rose even higher.

"We definitely can't miss this! Look at this flyer! Just don't read the words! Look at the girls on this flyer!" he said, as he waved the paper in my face.

Kyle could be so annoying at times, but I tolerated him because he was like a blood brother to me. No matter how annoying he was, I knew that I could always trust and count on him when I needed him. We were always there for each other, which was why he didn't need to convince me to go to that party. If he was going, I was going. Not because I wanted to, but because I had to watch out for my brother. We were in a new place, and didn't know anyone except for each other. There was no way I was going to let him be out there by himself.

After trying to read the blank expression on my face, Kyle asked, "So are you going or not?"

"Are you going?" I asked sarcastically.

"You already know I'm there!"

"Well, I have no choice," I replied.

Kyle would get mad when I would say things like that because he would feel like I felt as though I needed to keep an eye on him. The truth was that I did. There was no telling where Kyle would be if I hadn't been around to keep him out of trouble. There had to be balance in a friendship, or any type of relationship, and we had a pretty healthy one. I was always the voice of reason when Kyle wanted to do something that was absolutely insane, but I can say that Kyle was also my voice of reason when I got too deep into my own thoughts. Especially after my mom and I lost my dad.

About a week after my dad died, reality completely set in, and it seemed as though everything hit me all at once. I couldn't do anything without thinking about my dad. I had already begun to miss our talks, and seeing his big bright smile that told the world how happy and proud he was. Seeing my mom alone every day hurt me even more. She hid her sadness and tears, but I knew how she felt inside because I knew how I felt. Hers had to be at least a thousand times worse. I just wanted to get away from it all. One day I decided that I didn't want to be around anything or anyone that reminded me of my dad, so one morning before school, I filled by bookbag with as many clothes that would fit, and left a letter under my pillow for my mom that I had written the night before.

The letter read:

"Dear Mom,

I'm writing you this letter because I know I seem to be doing ok, but I'm not. I miss dad so much and I can't handle this pain anymore. Everything in this house reminds me of him. I can't sit in the family room and watch TV without thinking of that horrible night when I watched dad die on that same television. I can't sit at the kitchen table without feeling like I should be waiting on him to come have dinner with us. I can't even go into my room without envisioning him sitting on my bed next to me, dropping some of that good ole daddy knowledge. I don't know what else to do except to go somewhere where there are no memories of him. I know you're trying to be strong for the both of us, but it hurts me to see you go through life without Dad. Please don't be mad at me, and please don't look for me. I love you so much, and you're the best mom that any kid could ever have. Thank you for loving me the way that you do.

Love,

Ezekiel"

When I left out the front door that morning, I had tears in my eyes that I had to wipe away before running into Kyle on the corner of the block where we would always meet up to walk the rest of the way to school. He didn't know what I'd planned on doing, but I knew I'd have to tell him something when he saw that I wasn't going to school.

"Hey, Kyle," I said, as I continued to walk past him with my head hanging down.

"What's up?" he said, as he began following behind me.

After I didn't answer, he said, "What's wrong? Why do you look like that?"

I knew he was going to keep asking me questions, so I said, "I'm not going to school today, and don't ask me where I'm going!"

"Where are you going if you're not going to school," Kyle asked, completely ignoring my request.

I stopped walking and turned to him. "Didn't I Just say don't ask me where I'm going?"

Kyle buffed up at me and said, "Man, I don't care what you said. Where are you going?"

I took a deep breath and exhaled. "I don't know, but I have to get away from here! I can't stop thinking about my dad when I'm in that house!"

Kyle looked at my bookbag and asked, "What do you have in there?"

"Clothes," I replied.

"You're really serious about this?"

"Yeah, Kyle. You don't know what it's like!" I said, as I continued to walk down the street in the opposite direction of our school.

Surprisingly, Kyle seemed to have given up and headed in the direction of the school.

As I began walking faster, I suddenly heard Kyle yelling, "You're right! I don't know what it's like!"

I turned around and saw Kyle running back towards me, and I began running away from him. I didn't want to hear anything he had to say. My mind was made up and there was nothing that he could do to change it. Like I'd said, Kyle had no idea what I was going through. No one did. I was hoping Kyle would stop running after me, but every time I looked back, he was getting closer and closer. He was on the track team, and I had asthma, so we both knew that he'd eventually catch me. Breathing heavily, I stopped, bent over, and put my hands on my knees.

When Kyle caught up to me, he put his hand on my back and asked, "You ok?"

I couldn't get my words out, so he said, "Stand up and raise your arms in the air."

I did what Kyle said and began taking deep breaths.

Once I caught my breath, I said, "How did you know that would work?"

"Something my coach taught me for when I get winded, but forget about all that. Have you lost your mind?"

As we began walking, I said, "Like I told you, you don't know what it's like!"

"I may not know what it's like to lose my father through death, but I do know what it's like to not have my dad around, or to have great memories of him."

Immediately after Kyle said what he did, I knew exactly where he was going with it, and I felt bad.

He continued, "At least you have memories because your dad wanted to spend time with you. My dad is still around somewhere, but has never wanted to have anything to do with me. It may sound harsh, but I don't know if knowing he's around and doesn't want to communicate with me in any way makes me feel worse or better than if he were dead and didn't have the option of spending time with me. At least if he were dead, I could maybe convince myself that he actually would have decided to spend some time with me and get to know me. Knowing he has a choice and chooses not to hurts, but I can't control other people, and I just have to enjoy the people around me who love and appreciate me . . . not just tolerate me. All I'm saying is, at least you have memories. Good memories! Why would you want to forget them?"

Looking down at the ground, I said, "It's just so painful to think about him."

"It won't always be painful. You just have to give it some time. This is fresh. One day you'll be able to smile when you think of him. Just appreciate the time you had with your dad. I appreciate the time I had with him and he's not even my dad."

As I listened to Kyle, he was making a whole lot of sense. It was almost as if he was saying exactly what my dad would've told me at that moment. I didn't know where I would've been if my dad hadn't been a part of my life.

"And another thing. Do you really want to do your mom like that? She already lost her husband. You're all she has left. She would completely lose her mind if she lost you."

Kyle really made me think about how my mom would've felt if I went through with my plan. I really hadn't thought things through, and I was acting on impulse and only thinking about myself, which wasn't like me at all. That actually was more of a "Kyle" thing. I was letting my emotions control me, and my dad would've been disappointed in me because he always reminded me that letting my emotions control my actions could make things worse than what they actually were or had to be. I was giving up and running from my problems because I was sad and angry at the same time, but like Kyle had said, I wouldn't always feel that way, and one day, those memories and thoughts of my dad that I was trying to run away from would get me through some of my toughest moments.

[9] "The heartfelt counsel of a friend is as sweet as perfume and incense." – Proverbs 27:9 NLT

Kyle was able to help me clear my head, and help me remember that God was with me through everything that I was going through, and he wouldn't put more on me than what I was able to handle. I had been blessed with two strong parents, so I knew that I was able to endure so much more than what I was giving myself credit for.

After realizing we'd been walking and talking for quite some time, but not knowing exactly how long, Kyle looked at his watch and said, "We're an hour late for school, and if we head that way now, it'll probably be another hour before we get there."

I looked around and saw that Kyle was right. We had been so deep into our conversation that we hadn't realized that we had walked way to the other side of town.

"So, what now?" I asked, depending on Kyle to have a great idea.

"Well, we're already in trouble, so we may as well enjoy the rest of the day!" he said, shrugging his shoulders.

That was his great idea. To skip the rest of the school day. The thing was, I couldn't think of anything better, so I had to go with it. That day, we spent part of the hundred dollars that I had managed to save up to get to wherever I was initially going, and went to the movie theater to see a movie that we'd been wanting to see, and then went to a pizza parlor that we'd walked past on our way. Kyle and I had never done anything like that before. I stayed out of trouble for the most part, but Kyle stayed in minor trouble. His biggest issue was talking too much in class or being the class clown. He was just always lively and had high energy, and all of the teachers knew this. The fact that he was an "A" student didn't hurt, so he never really got in trouble. They would mostly just give him a warning, and it seemed as though the warnings never ran out.

When we got home that day, my mom's car was already parked outside. Kyle always went home with me after school because it would be a while before his mom would get home from work and he would sometimes even have to eat dinner at our house. With my mom being a schoolteacher, most days we would get home around the same time, unless she had to stay after for a faculty meeting or parent/teacher conferences.

As soon as we walked in the house, we walked right into the family room where both of our moms were sitting, staring at us like they were ready to wring our necks.

Nervously, I said, "Hey Mom. Hey, Ms. Morgan," as I tried to quickly walk past to go upstairs, hoping that Kyle was following suit.

"Do you two really think you're going to just walk past us and think that we're not going to say a word to you about you skipping school today?" my mom said.

Kyle's mom, then added, "On top of that, we both had to leave work early, so that we could drive around looking for the two of you!"

We stared at them, not saying a word, which seemed to make things worse.

Kyles' mom stood up and said, "So, Kyle, you're just going to look at me like I'm stupid after you've had me worrying all day and missing money that I need to take care of you?"

With his hands in his pockets, Kyle said, "I'm sorry, Ma."

I felt bad for Kyle, but I knew I had it coming, too. My mom was silent, but her eyes were burning a hole straight through me. I couldn't let Kyle continue to get beat up over something that I'd caused. If it hadn't been for me being stupid, we would've been at school like we should have been.

"It's not Kyle's fault. I . . ."

Kyle then interjected and said, "It's all my fault. I thought it would be fun to skip school and go to the movies. Ezekiel tried to stop me, but I wouldn't listen. You know me. I can be hard-headed at times. The entire time he was trying to talk me into going to school, so I really didn't even get to enjoy it. I promise it won't happen again."

I stood there staring at Kyle in disbelief. I couldn't believe he had taken the blame for everything.

My mom then stood up, and as she walked towards me, she said, "Is that what happened, Ezekiel?"

While I still stared at Kyle, with his eyes, he was telling me to just agree so we could move past that moment.

I swallowed hard before saying, "Yes, Ma. That's what happened."

My mom was still angry at me for skipping school, which she knew was out of character for me, but I preferred her being angry at me than being sad if I had left, especially if she'd found and read the note that I had left. Kyle ended up being on punishment for an entire month for something that was all my fault. I really didn't want him to take the blame, and I wasn't sure why he'd done that for me, but I did recognize that Kyle had been a true and loyal friend to me that day and I would always appreciate him for it.

Chapter Seven

As we walked towards the Frat House, not far from campus, I cuffed my nose as I asked Kyle, "Why did you spray so much cologne?"

Smiling, and of course, brushing his hair, he said, "I smell good, don't I?"

I didn't even respond. I could tell we were getting close to the party by how loud the music was becoming. Carloads of people steadily rode past us with music blasting. Neither of our moms felt like it was a good idea to send us to school with a car the first year, so we'd be stuck walking or taking the bus for a while. At that particular moment, it was probably best that we didn't have a car, or end up riding with someone else because Kyle definitely needed to air out a bit. His cologne was so strong, I just knew I'd have a headache before even arriving at the party.

When we finally arrived, I was in awe of how big the house was. It could've made someone like me who had no desire to be a part of a Fraternity, want to pledge just to live in the house. I could tell there was a lot going on inside from the colorful LED lights flashing through every window. Cars were parked along both sides of the street, and there were even people standing outside talking and laughing with drinks in their hands. I let Kyle lead the way, making my lack of enthusiasm very obvious.

As soon as we walked in, I felt completely out of my element. There wasn't one person without a drink in their hand, and I was sure it wasn't just juice. I began to think that just maybe that was the reason everyone walked around campus with a smile on their face. That was, everyone except for the girl who had taken my breath away earlier that day. I didn't know how often these parties occurred, but if it was on the regular, I didn't know how anyone passed their classes.

The crowd was so thick, I almost immediately lost track of Kyle. I walked around, absolutely clueless of what to do next. It was so warm due to all of the bodies in one place, that I instantly became thirsty. I wanted something to drink, but all I saw were punch bowls sitting around, and I wasn't willing to sample them until I found one that was alcohol-free. As I looked around, I noticed the crowd looked to be a little older, which made me wonder if there were any first-year students there. Honestly, most of them looked like they could've been grad students.

"Hey there. You look like you may be lost," I heard a sweet voice say coming from behind me.

I quickly turned around and found a girl that looked even sweeter than what her voice sounded standing in front of me.

I smiled and said, "No, I wouldn't say I'm lost. Just a little out of my element."

"You and me both!" she said. She then corrected herself, seeming to not want me to think she was boring, and said, "Well, don't get me wrong, I like to have a good time, but I don't need all of this."

Letting her know that she didn't have to try to prove anything to me, I said, "I get it. It's ok to not like the big party scene. I'm the exact same way."

I then noticed she had a drink in her hand, and said, "Well, maybe not exactly like you. I don't even drink."

As she looked down at her cup and laughed, her pale cheeks turned pink.

She pushed her blonde hair that had fallen into her face, behind her ear and said, "Oh, neither do I. This is just punch. My mom would kill me if she knew I was starting out my first year of college by becoming a lush!"

"I was just about to ask you what year of school you were in, but you answered that for me. What are you doing here if this isn't what you like?"

"I agreed to come along with a few of my friends. They're around here somewhere."

"How uncanny is this? I'm here for the same reason. My best friend dragged me here. Well, he really didn't have to drag me. I just feel like I need to keep an eye on him."

"Hmmm. So, where is he?" she asked, as she looked around.

"I have absolutely no idea!" I said, laughing.

"Well, I don't think you're doing such a good job at keeping an eye on him."

"I have to agree with you . . .", I said, pausing, as I waited for her to tell me her name.

"Madison," she replied. "What's your name?"

"Ezekiel," I replied.

"Wow. That's a nice, strong, biblical name."

"That's what my mom was going for. You have a beautiful name, Madison."

"Thank you," she said blushing.

We then had an awkward moment of silence, and both began looking around as if we were looking for the people we'd arrived with, knowing that wasn't the case as all.

To break the uncomfortable silence, I said, "Madison, can you show me where you found that virgin punch?"

"Sure, follow me," she said, as she grabbed my hand as if she'd known me for years, and led the way.

After getting a drink, we snuck out the back and sat on the patio where it was a lot more quiet. We did a lot of talking, and learned a lot about each other in just a little time. She was actually born and raised in California, but lived in San Diego, which was still almost five-hundred miles from the university. She was a business major, and our dorms just so happened to be in the same hall. Madison seemed very mellow and laid back, and I could definitely see us becoming good friends.

"Oh my goodness!" Madison said, as she looked down at her watch.

"What's wrong?" I asked sounding extremely worried.

"We've been out here for two hours. I hope my friends didn't leave me."

We both stood up, and I said, "Well, if so, you can walk back with me and Kyle. That's if he hasn't left me."

When we walked back into the house, I noticed that the crowd had cleared out quite a bit, and the music was low. We stayed together as we looked for Kyle and Madison's friends. As we were walking around, I saw a group of guys standing around in a crowd.

I told Madison I'd be right back, and walked over to see if Kyle was in the midst of whatever was going on. I pushed my way through the crowd, and Kyle was still nowhere in sight.

I then heard one of the guys that was sitting on one of the sofas next to a girl say, "She'll be ok. She wants to stay right here with me."

One of the other guys said, "Well, if she's staying here with you, we're all staying!"

It wasn't until then that I looked into the girl's face. Her hair was all disheveled. Even with her beautiful eyes closed, I knew exactly who she was. It was the girl from earlier, and she was completely out of it. I didn't know if she'd had too much to drink or if someone had slipped her a roofie, but what I did know was that if I didn't do something, every one of those guys, and it had to have been at least twenty of them, were going to take advantage of her that night. It was only me against all of them. I didn't know what these guys were all about, whether they had weapons, or if they would try to put up a fight if I threw a wrench in their plans, but none of that really mattered in that moment.

This girl needed help and I seemed to be the only one around willing to help her.

The guy who was sitting next to her began trying to fondle her.

"What are you doing?" I asked, as I jumped in front of all of the spectators.

The guy stood up, and at that moment, I realized he was a lot bigger than he looked while he was sitting down.

"No, what are you doing?" he said in an aggressive tone.

"I'm trying to take my sister home where she belongs!" I said, getting aggressive right back with him.

"Your sister?" he asked, looking as if he wasn't sure whether or not to believe me.

He looked back and forth at me and her, then shook his head and said, "Nah. Y'all don't look anything alike. I think you're just trying to have a good time with her just like we're about to."

He and his boys began walking up on me as if they were about to toss me around like a basketball. All I could think to myself was how in the world I had gotten myself into this mess.

"Hey, Ezekiel, did you find your sister yet?" I suddenly heard Kyle yell out from the crowd.

Kyle always somehow came through for me. I didn't know where he had come from, but I was glad that he'd shown up when he did.

"Yeah, she's over here. She had a few people keeping her company," I said, cutting my eyes at the guy who had just called me a liar.

Kyle then made his way through the crowd and everyone began moving out the way as we attempted to carefully lift my "sister" up off of the sofa. I lifted her up by her arms, and Kyle had her by the legs as we carried her through the crowd. Throughout the entire ordeal, she never even opened her eyes. I was just hoping she was ok.

Out of nowhere, came Madison. I had forgotten all about the fact that she was waiting for me to come back.

"What's going on? Do you know her?" she asked, as she looked down at the girl with a concerned look on her face.

Kyle looked strangely at Madison, then back at me, and asked, "Who is she?"

Too many different questions were being asked when all I was concerned with was getting this girl to safety.

As we headed out the front door, I said, "No, Madison. I don't know her. She was in danger, and I just needed to get her away from those guys. They were getting ready to take advantage of her."

"That's sweet of you and all, but you just put yourself in a whole lot of danger. They could've killed you. She put herself in this situation," Madison said, sounding more concerned about me than the girl.

We gently laid the girl down in the grass, and I checked for her pulse.

"She has a pulse. I think she's just passed out," I said updating Kyle and Madison on her status.

After making sure that the girl did have a pulse, I looked at Madison and said, "Maybe she did put herself in that situation, but even so, she still deserves for someone to help her when she can't help herself."

Madison, turning red, said, "I'm sorry. I shouldn't have said that. I didn't mean it that way. I just would've hated for something to happen to you."

"Just forget about it," I said, slightly irritated.

"I don't know what's going on. I just know that I walked in on you being in some deep trouble, and that's normally my M.O. First off, are you going to tell me who Princess is?" Kyle asked, looking over at Madison.

"Madison, this is my best friend, Kyle, I was telling you about. Kyle, this is Madison."

"Nice to meet you, Kyle," Madison said.

Kyle nodded his head.

At that moment, the girl we'd carried out began coughing and choking on her own vomit.

People continued to come out of the Frat House, but no one offered to help. I think that either everyone was so drunk that they didn't even realize what was going on, or they were just used to seeing that type of thing.

"Help me roll her over on her side!" I said.

After rolling her over and patting her on her back, Kyle said, "What are we about to do with her? We don't even have a car to drive her back. Maybe we need to call an ambulance."

I tried talking to the girl to see if she was alert enough to give me any information.

"Hey, I'm trying to help you. Can you tell me your name?"

All she did was moan.

"Did she have a purse?" Madison asked.

"No. I didn't see one."

All girls carry a purse. I'll run back in and see if maybe it was left on the sofa where you found her," she replied.

"No! One of us guys need to go back in. Kyle, can you go check?"

"No problem," he said, as he jumped up and headed back inside the house.

I looked at Madison and said, "Where are your friends?"

She shrugged her shoulders and said, "I don't know. They probably either all left together when they couldn't find me, or they might've each left with a guy. Who knows with them?"

I looked at Madison and shook my head.

"What was that for?" she asked.

"You just don't seem like the type to hang with people like that."

"Look at what I found!" Kyle yelled, as he walked towards us with a red purse hanging on his shoulder and something else in his hand.

"I found her ID. I didn't want to go through her purse, but we really have no choice here."

"What's her name?" I eagerly asked.

"We have here, Stormie Summers," Kyle said, giggling.

"Are you joking?" I asked, not taking Kyle serious at all.

"No. That's her name!"

I snatched the ID from Kyle and looked for myself. Being the jokester that he was, I didn't know when and when not to take him serious sometimes.

"Yeah, you're right. Stormie Summers, and she's from New York. How in the world have I never seen her?"

"Um, maybe because she lives in Queens, almost a whole hour from New York City!" Kyle sarcastically replied.

"I guess you're right. Anyway, I need you two to help put Ms. Stormie on my back."

"You're going to carry her?" Madison asked.

"I really don't have a choice. She can't walk"

"You think she's going to hold on?" Kyle asked.

"All we can do is try," I replied, becoming frustrated with the both of them.

I got down on both knees as I waited for Kyle and Madison to try and lift Stormie up and lay her on my back. Madison had a very small frame, so I was hoping that all of the muscles that Kyle put so much effort into keeping intact would do all the work. Stormie wasn't big, but very curvy and tall. With her being passed out, she felt like dead weight.

"I'll get her top half and you get her legs," Kyle said to Madison.

Within a few seconds, I felt Stormie's warm body lying on my back. I then grabbed her dangling arms and wrapped them around my neck. I slowly stood up, making sure that her long legs were secured.

I looked around at Kyle and Madison and said, "Ok. Let's go."

"Wait. Where are we going?" Kyle asked.

"Back to the dorm. It isn't like we know where to take her, unless you want to walk her all the way to Queens," I said, sarcastically.

Kyle then looked at Madison and said, "And where are you going, Princess?"

Before Madison could answer, I said, "She lives in our same residence hall."

"Alrighty then. Let's go," Kyle said, looking bewildered.

As we headed back to the dorm, Madison said, "I know one thing for sure. I'll never forget my very first night on campus."

"I think the same goes for all of us," I said.

"You got that right. This will be the first time since we've been friends that I wasn't the one to find trouble, but I for sure found some girls!" Kyle said, as he pulled several pieces of paper out of his pockets with phone numbers he'd collected throughout the night.

Chapter Eight

"Where am I?!?!" I suddenly heard a female's voice shouting.

As I tried to open my eyes, I felt someone trampling on my back. I was then confused about where I was, but as soon as I got my eyelids, which seemed to be glued together, to separate, I realized where I was and what was happening. I was lying on the floor next to my bed. I had laid Stormie in my bed once Kyle, Madison, and I made it back to the dorm. Stormie had finally awakened, jumped out of my bed, stepping all over me, and immediately began running around like a wild woman.

I quickly jumped up and tried to explain to her what was going on, but she wouldn't be still, nor quiet long enough for me to get her full attention and say what I needed to say.

Kyle opened his bedroom door and stood in the doorway, also looking confused as to what was going on. He didn't look as if he was in any condition to help out, so I had to do something quick.

"Stormie, calm down!" I yelled.

I'd finally gotten her attention, and thought I'd be able to have a civil conversation with her as she stood motionless, staring at me. Or maybe I should say, glaring at me.

"Stormie, we brought you here last night because . . ."

She interrupted me, and said, "We?" as she looked around and realized that I wasn't the only one in the room with her.

"Did you two kidnap and take advantage of me?" she asked, as she looked down to make sure her clothes were intact.

"No! We were helping you. Some other guys were trying to take advantage of you, and we snatched you up and got you out of there!" I said quickly before she could interject.

Stormie looked at me in disbelief and said, "Don't you lie to me! All of you are the same! You just wait for a female to get a little tipsy so you can take advantage of her! I already know the game!"

"Stormie, believe me when I say you weren't just a little tipsy. You were completely passed out. There's no reason for me to lie to you. Why do you think you don't even remember getting here? My friend Kyle and I were just trying to help."

Stormie squinted her eyes as she walked towards me.

"How do you even know my name?" she asked.

Before I could answer, she said, "Wait, I remember you! You were that weird guy in the quad yesterday just staring at me like some serial killer!"

Stormie then seemed as though she'd had some type of epiphany, and said, "Oh my God! Did you follow me to the party and plan this? I'm reporting both of you perverts!"

She then noticed her purse hanging on the back of a chair, quickly snatched it, and ran out the door.

I looked over at Kyle as he folded his arms and shook his head at me.

"Could I at least have gotten some help?" I said, sounded irritated.

"You wanted me to help? That was all your doing. You should've left that girl where she was. Now we're both about to get kicked out of school because you were trying to be Superman."

Panicking a little bit by what Kyle had just said, but trying to still sound calm and in control, I said, "Look, if she reports this, we'll just tell our side of the story!"

"Listen to yourself, Ezekiel! Two Black boys who are new on campus took a drunk chick who was all the way passed out back to their dorm room! Yeah, maybe, you're right. They'll believe us," he said, sarcastically.

Knowing Kyle was right, I still had to figure something out. Right at that moment, a lightbulb went off in my head and I said, "Madison! She'll vouch for us!"

"We don't even know that girl! She doesn't know us! You think she'll get in the middle of something like that just to try to defend a couple of Black boys that she knows nothing about?"

Kyle walked back into his room and slammed the door.

"It'll be alright. Everything is going to work out!" I yelled, even though I knew Kyle had probably stopped listening.

Throughout the rest of the day, I tried to not worry and remove the thought of being kicked out of school for doing what I thought was a good deed as far from my mind as possible, but it was still stressing me out. I prayed to God about it, but I still continued to worry. I worried about something that might not have even been anything to worry about, especially after praying about it. I knew better than that, but Stormie had put worry and fear in my heart.

22 "Cast your cares on the Lord and he will sustain you; he will never let the righteous be shaken." – Psalms 55:22 NIV

The last thing I wanted to do was to worry my mom, especially after only my first day of being on campus, but I needed to talk to someone since Kyle was clearly avoiding me. She was true to her name, and definitely a woman of faith, but when it came to me, her faith was sometimes tested.

"Hey, Baby! I was going to call you today. I was sure you probably had a long day of campus activities yesterday after Sonja and I left you boys, so I was giving you some time to rest up," my mom said, sounding surprisingly upbeat.

I guess I'd expected her to sound a little down because I was gone, but it was nice to hear her sound as though she would be ok without me. I hated to ruin it by telling her what I'd experienced the night before and that early morning, but I knew it would be better for her to hear the truth from me at that moment, than to possibly have to hear Stormie's version from the school, police, or both, later.

"Hey, Ma," I said, obviously sounding a little shook because she knew there was something wrong right away.

"What's wrong?" she said, with the joy in her voice immediately leaving.

Hesitating, I said, "Well, there was an incident last night." I then paused.

"Ezekiel, stop beating around the bush. Just tell me what happened! I'm sure whatever it is will be alright."

"I don't know, Ma."

She took and deep breath and said, "I know Kyle had to have something to do with whatever it is. What trouble did he get the two of you in now?"

"Kyle didn't do anything. I saw a girl at a Frat party . . ."

Interrupting, my mom said, "Here we go! Didn't I tell you about these girls! You can't let them get in your head, having you do things you shouldn't be doing! Stay focused!"

"Ma, can I please finish? It's nothing like that."

As my mom became silent, I continued.

"She was about to be taken advantage of by a group of guys. She was completely passed out, so I pretended to be her brother, and got her out of there."

"I'm confused. What's the problem? I'm sure she's thankful to you for that, and hopefully she learned her lesson."

"The problem is, since she was passed out, Kyle and I didn't know where to take her, so I carried her to our dorm room and let her sleep it off in my bed."

"Ezekiel!"

"I know, but what else was I supposed to do?"

My mom sighed, and said, "Go on."

"When she woke up, she freaked out on me. I promise I slept on the floor. I was the perfect gentleman."

"You know I have no doubts about that, Son, but just think about it. She woke up in a strange room with two boys. I'm sure she had no idea what happened to her. I know the two of you didn't do anything to her, but she doesn't know you. What exactly did she say?"

"Before she stormed out, she said she was going to report us. I tried telling her that we took her out of a bad situation, but she didn't want to listen to anything I had to say."

My mom was very quiet, and I knew that meant she was upset, but trying to calm herself down.

After a couple of minutes of silence, I said, "Ma, you there?"

"Yeah, I'm here."

"So, what do you think I should do?" I asked, sounding helpless.

"There's really nothing you can do except to pray that she realizes that you saved her. If not, I'm sure there are witnesses who saw what happened, but hopefully it doesn't even come to that."

"Yeah, Madison was there and saw exactly what happened."

"Madison?" my mom said, intriguingly.

"Yeah, she's a girl I met at the party . . ."

"Ezekiel, Ezekiel, Ezekiel . . . All I'm hearing is girls, girls, girls!"

"Ma, I'm going to meet girls! Madison is really nice. I didn't want to go to that party. I was really just going to keep an eye on Kyle, and I ended up losing him. While I was standing around, I ran into Madison, who was also just there because her friends drug her along. We left the party scene, went outside, and talked. When I went back in looking for Kyle is when I saw the other girl in trouble."

I could picture my mom rubbing her head as she said, "And you just had to go over and save her."

"Of course," I replied.

"You are your father's child."

"Wasn't that the right thing to do?" I asked, sounding confused.

My mom hesitated at first, but then said, "Of course it was. I would want someone to help you if you were in a bad situation."

I felt relieved hearing that from my mom. She reassured me that I didn't do anything wrong. I had begun thinking that maybe I should've just minded my business and went on my way. If I had done that, I wouldn't have even been able to sleep, but I still wasn't quite sure how well I would be able to sleep knowing that there was a girl out there thinking I'd tried to harm her.

"These years away from home are going to teach you a lot of things. You'll also learn how to handle situations that you may experience, or even see others experience. Take mental notes from this one. You could've still helped her by anonymously contacting the police or campus security. No one would've known you did it, and it would've prevented what you're going through right now. God knows the truth, so everything will work out. Just trust Him," my mom said, reassuringly.

[28] "And we know that in all things God works for the good of those who love him, who have been called according to his purpose." – Romans 8:28 NIV

"You're right, Ma, as always. Thanks for the talk. I do feel a lot better."

"I'm always here for you Ezekiel. You know that. Just pray, and I'll be in agreement with you. Keep me posted."

"Ok, Ma."

Before hanging up, my mom said, "One more thing."

"Yes," I said, as I prepared myself for her next lesson.

"Don't be so impulsive. You need to think things through a little more before you make a move. I know your heart is always in the right place, but sometimes we tend to allow our emotions to take control of every part of us. That's when our good intentions don't always result in the best results. That's ok, though. Just keep sowing good seeds, and you can't do anything except reap greatness. You're on the right path. I'm proud of you, and I know your dad is, too."

"I love you, Ma."

"I love you, too, Ezekiel."

Stormie

Chapter Nine

As soon as I walked out of the dorm room from with the two weirdos who had claimed to try to help me, I knew my first stop would be to campus security, but I had to get my story straight. I knew I'd had too much to drink the night before, but I also knew that those two guys had tried to take advantage of me. I had to make sure that security, the police, and whoever else needed to become involved, completely understood that I had been the victim of a serious crime.

As I walked towards the exit of the unfamiliar dorm hall, I constantly looked back, making sure that I wasn't being followed. While looking back, and not paying attention to what was right in front of me, I ran directly into a girl that was seemingly familiar.

"I'm so sorry! Are you feeling ok, today?" the girl with the bright blue eyes and long, frizzy blonde hair said.

Immediately defensive, as I was most of the time, and not concerned with anything the girl was saying, I said, "Watch where you're going!"

I knew I hadn't been watching where I was going because my mind had been too occupied with whether the two guys back in the dorm room were possibly following behind me.

Most times, people would've backed down from me after realizing that I wasn't very approachable, but not this one.

She folded her arms and said, "I said I was sorry! You were the one who wasn't paying attention. You should actually have more of an attitude of gratitude after what you were saved from last night! Anyone else would've probably left you right where you were, but there were some angels watching over you last night, so girl, be grateful!"

> [8] **"For it is by grace you have been saved, through faith—and this is not from yourselves, it is the gift of God —"**
> **– Ephesians 2:8 NIV**

I couldn't get past this White girl's sass, and the audacity she had to try to come for me. I was so upset with the way she had spoken to me, that I almost didn't hear her mention the part about me being saved the night before. My entire demeanor and facial expression changed. I let down my guard for the first time since I could remember.

As the girl rolled her eyes and began to walk away, I grabbed her arm and said, "Wait."

She rolled her eyes again, and said, "Wait for what? For you to try to go off on me for no apparent reason? There are some good people around here, and you definitely aren't one of them."

"Look. I'm sorry. I'm new here, just as you probably are." I lowered my voice and said, "I have absolutely no idea what happened to me last night. I woke up in these two guy's dorm room and completely spazzed out on them. I'm on my way to campus security now to report them, but it seems like you might know something that I don't know. I'm a complete wreck right now. I'm sorry about how I just treated you. I was wrong."

I didn't know what was going on with me, but me being nice, especially to a complete stranger was not me at all. I had always kept my guards up because I was raised in a way in which I felt like

I had to. I had grown up in the system, and no one in the system could be trusted. Absolutely no one. I had been taken away from my mom when I was only four years old. She was an alcoholic and heroin addict, and unfortunately when she didn't have money, she would sell me so that she could get her fix. One night, she went to a dealer to get her fix, knowing she didn't have money, but had me right by her side, and knew exactly what she'd planned on doing. As soon as she tried to exchange me for a quick high to the undercover cop on the corner of one of the busiest intersections in Queens, she was immediately handcuffed. She dropped what she called her "Lucky Lighter", as she tried to resist arrest. I picked up the bright pink lighter that had a beautifully hued butterfly on it and stuffed it inside my pants. After they threw my mom inside the squad car, I'd never seen her again, but her lighter stayed with me wherever I went.

I was placed in foster home after foster home, but because I had never had a stable home environment, and had been abused and neglected so much, no one was willing to put up with my understandably horrible behavior. Family after family, my self-worth declined more and more. All I knew at that age was no one wanted me, and I would've been better off with my mom. At least she did seem to want to keep me around, even it was to just use me. That's when I learned I couldn't trust people because they cared about no one except themselves. I had to take care of myself and not worry about anyone else.

The blonde-haired girl folded her arms, made a deep sigh, and gave me a slight smile.

"Apology accepted. I was just headed out for a walk. Come with me, and I'll tell you all about last night."

As I walked and talked with the girl, she told me her name was Madison. I felt so bad for treating the guy, whose name I'd learned was Ezekiel, the way that I had. Madison told me everything that had happened and how Ezekiel had sacrificed his own safety just to help me, a complete stranger, who he knew nothing about.

Everything was fine until Madison said, "Ezekiel is a really good guy, and you owe him an apology. I tried to tell him to just stay out of it and he refused to leave you there like that."

As we walked along the walkway of the campus, I stopped and looked at Madison.

"What?" she asked, as if she had said nothing wrong.

I pointed my finger in her face and said, "So, you suggested that he just leave me there and let those guys have their way with me?"

"You put it that way, but what I suggested to him was to mind his business because you were the one who decided to get as drunk as you did off of whatever you were drinking in order to give those guys the opportunity to take advantage of you. You are not Ezekiel's responsibility. He doesn't even know you for Christ's sake. He had just met me last night and I would've never expected him or anyone else to do that for me after only knowing me for a few hours. That's all I was saying."

I felt like slapping that girl at that exact moment, but I controlled my temper.

"You know what, Madison? I appreciate the information you've given me, but I think our time here is up before someone gets hurt, and it wouldn't be me. Tell your friends, or whatever they are to you that they don't have to worry about me saying anything."

Madison looked at me as if she was confused and said, "That's it?"

"What do you mean?" I asked, as I folded my arms. "What else do you want me to say?"

"You don't want me to tell them that you're sorry? Even better, why not do it yourself? A 'thank you' might even be nice," she said.

"Me not going to campus security reporting them should be 'sorry' enough. They could be in a lot of trouble," I replied.

"Something is really not right with you. They did nothing to you, but help. On top of that, I helped them help you, and you can't even say 'I'm sorry? Thank you so much?' That is so ridiculous. Who raised you?"

Madison stood there squinting her eyes, staring at me as if I was some type of alien while I looked right back at her and shrugged my shoulders. I didn't feel like I owed anyone anything further. I flipped my hair, turned my back on Madison, and said, "You have a good day."

What Madison didn't understand was through all my heartbreak, rejection, neglect, and abuse, even if any of it was unintentional, no one ever told me they were sorry. I never received an apology for anything that ever happened to me. There were people who did things to me that they should've rotted in prison for, but they didn't because I didn't turn them in. Did they ever thank me? No, because no one ever felt like they owed me a thing, and that was exactly the way I felt the entire world was. I reciprocated the treatment that I received my entire life, and didn't feel the least bit bad about it.

> [8] **"Finally, all of you should be of one mind. Sympathize with each other. Love each other as brothers and sisters. Be tenderhearted, and keep a humble attitude. [9] Don't repay evil for evil. Don't retaliate with insults when people insult you. Instead, pay them back with a blessing. That is what God has called you to do, and he will grant you his blessing. [10] For the Scriptures say,"If you want to enjoy life and see many happy days, keep your tongue from speaking evil and your lips from telling lies.[11] Turn away from evil and do good. Search for peace, and work to maintain it.[12] The eyes of the Lord watch over those who do right, and his ears are open to their prayers. But the Lord turns his face against those who do evil." – 1 Peter 3:8-12 NLT**

One of my not so fond memories of being under foster care was when I was placed with a family that already had four biological children of their own. They had two girls and two boys, all ranging from the ages of five to eleven. The oldest two were the girls, named Aaliyah and Ariana. Aaliyah was eleven and

Ariana was eight. The boy's names were Julian, who was six, and the baby boy, Gabriel, who was five. I had been in the foster system for about five years, making me nine years old, and this had probably been my seventh home. Before even arriving at that home, as I always did, I told myself that I was going to be on my very best behavior and do whatever my foster parents told me to do without giving them any problems, even if I knew they were wrong. When my social worker dropped me off, I immediately began asking myself why they would want to take me in when they already had four children of their own.

Most families I had been placed with would only have maybe one or two biological children, if any, and a few other foster children, so this one, I just didn't understand. I was smart enough to know that four children were a lot to be responsible for, so why would people want to add on to that responsibility if they didn't have to? I didn't realize until later on in life that money was a huge motive for fostering for a lot of families.

I tried not to get too far in my head and question things too much because the house was amazing. It was very different from what I had been used to, and I couldn't ask for much more. Since all of the rooms were taken by the other children, the foster parents who owned the home, Mr. and Mrs. Edwards, set up my room in the basement. It wasn't what most people would think of whenever someone mentioned a basement. I wasn't dark, cold, and spooky with cobwebs everywhere. It was actually probably one of the nicest places I had slept in my entire life. It was very clean, just like the rest of the house, and it was fixed up very nice. I even had my own bathroom, just as the other children's bedrooms did.

The Edwards' explained that they just didn't want anyone to feel overcrowded, and by doing things that way, everyone still had their own, personal space. I understood and didn't mind, since I had been in far worse places. Whenever social services would come by to check on things, my foster parents, Mr. and Mrs. Edwards, would coach me as to what to say and pretend that I shared a bedroom with Ariana. It was against the law for a foster child's room to be on a separate level, so the Edwards' had even put a spare bed and some of my personal things in Ariana's room to make sure it looked like I was really sharing the room with her. I didn't question anything because I felt as though I was in a great situation and dared not to mess that up.

Just by looking at Mr. Edwards, anyone would be able to tell he was a businessman. He almost always wore a suit and tie, and if he didn't, he wore jeans, a dress shirt, and a nice pair of Stacy Adams. Mrs. Edwards wore dresses that hugged her perfectly shaped curves almost every day. They were both in very good shape. Mr. Edwards left home every morning with a briefcase and came home in the early evenings. Mrs. Edwards took care of the house, making sure the kids got breakfast and made if off to school. She also always made sure dinner was prepared by five every evening. Their family seemed so perfect. I knew Ken and Barbie weren't real, but whenever I thought of perfection, that's who I thought of because I had never had any positive role models or influencers in my life. The Edwards' reminded of the Black versions of Ken and Barbie.

One day, around a week after I had arrived at the Edwards' home, while the other two girls and I were outside playing, Ariana said she was glad that I had come to live with them because she wouldn't have to play "that game" with her dad anymore.

"Ariana!" Aaliyah yelled as she yanked her towards her.

"What game?" I asked inquisitively.

"Don't listen to her. There's just this game my dad likes to play, and Ariana isn't very good at it, so she's hoping since you're here, she won't have to play anymore. She's just a sore loser. You'll soon realize that you shouldn't listen to most of anything that she says."

Ariana pulled away from her sister and we continued playing hopscotch as if nothing was said, and I never thought twice about it. I had seen a lot of drama between both biological siblings and other foster kids, so this was nothing that seemed unusual to me.

Chapter Ten

It had been about a month since I had been living with the Edwards'. Everything had continued to seem normal. I felt like I'd finally been saved from the constant abuse that I had endured in all of the other foster homes. I would even have dreams that the Edwards had decided to adopt me and I would never have to worry about going and living with any other families. I was happy exactly where I was, and I hoped with everything that I had in me that nothing would change. That was until I found myself disappointed once again.

One night, while in my room in the basement, sleeping, I was awakened by the sound of footsteps coming down the stairs. It hadn't been long since I had fallen asleep, so my eyes immediately popped open, and I began looking around.

"Ari?" I yelled out.

I assumed it was Ariana because she would sometimes sneak downstairs and crawl into bed with me. Whenever I asked her why, she would just say she had a bad dream, which seemed a little strange to me because who goes into a basement after they've had a bad dream? It seemed to me that she would've gone straight to her parent's room if she had really had a bad dream. She not only had the option to go to her parent's room, but she also had all of her other siblings to run to. I didn't give her a hard time. It did sometimes get lonely down there.

After not hearing Ariana respond when I called out her name, I turned on the lamp that was next to my bed, and right before my feet could touch the floor, Mr. Edwards came from out of nowhere, startling me. It looked like I had startled him for a moment, too.

"Hey, Stormie! I didn't think you would still be awake," Mr. Edwards said with a huge smile on his face.

He seemed very different. He was more of the serious type, so I had never really seen him smile the way that he was smiling in that moment. I then got a whiff of a very familiar stench. The same stench of liquor that I would smell on my mother. I'd never forget it. It looked like he had just gotten home because he was fully dressed and hadn't even taken the time to take off his shoes.

"Hi, Mr. Edwards. Is something wrong?" I asked nervously.

"No. Nothing's wrong. I just realized that I'm so busy with work most of the time, I hadn't really gotten a chance to really get to know you."

"Well, I think you know most of everything there is to know about me," I said, naively, shrugging my shoulders.

Mr. Edwards sat at the edge of the bed, still smiling.

He gently put his hand on my shoulder, and said, "I'm sure there is plenty more I need to know about you."

A sudden fear came over me. I was no stranger to this type of situation. I just never thought that I would have to worry about that with Mr. Edwards. Everything had been going so well, but by what Mr. Edwards said next, he also apparently knew I was no stranger to the type of behavior that he was exhibiting.

"You know, I'm well-known, and a very important part of this community, so I find out a lot of things. Even things that may not be in your records because they weren't reported to your social worker. Is there anything you want to tell me about yourself that I may or may not already know?"

Trying to stay calm and control my breathing, I said, "I don't know what you're talking about."

Mr. Edwards' smile completely disappeared, and I suddenly saw an extremely terrifying darkness in his eyes.

"Well, I hear that you're a troublemaker. You've stirred up a lot of trouble in homes of very prominent men like myself, who happen to be friends of mine."

My eyes became big as saucers. I knew if Mr. Edwards was friends with any of the men whose homes I had been previously placed in, I was in trouble. Every one of them had abused me in some type of way, whether it was physically, sexually, verbally, or emotionally. Whenever I would try to tell my social worker anything, she would just brush off any of my accusations as if I was crazy, and never reported anything. It should've dawned on me back then that she was going back telling the families what I was saying because even though she never filed any reports, the families would suddenly begin treating me worse and worse. I was only a kid, so I didn't know. I just wanted help, and trusted that she would help me. Without ever having anyone to believe me, or do anything to help me, I just always felt defeated and did whatever I had to do to survive. Eventually, after I had been used up, each family that I lived with would tell my social worker that I wasn't a good fit for their family, and I would get placed somewhere else, dealing with the same types of issues.

Mr. Edwards continued, "I'm going to let you know right now, you will do as I say, and I won't tolerate those problems in my home. I'm one of the biggest names . . . Wait . . . I am the biggest name around here!"

Mr. Edwards then began looking off into space, sounding as if he were talking to himself.

"I'm the best criminal defense attorney in this state, and probably any other state. No other attorney out there can even come close in comparison, and my dad said I wouldn't amount to anything. Ha! He's probably turning over in his grave looking at how great I turned out to be!"

Mr. Edwards began laughing, and then turned his attention back to me and said, "So you should be honored that you're even allowed to step foot in my door. It's a privilege. Everything around here is a privilege! Remember that!" he said, raising his voice. Paranoid, he then looked around, obviously remembering that there were other people in the house.

[3] **"Because of the privilege and authority God has given me, I give each of you this warning: Don't think you are better than you really are. Be honest in your evaluation of yourselves, measuring yourselves by the faith God has given us.** [4] **Just as our bodies have many parts and each part has a special function,** [5] **so it is with Christ's body. We are many parts of one body, and we all belong to each other.** [6] **In his grace, God has given us different gifts for doing certain things well. So if God has given you the ability to prophesy, speak out with as much faith as God has given you.** [7] **If your gift is serving others, serve them well. If you are a teacher, teach well.** [8] **If your gift is to encourage others, be encouraging. If it is giving, give generously. If God has given you leadership ability, take the responsibility seriously. And if you have a gift for showing kindness to others, do it gladly."**
– Romans 12:3-8 NLT

He then said, "Now we're going to play a game that I'm sure you're familiar with."

I immediately realized what Ariana was talking about when she mentioned "the game", and that was when it happened. The first man I'd actually looked up to sexually molested me. Even though it had not been the first time I had been molested, it felt even worse this time because I thought Mr. Edwards was someone I could trust. I had never trusted the other men. One thing Mr. Edwards taught me was that I could trust absolutely no one.

Life went on in the Edwards' household as normal. I kept my mouth closed about everything, even to Ariana and Aaliyah, but I had a strange feeling they already knew. Ariana would look at me as if she wanted to say something, but Aaliyah was always lurking around. She seemed to have a lot of control over her little sister and seemed to want to protect her dad. I also noticed that when Mr. Edwards did get out of his super serious moods, he played and joked around a lot with Aaliyah. I wondered if he had also molested her, or if he still was. If he had, or was, it seemed like she thought it was ok. It was as if her dad had her brainwashed, making sure she kept the secret between only the two of them.

Mrs. Edwards just walked around cooking and cleaning, seeming oblivious to everything that was going on right in front of her in her own home. I didn't know how long I would end up living with the Edwards, but I knew that I didn't have anyone on my side. I knew if I had even tried to go to a teacher at school, it would backfire on me because my social worker was always sure to get to them before I could, telling them how I "liked to make up cruel stories" about the families that would take me in. I wondered if she was getting a cut out of the deal for keeping the authorities and anyone else out of the situation. The only person that I felt that could possibly help me out of the situation I was in was Ariana, but Aaliyah made sure I never got too close to her. She wouldn't even come sneak in the basement with me anymore when she would "have a bad dream", so I was sure someone had told her to stay away from me.

Each year that went by, I began accepting the situation more and more. I had become less afraid of Mr. Edwards because even though the molestation continued, he'd actually begun treating me like a person instead of a prisoner. As sick as that may sound, it was true. As long as I tried fighting him each time he came down those basement stairs, like I would in the beginning, he would punch me, kick me, spit on me, and even push my head down in the toilet and act as if he was going to drown me. After going through all of that, I finally realized that as long as I followed his instructions, and did whatever he wanted me to do, I received the same treatment as his other children. I had to do what I had to do to survive, and that was how I learned to live in survival mode at all times.

With each year that went by, the taller and more developed I became. By the time I was thirteen, I was already 5' 8" tall and very curvy. Everywhere we went, the boys were looking, and trying to get my phone number. Mr. Edwards would be with us a lot of those times, and if looks could've killed, those boys would've been dead. Aaliyah was fifteen at the time, and the looks she would give me weren't very pleasant either. She and her dad had been very close, but he seemed to start paying more attention to me than her, and I could tell she was very bothered by it. Mr. Edwards had his entire family brainwashed. They all thought he was bigger and greater than anything in this world and felt like no none could love them more than he could. I began to feel the same way. Being a foster child, I never really had any confidence, and felt rejected, but after a while, Mr. Edwards took advantage of that, and knew exactly what to say to make me feel loved and desired. Despite the things Mr. Edwards was making me do, I trusted him again. I knew what he was doing was wrong, but no one else had ever made me feel the way he made me feel.

[4] "Everyone who sins is breaking God's law, for all sin is contrary to the law of God. [5] And you know that Jesus came to take away our sins, and there is no sin in him. [6] Anyone who continues to live in him will not sin. But anyone who keeps on sinning does not know him or understand who he is. [7] Dear children, don't let anyone deceive you about this: When people do what is right, it shows that they are righteous, even as Christ is righteous. [8] But when people keep on sinning, it shows that they belong to the devil, who has been sinning since the beginning. But the Son of God came to destroy the works of the devil. [9] Those who have been born into God's family do not make a practice of sinning, because God's life is in them. So they can't keep on sinning, because they are children of God. [10] So now we can tell who are children of God and who are children of the devil. Anyone who

does not live righteously and does not love other believers does not belong to God." – 1 John 3:4-10 NLT

One morning before school, Aaliyah, Ariana, and I sat at the breakfast table eating cereal while Mrs. Edwards checked on the boys, making sure they were up getting dressed. Aaliyah kept looking at me as if she wanted to say something, but then she'd just roll her eyes. She was a fifteen year old hormonal girl, so I really didn't think anything of her rolling her eyes. When she realized I wasn't paying her any attention, she began to sigh, loudly.

"What's wrong with you?" I finally asked, giving her what she wanted.

"You just always sit here as if you're part of this family. You do get that you don't have a mom or a dad, right? They didn't want you then, and they still don't want you now! If they did, they would've tried to come back for you a long time ago."

Here I was, thirteen with a fifteen-year-old picking on me for no apparent reason. Aaliyah was never too fond of me, so it didn't surprise me, but this time she had hit below the belt.

"I have a mom and a dad. If I didn't, I wouldn't exist," I replied.

"That doesn't take away from the fact that they still didn't want you!"

"What? Are you mad because your dad would prefer me to be his daughter over you? Is that what this is about? Because he treats me the way he used to treat you?"

I could see the fire in Aaliyah's eyes. I looked at Ariana and she looked as if she wanted to cry, but remained quiet.

"I could care less how my dad is treating you! It doesn't mean anything. Don't you see that? He has done the same thing to all of us! You're not special. He doesn't care about anyone but himself, but you think he loves you? I used to think he loved me, too. To the point that I didn't protect my little sister. I'm old enough now to realize that this life is a big lie! This isn't normal and no one here seems to care. Not even our own mother!"

Aaliyah was shouting so loudly, Mrs. Edwards walked in and said, "Aaliyah, what is going on?"

"Nothing," Aaliyah said, as she grabbed her bookbag and walked out the door.

Mrs. Edwards looked at me and Ariana, waiting for an explanation from us. We both shrugged our shoulders. I felt the entire outburst was out of jealously because Aaliyah wasn't getting the attention she was used to, but later in life, I realized it was out of guilt. As the oldest child, she felt guilty about the things she allowed to go on in the house without saying anything. She was the first it had happened to, and she protected her dad and allowed it to continue to happen.

[22] "let us go right into the presence of God with sincere hearts fully trusting him. For our guilty consciences have been sprinkled with Christ's blood to make us clean, and our bodies have been washed with pure water."
– Hebrews 10:22 NLT

After Ariana and I finished eating, we walked out the door and headed to the bus stop.

On the way there, Ariana asked, "Do you think Daddy loves us?"

"Of course he does," I replied. "Do you think he loves you?" I asked, Ariana.

"Now I do, but when he used to make me play that game, I didn't. I didn't think my daddy would hurt me like that if he loved me, but when you came, he didn't hurt me anymore. Does he still make you play the game?" she asked.

I was about to tell Ariana the truth, but I was so confused about how I should've felt about everything. I didn't feel hurt anymore. I felt loved. I had a family, so I felt I should've been grateful and not complain about anything. Aaliyah, Ariana, and I were in different situations. I was only a foster child. I could've been made to leave at any moment, and I didn't want that. I didn't want to have to go through getting accustomed to another family. I had been with the Edwards' for almost five years, and after everything I had gone through to get in the position that I was in, I wasn't trying to go anywhere else. Others may call me stupid and wonder what was wrong with me, but those same people don't understand the meaning of Stockholm Syndrome, which is what I was experiencing. Back then, I didn't even know what it was, but it is real, and people suffer from it every single day.

Stockholm Syndrome – "Stockholm syndrome is a psychological response. It occurs when hostages or abuse victims bond with their captors or abusers. This psychological connection develops over the course of the days, weeks, months, or even years of captivity or abuse."
– Healthline.com

When we got to the bus stop, Aaliyah was standing there talking to one of her friends. She glanced over at me and Ariana, and then continued her conversation. She smiled and laughed with her friend as if nothing had just occurred between the two of us.

"Don't worry about her. She just gets in these weird moods sometimes," Ariana said.

"I already know," I said.

When the bus pulled up, Aaliyah and her friend got on and went all the way to the back as they always did. Ariana and I sat upfront since the bus stopped at the junior high school first, which was where we both attended. When the bus stopped for us to get off, I stood up and looked back at Aaliyah. Something just didn't seem right. We argued often, but today seemed different. She seemed more bothered than she had ever seemed, and she had never talked about her dad the way she had this particular morning.

She grinned at me, and I didn't know whether to smile or roll my eyes, so I did neither. Ariana and I got off the bus with all of the other students, and as the bus drove away, Aaliyah shouted through the window, "See you at home!"

I thought about Aaliyah saying she would see us at home all day. It was strange. First of all, in the past, she would never say anything to us when Ariana and I got off of the bus. Secondly, she would see us back on the bus at the end of the day before we got home. It almost seemed as though she had planned to be home before we got there. With Aaliyah, nothing was ever black and white. I sometimes thought I didn't understand her because she was older than me, but I was pretty mature for my age and understood a lot of things she didn't even understand, so she kept me pretty confused.

At the end of the day, Ariana and I got on the bus and Aaliyah was nowhere in sight. The highschoolers were always picked up first at the end of the school day. I looked around and everyone else who was normally on the bus was there. Everyone except Aaliyah.

"Where's Aaliyah?" Ariana asked.

"I don't know. Maybe she had after school detention, or got sick and went home early," I said, trying to think of any and every reason why Aaliyah wasn't on that bus.

"I hope she didn't get detention. If she did, she's gonna be in a lot of trouble with Daddy."

"Yeah, I know," I mumbled, as I sat down and looked out of the window, as if I thought she was going to suddenly appear.

Ariana and I were quiet the entire ride home. When we finally came to the corner of our street where the bus stop was, we jumped up before the bus driver even had a chance to open the folding doors. When we got off of the bus, we looked down the street and noticed police cars and news vans everywhere. Ariana and I looked at each other and immediately began running home. As we shoved our way through the crowd in front of our house, people tried to stop us and ask us questions. They were asking us what our names were, and if we were children of Attorney Jackson Edwards. We kept running until we made it to the front door. The door was locked, so we began banging on it, and ringing the doorbell. I knew we had to be thinking the same thing, and if we were, we were both thinking that something really bad had happened to Aaliyah.

A police officer finally opened the door, and I immediately saw Aaliyah sitting on the sofa.

The police officer looked back at her, and by nodding her head at him, she confirmed that we lived there.

We still had no idea what was going on, but the police officer told us to sit on the sofa next to Aaliyah, and we did as we were told.

I whispered to Aaliyah, "What is going on?"

Before she could answer, we saw another officer walking Mr. and Mrs. Edwards out of the kitchen in handcuffs.

Mr. Edwards shouted, "She's lying! Are you going to believe a kid over me? Do you know who I am? Stormie, tell them the truth. You know I love all of you!"

In a low, solemn voice, Aaliyah said, "I did what I should've done a long time ago."

Frantically, I said, "Aaliyah, what did you do?"

Looking at me as if I was crazy, Aaliyah said, "I told the truth! Daddy has been abusing us for years, making us believe that it was love! What he did to us was not out of love and I'm so ashamed of myself for letting him manipulate me into thinking it was! Even Ari was smart enough to know it wasn't right!"

Aaliyah looked at her little sister and said, "Ari, you do understand that what Daddy did to us wasn't right, don't you?"

With tears in her eyes, Ariana replied, "Yeah, but you told me it would be ok, and I believed you."

Aaliyah, jumped up, grabbed, and hugged her sister, and said, "I'm so sorry for letting him do that to you. I'm sorry for not being a better big sister and helping you. You needed me and all I was concerned about was being loved by someone who didn't really care about any of us. I should be punished because I feel like I neglected you and left you to fight a battle you should've never had to fight on your own."

[20] **"The person who sins is the one who will die. The child will**

not be punished for the parent's sins, and the parent will not be punished for the child's sins. Righteous people will be rewarded for their own righteous behavior, and wicked people will be punished for their own wickedness."
– Ezekiel 18:20 NLT

I jumped up and said, "Do you know what you did, Aaliyah? Mr. Edwards is the only man who has ever really loved me! He told me he loved me, and he would do anything for me! Now I have no one! Now I'm going to be put back into the system. Do you understand everything I have already gone through?" I asked Aaliyah, as she continued to hold Ariana.

Before she could respond, I said, "Of course you don't understand because you've always had a family that loves you!"

"This is not a family! This is a dysfunctional mess! People look up to us, and our dad has sexually molested all of us, and our mom stood around and let it happen! Is this what you really think a family is? Is this what you really call love? Did you see how quickly my own dad threw me away once he had you to do whatever he wanted?"

"That's all this is about! You're jealous because your dad loves me more than you!"

"You are insane!" Aaliyah shouted. "You just don't get it and I don't think you ever will! I feel so sorry for you."

"Ladies!" one of the officers yelled. "I know this is an emotional time, but we're going to get all of this sorted out. I'm just glad that one of you were brave enough to finally report what was going on here. You all will be safe from now on. We're going to make sure of that."

That day seemed to be one of the worst days of my life. Mr. and Mrs. Edwards were going to jail for a very long time after testimonies from their own children, and a search warrant that exposed child pornography and other evidence of the abuse that was taking place inside of the home. The Edwards' children went to live with their aunt and uncle, and I, of course, went back into a group home and had to wait to be placed with another family.

This time would be a little harder because there weren't too many families who wanted a thirteen-year-old foster child in the home. The older we got, the more problems we seemed to have. I wasn't going to get my hopes up of getting out of the group home. I accepted the fact that I would probably be there until I was eighteen and then would have to figure life out on my own.

Ezekiel

Chapter Eleven

After talking to my mom on the phone, I just sat at the end of my bed wondering how in the world I had gotten myself into so much trouble in so little time, but like my mom said, God knew the truth. My intentions were good, so I knew everything would work out in the end. It was the in between stuff that I was a little concerned about.

"Kyle," I yelled out as I stood up from my bed, getting ready to do the inevitable.

Kyle didn't answer, so I figured he was probably still upset with me for getting him into this mess.

I went and knocked on his bedroom door and said, "Kyle! Man, open up. I know this is my fault and I'm gonna fix it. You know I wouldn't let you go down like this."

I finally heard the knob turning, and Kyle opened the door.

"What's the plan my man?" Kyle said after looking at me, shaking his head.

"We have to go to campus security and tell them what happened."

Kyle covered his face with his hand, and shook his head at me once again.

"So, this is your great plan? To go tell campus security that we took a drunk girl back to the dorms with us last night? And not only was she drunk, but she was also passed out! Yeah, that sounds like a winner!" Kyle said, sounding irritated.

He attempted to shut the door in my face, but I stuck my foot in the door, forcing him to hear me out.

"That's exactly what we're going to tell them! Listen to what you just said. We took a girl who was drunk and passed out back to the dorm. If she reported us, how could she even give them a full statement about what happened if she was passed out? She has no idea of what really happened. If we just sit here and let them come get us, then we'll look like we're guilty. I know you're not feeling this, but just trust me, Bro."

Kyle took a deep breath and said, "Whatever. Let me put my shoes on."

"I'll be waiting out in the hall," I replied.

While waiting on Kyle, I saw Madison quickly coming down the hall.

"Just the person I was coming to see," Madison said.

Madison looked as if she was upset about something, and one thing I didn't need was for one more person to be mad at me about something.

"Hey, Madison. Is everything ok?"

"Well, I have good news and bad news," she said.

Just then, Kyle came walking out, brushing his hair.

"Hey there, Princess," Kyle said with a big smile.

"Nice to see you smiling again," I said, sarcastically.

"Anyway, don't mind him. He's just in his feelings a little because he's so full of horrible ideas. What's on my mind right now is you, and what you're doing here. My boy, Ezekiel, didn't plan another "Save a Drunk College Girl" adventure, did he?" Kyle said, trying to be funny and flirtatious at the same time.

Madison, not cracking one smile, said, "I actually came by to tell the two of you that I ran into Miss Stormie a little while ago, and she is something else!"

"We know," I replied. This morning didn't go very well when she woke up. She didn't believe anything we had to say, and she ran out of our room threatening to go to campus security."

"Yeah, that's where she was on her way to until I stopped her. She is so rude it's ridiculous! I told her exactly what happened, and I was finally able to get her to say that she wouldn't go to campus security and report you guys."

My eyes lit up and I looked over at Kyle and said, "I told you it was going to be ok."

I then looked back at Madison and said, "So what was the bad news?"

"She's a horrible person. After I told her all of what had happened, she still didn't seem grateful. She didn't even feel like she owed you two an apology, and she couldn't even say 'thank you'."

I raised my eyebrows and said, "That's what you call bad news? I'm just glad she's not reporting us. I don't care about an apology or a thank you."

"Speak for yourself. She was kind of heavy," Kyle said.

"Come on, Man. We need to be grateful right now that we don't have to worry about that trouble anymore. It's over now, so let's just move on from it."

"You are too nice for your own good," Madison said. I felt like slapping her for you!"

"Yeah, I guess I get it from my dad. He was the nicest man I've ever known."

[31] "Get rid of all bitterness, rage, anger, harsh words, and slander, as well as all types of evil behavior. [32] Instead, be kind to each other, tenderhearted, forgiving one another, j ust as God through Christ has forgiven you."
– Ephesians 4:31-32 NLT

After Madison delivered the good news, I felt one hundred percent better, and of course, I had to call my mom and let her know everything was all good. Kyle and Madison waited outside while I made that call. She said she had been praying, which I already knew. She was glad that Madison had spoken with Stormie and that she had decided not to report us, but she still wanted Kyle and I to report what happened, just in case Stormie decided to go back on her word. That way, if she did, we wouldn't look guilty. My mom was a very smart woman and always gave the best advice. What she said made a lot of sense, and when I told Kyle and Madison what she suggested, they both agreed. I just hoped that Stormie wouldn't get in trouble for being drunk and passed out at a party, because I was sure campus security would want us to give her name. That was one name I could never forget. Stormie Summers.

Madison offered to go with us since she was a witness and helped us get Stormie to the dorms.

Kyle smiled, and said, "Cool. Then maybe I can take you to lunch, Princess."

Madison shook her head at Kyle, and then said, "Maybe. Only if you stop calling me 'Princess'."

"Oh. That's not your name?" Kyle said, trying his best to look and sound serious.

Madison folded her arms and cut her eyes at him.

"You need to quit it, Kyle," I said. "Come on. Let's go and get this over with."

As I started walking towards the residence hall's double doors, I looked back and saw that Kyle and Madison were several feet behind. He had put his arm around her as he whispered who knows what in her ear. When it came to girls, Kyle always had to shoot his shot when he felt he had a chance. Madison was no exception.

When we finally found the campus security building, Kyle said, "Man, you know I trust your mom like I trust my own, but are you sure we should do this?"

"Are you having second thoughts now?" I asked, squinting my eyes at Kyle.

"I just don't know . . ."

Madison interjected, and said, "Well, I think it's the absolute right thing to do. I don't trust Stormie. My mom taught me to always cover my butt, and that's what you guys are doing."

"Ok. Princess said . . . I mean Madison said it's all good, so let's go," Kyle said.

I could do nothing but laugh. He was laying it on extra thick for Madison. She just didn't know how persistent Kyle was. Once he laid his eyes on something he wanted, he didn't give up very easily, and it looked like this was the case with Madison.

I held the door open so that Madison and Kyle could walk into the building.

As soon as we all stepped in the door, a very tall, heavy set, dark complected woman, wearing a security uniform said, "Can I help you?"

She sounded just as intimidating as she looked.

Kyle and Madison both looked at me, so from that I assumed I was the designated spokesperson.

I stepped forward, feeling myself fidgeting, and said, "Yes, Ma'am. I'm Ezekiel Whitfield, and my friends and I want to report an incident that occurred last night. Even though no crime was actually committed, we just felt like the right thing to do would be to report it."

The woman stood directly in front of me. We stood face to face, so I knew she had to be at least six feet tall. She put her hands on her hips and gazed into my eyes for a moment as if she was trying to read me.

She then said, "So if no crime was committed . . . I did hear you correctly when you said that, right?"

"Yes, Ma'am," I replied.

"Ok. I just wanted to confirm I was hearing everything correctly. So, now that I've confirmed there was no crime committed, please tell me again why you're here.

"You know, just in case there are any issues or misunderstandings later. We just want it on record that we did come in because I know sometimes things can be misconstrued. I'm an honest person, and so are my friends here. We just don't want any problems. That's all."

"Uh-huh," she said sarcastically, as she walked around me and stood in front of Kyle.

"And what's your name?" she asked Kyle.

"Kyle Morgan, Ma'am."

"So, Kyle, you want to tell me about this incident that occurred last night?"

Before Kyle began talking, I said, "Ma'am, can we please go somewhere in private and talk?"

The woman looked around the empty lobby and said, "This is as private as it's going to get, Baby," she said, turning up her mouth and raising her eyebrow.

"I don't mean to interrupt, but what I think he means is in an office somewhere so we can sit down and talk, and so that maybe you can grab a pen and paper to actually write down what happened," Madison said.

"You don't mean to interrupt, huh? Well, I don't mean to disappoint you, but I don't take statements," the woman said, laughing. "All of our guards are out walking around campus, keeping an eye on things, and everyone else is out to lunch."

Looking confused, I said, "But you have on a uniform!"

"Yeah, because I complained long enough about everyone else having some sort of uniform, and looking official except me. That's how you get your way around here. Just keep complaining. They'll get tired of hearing you talk sooner or later. It took me three years, but I got my uniform! I'm actually the administrative assistant here, so I'll be happy to take down your name and number so security can get back with you. Come follow me."

The woman walked towards her desk, and I felt like turning around going home. I felt like nothing we had to say was going to be taken seriously, even whenever we did get to speak with someone. Especially if everyone had the same type of sense of humor as this woman did.

When the woman got to her desk and sat down, she noticed that we were still standing, and asked, "What's wrong? Don't you want me to take down your information?"

"We did, but it doesn't seem as if any of this is going to be taken seriously, so I don't even know if we should waste our time," I said.

The woman's face became very serious, and she said, "I'm sorry. I didn't mean to make you feel like that. Most people around campus know me, and that's just my personality. You all must be Freshmen. You'll get to know me. I don't mean any harm. Come on over and have a seat. My name is Claire Jacobs. Most, especially the kids around here call me Miss Jay."

The three of us slowly walked towards her desk. Madison and I sat in the two chairs that were available while Kyle stood.

"Ok, Babies, now just give me a brief summary of what happened."

I began by saying, "Before we go into this, I just want to know if one of the people involved could possibly get in trouble."

"Depends on what they did, and like I said, I'm not in the position to make those decisions. I've seen a lot around here, so I may have an idea whether they would get in trouble or not."

I hesitated before saying anything, and then Madison whispered in my ear.

"Ezekiel, we can't worry about her getting in trouble. You have to worry about yourself. Her punishment will be a lot less harsh for getting drunk at a frat party than you and Kyle's punishment would've been if she had told campus security what she had planned on telling them before I talked her out of it. She wasn't thinking about you at all. Stop feeling like she did you guys a favor. You helped her. She didn't help you."

I looked at Miss Jay and could tell she was trying her best to hear what Madison was saying. I understood everything she was saying, but what she didn't understand was that I wasn't like other people. I had a lot of compassion for other people and would never want anyone to be harmed by something I said or did. However, I did know that if I didn't do what needed to be done, it could've backfired on me, and Kyle and I could've possibly gotten into a lot of trouble.

I took a deep breath and began. "Ok. We went to a frat party last night and I found a girl laying on the sofa passed out, drunk. Some guys were about to take advantage of her, so I stepped in and pretended to be her brother and we took her back to my dorm room, where she didn't wake up until this morning, and when she did, she freaked out. I promise we didn't do anything to her. I even put her in my bed, and I slept on the floor."

Miss Jay, the woman who had just intimidated me not ten minutes prior, looked as if she was tearing up.

"Is everything ok?" I asked.

She began shaking her head, and said, "I wish I had a son like you. You risked your own safety to save someone else. There aren't too many people like you around these days."

Kyle, of course, interjected and said, "What about me? Oh, and Madison. We both helped."

Miss Jay smiled and said, "Oh, yes. The two of you also. You're all good young people. Your parents should be proud."

Kyle folded his arms and nodded his head with pride that he had been acknowledged for his good deed. I didn't care about that.

"So, since you told me what happened, I find that it's not necessary to make a huge issue out of this by making a formal statement. No one was hurt, no one needs to be arrested, and there are no other accusations being made. I do have the authority to make a Preliminary Statement, in which I will just give your names, a briefing of what happened, and where it occurred. This way, it is on record that you came in just in case anything else comes of it, but I seriously doubt it."

We all agreed that would be fine and gave Miss Jay the information she needed.

After Miss Jay finished getting our information, and gave me a copy of the preliminary report that she wrote up, she said, "You all stay out of trouble, but I'm pretty sure you won't have a problem doing that!"

She ended up being very nice and understanding. I guess that's why people say to never judge a book by its cover. Everyone is different in their own ways, and have different personalities, and God made us all different for his own personal reasons.

24 "Look beneath the surface so you can judge correctly."
– John 7:24 NLT

Chapter Twelve

After finally leaving the campus security office, Kyle, Madison, and I decided to go to a popular burger joint a few blocks down from campus called "Burgers, Wings, and Things". On the way, Kyle continued flirting with Madison. I couldn't tell whether she liked it or not, but she definitely wasn't complaining. I was feeling pretty good. Even though I really didn't want to go to campus security about our little situation, it did make me feel more at ease. I felt like I could relax without someone coming to me later accusing me of something I didn't do.

The first thing we noticed when we walked into the restaurant was how crowded it was. We all looked around for a table that would seat the three of us. I felt like it probably looked strange for two Black guys to be walking around all day with a White girl tagging along, and it probably would look even more strange to see us sitting at a table together, but I was never one to look at color. I just knew how a lot of other people viewed certain things. Madison certainly didn't seem uncomfortable, so if we were cool with it, everyone else would have to be. I'd only known Madison for one day, and she had been more of a friend to me than a lot of other people who had once claimed to be my friend back in New York. I already knew she was one of those friends that would be there for me whenever I needed her, just like Kyle was.

"Over here!" Madison yelled from a few feet away.

She had found an empty booth for us to sit in.

Kyle and I walked over and stood next to Madison while the busboy finished cleaning the table.

"Lucky me, huh?" Madison said, laughing.

"Blessed," I replied.

Looking confused, Madison squinted her blue eyes at me and said, "Huh?"

"I said blessed. My dad always taught me there's no such thing as luck."

"Kyle, is there anything wrong with your boy? He seems too perfect," Madison said, jokingly.

As she slid into the booth and Kyle slid in next to her, he replied, "There's just one thing wrong with him."

As I sat across from Kyle, I said, "And what's that, Kyle?"

"You already know, Bro. You're not as handsome as me!" he said, laughing hilariously.

Smiling, Madison said, "Do you joke around all day?"

Before Kyle could respond, I said, "Absolutely. He's always been that way!"

"Not always!" Kyle said, attempting to defend himself. "I'm being serious when I tell you I'm really feeling you, but I don't think you're trying to hear all that."

Seemingly speechless, Madison looked down at the menu. The whole table became quiet, and just in time to break the uncomfortable silence, the waitress stopped by to take our orders.

"Hello! Are you guys ready to order?" the thin, short girl with freckles said.

It was like I was able to see what was about to happen before it even happened.

Kyle looked up at the waitress and his eyes instantly bucked.

"Hey, Slim. I actually don't know what I want, but I'm sure a girl that looks like you always knows exactly what she wants, and it's always the best of the best, so what do you recommend?"

Madison sat back with her arms folded as she watched Kyle in action. I didn't know if he had forgotten that he had just been all up in her face, telling her how he was feeling her, or if he had just completely forgotten that she was even there at all, but I just sat back and minded my business. I couldn't save him from this.

The waitress, whose name badge said "Mandy", smiled at Kyle, blushing from his tired pick up line, and said, "Well, I love the jalapeno bacon burger, but only get that if you're ok with a little spice. If you're more of the safe type, I'd just go with the sweet barbecue bacon cheeseburger."

"Oh, I don't think he's the safe type at all," I said laughing, as I quickly glanced over at Madison, trying to remind Kyle that she was still sitting there.

Kyle quickly caught on and said, "I'll take the jalapeno bacon burger with fries and a Coke."

He then looked at Madison and said, "Put whatever she wants on my bill. We're together."

It was the most hilarious thing I had seen in a while. The way Madison and Mandy both looked at Kyle was priceless. I could barely hold in my laughter, until something happened that took my mind completely off of what was going on at the table.

Stormie walked through the door, more beautiful than ever. It was just something about her beauty that was like no other. Even after the way she had treated me and Kyle that morning, I still could do nothing except admire her flawless beauty. Her long black lashes made her already beautiful almond-shaped eyes pop even more, and her lip-gloss made her perfect, voluptuous lips shimmer. She and another girl that she had walked in with were talking and laughing. Her smile was angelic as she showed all of her sparkling white teeth. I wanted so badly to get up and talk to her, but what would I even say? Especially after what had happened earlier that morning.

"Earth to Ezekiel," I heard Kyle say as I stared at the young woman who I felt I already loved.

When I came to, all I could see was Kyle waving his hand in my face.

"Where did you just go, Bro?" Kyle asked. "It's your turn to order."

"I'm sorry about that," I said to the waitress.

I was sure she was already irritated enough by Kyle's antics, so I quickly ordered while trying to keep my eyes set on Stormie, but I kept hearing my mom's voice in my head telling me, "Always look at a person in their eyes when you're talking to them," so I stopped being rude and looked up at Mandy as she took my order. Of course, when I did that, I lost total sight of Stormie.

When Mandy walked away, Kyle said, "Now are you gonna tell me where your mind was just a minute ago?"

I didn't want to say anything about Stormie to Kyle or Madison because I knew they weren't too fond of her.

"I was just in a daze for a second. I guess I'm just a little tired from all that's been going on in so little time."

"Yes, it has been a lot, especially dealing with your friend over here," Madison said, as she cut her eyes at Kyle.

"What did I do?" Kyle asked, trying to sound innocent.

While they were having their discussion, I said, "You two continue on. I'm going to the bathroom."

I didn't know if whether or not they had heard me, but I made a quick getaway. I walked around the restaurant, looking in every booth and at every table hoping to see Stormie. I didn't even know what I was going to say to her, but I felt like I needed to say something. I knew there was even a possibility that she might've gone off on me in front of everyone if I approached her, but I was willing to take that chance. As I continued to walk through the restaurant, it didn't look as though I would even get that chance.

After probably making everyone feel uncomfortable as I slowly walked past each table, I finally gave up. She had obviously left. I saw the "Restrooms" sign and headed that way while I was up. As I turned to go down the hallway where the restrooms were located, to my surprise, Stormie was coming down the hall in my direction. My heart began beating extremely fast. I took a deep breath to help control my breathing, and felt as though I needed my inhaler for my asthma. I couldn't understand why this girl that I didn't know much of anything about had the type of effect on me that she did. I had never seen or met a girl that made me feel the way that she made me feel.

As I almost let her walk right past me, I pulled some nerves from somewhere and said, "Stormie."

I don't even think she saw me when she walked past, but I couldn't let her get away again. I just had this strong feeling that she was meant to be a part of my life.

She looked back at me, and nonchalantly said, "Oh, it's you. I told your little friend that I wasn't going to say anything, so you're all good. You don't have to come begging me not to get you in trouble. It's in my past and I prefer not to think about it anymore."

I realized by just the little bit she had just said, she felt as if she was innocent and that I had done something wrong. I began to think Madison may have been right about her, but I was all about giving people a second chance, and not just assuming what they were thinking or how they felt.

As Stormie got ready to continue walking, I said, "Actually, I didn't just get your attention to beg you not to say anything. My friend, Madison, did tell me she spoke with you. I just wanted to see if we could talk. We don't have to talk about last night. You just seem intriguing, and I'm interested in getting to know you in a better light."

Stormie rolled her eyes and said, "No."

That was it. She said nothing else. Just "no" with no explanation whatsoever, and stood there looking at me as if I was small.

Whenever I wanted to know something, I asked, so I said, "Why not?"

"Because I'm not interested in you getting to know more about me. That means you would eventually want to date me, and to be perfectly honest, if I saw you out in public, I wouldn't even give you a second look. You're just not my type."

This girl was brutal. She said exactly what was on her mind, but I kind of liked it.

"What is your type, if I may ask?"

Stormie took a deep breath as if she was becoming irritated, but answered me anyway.

"You just seem too nice. I'm more into the bad boy type. Someone who can handle a girl like me. You're not that person. Trust me."

"You don't even know anything about me, so how could you possibly know that I'm not that person. Do you have a boyfriend now?"

Hesitantly, she said, "No."

"So it doesn't seem like that bad boy type thing you're talking about has been working out too well for you."

As soon as I said that, I saw the girl that Stormie had walked into the restaurant with coming down the hall from the direction of the women's restroom. She looked me up and down as she approached us.

"You ok, Girl?" she asked Stormie.

"Yeah, I'm fine. You know how these boys are," she said, while staring directly into my eyes, pulling me in even deeper without even knowing it.

She then said, "Bye . . . What was your name?"

"Ezekiel. My name is Ezekiel," I said, sounding defeated.

"Oh, yeah. Your friend, Megan, did tell me that."

"Her name is Madison," I replied.

"Bye, Ezekiel," she said, as she walked away with her friend right behind her, laughing. I was sure she was laughing at me, because to them, I just seemed like some desperate guy trying to get with a beautiful girl.

With my head hanging low, I walked towards the men's bathroom until I then heard my dad's voice say, "Boy, hold your head up. Never let them see you sweat, and when you're passionate about something, never give up on it. If it's for you, it'll be yours. If not, you'll soon find out."

Hearing that made me smile because I knew that was exactly what my dad would've said to me in that moment. I walked into that men's bathroom with my head held higher than I'd ever held my head walking into a bathroom. Even after just being rejected, I knew it wasn't over until God said it was.

On my way back to the booth where I was sitting with Kyle and Madison, without even looking, I happened to run into the booth where Stormie and her friend were sitting across from each other. I boldly slid into the booth right next to Stormie. I could tell that her friend was taken aback by my boldness as her eyes bucked and neck snapped back.

"Whoa," she said.

Stormie looked over at me and said, "What now, Zeke?"

"Zeke?" I said.

"Yes, Zeke. I like that better. Ezekiel has way too many syllables. What was your mom thinking?"

"Actually, that name means a lot to my mom. It means 'God's strength'. She always wanted me to be strong in God. She and my dad both did. The day I was born, she told my dad that no one was ever to shorten it because it was such a strong name. No one has ever called me Zeke."

"Not even your best homeboys?" she asked, sounding intrigued.

"Nope. . . See there's a lot of interesting things about me that you could learn, and I'm sure there's a lot about you that I could learn, but you're not even interested in being friends. I'm not asking you to marry me or even date me. We're both new around here, and I know I could use some friends. I don't know about you."

Stormie sat there tapping her freshly manicured nails on the tabletop, then looked up at me and said, "Zeke . . ."

I raised my eyebrows, waiting to hear what she was about to say.

"That's what I'm going to call you if we're going to be friends. You'll just have to keep that from your momma. No disrespect." She looked across the table and said, "This is my roommate, and the only person I kind of know so far, Brittney."

"Nice to meet you Brittney," I said with a big smile.

I had caught on to what Stormie said about being friends as long as she could call me "Zeke" and I was absolutely ok with it as long as my mom didn't get wind of it.

Brittney replied, "Nice to meet you, too . . . Is it ok for me to call you Zeke, too?"

I smiled and said, "I would say yes, but . . ." I looked over at the booth where I had been sitting, and said, "You see that guy over there? That's my best friend, Kyle. We've been friends since we were two years old, and we've practically done everything together, including this college thing. He has never even called me anything besides 'Ezekiel' . . . Oh, and 'Bro', of course. That's his favorite," I said, smiling. "But he is definitely like a brother to me."

"Ok, Ezekiel. I can understand and respect that," Brittney said.

Right at that moment, Stormie and Brittney's waitress came over with their food, which reminded me that I had also ordered food that was probably cold by now, but it was worth it.

"Ok, Ladies. I'll let the two of you eat, and hopefully I'll be seeing you around campus. It was good talking to both of you."

I could tell Stormie still had a wall up. From our short conversation, I could tell she was used to living a certain type of life, and dealing with certain types of people, and really wasn't willing to steer away from her norm. From what I'd seen happen the previous night, her norm wasn't safe at all, and it would probably be a while before she would realize that there was a better way of life out there. Sometimes God puts people in our lives for us to help them get on that right path, and I really felt that God had placed us in each other's paths so that I could help her do just that. It was going to be a challenge, but whenever I felt the Spirit of God trying to tell me something, I had to listen and be obedient. I didn't know why I felt such a strong connection to Stormie. Yes, she was beautiful, but that wasn't all to it. There was something else. Something mysterious, and God was always intentional in His actions, and I knew deep in my heart this was no different. Whether she would be a blessing or a lesson, I didn't know, but whatever the case may have been, I was sure I would learn something from it.

As I stood up to go back to my table, I said, "See you ladies later."

When I began walking away, feeling as though I had redeemed myself from the short moment that I had felt defeated, I felt Stormie grab my arm.

I looked down at her, raising my eyebrows because I certainly wasn't expecting that.

She looked me in the eyes with sincerity and softly said, "Thank you for last night, and I'm sorry for the way I treated you this morning. Tell your friends that I said, thank you, too."

"You're welcome, Storm, and I understand," I said.

"Storm?" she said, with a slight grin.

"We're friends, right?" I said with confidence, as I walked away smiling.

As soon as I got back to my table with Madison and Kyle, Madison couldn't wait to speak.

"We saw you! So, you decided to still talk to her after all she put you guys through and couldn't even say 'thank you' or 'sorry'?" she said, uncomfortably rolling her neck, with her arms folded.

"She actually said she's sorry and told me to tell you guys. She really meant it. I could see it in her eyes."

"Bro, you got it bad. If she wasn't fine as she is, would you even be trying to have a conversation with her right now?" Kyle asked.

"Kyle, I honestly think I would."

"Well, I still don't trust her," Madison said.

"You don't have to trust her, but you have to forgive her," I replied.

"Why do I have to? Because you said so?" Madison asked.

"No. Because God said so."

[32] **Instead, be kind to each other, tenderhearted, forgiving one another, just as God through Christ has forgiven you."**
– Ephesians 4:32 NLT

The entire table became quiet, and I took that time to eat my ice-cold cheeseburger and fries that I'd ordered.

Chapter Thirteen

After the talk I'd had with Stormie at the restaurant, I realized that the only way I'd be having any other talks with her would be if we ran across each other on campus, which is what I was hoping would happen. I wouldn't dare ask for her phone number after I'd finally gotten as far as I had gotten with her. I had broken down only a small fraction of her wall, and there was no way I was going to regress by asking her for her number. If I never ran across her on campus ever again, at least I did know that all I had to do was go to the next Frat party. I'd be sure to find her there.

Thankfully, I didn't have to wait to see her again in that party scene type of setting. It was a couple of weeks before I actually saw her again, but I was just thankful to see her. Everything happens in God's timing. One afternoon when I was leaving my second class of the day and had a break in between, I walked through the campus courtyard, just enjoying the weather. I was actually looking for somewhere to sit so I could start on one of my assignments when I saw Stormie sitting alone underneath a tree.

"Stormie!" I yelled from the walkway.

She looked up from the book she was reading, waved, and looked back down at her book. I was a little disappointed that she didn't call me over, but I didn't let that keep me from walking over anyway.

"Hey, there!" I said, as I walked in the grass, close to where she was sitting.

Dryly, she said, "Hey, Zeke," without even looking up.

"Are we about to start this all over again?" I thought to myself.

"I haven't seen you around since the fast food joint."

"Yeah, I've been doing my own thing," she replied.

"Are you even going to look up at me?"

"I can hear you. Why do I need to look at you?"

"My mom always said to look a person in the eyes when you're talking to them."

"Why, momma's boy?"

"Wow," I said. "So, because I respect the things my mom taught me, I have to be a momma's boy?"

"During the couple of times we've spoken, you've always brought her up, but forget all that. Why do I need to look a person in their eyes when I'm talking to them? I might can learn a few things from your mom's teachings."

"First off, it forms a sense of trust, and you can learn a lot from a person when you look into their eyes. Secondly, it's just out of respect. It shows a person that you're paying attention to, or interested in what they're saying."

"Well, maybe I'm not interested in what you're saying."

As I sat down in the grass next to Stormie, I said, "I haven't even gotten a chance to say anything yet, and I know I talk about my mom a lot, but she's just important to me. She's all I have. My dad died when I was thirteen. He was a fire chief and ran into a burning house to save a girl who was around my age around that time."

Stormie glanced up at me for a moment as if my story had interested her, but she didn't say a word, and placed her focus back into her book. I glanced at the cover of the book she was reading, and it definitely didn't look like something she was reading for a class.

"Are you listening to anything I'm saying, or are you too deep into that book?"

She finally looked up at me and said, "I am into this book, but I was also listening to you. I heard you say how much your mom means to you, and how your dad died when you were thirteen, saving some girl from a fire who probably didn't even appreciate it. I wish someone would've saved me on several occasions. She has probably never thought about your dad ever again."

I looked at her in shock, not knowing what to say. I never shared that story with anyone and she had just made it seem like what my dad did meant nothing. Like it was in vain. The saddest part was that she said it without any type of emotion whatsoever.

She must've realized how that must've made me feel, and felt the need to explain herself.

"I just don't know how to respond to things like that when my mom used to sell me for a fix, and I never knew who my dad was, so I ended up in the foster system when I was four. I never really had anyone to care for me, and the people who I thought cared for me let me down, so now I don't have any space to care."

She went into her bag and pulled out a pink lighter with a beautiful violet, black and teal butterfly design that matched the one that I'd noticed on the back of her left shoulder the first time I'd seen her.

"This is the only thing that I have left that reminds me of my mother. A freakin' lighter! Every time I see a butterfly, I believe that it's a sign from my mother, wherever she may be. It's probably nothing, but it makes me feel better to believe that my mother is thinking of me. My childhood was so jacked up, so I try to do whatever I can to enjoy this part of my life. Maybe my mom's childhood was jacked up, too, and that's why she tried to keep herself feeling good with coke, heroin, alcohol, and whatever other demon she could find to soothe her pain. Who knows? It wasn't like I had family to tell me about my mom's childhood. I don't know anything and never will. All I know her as is a crackhead and alcoholic who I once adored."

Stormie had thrown a whole lot on me in a matter of minutes. It made me feel bad to know I lived a pretty good life while Stormie was suffering, living from foster home to foster home. I'm sure if my mom and dad would've known about her situation back then, they would've taken her in and even possibly adopted her with no questions asked.

"You're real quiet now. Did I scare you?" Stormie asked.

"No. Not at all. Just trying to digest everything you've gone through. I can't even imagine."

"Trust me. You don't even know the half of it, and talking about it makes me feel no better, but this book right here makes me feel pretty good and keeps me away from some of my other demons."

When Stormie held up the book to show me that she was reading an erotica romance novel, a packet fell out of it into the grass. She tried to hurry and pick it up, but I grabbed it before she could. It was a small packet of what looked like cocaine. She quickly snatched it out of my hands.

"Like I said, I have some demons, but don't we all?" she quickly said defensively.

"We do, but that doesn't mean we can't be saved from them. None of us are perfect, and no one is in a place to be able to judge anyone else."

"So after seeing that, you're going to try to tell me you don't think I'm some type of dope fiend or crackhead?" she asked.

"No, I don't. I don't know what you go through from day to day. I don't know the type of pain you deal with from your past. I'm sure you have a void, and probably try to fill it with other things. Things that aren't of God. You know, He puts people in our lives to help, and you may not think so, but I'm here for a reason."

[1] **"Do not judge others, and you will not be judged.** [2] **For you will be treated as you treat others. The standard you use in judging is the standard by which you will be judged.** [3] **"And**

why worry about a speck in your friend's eye when you have a log in your own? [4] How can you think of saying to your friend, 'Let me help you get rid of that speck in your eye,' when you can't see past the log in your own eye? [5] Hypocrite! First get rid of the log in your own eye; then you will see well enough to deal with the speck in your friend's eye." – Matthew 7: 1-5 NLT

"Listen here, Zeke. I know you're all sanctified, religious, and filled with the Holy Ghost, and I'm sure your entire family probably is, but the thing is, I'm not. I believe in a higher power, and I'm nowhere near holier than thou. I know that I didn't come into existence without any help, but I fail to understand why I was created at all if I was going to be thrown into such a miserable life."

"Storm, I have no idea of what all you went through so I can't tell you how you feel, but what I do know is, unfortunately, people go through things, and all we can do is use those things to make us stronger. I know lot of people in your life hurt you, but you still have to forgive them and move on. Your past is your past, and now you have an opportunity to make a great future for yourself. Your love for butterflies, and the way they give you hope isn't a coincidence either. I don't know if you realize it, but butterflies are a sign of transformation and spiritual growth. I pray and believe that you will experience that, and when you do, you'll have a totally different outlook on life, regardless of the things you've gone through."

Stormie looked up and rolled her eyes at me.

"Everything you're saying sounds real simple, but the thing is, I can never forget the things that people have done to me. I'm damaged for life because of those people, and just because I have a butterfly fetish doesn't mean I'm going to go through some type of miraculous transformation. I understand the metaphor you're trying to use to compare the transformation of a caterpillar into a beautiful butterfly to me and the change that you would like for me to experience. I'm sorry to tell you, but my transformation period seemed to be tainted. I won't be turning into this perfect, loving person any time soon. I am who I am. I have to stay high and drunk half the time so I can forget the past and function in life. These people ruined me, and you just expect me to forget? Never! This is why I don't go to church. Those people just act like life is so perfect and all I have to do is pray and things will get better. The higher power, whoever that may be, just decided to drop us here in the middle of this mess with other people who don't care about anyone except themselves so that we can fend for ourselves. Nothing is fair about that."

"Listen, Stormie. I'm sorry about everything you went through, but I want to be there for you to show you how great life can be, and show you that there are people who will care about you and want what's best for you. I know you don't believe in God, but prayer does help. You may not see things happen right away, but if we pray and have faith in our prayers, God is always working things out for our good. I may not seem like the type of guy you'd enjoy hanging out with, but I promise I can prove you wrong."

Stormie put her book down for the first time, put her cheek in the palm of her hand and grinned at me as she batted her thick eyelashes. I felt as though I might've been finally getting somewhere with her.

Chapter Fourteen

After that day of sitting underneath a tree having a real conversation with Stormie, we began spending more and more time together. I called them dates, but she never wanted to refer to them as such. We would go out to dinner, to the movies, and even breakfast sometimes before class. Although we had different classes since she was an Accounting major and I was an Engineering major, whenever we had to be in our first early morning class at the same time, I would pick up coffee for the both of us and walk her from her dorm to class. The more I got to know her, the more beautiful she became. There was nothing we couldn't talk to each other about. I was a little nervous about how Kyle would handle my newfound friendship with Stormie, however, he wasn't paying me much attention because his attention was so set on Madison that it was hard for anything else to distract him. For that, I was very thankful because I definitely didn't want him to feel as though I was neglecting him after all of the times he'd been there for me. Kyle and I had all the same classes since we were both majoring in electrical engineering, but I didn't see him most mornings because he would be over at Madison's room. Stormie and I hadn't even kissed yet. I didn't complain though. I wanted to be a gentleman. That's what my parents would've expected of me, and those were the expectations I had for myself. I was young, but I believed that a woman should be treated like a queen. That's how my dad treated my mom, and I would treat my woman no other way.

One thing about hanging out with Stormie was it was exhausting. I couldn't understand how she functioned the way she did every day. She went to every single party on campus and dragged me along. The next day, I would be so tired that I would be late for class, and when I'd get there, I'd end up falling asleep. On top of that, I'd end up having to stay after class to listen to the professor lecture to me about how much better I was than the grades that I had begun receiving on my assignments and tests. Stormie seemed like none of that bothered her. She was always bright-eyed and bushy-tailed, and I began wondering if it had to do with the packet of what had looked to be cocaine that I had seen fall out of her book. She was either doing something she had no business doing that kept her energized all day, or she wasn't human.

Things were going well between us, and I didn't want to ruin it by trying to be in her business, but I was genuinely concerned about her well-being. She was such a joy to be around, and I was having the most fun I'd had in a long time. We always found something to do that we could both enjoy, but the parties would be a little uncomfortable because she always tried to get me to drink, and that just wasn't my thing. That was one of the things that I found very unattractive about Stormie, but I figured that was just a part of college life. Partying and getting drunk seemed like the norm, but I wasn't the least bit interested. Plus, I needed stay sober to make sure she was ok.

One night, Stormie and I were at Frat party, and I sat on the sofa with a Coke while I watched her socialize with everyone that walked by. She was loved by everyone, and I started wondering what in the world she would want with me. I began questioning myself as to what I was doing. All of the people she socialized with had a drink in their hand, and of course, all of the guys she danced with looked like they were ready to have a good time with her. They looked more like the bad boy type that that she was attracted to that she had initially described to me. I was easy on the eyes and had plenty of girls that tried to hit on me, but I knew who I wanted. I just didn't think that she wanted me. Stormie liked me as a friend. She enjoyed our conversation and our outings, but I could tell that she had absolutely no romantic feelings for me and there was nothing I would be able to do to change that. I would just have to accept that we would always be friends and appreciate the fact that she at least enjoyed my company.

"Hey, Bro!" I heard Kyle say as he slapped me on the back of the head.

I was sitting on the sofa in a daze, watching the woman who I someday wanted to be my queen, have a good time with everyone else.

"Hey. What are you doing here?" I asked Kyle.

"I just thought Maddie and I would get out for a little while and see what's going on over here. I didn't think we would run into you."

I looked over and saw Madison smiling and waving as she fixed herself a cup of punch.

"Hey, Man. You better make sure that punch isn't spiked," I warned Kyle.

"A little spike won't hurt her. She's a good girl. What's going on with you and Stormie? She looks like she's over there having herself a good time," Kyle said, looking over in Stormie's direction.

"I'm basically just here to make sure she gets home safely," I said.

"You don't mind all of those guys all over her?"

As I watched Stormie take off her heels and pull her thick hair out of the ponytail holder that was holding it into a bun, I said, "Nah. We're just friends. What can I say?"

"Friends, but you buy her coffee every day and walk her to class? And on top of that, you hang out with her all the time! That sounds like more than friends to me. I think the two of you have some things to talk about. She may not be the one for you, Bro."

Madison walked over and said, "Did I hear you right? Stormie's not for Ezekiel? I thought you guys were doing well."

I looked over at Stormie, and Madison's eyes followed mine.

"Oh, I see," Madison said.

"Yeah, I'm beginning to think I'm wasting my time. I'll never be the type of man she wants. I just can't hang with all of that."

Madison, trying to be optimistic, said, "Well, you never know. People change, and their taste in people change."

"Yeah, you're right, but I don't see that happening too soon," I replied.

At the end of the night, as usual, Stormie wrapped her one arm around me as I held her up, holding her shoes in my hand until we got outside onto the sidewalk. She then hiked up her black minidress and jumped on my back after I knelt down. She passed out on my back, as she always did, with her hair flopping around in my face.

Kyle and Madison walked out with me and said they were going to walk over to "Burgers, Wings, and Things" to get some food before heading in.

"I would join you guys, but as you see, I'm a little preoccupied," I said sarcastically.

"I get it, Bro. We're going to have to talk. For real."

"I know. I'll see you in the morning," I replied.

I knew what Kyle wanted to talk to me about. I was being a sucker and I knew it. Stormie had me sprung by just being her. I truly felt like I loved her, and I had no idea how she felt about me. One thing I did know was that she showed absolutely no type of guilt about being in other guy's faces, smiling, laughing, and being so close in proximity that they may as well had been kissing, while I stood there watching.

When we got to Stormie's dorm room, as I was getting her keys out of her purse, Brittney came and opened the door.

"This is getting really old," Brittney said. "You have to stop enabling her. If she doesn't have someone to rely on to watch over her while she gets drunk like this, maybe she'll stop."

"I don't think she will. That's why I do it. I don't want her to get hurt," I replied.

Brittney shook her head and said, "Come on. Let's get her in the bed."

The most I had ever been in Stormie's room was to put her in her bed after a night like tonight. I threw the blanket on top of her, kissed her on the forehead, and told her goodnight, as if she knew, or could hear anything that was going on.

Brittney walked me to the door and said, "Ezekiel, please don't take this the wrong way and think that I'm trying to destroy your relationship with Stormie. You're a good man, and you deserve better than this. Stormie has a lot of issues, and she needs professional help. You can't help her. Enjoy your college life and let her go. She's not the type of woman for you, and she doesn't think of you as the type of man for her. If you want to be her friend, fine, but please don't waste your life trying to be someone she wants you to be."

"Thanks, Brittney. Believe me, I've been doing a lot of thinking on this, and I totally agree with you. We don't have anything in common except for being enrolled in this school. I just wish that there was something that I could do to help her."

"I know you do, but right now she's not open to help. Maybe someday, but not now."

Brittney gave me a hug and told me goodnight. On the way back to my room, I decided that the next day I would start the process of weening myself off of Stormie. I wouldn't pick up her coffee and I wouldn't be walking her to class. Those were things that a man would do for their woman and that wasn't the position that I held in Stormie's life. I began to feel at peace with that after talking to Brittney.

Chapter Fifteen

I had talked to Brittney and Kyle about my "relationship" with Stormie, and a couple of weeks had gone by since I'd seen or spoken to her last. I figured that she probably had been busy like the rest of us, preparing for midterms, so that gave me an excuse to not even attempt to contact her, knowing deep down inside I wanted to call her or knock on her door so badly. I decided to wait until after midterms were over to see what happened. It hurt my feelings a little bit that she hadn't even tried to check on me, especially when I would be the one to bring her coffee every morning and walk her to class. What if something had happened to me? Was she even concerned about me at all? I was used to surrounding myself with caring individuals. People who checked on you if they hadn't heard from you in a while, whether it was by calling, stopping by, or just dropping a quick text.

The day after the last day of midterms, even though Stormie seemed to not care anything about me, I decided to stop by her dorm room just to see how things were going. When I walked into her residence hall, there was a guy walking about one hundred feet ahead of me. He was a few inches taller than me and looked like he had just come from the gym. Coincidentally, he stopped and began knocking at Stormie's door. I hid around the corner because I didn't want to look like a fool. He could've easily been going to see Brittney, but I wanted to be sure. When I heard Stormie's door open, I heard the sweet voice that she would put on only for people that she really liked. I peeked around the corner and saw the guy lift her up and twirl her around. He then put her down and kissed her. My heart immediately shattered into a million pieces. I stayed long enough to watch her invite the guy inside and shut the door. It hurt even more knowing that Stormie had never even invited me in just to visit. I only had the privilege of putting her to bed on her drunken nights. That was all of the confirmation that I needed to know that Stormie really had no intentions on furthering our relationship into anything more serious than a friendship. I had allowed myself to basically only be her savior, and that's how she looked at me.

After letting Stormie go, I vowed to keep my head in my books and focus on the things that were important to me before Stormie had entered my life.

"Hey, Bro. What's up?" Kyle said when he got home from class.

"Nothing. Just studying."

"Midterms are over, and I can't remember the last time I saw you sitting at that desk with a book open," Kyle said.

"That's because you're never here," I said sarcastically. "You and Madison might as well be roommates."

"Wait a minute. Are you trying to throw a guilt trip on me when you were spending all of your time with a chick that didn't even want you?"

There were so many things I wanted to say to Kyle in that moment, but I just looked at him, shook my head, and continued to read.

Kyle stood there for a moment and said, "I'm sorry. That came out the wrong way."

"No, it didn't. You said exactly what you meant to say. It's ok, though. You're right. You were right from the beginning when you said I could never get a girl like that. She wants something different, and I saw exactly what that was today."

Kyle sat on my bed and said, "Don't tell me you saw her with another guy."

"Yep, and she looked happy. She even invited him into her dorm room. Do you know she hasn't even checked on me to see if I'm ok?"

Kyle took a deep breath and said, "I don't know what to say. I'm sorry, Man. I should've protected you from her."

"You tried, and Madison tried, but it was just something that kept telling me I had to have her. Even after what I saw today, I still feel like I love her."

"Just try to focus on other things. You can come hang out with me and Maddie. We're going to play pool tonight if you want to come."

"No, thanks. I don't want to be a third wheel. I was hoping we'd be double dating by now."

"Don't worry. We're still young. You have plenty of time to fall in love and all that good stuff. I'm with Maddie today, but who knows who I'll be with tomorrow? It just might be Beyonce'," Kyle said, raising his eyebrows and shrugging his shoulders.

Kyle always knew how to make me laugh.

"Dude, you are crazy! You and I both know that Madison isn't going anywhere any time soon!"

Kyle laughed, and said, "You're probably right. She's great. I can't complain . . . yet. I'll leave you to studying, but promise me you're going to keep your mind off of that girl. Go work out or do something. Go meet some new girls. There's someone out there just for you."

"I know. I'll find something to do. Have a good time and tell Madison I said 'hi'."

After Kyle left, I studied for a little while longer, but found myself reading the same sentences over and over again, so I closed my book and decided to take a nap. I was willing to do anything to keep my mind off of Stormie, and sleeping seemed like the thing to do at that time. While awake, I couldn't help but to wonder what she and that guy were doing in her room. Before I dozed off, I said a short prayer. I knew that prayer was the only thing that could get me through anything. Even heartbreak.

"Dear God,

I know that you already know what I'm going through, but I need you right now. My heart is broken, and I need you to heal it. I don't know if Stormie is for me, although I thought she was. I know that everyone is put in our lives for a reason, Lord, but what was the reason for Stormie? I know it just wasn't to break my heart, and I know your plan is always better than mine. Please just do Your will in my life. It isn't about what I want, but what you want for my life. Please give me the Spirit of Discernment so I will know what's for me and what's not, and what path to take. Place me in front of all of the right people and in all the right places at the right time. Keep me protected and covered with your blood from anything and anyone trying to destroy me. Keep me in perfect peace. Thank you, Lord, for always watching over me and making sure that I'm always doing Your will. Thank you, Father, in the name of Jesus. Amen."

After I finished my prayer, I went to sleep in peace, knowing that I had left everything in God's hands, and He would take care of me. I had to remember to never let my faith waver, which I felt as if I had done for a moment.

I didn't know how long I had been asleep, but I was awakened by a knock at the door.

As I rolled over to get up out of bed, I said, "Kyle, did you forget your key again?"

Kyle was known to always leave his key and would have to wait for me to get home to let him in if I wasn't there.

When I swung the door open, to my surprise, it was Stormie, looking even more beautiful than usual. She wore her hair naturally curly, as she normally didn't, and wore absolutely no make-up. I was all for the natural look. It made me even more attracted to her.

Although I was totally taken aback, I took a deep breath and said, "What do you want?" trying to sound as if I wasn't interested in anything she had to say.

"What do you mean? You're the one who ghosted me. I should be the one upset, but here I am, standing at your door, wanting to make things right."

"Make what right, Stormie? Tell me? I don't know what it is that we even had. You never made that clear."

Stormie looked down at the floor and sighed.

"Are you going to invite me in?" she asked.

"Is it really necessary? You never wanted to come in before, and you sure as hell never invited me into your place."

"Zeke, please," she begged.

"Don't call me that," I said.

"Now I can't even call you, Zeke? What's going on? I Just want to talk to you."

I stood there silently staring at her while the soft spot in my heart for her kept telling me to let her in. I pushed the door open so that she could enter.

As she walked in, she said, "Thank you."

"You have ten minutes, Stormie," I said, still trying to play hard.

As she sat on my bed, she said, "I still don't understand why you're the one mad at me."

I stood in front of her and began completely pouring my heart out to her.

"Stormie, you know how I've felt about you from the very beginning. We became close and did everything together, but you still seemed like you wanted nothing out of me except a friendship. I felt like I was your bodyguard to make sure you made it home safe after flaunting yourself and having a good time with other men. I finally realized I was making a fool of myself by waiting on you to want me as more than just a friend. I couldn't do it anymore. None of it. The morning coffees, the walking to class, the breakfasts, the dinners, none of it. I really realized exactly what I meant to you after I stopped doing all of that and you didn't even check on me. Anything could've happened to me, but you didn't seem to care."

The entire time I spoke, Stormie's eyes followed me with every step I took as I paced the floor in nervousness and frustration. When I finished my rant, I took a deep breath and plopped down beside her.

Softly, Stormie said, "I understand." She looked at me and said, "We're too different and I'm not willing to change. I am who I am, and I don't take kindly to being judged."

"I never judged you," I quickly interjected.

"You don't have to say anything. I can see it in your eyes and by your facial expression every time I party and get wasted. You have a look of embarrassment on your face. I don't need a man who's embarrassed of who I am. Even when my bag of coke fell out of my book that day when you came and sat with me underneath the tree, I saw the look on your face. Like I told you that day, I have my demons, and I have them for some very valid reasons. I didn't grow up like you. Like I said, I am who I am, and I know you'll never be able to accept who I am. Even if you don't say anything, you'll always be judging me in the back of your mind."

"So, the guy you had in your room today accepts you for who you are?" I asked, catching Stormie off guard.

Stormie's eyes almost popped out of her head.

"How do you know that I had someone in my room today?"

"Because I was on my way to check on you, but I guess he beat me to the punch."

"We're just friends," Stormie replied.

"Oh, so he's a friend like I was, but he has different privileges than I had. He was actually invited into your room. So, are you sleeping with this friend? What makes him so different than me? Am I just too soft for you?"

"Can you please give me a chance to answer one question before you throw a million more at me?"

I sat quietly and gave Stormie the motion to proceed.

"The guy that you saw was Chris. He was an ex from high school. He doesn't even go here, but is thinking about enrolling next semester. He just came to visit the campus to see how he liked it. While he was here, he stopped by to visit me. That was it. Nothing happened."

"Except a kiss?" I asked, curiously wondering how she would answer.

"Yes, a kiss," she said sounding regretful. "Like I said, I just wanted to come over here and talk face to face to let you know why I handled things the way I did. I saw things between us ending badly and I didn't want things to go any further because I knew that the further they went, the more I would hurt you and I didn't want to do that. There are some real nice girls out here. I'm not one of them. I'm not the one for you. Please, just trust me."

"I want you, Storm. I knew that you were who I wanted the first time I saw you even though you were rude to me. There's just something about you. I know you say you are who you are, but you can change. We all change. You may just need someone who's different than you to help make that change."

"Stop right there," Stormie interrupted. "You should never go into a relationship expecting a person to change. That's where people go wrong. I may never change, and what if I don't? You'll be in a relationship with me, unhappy because you expected me to change into this perfect woman that you created in your head."

"I trust my instincts, Storm. I prayed about you today. I've never felt for a girl the way that I feel for you. How about we both just try to get a taste of each other's worlds with no judgement for a while in a more romantic type of way and see where it goes from there? If you're not comfortable with that, I understand. I just really have this feeling that something is there. I don't want you to feel like I'm desperate, or begging you, but as you know, I have total faith in God, and when I prayed today, I asked Him to do His will when it came to me and you."

Stormie hesitated for a moment, and then said, "No judgment?"

"Absolutely none," I replied.

"Ok. Let's do this. I just hope you're ready for the ride, Church Boy."

Stormie

Chapter Sixteen

A month or so went by, and all seemed ok with Zeke, but I felt as though I was still missing something. I was more of a free-spirited type of person and just liked to have fun and enjoy life. It was like he had to think about everything before he did it. If I felt like doing it, I did it. There was never much of a thinking process that went behind it. That was what most of our arguments were about. I'd want to do something, and he never thought it was a good idea. Most of the things I did get him to do, I had to force him to do them. I knew I couldn't live like that. Especially during my college years, which were supposed to be the best years of my life. I would either have to let Zeke go, or get him to open up to more exciting things in life.

20 "Walk with the wise and become wise; associate with fools and get in trouble." – Proverbs 13:20 NLT

Zeke was a good guy. Too good, and I knew I wasn't the type of woman that the universe had created for him. We had different beliefs, values, and morals, and even though we would probably never get married, I felt that those things were important in any type of relationship. I had to hide things from him, such as my occasional coke habit, and when I badly wanted another drink at a party, I'd have to bite the bullet and seem to be ok with the one drink I'd had for the night, knowing I could've downed at least four more. I had a strong feeling that he thought that if I stuck with him long enough, I would change. The problem was, I didn't want to change. I liked myself just the way I was. It had taken me a long time to even like myself, and now, I was actually in love with myself. I didn't have to answer to any so-called god, or feel any regret for the things that I chose to do. I had no idea what happened after death, and never believed anyone else really did, so I chose to enjoy myself in the "now". I only had one life to live and wasn't going to worry about the things that probably weren't real. I was a storm to be reckoned with and I intended to live life to the fullest. I didn't need anyone or anything holding me back. Zeke either needed to loosen up and enjoy some of the things with me that I enjoyed, or he needed to find someone that was more like him.

After final exams were over, it was time for winter break. I knew I had nowhere to go. I had no family to visit, so I planned to stay on campus and get into whatever I could find to get into. Brittney had invited me to come home with her, but I didn't want to intrude on another family's plans. Madison was also going home to visit her family, and Zeke and Kyle had purchased tickets an entire month in advance to fly home together. He never even hinted for me to go home with him, so I just figured that he already knew that his mom wouldn't be ready to meet a girl like me. I was probably the opposite of what she would have ever expected, and wouldn't have accepted me. Even when Zeke would talk to her on the telephone when I was around, he'd put his finger to his lips so that I'd be quiet, and then walk out of the room. I knew he didn't want her to know anything about me. The way he talked about his mom seemed like she was just the perfect woman, and I had a feeling he was looking for someone just like her.

When the day had finally arrived for Zeke and Kyle to leave, I felt a little sad. Even though I had plenty of other people who I knew that would be sticking around, I knew that I would miss Zeke. It would only be for a couple of weeks, but even though Zeke wasn't the person that I would've like for him to be, I could honestly say that during my entire life, I had never been so close to anyone who always seemed to be a breath of fresh air.

I met Zeke and Kyle at their residence hall before their Uber picked them up. They sat on the steps of the building with their suitcases. Kyle looked excited, but Zeke looked a little uncertain.

"You ok, Baby?" I asked Zeke, as I stooped down and gave him a kiss on the forehead.

"Yeah, I'm good. I'm just going to miss you, but I'll be back before you know it. I just hope you don't get too lonely."

"Don't worry about me. I'll be fine. I'm sure your mom is going to be ecstatic to see you!"

"I'm sure she is. I could hear her excitement through the phone when I talked to her earlier today," Zeke said, as he stood up fixing his gray sweatpants and hoodie.

"I know I'm ready to be back in New York for a little while. That's where my roots are," Kyle said.

"I know what you mean. I miss my girls from Queens, but I feel like I stay out of a lot more trouble where I am," I said.

Suddenly, I saw an SUV slowly riding through the parking lot looking as if it were lost. It finally stopped in front of Kyle and Zeke's residence hall and I knew it was time for us to say our goodbyes.

"See ya in a couple of weeks, Stormie," Kyle said as he ran over to the Uber and put his bags in the trunk.

Zeke wrapped his arms around me and told me how much he was going to miss me for like the twentieth time.

I hugged him back, and whispered in his ear, "It's only two weeks. We'll be ok. I'll talk to you every single day. I promise."

"I know," Zeke said. "I just don't feel right leaving you."

"I'll be fine!"

The Uber driver honked his horn and Zeke said, "Well, I'll see you later."

He gave me one last kiss, grabbed his luggage, and headed over to the Uber. He waved goodbye as he got into the backseat, and watched me through the back window until they were no longer in plain sight. I sighed, and headed back to my own residence hall.

When I got back to the dorm, I did what I did best. I grabbed a bottle out of the cabinet, and my stash of coke from the hidden, inside pocket of my purse. I poured a little of it out on my desk, and lined it up. I poured myself a glass of red wine, and as soon as I got halfway done with it, someone knocked on my door. I immediately looked over at my desk where my coke had been prepared for when I was ready for it, and wondered who it could've possibly been interrupting my solo party.

With the latch on the door, I cracked the door open, and saw that it was Damon. Damon Spears was my math professor, but we had an understanding and would get together sometimes just to do whatever it was we wanted to do. I could be myself around him, and he could do the same.

"I heard you were going to be alone during winter break, so I thought I'd come keep you company," he said, through the small crack.

I unlatched the door and said, "Yeah, I did tell you I'd be alone, didn't I?"

Damon looked around and said, "It looks like you were about to start the party without me."

"Well, I honestly wasn't expecting company, but I don't mind sharing."

"Well, thank you. I appreciate that."

Damon was young. He couldn't have been any older than twenty-six. I know that sounds old since I was only eighteen, but compared to the men I'd been molested by, that was nothing to me. I had never had sex with Damon. We just enjoyed each other's company, getting drunk and high. He was the type of man I needed in my life, but unfortunately, student/faculty relationships were frowned upon, and I couldn't afford to get kicked out of school since I'd received a grant due to my unfortunate circumstances.

"Wine?" I asked, as I grabbed a glass out of the cabinet.

"Sure," he said, as he grabbed my straw off of my desk and snorted the line that I'd prepared for myself.

"Really? You could've asked."

"I have more if you need some", Damon replied.

"That's not the point. The point is you should ask before using someone's stuff."

"My bad. I apologize."

After I handed Damon his glass of wine, he sat it down on the table and grabbed me.

"Let's dance," he said, already feeling his high coming on.

"Wait. Can I at least get a little something in me?"

While Damon found something to play on the radio, I poured some more coke out of the bag for myself and snorted it. I lied back on the sofa and closed my eyes to let it marinate. Next thing I knew, I felt Damon's lips up against mine. I slowly opened my eyes, not really sure of what had just happened, but by the looks of it, what I thought had happened, had actually happened. Damon and I had never been intimate. We just always had innocent fun with a few illegal practices in the privacy of our own space, and then would go our separate ways. I can't say that I was never attracted to Damon. He was tall, muscular, caramel complected, with a bald-head, and goatee, but I knew nothing was happening there. All of his female students had crushes on him, and none of them knew that I was the only one who got to spend time with him outside of class. I really couldn't say that without my doubts. I may not have been the only one, but I liked to believe that I was.

After Damon kissed me, he pulled me up off the sofa and we danced to Jodeci. That was the closest that I had ever felt to Damon. The physical attraction was definitely there on both ends. As soon as I felt that things were about to go too far, I heard something at the door.

My eyes bucked, and I said, "Did you hear that?"

Damon, not trying to hear what I was saying, and still trying to fondle me, said, "Nah. It was probably just someone outside in the hallway going into their dorm.

Next thing I knew, my door was flying open and on the other side was Zeke. He immediately dropped his luggage and said, "So this is what you were waiting to do while I was gone?"

He quickly skimmed the room to get an idea of exactly what was going on.

I ran over to Zeke and said, "No. This isn't what it looks like. We were just having a couple of drinks . . .

"And snorting cocaine. I thought you were done with that!" Zeke said.

"This is exactly what I mean about you trying to change me. This is what I do from time to time, and I never told you I was done. Just like people smoke weed. This is what I do. It's not like I do it every day!"

Damon walked over to Zeke and said, "Young Brother, if this is your woman you have a good one. All she's doing is sitting in her room minding her business."

"Yeah, with another man in her room. And aren't you a professor?"

"Yeah, I am a professor, and hopefully we can keep all of this right here in this room. You wouldn't want to get your girl in trouble, would you?"

Damon grabbed his glass of wine and gulped it down. He then walked past Zeke as he headed towards the door and said, "Man to man, study your girl. Learn what she likes. If you do that, she won't need people like me around, even though I'm not complaining about being able to keep her company."

Damon then walked out the door, leaving Zeke standing there, speechless. I knew that if he had been any other guy, there would've been a fight in my dorm room that night, but Zeke wasn't that type. He rationalized through everything and didn't let anything get him out of character. That was one of the qualities that I adored most about him.

"Zeke, why aren't you in New York?"

"Is that really all you can think about right now? I'm not in New York because I didn't want you to be alone, but I guess you didn't have that problem."

I don't think Zeke ever meant to, but he threw a lot of guilt trips on me very often and I would allow him to, just so I wouldn't hurt his feelings. I knew I could be pretty harsh at times, but this time I had to let him know what was really on my mind.

"Zeke, honestly, I was looking forward to this time alone. It was time that I knew that I would be able to be myself. We don't have the type of fun that I like to have and it's really starting to get to me. I feel like I'm losing myself, and I sometimes even feel depressed. I really like you, but I just wish we could enjoy the same things together. I know you don't agree with most things I do, and a lot of things that I say, but we're going to have to come to some compromise if you want to be with me. Look around this room. Music, coke, a little wine, and maybe some dancing. That's a good time to me. You, on the other hand, only enjoy stuff like going to the movies, dinner, bowling, playing pool, and reading that damn Bible. That's all cool, but what I'm saying is, we can incorporate both sides of our lifestyles and you'll see how much fun we can have together."

"I get it. I just have morals and values that I can't go against. I don't even know how I'm sitting here as calm as I am talking to you when you've been messing around with Professor Spears."

"We haven't been messing around. We just hang out in my dorm room. Most times, Brittney is here, and we have some drinks, talk, and laugh. I promise."

Zeke looked disappointed and very doubtful, but he still had it in him to say, "Stormie, I want to believe you because I love you. I don't love everything that you do, but I'm not going to love everything anyone does. I just want to be with you, and I want you to be with me, but not because I'm forcing you to, or because you feel sorry for me. If that's the case, let me go for good right now. I'm supposed to be on the plane right now visiting my mom, and the fact that she doesn't even know I'm not coming is one of the most hurtful things I've ever done to her. I don't even know how I'm going to explain this to her, but I know I have to. The first thing I want you to do is to tell me if this is something you want. If not, I'll leave and will never look back."

Zeke was so serious, and I was so confused. Zeke was probably a man that so many other women wanted, but he had chosen me. He was extremely smart, tall, dark, handsome, and loyal. Most women would've considered his relationship with God one of the best traits a man could have, but that wasn't on the top of my list when it came to choosing a man. In fact, it wasn't on my list of prerequisites that a man needed to have in order to have a chance with me at all. I felt a man could be a good man without believing in or having any sort of relationship with a so-called god.

I needed to lighten the mood, so I poured Zeke a glass of wine and said, "Here, drink this, and let's talk."

"Stormie, you know I don't drink."

"I know, but I think this will really help, and we can have a real heart to heart conversation."

Zeke looked at me with the eyes of a man who had all of the trust in the world for his woman and grabbed the glass from me.

He took a small sip and said, "This isn't too bad."

As Zeke sipped on his wine, I thought I'd try my luck and pour a little bit of coke for him to try.

He looked at me and said, "What are you doing?"

"Can you just try a little bit for me? Just this one time, and if you don't like it, I won't ask you again."

[11] "Put on the full armor of God, so that you can take your stand against the devil's schemes." – Ephesians 6:11 NIV

Zeke sighed, then put his glass down. "Let me call my mom first. I don't want Kyle to get to her before I call and try to explain. We discussed what we would say, but he sometimes has a way of adding his little two cents to it."

Zeke grabbed his phone and went out in the hall. Being nosey, I put my ear to the door. I knew I would be able to hear the entire conversation since Zeke almost always put his phone on speaker.

"Hey, Zeke! Where are you? You should be here by now," his mom said, sounding worried.

"Well, I got to the airport with Kyle, but I suddenly didn't feel well, so I caught the Uber back to campus. I think I'm just going to stay here for winter break."

There was dead silence for at least thirty seconds.

"Ma. You there?" Zeke finally said to break the silence.

"Yeah. I'm here. I'm just trying to comprehend the fact that you won't be here for the holidays. We've never been without each other this time of year."

"I know. I'm sorry, Ma. I miss you and I was really looking forward to seeing you."

"I was too, Baby. Maybe you'll feel better in the next couple of days and can still make it, but no pressure. I may be able to make my way that way soon, or, if not, spring break will be a nice time to come. The weather should be much better."

"Yeah, Ma. Thanks for understanding. Kyle should be there soon. I'm sure that you, him, and his mom will get together and have a good time."

"Yeah, but it won't be the same without you. I love you, Son."

"I love you, too, Ma."

When I heard Zeke hanging up the phone, I hurriedly ran and jumped on the sofa as if I had been there all along.

"How'd it go?" I asked.

Looking sad, Zeke said, "I feel bad. She already doesn't have my dad there, and now she doesn't have me."

"You never really talk about your dad, besides the things he taught you. You only brought up how he died one time, and when you did, I was really disrespectful and inconsiderate. I apologize for that."

"Thank you. To be honest, talking about him makes me sad a lot of times. He was a really good dad, and I just like to remember the good times. Little things remind me of him. Even things I see in myself, so even though I don't talk about him, I'm almost always thinking about him."

"I understand," I replied. "Well, this may make you feel a lot better," I said, as I put a tray in front of Zeke with a line of coke.

I handed him a straw. He held it and looked me in the eyes.

"Trust me. You'll feel better," I reassured him.

Zeke put the straw to the tray and snorted the entire the line. He looked at me and said, "That's it?"

"Oh, just give it a minute," I said.

After that one experience, Zeke was hooked, and I finally had my wish of having one thing we could experience together and enjoy.

41 "Watch and pray so that you will not fall into temptation. The spirit is willing, but the flesh is weak."
– Matthew 26:41 NIV

Ezekiel

Chapter Seventeen

When I woke up on the couch with Stormie laying on my lap, I rubbed my fingers through her hair as she slept, and I thought long and hard about what I'd engaged in the night before. I knew that my actions were unacceptable, and my father was probably rolling over in his grave. I began thinking about the fact that I should've left when I had come back and seen Stormie with another man in her dorm room. Especially a professor. What was I thinking? In the back of my mind, I knew that Stormie wasn't right for me. I had learned that anyone that led me onto the wrong path, tempting me to do things that I wouldn't ordinarily do were not the type of people that I needed to involve myself with. It was just something about Stormie, and I know I kept saying that, but it was because I truly believed it. I couldn't put her in that same category as those other people that I knew I shouldn't associate with. She had something over me, and I didn't know what it was, but I couldn't imagine my life without her.

[12] **"For we are not fighting against flesh-and-blood enemies,**

but against evil rulers and authorities of the unseen world, against mighty powers in this dark world, and against evil spirits in the heavenly places." – Ephesians 6:12 NLT

As I was deep into my thoughts, Stormie woke up and looked up at me. Her smile gave a sense of reassurance, and her eyes were just so tantalizing. I felt comforted just by looking at her. I always used to say I wanted someone like my mom, and she was the complete opposite. My mom would've never approved of her if she really knew her, so I knew I would have some work to do before introducing the two. I needed for my mom to love her just as much as I did, but I knew she wouldn't, knowing that she wasn't anything like the type of girl that she expected me to be with, or thought I deserved.

Stormie sat up and gave me a kiss on the cheek. "Good Morning, Babe," she said in the middle of a yawn. "How are you feeling this morning?"

I felt ok physically, but mentally, I was a mess. I still lied and said, "I feel great."

I didn't want Stormie to worry, or think that I didn't enjoy my time with her. I just didn't want to lose her.

"I knew you would, so now it's time for something else," she said as she got up and walked towards the kitchen.

"Something else?" I mumbled to myself. The only thing I wanted was to go to my dorm room, take a shower, and get into bed.

A few minutes later, Stormie walked back into the room with two glasses.

"I'm good. I'm not thirsty," I said. "In fact, I think I'm going to head back to my dorm and freshen up."

"Come on. Please?" Stormie begged. "Just one drink."

She began pouring Tequila in both glasses, filling them halfway and adding orange juice.

I had never been a drinker and didn't want to start. I had never snorted coke either, but somehow, Stormie got me to do that.

"Storm, I'm good. You know I don't really drink," I said, trying to be honest.

"I thought that we had decided since we were going to be together, we were going to have to compromise on some things. I like to drink, so can you please just have a drink with me? I promise I'll do something with you that you like to do, whatever that is. It really doesn't seem like you like to do much of anything except study," she said, giggling.

I looked at my watch, and said, "Stormie, it's ten-thirty in the morning. Who drinks this early?"

She cut her eyes at me and said, "Me, and stop judging. It's happy hour somewhere."

I took a deep breath, still unable to resist her undeniable beauty. She seemed to be even more beautiful when she woke up than she did when she would fix herself up for the day. I just had never met anyone who thought that life should be a party every single second of every day.

"Ok. Just one," I said, already regretting my decision.

Before I knew it, we'd each had three glasses. We talked to each other as we laughed with our speech slurring. We could barely even walk to the bathroom without holding on to the wall. That's the way our entire winter break went. All we did was eat, drink, smoke weed, and snort coke. That had become the way that we connected in ways that we would've never naturally connected. My initial intentions were to get to know Stormie better without all of the noise of other people around, but instead, I began the same bad habits that she had, and that seemed to be the side of me that she enjoyed the most. We did happen to have some serious conversations, and one of them involved memories of my dad, including the last evening my mom and I had spent with him. She seemed really compassionate, and comforted me as I uncomfortably divulged information that I had never discussed with anyone since it had happened.

I had a conversation with my mom on Christmas, and I was so high that I had barely hidden it.

"Ezekiel, are you ok? You don't sound right," she said, sounding concerned.

"Yeah, Ma. I'm fine. I'm just a little tired. I've been staying up late watching TV."

I had never mentioned to my mom the fact that I was dating the girl who had almost gotten me kicked out of school by accusing me of raping her, and I hadn't planned to anytime soon, but as I was talking to her, Stormie walked in and made sure that my mom was aware that I wasn't alone.

"Zeke! What's taking you so long?" she said, smiling and winking at me.

"Ezekiel! Is that a girl you're with? Who is she and why haven't I heard about her? And why is she calling you Zeke? Your name is Ezekiel, and you know how important that is to me!"

"Ma! She's just a girl I've been dating, and she chooses to call me Zeke, and I don't mind it."

Stormie became very angry and said, "Is that all I am? Are you so embarrassed of me that you can't tell your mom that we've been dating the past few months?"

"Few months?" my mom said, angrily. "Is that why you couldn't come home and spend some time with me?"

I felt horrible because I could hear the shakiness in her voice that I would hear when she was either crying or about to cry.

"I'm sorry, Ma. I just wanted to make you proud. I wanted to make sure she would be someone you would approve of."

"Listen to me, Ezekiel. I trust your judgement in character, but I don't like the fact that someone can cause you to lie to me. That makes me feel as though you're hiding something from me. I can't believe Kyle didn't even tell me. You don't have to lie to me about anything, Ezekiel. You've never had to lie me and never will. I want you to be able to talk to me about anything, no matter how old you get, so the next chance you get, I want to meet this girl."

"Ok, Ma. I promise. Please forgive me. I'm so sorry for hurting you."

"I'll always forgive my baby. I know how it is when it comes to relationships. Nothing could keep me and your daddy apart.

Nothing but death, and I can still feel him even now, so I can't even say death can keep us apart. I'm not going to get all sad and sappy on you. I did enough of that when I received the locket from you with the picture of me, you, and your dad inside. That was the most beautiful gift you could've gotten me. I hope I sent you enough money for you to get by for a while. I know college life is rough."

"Don't worry about me, Ma. I'll be ok."

"Go ahead and enjoy yourself, and I'll be looking forward to meeting your new friend."

When I got off of the phone from with my mom, Stormie was sitting on the sofa across from me with her lips poked out.

"What's wrong with you?" I asked.

"Mama's boy!" she shouted. "That's the last thing I need in my life. You'll never be able to be anyone's man or husband because your mom will always come first in your life!"

"Stormie, you're drunk. We both are, but I'm sober enough to know that what you're talking about is some nonsense. I grew up in church, and I know the Bible very well. The Bible tells me to respect and honor my parents, and when I get married to cleave to my wife."

24 "Therefore shall a man leave his father and his mother, and shall cleave unto his wife: and they shall be one flesh."
– Genesis 2:24 KJV

"Blah, blah, blah! Here you go about that Bible stuff with a system full of alcohol and weed. This is exactly why I don't believe in any of that stuff. Look at you sitting here being a hypocrite. Look at yourself and tell me honestly what your "so called" god thinks of you right now."

The words that Stormie had just said to me resonated within my soul and left me speechless. What was God thinking of me at that moment? I knew that I could repent and God would forgive me, but I had never felt as though I had disappointed God so much. I had to stop what I was doing, and I knew I had to do it immediately. My integrity was very important to me, and I felt as though Stormie had purposely caused me to sacrifice my integrity just so she could try to prove a point. I couldn't completely blame her, though, because it was my choice, and no one had put a gun to my head.

"Stormie, God is real. I've always believed in God and I know I'm not perfect. I've never done any of the things that I've been doing since being with you."

Stormie interrupted and said, "So now you're going to blame your actions on me? I didn't put a gun to your head. You did what you did because you wanted to! I thought God was supposed to protect you from doing things that are supposedly "ungodly". How is that working for you?"

"I'm not blaming you, Stormie. I did it on my own free will. I really just wanted to have a good time with you."

"Right! And we've been having fun, haven't we? Since God is supposed to be so good and mighty, and wants the best for us, don't you think He wants us to have fun?"

"Of course, Storm, but not the kind of fun we've been having. We have to do better. I can meet you halfway on some things, but I can't compromise my morals and integrity, and that's exactly what I've been doing."

Stormie sat down and put her head in her lap. She then raised her head and said, "Every time I find someone that I think I might like, they want to change me. Why do I have to change? Why won't they change for me? No one ever does anything for me and I find it to be quite selfish. All you're thinking about right now is you and how you feel. How about how I feel? This is all I know, and if I don't have it, it might destroy me. You have no idea what I've had to go through to get to where I am now, but then again, you probably don't even care. All you care about is you, your momma, your dead daddy, and a god that doesn't even exist."

My eyes bucked because I couldn't believe what Stormie had just said. I tried to remain calm, and I softly said, "Storm, you're hitting below the belt. Please don't say anything about my daddy. You know nothing about him, but what I can tell you is that, yes, I do care about my mom and dad, and my dad was the best man that I've ever known in my life."

Stormie looked remorseful, and quickly came over and gave me a hug.

"I'm so sorry, Zeke. I'm just frustrated. I want a good man, but it seems like a girl like me just can't have one."

I sat right next to Stormie and put both of her hands into mine. I looked into her beautiful eyes and said, "Stormie, listen to me. I know you've had a hard life, and I know you're still holding in a lot of your anger, but trust me when I say, I'm here for you and I'm not going anywhere. I hope I don't scare you, but I love you. There is just something that draws me to you, and it may just be that you're so different from any other girl that I've ever known, but that's enough for me to want to continue to get to know who you are. I just want what's best for you, and you're better than all of this drinking and smoking. Others in your life have tried to destroy you, but the person you're meant to be is still in there," I said, putting my hand over her heart. "Let me just help you."

A tear dropped from Stormie's eye, which I had never seen. She then said the last thing that I would've thought she would've said after all that.

"Can we just have a long night of fun for just one more night? It's Christmas. Then you can help me start on this new journey of finding myself. I want you to be there for me and help me, but I've been doing this for a long time, so just one more night. Please."

I put my hands over my face, not knowing what to do. Stormie sounded like she wanted help, but needing another night to get high just seemed crazy. That was when I realized she was truly an addict. A functioning one at that, because if no one actually saw Stormie get high, they would've never known that she did every single day. I knew what my answer should've been. I should've told her she needed real help and walked out at that moment, but she needed me, so I stayed. Not only did I stay, but I also partook in all of it, feeling ashamed that I was enjoying myself once again the entire time.

That night almost messed up my entire life. All that I could assume was that I passed out and Stormie was still sober enough to call 911 because she couldn't get me to wake up. When I finally did wake up, several hours later, I looked around and saw my mom standing over me with more disappointment on her face than I'd ever seen. I then looked over at the chair in the corner, and Kyle was lying there sleeping. I tried to speak, but there were tubes everywhere.

"Shhh. We have a lot to talk about, but not right now. I'm just glad that the doctors were able to save you. I don't know what I would've done if I lost you," my mom said with tears in her eyes.

I didn't see Stormie anywhere around, and I was wondering if she was ok, but I couldn't speak. Even if I could have, I wouldn't have dared to ask my mom about Stormie because I knew by now she had some type of idea about the type of girl Stormie was. At that moment, my mom didn't care about anything except for the fact that I was ok, and I was thankful to God to still be alive.

[21] "This I recall to my mind, therefore have I hope. [22] It is of the Lord's mercies that we are not consumed, because his compassions fail not. [23] They are new every morning: great is thy faithfulness." – Lamentations 3: 21-23 KJV

Chapter Eighteen

Hours later, I heard a voice that sounded a lot like Stormie. "Hi, Faith. It's nice to meet you, finally," I heard Stormie say as I laid in the hospital bed with my eyes closed.

I knew right at that moment that there was about to be a problem. My mom was God-fearing and always did her best to say and do the right things, but when it had something to do with endangering her family, or putting them in harm's way, she had a real problem with that, and it was extremely hard for her to control her temper.

I immediately opened my eyes and saw my mom's petite figure standing in front of Stormie's tall frame. I was hoping Kyle would get up and stand in between them, but I looked over in the chair where I had last seen him sleeping, and he was gone.

My mom put her hand on her hip, looked Stormie up and down, and said, "Excuse me, but who are you, and did you just call me by my first name? If you did, my next question is going to be who raised you?"

Stormie looked speechless, but I knew she was trying to gather her words without being disrespectful. She knew exactly how I felt about my mom.

Struggling to speak, I said, "Ma, that's Stormie, my girlfriend."

My mom was taken aback and said, "Girlfriend? Isn't Stormie the girl who accused you and Kyle of trying to rape her when you did nothing but help her? This is just too much for me right now."

"But, Ma, she saved my life."

My mom sat as closely to me as she could on my bed and her mouth was so close to me that I could feel every one of her words tremble through my body.

"Listen to me, Ezekiel. This woman did not save your life! She almost killed you! You would've never had liquor and drugs in your system if it wasn't for her! I know this was all of her doing! You are not, and never have been that kind of young man! Your dad and I raised you better!"

Stormie interjected, and said, Ms. Whitfield . . .

"Mrs. Whitfield!" my mom said, correcting her.

"I'm sorry, Mrs. Whitfield. It is my fault. Zeke didn't want to do any of what he did, and I pressured him."

My mom stood up and said, "First of all, his name is Ezekiel! Secondly, you didn't pressure him to do anything because a strong man thinks on his own. Ezekiel allowed his flesh to take over instead of listening to his spirit, and this is where it got him. Little girl, you don't have enough power to pressure anyone into doing anything! That was his decision, unfortunately! He has a soft heart, and unfortunately, his heart sometimes gets him in trouble, especially when he finds himself really caring for someone."

Stormie looked as if she had no idea what my mom was talking about. She wasn't raised in the Word like I was to understand what walking in the flesh and walking in the Spirit meant.

[17] **"Remember, it is sin to know what you ought to do and then not do it." – James 4:17 NLT**

"I just wanted to say that I'm sorry. I think I should leave," Stormie said.

"I think you're right, and please don't come back," my mom said, furiously.

Stormie secretly rolled her eyes at my mom behind her back, and told me that she'd talk to me later. When she left, my mom really had a mouthful.

"Is this what you've been doing during your break? Do you know how much trouble you can get into? If the school finds out about this, you can possibly lose your scholarship, or worse, get kicked out completely! This girl is no good for you. It doesn't matter how pretty she is, or whatever else she does for you. What does she have offer you that will improve your life in a positive way? If you can answer that, I just may be willing to give her a chance."

"She had a hard life. She grew up in foster homes, and I don't think they treated her too well. I've been trying to talk to her about God, but her mind has just been all messed up by what she's gone through."

"So you thought you'd make it better by drinking and getting high with her?"

"No. I had talked her into quitting. She begged me to do it with her one last time, so that's what I did. I never thought the night would end up like this."

"Getting a call from Kyle at one in the morning was no fun! She didn't even have the decency to call me! I'm your mother."

"Well, she must've gone through my phone, and maybe Kyle's number was the first one she ran across. I'm sure she was panicking. We do crazy things when we panic."

"There you go. That's what I love about you, Ezekiel. You always look for the best in people, but from the feeling I get from just being around her, she is not good for you. Her spirit isn't right. You don't need anyone like that in your life."

"But she needs me, Ma."

"She doesn't need you. She needs a whole lot of help, but way more than you can give her. She is not your project. All you can do is pray for her. She's been doing ok without you all of this time, so trust me when I say she'll be ok."

I sighed just thinking about not spending time with Stormie. Even though I knew the things that we were doing weren't always right, she showed me a different, exciting part of life that I didn't know anything about. I began to think that maybe that was what caused me to be even more intrigued by her. It was such a thrill to be with her, but I didn't know what would happen once that thrill was gone. Maybe I had just been addicted to the things that I was never allowed to do and had never done. Whatever it was, all I knew was I felt as though I was in love and even though it was probably infatuation, no matter how many times my mom said she wasn't right for me, I didn't know how I was going to let her go.

I was tired of talking about Stormie, knowing my mom wasn't going to have anything good to say about her, so I asked her how long I'd have to be in the hospital.

She answered by sarcastically saying, "Well, let's see. You came in with alcohol poisoning and an overdose of cocaine which started to shut down your organs, so I would say at least for a few days! They may even try to put you in a rehab program."

"But, Ma, I just started doing this stuff!"

"I understand, but before you leave here, they want to make sure they do all they can to make sure that you don't continue down the same path. It's not up to me at this point. It's up to the doctors."

"You can tell them I'm a good kid and this is my first time getting into this type of situation."

"And it will be the last!" my mom said with force.

"I promise it will, Ma."

"I know, because the rest of your break, you'll be spending at home with me."

"But, Ma!"

"No buts! My mind is made up. There is no way I'm leaving you here with that girl, especially without Kyle here to watch you."

"But Kyle's still here, right?"

"Yeah. I gave him money to get a hotel room at the hotel where I'm staying. I didn't want him sleeping in that chair all night, but he's leaving going back to New York when I leave, so the three of us will be leaving together."

I was distraught. I didn't want to leave Stormie. I didn't want her to get right back into her same ways, and I definitely didn't want that professor coming by spending time with her. I knew there was no talking my mom out of her decision. Once her mind was made up, it was made up, so I didn't even try to change it. Stormie kept calling my cell phone, which was sitting on the table next to my hospital bed, but after around the fifth call, my mom grabbed it and threw it in her purse.

"Ma, can I at least talk to her. She may really need to talk."

My mom put both hands on her hips and said, "Absolutely not! I think that you feel like you need to talk to her, and you don't need to talk to anyone right now except for Jesus Christ, so with that, I'm going to leave you for a little while, go get myself a little something to eat, and I'll be back later. That'll give you some time to think about who you were raised to be, and to have a much-needed conversation with God."

My mom walked out of the room without looking back. I couldn't even use the hospital phone to call Stormie because I didn't know her number by heart, so I did what my mother said I needed to do. It had been a long time since I'd had an intimate moment with God. As much as I had tried to force my beliefs on Stormie, I hadn't been practicing what I preached.

6 "I am praying to you because I know you will answer, O God. Bend down and listen as I pray.
7 Show me your unfailing love in wonderful ways.
 By your mighty power you rescue
 those who seek refuge from their enemies.
8 Guard me as you would guard your own eyes.
 Hide me in the shadow of your wings.
9 Protect me from wicked people who attack me,

from murderous enemies who surround me."
– Psalm 17:6-9 NLT

After spending a couple of more days in the hospital, I was finally released to go home. Kyle, my mom, and I hopped on a plane back to New York. Stormie never tried to make her way back to the hospital to see me, and I still didn't have my phone to see if she had called. I couldn't imagine that she wouldn't have tried to contact me in one way or another. My mother could be very intimidating, even to be so small, so I was sure Stormie probably had decided she'd just wait until I contacted her whenever things cooled down.

Chapter Nineteen

"**M**an, what were you thinking?" Kyle asked me as we sat in my bedroom in New York that hadn't been changed one bit since I'd left.

I sat on my bed and cuffed my face inside my hands as I said, "Bro, I don't know. I knew what I was doing was wrong, but I wanted to make her happy."

"You can't make anyone happy. Joy is inside a person's heart. That's one thing I'll remember your dad telling me to always remember. If she likes you, she's going to like you whether or not you're drinking and getting high with her. You are not that person. Don't let anyone change who you are. There's someone out there who will love everything about you. Well, maybe not those big ole crusty lips, but everything else," Kyle said, trying to add some light to the situation.

"I knew you had to throw a joke in there somewhere," I said, laughing, as I licked my lips.

Kyle continued, "I never thought I would be compatible with someone like Madison, but she loves everything about me. She even laughs at my corny jokes, and would never expect me to do anything that goes against my morals. I feel the same about her. If we wouldn't have met her that night at that party, I probably would've missed out on someone special because of my expectations of perfection. If I'd just seen her walking around on campus, I probably would've just kept walking."

[24] "Look beneath the surface so you can judge correctly." – John 7:24 NLT

"Stormie has some issues she needs to figure out on her own. You are just like your dad. You want to save the world, but you can't save everyone, Dude," Kyle continued, being completely sincere with every word he spoke.

"I know I can't. I'm just going to see how things go. Maybe we just need a little time apart to see clearly and know whether or not we're meant for each other," I said.

"Ezekiel, are you hearing me? Unless she goes to some type of rehab and God performs a miracle on her, she is not the one for you. I don't like judging people, but I'm just going by what I've seen and what just happened to you. A good woman is supposed to help elevate you, not deplete you of everything good that you have inside of you. I know you're not talking about marrying the girl, but there's no point in getting deeper into this than it needs to go. The deeper you get in, the harder it's going to be to get out. The two of you lived two totally different lives. You lived in a home full of love. No telling what she went through in all of the homes she passed through."

"You may not think I'm hearing you, but I am, and I agree with you. I'll figure it out. Don't worry about me. I'll be ok."

That evening, Kyle went back to his mom's place, and I laid in my bed with a million thoughts running through my mind. I wondered what Stormie was doing, who she was with, if she was thinking about me as much as I was thinking about her, and if she was the one. My mom finally came into my room and relinquished my phone.

"I'm only giving this to you because I believe I can trust you to do the right thing," she said.

I looked at the screen and there were no missed calls.

"Did you check or answer any of my calls?" I asked my mom, figuring that was the reason why it seemed as though no one had called.

Well, unfortunate for me, I was wrong.

"Nope. Your phone hasn't rang since I've been holding it hostage. Not even a text message. I don't want to sound negative, but that should tell you a lot about the girl that you care so much about."

I knew there had to have been an explanation as to why Stormie hadn't contacted me. Maybe my mom had completely scared her off, or maybe the entire situation of me having to go into the hospital freaked her out.

"I'm about to go take a shower and get in bed. You need anything before I turn in?" my mom asked.

"No, Ma. Thank you so much for everything, and for loving me regardless of my mistakes."

My mom smiled and said, "That's what moms are for. You may upset or disappoint me, but you will always be my baby and I'll always love you unconditionally. I know you have a heart of gold, just like your daddy, and I'll never stop loving you."

She gave me a kiss on the forehead, and said, "Goodnight, Baby. I'll see you in the morning."

After my mom walked out of my room and closed the door, I stared at my phone. I wanted to call Stormie so badly, but I wasn't sure if that was a good idea. What would I even say? What would she say? I sat my phone on the nightstand and rolled over, trying my best to fall asleep. I laid there for about a half hour, and I still couldn't doze off. All I could think about was her smile, her eyes, her hair, her perfect body, and how if I could just show her the way, she'd be ok.

Next thing I knew, I was picking up my phone. I went to Stormie's number in my contacts and called her. The phone rang about three times, and right before I was about to hang up, she answered, sounding like she was asleep. I looked at the time, and it was only around ten-thirty, and there was a three hour time difference between New York and California, so it was only about seven-thirty where she was.

"Hey, Storm. You sleep already?"

"Zeke! Are you ok?" she asked, sounding as if she had perked up.

"Yeah, I'm ok. I was wondering the same about you. I hadn't heard from you."

"Sorry. I was going to call tomorrow. I kept trying to call you after I left the hospital the first day and I never got an answer, so I just decided to let you get your rest."

"It's been three days, and you haven't even checked on me. It doesn't sound like you really cared about how I was doing."

Stormie immediately became defensive and said, "Is this why you called me? To antagonize me? Your mom already beat me up and cut me with her words, and now you want to beat me up some more? You aren't the only person going through some things. I was the one who had to see you lying there, helpless, foaming from the mouth. I thought you were dead! Did you ever think about my mental state?"

Stormie was right. She had been through a lot that night, too. I couldn't even imagine myself going through what she did, watching me lying there unconscious while she sat there trying to perform CPR, not knowing whether or not I going to live or die. I knew it had to be traumatizing for her as well.

"I'm sorry. I didn't think about things from your perspective."

"It's ok, and I'm sorry I didn't at least send you a text. I could've done that much."

"Thanks. I appreciate that," I said.

There was a brief, uncomfortable silence, and Stormie finally asked, "Are you still at the hospital? I can come see you tomorrow, if your mom doesn't mind."

I hesitated for a moment and said, "I'm actually in New York."

"In New York? What are you doing there?"

"My mom wanted to keep an eye on me."

"Um hmm. Keep an eye on you, or keep you away from me?"

I didn't want to hurt Stormie's feelings, but I also didn't want to be untruthful with her.

"I guess a little bit of both. I'm sure once all of this passes, she'll get to know you and love you. She was just upset and wasn't in the mindset to meet you and have a conversation with you, but who could blame her?"

"Zeke, be honest with yourself. After all that has happened, you mom will never like, nor respect me. In her mind, I'm the girl who almost killed her baby boy. That's hard to come back from."

Suddenly, I heard a voice in the background, and it wasn't a female.

"Is someone there with you?" I asked inquisitively.

Stormie hesitated and said, "Nope. Just me. I've been alone since you left."

"I could've sworn I heard someone," I said, letting her know I wasn't completely buying what she was trying to sell.

"You probably just heard the TV, but I'm pretty tired, and I'm sure you are, too, so I'll call you tomorrow," she said, seeming to rush me off of the phone.

"Ok, Storm. Sweet dreams."

"Only if you're in them", she replied as she always did when I told her "sweet dreams".

As we hung up the phone, I knew she was lying to me, but I didn't want to believe it. If you truly care about someone, I don't care how uncomfortable someone makes you feel, you're still going to be there by any means necessary. She didn't even try to be there, and then when I contacted her, she had the nerve to act as if she didn't even want to talk to me. I knew this next week was going to be hard on me because I wasn't in California to be able to see what Stormie was doing, but then again, what type of relationship was that to have to even feel the need to worry about what she was doing? My heart was telling me one thing, and my mind was telling me something totally different.

[9] **"The human heart is the most deceitful of all thing sand**

desperately wicked. Who really knows how bad it is?"
– Jeremiah 17:9 NLT

I knew I needed to listen to my mind. I asked for it to be renewed every day so that I could have a mind more like Christ, but it seemed to be way easier said than done.

[8] "And now, dear brothers and sisters, one final thing. Fix your thoughts on what is true, and honorable, and right, and pure, and lovely, and admirable. Think about things that are excellent and worthy of praise." – Philippians 4:8 NLT

The rest of the time I stayed in New York, I decided not to call Stormie, which was a very hard decision, but it became easier when she didn't attempt to call me either. I just wanted to enjoy my mom as much as I could because if anyone else in the world didn't care about me, I knew beyond a shadow of a doubt that she did, and would always want what was best for me.

The Sunday before I had to head back to school, my mom and I went to church. It was the same church we had gone to my entire life, which was called Fountain of Renewal Christian Center, pastored by Pastor Drew Ervin. Pastor Ervin had known me all of my life, and every time he saw me, he would tell me that I was a special young man.

After the sermon, Pastor Ervin called me up because he had a word from God for me.

He placed his right hand on my head and began by saying, "And I hear the Lord saying, you have so much love to give, but you tend to give it to people who don't want to accept it. You want to change people to be the people that you think they ought to be, but you can't change them. Only I can. I made you to be someone great, and others will see that and want to destroy you. Stand strong in who you are. You are my child, and I want what's best for you. You have so much to do in this world, and the things that you do will blow your mind. They will be things that you would've never thought that you would do. Things that have never even crossed your mind. You will meet people in your life that will come and go, but some are meant to stay, and they have a very specific purpose in your life. You will know exactly who that person or those people are when you meet them. There will be no doubt nor confusion about them. You don't only have an abundance of love inside of you, you have so many gifts, and those people who are meant to be a part of your life will stand by your side and help expand your gifts and they will be just as important to them as they are to you. I will reveal those gifts to you when it's time, but for now, just keep your mind, heart, and soul open to me and follow my lead. I won't lead you astray. You will know if something isn't for you. You won't feel my peace. My peace and joy are inside of you, and anything that disturbs it, is not of me. Remember that and never forget it. Follow me, talk to me, listen to me, and continue to allow me in. I will never leave you nor forsake you. Just continue to allow me to prepare you, saith the Lord."

Pastor Ervin hugged me and whispered in my ear that we needed to get together very soon. When I turned and walked back towards the congregation, the first thing I saw was my mom standing there, clapping and crying. That word was definitely something that I needed. I knew I was better than my recent behaviors, but that word was just confirmation from God. I needed Him in my life, and I shouldn't have been putting anyone before him, no matter how much I cared for them.

[33] "Seek the Kingdom of God above all else, and live righteously, and he will give you everything you need."
– Matthew 6:33 NLT

When my mom and I walked out of church that day, we heard someone calling after us as we walked down the sidewalk towards the church's parking lot. When we looked back, we saw Pastor Ervin jogging towards us in his grey suit and freshly polished dress shoes.

When he finally reached us, my mom said, "Hey, Pastor! That was a very good sermon today, and thank you so much for the word you gave Ezekiel."

"Well, I just tell people what God wants them to hear, and that was something that God told me that Ezekiel really needed to hear."

Pastor Ervin then reiterated to me and my mom of how special of a young man I was and that I had a huge calling on my life that God would be revealing to me in due time. This was an honor coming from Pastor Ervin. I could tell that he saw something in me that truly amazed him, and I didn't want to let anyone down. Especially God.

Chapter Twenty

My mother was extremely happy to hear what Pastor Ervin had to say, and was even more happy that we were able to spend some time together during my break. Even though those weren't my initial plans, that was the best thing for me. God definitely knew how to make things work out in the way in which they needed to. I needed to be around my mother so she could help remind me of how I was raised and who the ruler of my life was. I had seemed to forget during the short period that I was in school, but I was quickly reminded that one day I could be here and the next day I could be gone. Every day was a blessing and I needed to continue to be obedient to the person that gave me life so I could stay on the path of completing my assignment.

While Kyle and I were on the plane heading back to school, we had a long talk. I talked to him about the conversation between me and Pastor Ervin.

"So, what are you going to do about Stormie when we get back?"

"Stormie hasn't even called me one time since I've been gone, so I think all of that is over."

"You think?" Kyle asked, raising one of his eyebrows.

"I mean, who does that to someone they really care about?" I said.

"Exactly!" Kyle said. "So, you shouldn't think that it's over. You should know! I know she's fine and all, and these girls can do something to us, but you just have to let it go, Bro. That's probably her problem. She's so pretty and used to getting her way that she's not even worried about you going anywhere. You need to let her know that your values and morals are more important than being with her. Her looks can't get her everything she wants, and she needs to know that."

> [6]"Even if I should choose to boast, I would not be a fool, because I would be speaking the truth. But I refrain, so no one will think more of me than is warranted by what I do or say, [7] or because of these surpassingly great revelations. Therefore, in order to keep me from becoming conceited, I was given a thorn in my flesh, a messenger of Satan, to torment me."

After Kyle and I landed back in California and got to our dorm, I went straight to my room, threw everything down, and sat on the edge of my bed. I could hear Kyle rummaging around in his room, making all kinds of noise.

"Dude, what are you doing in there?" I asked, taking my frustration out on him.

Next thing I knew, Kyle was walking into my room with a handful of clothes.

"I'm trying to unpack if you don't mind. I do have a couple of week's worth of clothes to wash, as should you, too."

"My bad. I'm just feeling some type of way. My emotions are all over the place," I apologized.

"You just need to occupy your mind. You want to go hang out and find something to do? Madison won't be back until tomorrow, so I definitely don't have anything to do, and even if she was here, you know I'm always here for you, Bro."

"I know. I just feel like I need to see her. I need closure."

"The closure should've been when she didn't call you, but I know you're different from me, and I can't tell you what to do. All I can say is do what you feel like you need to do for your own sanity."

Kyle walked out and went back into his room, continuing to sort out his own mess. I wished some dirty clothes had been the only type of mess that I had going on. Mine went so much more deeper than that, and I needed to clean it up.

I grabbed my keys off of my dresser and yelled, "I'll be back!"

Kyle came running out of his room and asked, "Where you going?"

"You said to do what I feel I need to do, and I need to see her."

Kyle shook his head, and said, "Ok. I trust you'll do the right thing. Just be careful."

As I walked to Stormie's residence hall, I began to think maybe I should've called first, but I felt as though I'd get more of the truth that I needed if I just showed up. As I was walking up to the building someone was walking out, so I didn't have to get buzzed in as normal. When I knocked on the door, I heard movement inside, so I knew she was there, unless her roommate, Brittney, had gotten back.

"Who is it?" Stormie asked from the other side of the door.

I cleared my throat, and said, "It's Zeke."

"Zeke?" she said as she slowly opened the door.

She was dressed in some grey sweatpants and a white tank top with her hair messily pulled up into a knot at the top of her head. She didn't have on any make-up, so all I saw was her naturally beautiful brown skin.

"I'm back," I said.

"I see," Stormie said, not seeming very excited to see me. "You could've called to let me know. I could've gotten myself together. I look horrible," she said, as she looked down at her clothes.

"You look beautiful," I replied.

I thought I was going to have to ask, but she finally invited me in. As I walked in behind her, she looked around the room as if she had never been there, so I began looking around, too.

"Are you looking for something?" I finally asked her.

"No. I'm just embarrassed. I'm a mess, and it's a mess around here."

As we walked past the kitchen table, I noticed two wine glasses sitting there. One with the same colored lip-gloss that Stormie normally wore, and the other with no sign of any lip-gloss or lipstick.

"Is Brittney back?" I asked Stormie.

"No. She should be back tomorrow evening," she replied.

That made me wonder who the other glass belonged to. When we got to her room, I noticed at least three bottles of liquor sitting on her dresser, and a tray on her nightstand next to her bed. Just from the looks of everything, I could tell what Stormie had been up to.

She looked back at me and saw me looking at every inch of the room.

Sounding guilty, she said, "I didn't drink all of this. I was just doing some deep cleaning and found some old empty bottles underneath the bed."

To try to distract me from everything else, she gave me a hug.

"I missed you so much, Zeke."

"You missed me so much that you never even called, huh?"

"I just didn't want to bother you. I knew you were spending some quality time with your mom and figured you would call me when you had time."

"Listen to yourself, Stormie. I'm the one who was in the hospital and almost died. Don't you think you should be the one checking?"

"I'm sorry, Babe," she said as she kissed me on the lips. "I'm just so glad you're ok, but you seem like you're on edge. I don't like you like this. Sit down."

She sat me down on the bed and straddled her long legs around me. She then began to massage my shoulders.

"You're so tense. What has you like this?"

"You do."

She quickly jumped up and said, "Me?"

"Yeah, you. The entire time I was gone, all I could think about was you, and it doesn't seem like you thought about me at all. It seems like you've already come to a conclusion about our relationship status, but I had to see one last time for myself."

"What conclusion?" she asked curiously.

"We're not right for each other."

Seeming surprised, Stormie said, "What do you mean? You bring out the best in me."

"Do I really? It seems like I've only seen the worst in you lately. When I first met you, that seemed to be the best version of yourself. I can definitely say you don't bring out the best in me."

"Yes, I do. You just can't see it because you've never seen that version of yourself before. You just have to learn how to control that version and you'll be fine. Please don't leave me. Don't be like everyone else."

"It doesn't look like you were alone while I was away. Did Damon come by?" I asked, changing the subject.

Stormie was silent, but I could tell what the answer was by looking into her eyes.

She finally said, "I told you, it's nothing intimate, but I promise if you find it a problem, I'll tell him that he can't come around anymore."

"Storm, we're supposed to be in an exclusive relationship. Of course I have a problem with another guy coming around, especially when I'm nowhere around, and I don't feel I should have to tell you that. You wouldn't want another female coming around me, would you?"

She hesitated, and then said, "I guess not."

"Stormie, I'm going to ask you a question, and please be honest with me."

Stormie looked nervous, but said, "Ok. Go ahead."

"Do you have any coke around here?"

She smiled and said, "Yeah, I do," as she got up off of the bed and walked out of the room.

I shook my head, not being able to believe after all that had happened, she continued on doing her thing without any type of regard for me.

She came back into the room and said, "Here you go," as she held out a can of Coca-Cola in front of me.

"Stormie, that's not funny. You know what I mean."

Stormie sighed and plopped down on the bed.

"If you want to ask me if I've been getting high, just ask."

"Ok. Storm, have you been getting high?"

"Yes, I have, and yes, I do have some coke underneath the mattress. I had good intentions to quit, but without you here to motivate me, it was so hard."

I knelt down on the floor and stuck my hand underneath Stormie's mattress and couldn't feel anything.

"What are you doing?" Stormie asked, with her face frowned up.

"I'm looking for the coke so we can get rid of it."

"I never said it was underneath my mattress. That would just be dumb on my part."

"Stormie, please tell me you didn't . . ."

"Didn't what? Put it underneath Brittney's mattress? Yes, I did. I have gone through too much in my life to get to where I am for someone to take it from me. Brittney has had it good. If she got caught, she would just get a slap on the wrist."

"But that's your friend, Stormie. How could you do that to your friend?"

"We're not friends. We're roommates that hang out from time to time."

I kept hearing a voice in my head that kept telling me over and over again to walk away right at that moment, but I still couldn't. I didn't know how I would ever be able to trust her after finding out what she had done. Brittney truly cared about Stormie and would have never done anything like that to her. What made it worse was that she had no shame about it, but I still felt as though I was supposed to be there for her.

I walked over to Brittney's bed and lifted her mattress, immediately finding the bag of coke.

"Now what?" Stormie asked.

"Now we're going to go to the bathroom and flush it."

Stormie looked very uneasy about what I'd just suggested, but it needed to be done.

"You good?" I asked Stormie as she sat on the bed staring at me as I prepared to take the bag to the bathroom.

"I'm fine," she said, trying to sound as if she didn't have a care in the world. She then got up and followed me to the bathroom.

When we got to the bathroom, I found that Stormie had a night of praying to the porcelain god and hadn't even cleaned up yet.

"Let's clean this up first," I said.

"I don't have a problem, Zeke. I'm ok. I can handle myself. I've been doing this and functioning just fine for a long time. If we never dated, you would've never even known."

"But we are dating, and I do know, so now it's up to me to help you."

I bent down to open the cabinet with the cleaning supplies and found there were none. There wasn't even any space for cleaning supplies because bottles of liquor took up every inch of space in the cabinet.

I looked up at Stormie and said, "But you don't have a problem?"

She rolled her eyes and said, "Just do what you came in here to do."

I stood back up and opened the bag. I stared at it for a moment and suddenly felt the sensation that I felt each time that I snorted it. I could see Stormie staring at me from the corner of my eye, and she began grinning.

"I know exactly what you're feeling right now. It gets you high just by looking at it. Just by thinking about it. You can't do it, can you?"

Stuttering, I said, "Yeah, I can do it."

My flesh had taken over, and I honestly couldn't get enough strength to poor the coke down the toilet. I suddenly got a strong urge to take it back into Stormie's room and enjoy just a little bit. *"Am I addicted?"* I thought to myself. I couldn't have been. I'd only done it a few times.

Stormie softly caressed my back as she grabbed the bag, and said, "Come on. One last time. I'll make sure you're ok. I promise."

I looked into her eyes, and once again, she drew me in. That didn't end up being the last time, but throughout our entire college career, it remained our secret. I accepted that was who Stormie was, and if I wanted to be with her, I needed to be the type of man that she desired for me to be. The man that she could enjoy, and completely be herself around. Ezekiel wasn't that person that enjoyed doing the things that Stormie did, but obviously Zeke was.

Chapter Twenty-One

After finishing college, Stormie and I decided to both move back to New York. Although Stormie was originally from Queens, we still found an apartment in New York City where we had both landed jobs in our fields. I also wanted to be close to my mom, who still lived there. My mom never straight out and said it, but she still couldn't stand Stormie. She didn't have to say it. The way that she looked at her, and the tone in her voice when she spoke to her said it all. She definitely made it known that she did not agree one bit with our decision to move in together. I got to the point that whenever I would go visit my mom, I would leave Stormie at home because when they were around each other, the tension was so thick that I couldn't genuinely enjoy my time with my mom. Stormie didn't mind one bit.

Kyle decided not to move back to New York. He and Madison broke up due to him being unfaithful, but he liked California so much, and received a job offer that he couldn't turn down, so he decided to stay. Deep down, I felt like he and Madison would eventually get back together. He still never approved of me being with Stormie either, but he just wanted me to be happy, but safe at the same time. I had to say, it did feel strange without him being around, but no matter wherever we were in the world, we would forever be brothers and always kept in touch.

One morning, my mom invited me over for breakfast since it was the weekend and I didn't have to work. She was so happy to have me back in the area, so whatever chance she got, she made it a point to make plans with me. This particular morning, I had some news for her that I knew she wouldn't be very happy about.

Before I could get to the front door, my mom opened the storm door, ran out in her robe and house shoes, and hugged me.

"You are looking more and more like your daddy every day!"

"Ma, you say that every time you see me."

As I held the door open, so that we could walk into the house, my mom said, "Because it's true! He would be so proud to have a college graduate with a promising career as an electrical engineer!" While she began fixing my plate as I sat at the table, she continued by saying, "I don't know how he would feel about that girl . . ."

"Ma, her name is Stormie, and Dad always told me that I would have a great woman beside me. Someone like you."

"That doesn't mean she's that woman."

"But I've never felt this way about anyone."

"You haven't even given yourself a chance to feel any way about any other woman," she said.

I took a deep breath, and said, "Well, while we're already talking about Stormie, I wanted to tell you that I proposed to her last night."

My mom put my plate of pancakes, eggs, and sausage in front of me and said, "You did what?" sounding disappointed.

"I proposed to Stormie. I love her and she loves me."

"Do you not recall the day she almost let you die? She had you involved in some things that you would've never been involved in had you never met her. People like her just don't stop that stuff on their own either."

My mom sat across from me and said, "Ezekiel, be honest with me. Does she still get high?"

I looked at my mom directly in the eyes and said, "No."

I lied to her right to her face. Stormie and I both still got high. We had never stopped, and our first drink of the day was always a double shot of Tequila. If I had told my mom the truth, she probably would've gone over to my house herself and made sure that I never saw Stormie again. We just had a different type of relationship. One that no one would've ever understood, so we kept to ourselves for the most part. We would go out and have a good time, but I preferred to keep people out of our business. I knew that it was all a part of my shame and conviction, but I wanted to keep Stormie happy.

"Ezekiel, I'm just going to tell you like this, because you know that's what I do. That girl is not good for you. I just don't feel like she's the one. You have changed so much since you've been with her. Just like right now, I can already smell liquor on you and it's not even 10 am. I want my baby boy back and I feel like she stole him and buried him away somewhere."

"Ma, if you just gave Stormie a chance, you might actually like her. What happened to 'everything happens for a reason'?"

"Everything does happen for a reason, but I just can't figure out what the reason is for her entering into your life," my mom said.

"You know what Dad would say to you right now, right?"

She looked at me sternly, and said, "Yeah. He would say, Faith, go talk some sense into that boy!"

"Now you know that's not what he would say. He would calm you down and ask you, 'My dear Faith, where is your faith'?"

My mom took a deep sigh and said, "You're right. You're a grown man. I have to let go and trust you, whether I like it or not."

"Thank you, Ma. I appreciate that. And while you're all in my love life, when are you going to start dating?"

"Never!" my mom said, giggling.

"Yes, you will."

"Every time I see someone who I may be even the least bit interested in, I start comparing them to your dad, and there's absolutely no one that comes even close to being the man that he was. I refuse to settle, and your dad wouldn't want me to, either. I sometimes wonder what life would be like if he were still around, but as you have already said, everything happens for a reason. So, let's stop talking about me. You must be excited about tying the knot. Have the two of you decided on a date?"

"Yes. We're actually not going to have a wedding. We're going to the Justice of the Peace next weekend, and I hope you'll agree to be there. You're all we have."

"Next weekend! No wedding? I always imagined a big fancy wedding for my son and his wife to be. Why the hurry?"

"Wait. Didn't you and dad go to the city court and get married?" I asked my mom.

"Yes, we did, but that was different. We were straight out of high school and very much in love. We didn't have any money to do much else, but we wanted to be married so we didn't care about all the extra stuff."

"Well, we're straight out of college and we're also in love, so what's the difference? You still don't think I'm really in love, do you?"

"Ezekiel, I shielded and protected you from a lot, and I think I regret that now. I think you may be infatuated with Stormie, but not truly in love. Like I said, it's your decision, and if that's what you want to do, I will be there, whether I'm in agreement or not."

"Well, I guess that's better than nothing," I said, sounding discouraged.

"Listen, Ezekiel, I may be all wrong about you and her. This is your life, so don't let how I feel or what I say make you feel any differently because there was nothing anyone could say to me or your dad to change our minds, so we did it without anyone even knowing. I appreciate you at least telling me and inviting me to be there."

That next weekend, I put on the best suit I had, and Stormie put on the most beautiful dress that I had seen her in, and we became Mr. and Mrs. Ezekiel Whitfield. I hadn't even talked to Kyle and told him because he felt the same way about Stormie that my mom did. After the short, but momentous event was over, my mom walked over to Stormie and gave her a big hug.

I saw her whisper something in Stormie's ear, and Stormie's smile quickly dissipated.

Then aloud, my mom said, "Well, Stormie Whitfield sounds a lot better than Stormie Summers. Who likes stormy summers anyway?" my mom said with a slight giggle.

It was a bit uncomfortable, but I think my mom did the best that she could've possibly done under the circumstances. Honestly, she had every right to feel the way that she did, but I felt like I could fix everything, and Stormie would be that wife that both of my parents would've wanted me to have.

After the wedding, I took Stormie to a fancy restaurant where we could have a nice dinner together. It was an Italian restaurant that was a lot fancier than all of the other restaurants we'd previously dined at. That was another thing about Stormie. She never cooked. I asked her to cook one time and she looked at me as if I had asked her to go out and murder someone. Most times, she would pick herself something up to eat after work and leave me to figure things out on my own. I know anyone in their right mind would ask me what I was thinking, but I loved that woman. There was absolutely nothing anyone could ever tell me about her that wasn't positive. Sometimes I felt like I wanted a relationship like my mom and dad so badly that I was willing to do whatever it took, and wait however long it took, for that woman that I felt was inside of Stormie to come out.

After we ordered our food, Stormie looked at me smiling, and whispered, "I can't believe we're married! I can't wait to get home and really celebrate!"

I knew exactly what Stormie was talking about. She was ready to get higher than a kite, and I felt a little sad because that was all she could think about when all I could think about was that I had married the woman of my dreams who I was madly in love with. I was speechless, and I was sure I probably had an extremely disappointed look on my face, but she didn't seem to pick up on it. I didn't even feel as though I really had the right to be upset because I had allowed her to continue to be this woman that she was by accepting her that way.

After we finished eating our meals, and having a couple of glasses of the most expensive champagne on their menu, we headed home. The drive was around forty-five minutes, and for at least forty of those minutes there was dead silence.

When we got around five minutes away from home, Stormie asked, "Are you ok? You've been pretty quiet."

"Continuing to look straight ahead, I said, "Yeah, I'm good. It's just been a long emotional day."

Stormie rubbed the back of her hand down the side of my face and said, "Yeah, it has, but when we get home, you'll feel a whole lot better," she said, as she giggled with excitement.

I felt as though she was more excited about getting home than she did about marrying me.

I took a deep breath and asked, "What did my mom whisper in your ear?"

I could see her look over at me from the corner of my eye.

"What?" she asked, trying to sound as if she didn't know what I was talking about.

"When we were at the city court, at the end of the wedding, I saw her whisper something in your ear when she hugged you."

"Oh, that. She just told me not to hurt her baby boy."

I nodded my head and said, "She meant it."

At that moment, I looked over at Stormie and made eye contact with her. She looked at me as if what I'd said was the most disrespectful thing anyone had said to her. I only said what I knew. My mom wasn't going to be a happy woman if Stormie did anything to hurt me. That went for anyone. I didn't realize it then, but God was showing me some things. My mom was a praying woman, and I was sure from the day I'd told her that Stormie and I were getting married, she'd prayed extremely hard that entire week, and I can almost guess what her exact prayer was. I'm pretty sure that she asked God to give me the Spirit of discernment and reveal the things that needed to be revealed to me in due time. It was just the beginning.

When we finally pulled up at home, I got out of the car and went and opened the passenger door for Stormie, as I always did. She ran straight into the house, hopped in the shower, and put on the lingerie that she had bought specifically for our wedding night. While she was in the shower in our bedroom, I took a shower in the guest bathroom. A strange feeling had suddenly come over me from the time we left the restaurant until the time we got home.

After I got out of the shower and put on my robe, when I walked out of the bathroom, I found Stormie sitting on the living room sofa with her favorite tray right in front of her.

"Don't worry. I didn't start without you," she said with that beautiful smile that used to always give me butterflies. Her smile was one of her most beautiful qualities, and when she smiled, I could never tell her "no". She knew it.

"Thanks," I replied, as I sat down on the sofa.

"Are you sure you're all right?" she asked me again, as she sat on my lap and wrapped her legs around me.

"I told you, I'm fine."

"You want me to make you a drink?" she asked.

"Yeah, sounds good."

Stormie knew something was up. She kept looking at me as if she was trying to read me by looking straight through me.

Before she went to make me a drink, she began lining up her coke and took a sniff. I watched her, and I had watched her dozens of times, but this time felt different. It was almost as if it was a turn off. This was my wife snorting coke right in front of me. I began trying to imagine my mom doing something like that in front of my dad, or any man. The sad part about it was that I couldn't because my mom would've never done anything like that.

When Stormie came back, she sat two glasses on the table.

"You haven't had any yet?" she asked.

"No. I'm just relaxing, trying to take everything in."

"I know what you mean," she said, as she lined up the coke for me.

We had a mirror right in front of the sofa, so as I sniffed it, I looked up at myself and felt ashamed. I didn't feel like a man. My dad told me I was going to be a great man, and here I was snorting coke with the so-called great woman that was supposed to be by my side. I knew my dad couldn't have been wrong when he told me those things. I couldn't think of one time that he had ever been wrong about anything. I then watched Stormie lace a blunt with coke and smoked until the entire apartment looked like it was covered in fog, and she drank until she couldn't drink any more. The entire time, it seemed like I wasn't even there. She acted as if she was having the greatest time of her life all by herself.

I was doing things all wrong, and I had to figure out how to make them right. I had to become the man that my dad knew that I would become. I couldn't disappoint neither him nor my mother, and I vowed that day, which was my wedding day, that I wouldn't. I picked Stormie up and carried her to bed. I then laid in bed next to her and turned over in the opposite direction.

"Zeke, what's wrong? Didn't you enjoy our day? I didn't think it would already be coming to an end."

"Storm, I really don't think we should talk about this right now. I don't want anything to be said that can't be taken back. Let's just go to bed, get some rest, and have a civil conversation tomorrow."

It was completely quiet for a moment. Stormie then said, "Ok", as I felt her turn over and pull the covers up over her body.

[23] From a wise mind comes wise speech; the words of the wise are persuasive. [24] Kind words are like honey— sweet to the soul and healthy for the body.
– Proverbs 16:23-24 NLT

Stormie

Chapter Twenty-Two

I didn't know what was going on with Zeke, but he had made me feel completely rejected on my own wedding day. I never took rejection well because I was rejected basically my entire life. It made me feel as if I wasn't enough, and growing up, I taught myself to never let anyone make me feel that way. I didn't know if Zeke realized the damage that he was doing to our relationship by trying to destroy my self-confidence, but what he obviously didn't realize was that I was Stormie, and I could've had any man that I wanted, but I had chosen him. Any man would've loved to have me, and I wouldn't have had to put up with his hateful, judgmental mother either. I chose to put up with Zeke's. Why? I didn't even know. Maybe because Zeke did make me feel like a queen. Men loved me to death, but I had never had one to treat me as if I was the only woman in the world, so dealing with his mother seemed like it would be a piece of cake, and well worth it in the end.

The last time I had been rejected by a man hadn't gone too well, so I was trying not to let myself get too far into my head. I kept telling myself that Zeke and I were just having one bad day.

Zeke finally came down the stairs after getting dressed the next morning, and I couldn't help but to be curious as to what he wanted to talk about, because it was very apparent that something had been on his mind the previous night.

He walked over to me as I finished attempting to scramble eggs for breakfast and gave me a kiss on the forehead.

"Good Morning, Baby. How are you feeling today?" he asked, as if everything was on the up and up.

"I'm feeling great. I think I should be asking you how you're feeling."

"I'm good," he said, sounding like he was just trying to pacify me.

"So, what was up with you last night? You were acting a little strange. Like you weren't having a good time," I said, trying to address the elephant in the room.

Zeke sat at the round, wooden kitchen table and clasped his hands together. That's what he always did when he had something serious going on in that mind of his.

"Storm, I just don't feel like this lifestyle is for us anymore. We're really adults now. We have real jobs, real bills, we're married, and someday we'll probably have kids. We have to be positive role models for the people who look up to us as a couple. When will this end?"

I placed Zeke's plate of the only meal that I halfway knew how to cook, which was pancakes, bacon, and eggs, in front of him, and said, "I'm not following you. I think we're living the perfect lifestyle. People do way worse things than what we do. We get wasted in the privacy of our own home. Nobody knows."

Zeke looked at me and said, "God knows."

"Zeke, you can't possibly feel guilt over someone who more than likely doesn't even exist! Would you feel ok about the things we do if I was able to prove to you that God is a non-factor?"

"Storm, you're making matters worse by the words that you're allowing to come out of your mouth. You know, and have always known how important my faith is to me."

"So, are you actually talking about how important your actual 'faith' is, or are we now talking about your mother?" I asked, laughing.

Zeke mumbled, "Maybe she was right."

I slammed my glass of orange juice down on the table and said, "Look! I don't have to take this! Do you know how you made me feel last night? You made me feel just like . . . never mind."

"No. Finish," Zeke said. "I made you feel just like what?"

I sat down in front of Zeke and said, "Not like what. Like who. You made me feel like Gavin."

Looking completely confused, Zeke said, "Gavin? Who in the world is Gavin?"

That's when I began to tell my story. "Gavin was the last real foster father I had. He was so nice to me, gave me whatever I wanted, and treated me like I was his own. He had a daughter, but he treated me just as well as he treated her, and I knew beyond a shadow of a doubt that their home would be my final residence while in foster care. His wife, Mena, even loved me. Coco was their daughter, who was a year younger than me, and Mena would often take us out on shopping sprees and out to lunch."

I took a deep breath and decided I had said enough, but obviously Zeke wanted to know more. I realized that I'd opened a can of worms. I really didn't want to go back into that part of my life after all, and had to figure out how to end the story without Zeke trying to force me to continue.

"So, what happened?" Zeke asked, before putting a forkful of eggs into his mouth.

"Gavin just started treating me differently. It was like he didn't want me around anymore and I didn't know what I'd done, but of course, Mena went along with it because she was a weak woman! She let her husband reject me and I was only a thirteen year old little girl! After being removed from their house by the request of Gavin, I was placed into an orphanage for the next five years."

Zeke got up and hugged me and said, "I'm sorry for making you feel that way. Those weren't my intentions. I just know that we are better than what we've been doing, and I had a true epiphany last night. I want us to be better, but I need for you to want the same thing. I want to be that couple that can bless others. That couple to give others hope and faith in true love. We have to do this together as a team. I'm not trying to push you away. I don't want you to go anywhere, and I'm definitely not going anywhere. Are you with me in this?"

I could see that Zeke had so much faith in us. I knew that he would probably have no problem giving up our current lifestyle of drinking and getting high, but for me, that was all I knew. That's what made me happy and kept me going. To be honest, I didn't even know if I would still even want Zeke if I chose to let that part of my life go. Maybe that was the only thing keeping me halfway content, and had nothing at all to do with him. I knew that was sad, but it was the truth. Drinking, smoking, and snorting coke was what made my life feel like it was worth living. It made me feel good. In fact, it made me feel like I was living life, and not just existing. I felt invincible. Honestly, I knew that it had nothing to do with Zeke, but, of course, I couldn't tell him that.

"I'm in, but please be patient with me," I told Zeke. "I've been doing this for a long time, so I'm sure I'll go through a terrible period of withdrawals."

"We'll be in it together. I'm sure I will, too, but with prayer and faith in God, He'll bring us through."

When Zeke said we needed to change our lifestyle, I didn't think he meant immediately. As soon as he finished his breakfast, he emptied the liquor cabinet, pouring out every single bottle of liquor that we had, even the stash that I had on my side of the bed. I couldn't bring myself to get rid of any of it. I just stood there and watched him as he poured what I considered to be much of my joy and happiness down the drain.

13 "May the God of hope fill you with all joy and peace as you trust in him, so that you may overflow with hope by the

power of the Holy Spirit." – Romans 15:13 NIV

He then went to our stash of coke and opened every single plastic bag and poured it all out into the toilet without hesitation this time. I could feel tears forming in the corners of my eyes. Zeke was so serious, and I just wasn't ready. When he had gotten rid of everything, we stood in front of each other not knowing what to do next. The things Zeke had just gotten rid of had become our lives.

"What now?" I asked Zeke, with tears in my eyes.

"Are you about to cry?" he asked. "Is all that mess that we've been pumping into our bodies that important to you?"

"I just wasn't prepared, and now I don't know what I'm going to do," I cried, as I hugged him and laid my head on his shoulder.

"Look, this is just the first step. We have a long way to go, but once we beat this thing, we'll be ok. We have each other, and we have God, but you act like that stuff was more important to you than I am. All that poison did was give us temporary happiness. We both have voids that we need filled, and to be honest we already have everything inside of us that we need. You have to trust me. As the man of this house, I have to do what's best for us, and this was definitely one of the best things I could've done. That is not who I am. It never was, and it's no longer who you are. It was never who you were. It's just a way Satan has found his way in to use the both of us, hoping that he'd destroy us. He knows what we can become by staying on the path that God has set for us, and he doesn't like it. We just have to dig deep inside of ourselves and find the peace and joy that God has already gifted us with. We're going to be ok. You'll see. Just watch."

I heard everything Zeke was saying, but he was in a different place than I was. He believed God would help us through this, while on the other hand, I didn't believe there was a god so who was going to help me? I felt like I was alone in this, and had to do it on my own.

We took the next couple of weeks off of work on sick leave. We knew we would struggle through withdrawals, and I was a little afraid, but I also didn't want to go to a facility as Zeke had suggested. Zeke didn't have it as bad as I did, which I had already suspected. During the entire two weeks, I was irritable. I didn't want to talk to anyone, and I didn't feel anything like myself. I always felt so confident and content, but I found myself just wanting to lay in a dark room and sleep to keep my mind off of the things that I really wanted. I was so depressed, and I just wanted all of what I was feeling to go away. I even had suicidal thoughts, and if Zeke hadn't been there with me, I probably would've gone through with it. It seemed like life was coming towards me at full speed and I had no idea how to handle any of it. I had never felt so overwhelmed and anxious at the same time.

After the two weeks passed, I began to get better. I began feeling more like myself again, and didn't think about getting high as much as I had been. Zeke seemed to be doing ok after dealing with a lot of nausea and vomiting, and getting a lot of rest. I also noticed him doing a lot of praying. I would sometimes leave the room and come back, thinking he was asleep, but then he would begin talking. It would take a moment for me to realize he wasn't talking to me, and was actually praying to God. I just couldn't comprehend how someone could have so much faith in an entity in which there was no definite proof of existence. Zeke thought I was crazy for not believing, and I honestly felt he was completely insane for believing.

Zeke finally felt he was well enough to be able to function at work and asked me if I'd be ok if he left me at home while he went back. I knew I wasn't quite ready to go back to work, especially having to deal with numbers and other people's money. I felt strong enough to stay home alone, and no longer felt sick or having many cravings, so I told him I'd be fine. He told me to call him if I needed anything, and I agreed.

That first morning that Zeke went back to work, I opened the blinds to let the sunlight shine through, and popped a coffee pod in the Keurig to make myself a nice hot cup of coffee, which seemed to be getting me through each day. That particular morning, as I poured a couple of scoops of sugar into my cup of coffee, other things began to cross my mind as I watched the sugar pour slowly from the spoon. I began to feel nauseous, so I quickly sat down with my cup. I stirred my coffee and took a few small sips.

In my head, I began hearing my own voice saying, *"I can't do this. This isn't me."*

I began feeling like I was changing for someone else, and I just wanted to be me again. My mind was too idle, and as people always say, an idle mind is a dangerous one. Everything that Zeke and I had agreed on no longer meant a thing to me, and I had to figure out how to get what I needed without him knowing.

"Just one time won't hurt," I said to myself. "I just need a little bit, and he'll never know."

13 "Therefore put on the full armor of God, so that when the day of evil comes, you may be able to stand your ground, and after you have done everything, to stand."
– Ephesians 6:13 NIV

I felt excitement come over my entire body just thinking about getting even just a quick high. I hurriedly jumped in the shower and put on clothes. I brushed my hair back into a ponytail and put on a little makeup. I wanted to feel completely like myself, and when I finished getting dressed, I almost did. I was just missing one thing, and I was only moments away from getting it.

I grabbed my keys and purse and headed out the door. As soon as I got into my car and started it up, my phone rang, and I saw that it was Zeke. I started not to answer, but I didn't want to seem as if I was trying to hide anything.

"Hey, Babe," I said, as I answered the phone.

"Hey. I was just checking on you, but you sound like you're doing pretty good. What are you doing? You sound like you're outside."

Trying to stay calm and sound as if I was being truthful, I replied, "Yeah, I just got in the car. I got myself together and wanted to get some fresh air, so I thought I'd go out and pick up something to eat."

"Sounds good. What are you going to get?"

"I'll probably just stop by the store and get some things to make a good salad. I have to ease my way into eating anything more than that. I don't think my stomach is ready."

"Ok. Well, the weather's nice, so enjoy. Remember, I'm here if you need me."

When I got off of the phone with Zeke, I regretted telling him I was going to the store to pick up some things because now I would really have to go to the store. I could've said I was going to pick up a salad from McDonald's, but he caught me off guard and I wasn't thinking straight.

I pulled into the parking lot of the local grocery store and quickly grabbed a shopping cart. I pushed that cart through the store like a mad woman, throwing lettuce, onions, cucumbers, tomatoes, grilled chicken, cheese, croutons, and salad dressing into the cart within only about five minutes. As I was headed towards the cash register, I found myself in the liquor aisle and tried my best to look straight ahead and keep going, but I failed. I stopped and grabbed a bottle of Don Julio Tequila. When I got to the cash register, I decided to pay with cash just in case Zeke would notice the extra money I'd spent on the alcohol.

After I left the grocery store, I headed to our dealer's spot and purchased a bag of coke.

Our dealer's street name was Rocko. He was Mexican, and by the way he carried himself, he looked more like a cop than a dealer, but I guess that was how he stayed under the radar.

As soon as he saw me, he said, "Hey, Storm. I thought y'all had let me down for someone else."

"Not at all," I said smiling. "We're just trying to slow down."

"I feel you. Smart move. No good for me, but I get it," he said, as I handed him the cash and he handed me my package.

The strange thing was, I felt so guilty about everything I'd done, and would have to hide from Zeke, but not guilty enough to stop me from wanting to do what I'd planned on doing. I couldn't wait to get home. I felt like a kid on Christmas morning.

When I got home, I ran straight into the house, threw all of my shopping bags, besides the one with my tequila, on the kitchen counter, and went straight upstairs to our bedroom. I quickly poured the coke onto my nightstand and opened my nightstand drawer to try and find a straw. I couldn't find one, so I grabbed a dollar bill, rolled it up, and finally experienced by first high that I'd had in two weeks. I opened the bottle of tequila and drank it straight from the bottle. I felt like I was in Heaven. I plunged onto the bed on my back and the next thing I knew, I was out of it. I had to have been passed out for at least four hours when I suddenly heard footsteps coming up the stairs. I quickly jumped up and tried to gather up all of my paraphernalia before Zeke walked in. I got on my knees and tried to quickly scoop the rest of my coke back into the bag, and grabbed the bottle of tequila off of my nightstand. As I was trying to hide the bag and the bottle, Zeke walked in.

He stood in the doorway with his arms folded.

"Stormie, are you serious right now? I thought I could trust you."

Still feeling my high, I ran up to him and said, "You can! I promise you can. I just needed one more hit. I really just wish you would love me for me. I was fine just the way I was and now you want to change me! You knew who you were marrying when you married me!"

"You need help, Stormie, and I can't help you."

"I'm not going into a facility. I can't!"

Zeke wiped what must've been coke from my nose, grabbed the bag and bottle out of my hand, and said, "No, I'm not going to make you to go a facility. You're going somewhere even better. We both are."

Ezekiel

Chapter Twenty-Three

That following Sunday, Stormie and I went to Pastor Ervin's church. I felt comfortable going there since that's where I'd gone all my life, but I can't say that it was an easy task getting Stormie to agree to join me. She continued to remind me that her beliefs weren't the same as mine, but my argument was that she had never really had anyone that she could trust to teach her the truth. I felt that was for me to do as her husband. I wasn't anywhere near perfect, but I had grown up in church. I also didn't claim to know everything about God and the Bible because there was so much to know, and frankly, no one could ever know everything, but I knew enough to get us started on the right path. I knew who created me, and I also knew that it was my responsibility to have faith in Him, obey Him, and lead others to Him. I had lost focus for a while, but I knew that God would always welcome me back with open arms, along with anyone else.

Stormie and I walked through the doors of the church house and walked down the aisle, hand in hand, until I found the row of pews where my mom was sitting. There were coincidentally two empty seats right next to her, and when she looked up and saw me, the smile on her face was priceless. I hadn't been to church in a very long time, and I had kept it from her that Stormie and I would be coming on this particular Sunday.

My mom quickly patted the seat directly next to her, gesturing for me to sit down, and waved at Stormie. Stormie gave her a quick wave and sat right next to me on the other side. I had to admit, it felt wonderful to sit in between my two favorite women in the house of the Lord. I just wished that they had gotten along better, and that I could feel that my mom was being completely sincere when she would hug, or address Stormie in a positive way. The same went for Stormie. I knew that she really couldn't stand my mom, but she knew how much my mom meant to me, so she tolerated her without being disrespectful. My mom was a God-fearing woman, so she knew that my wife would always come before her, and she would expect nothing less from me. I just prayed that I would never be put in the position to have to hurt my mom's feelings due do her behavior towards Stormie.

As I listened to Pastor Ervin's sermon, it had come right on time. He preached on bad habits, and how we couldn't allow them to control our lives. We had to let them go, and the only way we would be able to do that was by asking for God's help, trusting that He would help us through it, and renewing our minds every day in order to protect us from those sinful thoughts. Habits begin as thoughts before they are put into action. I had never thought of it that way, but as long as we kept clean thoughts, we would have a pure heart, and then would be able to develop good habits in place of those bad ones.

I looked over at Stormie, and I couldn't tell if whether she was truly listening, or if her mind was completely somewhere else, but I was just happy to get her to the point of sitting inside of a church for Sunday service. It was definitely a start for her, and for us as a married couple. I grabbed her hand and put my fingers in between hers. She looked down at our intertwined hands, and then looked up at me with a slight grin before looking back up towards the pulpit.

At the end of service, everyone greeted and shook hands with Pastor Ervin.

As soon as he saw me, he gave me a hug and said, "Good to finally see you again, young brother, Ezekiel!" He then lowered his voice a bit and asked, "So did God reveal that calling to you yet?"

He then looked up at Stormie since she was wearing heels that were probably five inches high, and Pastor Ervin wasn't very tall.

"And I don't think I've ever met this lovely young woman," he said.

"No, you haven't. This is my wife, Stormie."

"Nice to meet you, Stormie," Pastor Ervin said, as he gave her a Godly hug.

My mom was right behind Stormie, and when Pastor Ervin saw her, he grinned from ear to ear and said, "And there is one of my favorite ladies, Sister Whitfield!"

She smiled as they hugged. Everyone loved my mom, which was why I wished she and Stormie hadn't gotten off to such a rough start while we were still in college.

Pastor Ervin said, "I was just asking Ezekiel if God had shown him his purpose."

My mom replied by saying, "I believe He has, and I also believe we both know what his calling is, but we can't hear God when it's too noisy, and I believe that's the problem. My baby boy just has too much going on right now to hear God."

Pastor Ervin looked at me and said, "Your mom has always been a smart and wise woman, and what she just said has a lot of truth to it. You have to make time for God. Even if you just sit silently in a quiet room. You don't have to say a word, but you'll eventually hear God tell you exactly what He wants you to know."

³ "The gatekeeper opens the gate for him, and the sheep recognize his voice and come to him. He calls his own sheep by name and leads them out." – John 10:3 NLT

Those words that Pastor Ervin spoke to me that day spoke volumes and truly resonated within my soul. I felt like God moved through my entire body at that moment, and with that, I knew I needed to get into God's word and give Him more of my time. That's exactly what I began to do.

I began studying the Bible every chance I got. I even carried a Bible to work, and studied during my lunch breaks. I could tell that Stormie sometimes felt as though I was neglecting her, and I tried to explain to her that God had to come first and be at the center of our marriage. I kept trying to get her to read and study with me, but she wasn't trying to hear anything I had to say. I wasn't going to force her, because one thing I did know was that no one could make someone want to be closer to God if they didn't want to be. They had to make that decision on their own, and only God could change them. I had to be happy that she was at least going to church with me every Sunday. I looked at it as progress, and she and my mom had time at least once a week to see each other and attempt to form some type of bond. My mom seemed to become more open to it, but Stormie seemed to put no effort whatsoever towards it. If my mom didn't say anything to her, she didn't say anything to my mom. I prayed that they would someday develop a healthy relationship, but until then, it seemed God had other plans for me that he wanted me to focus on.

Eventually, Pastor Ervin asked that I teach Bible study, which I truly enjoyed, but Stormie wanted no parts of that either. When I first mentioned it to her, her response was that she was already compromising by going to church every Sunday, and definitely wasn't stepping foot into a church twice a week. I prayed that God would work on her, and work on me to be able to continue to have patience with her. That was all that I could do, and continue to stay on the path that God had me on. I knew that He had a perfect plan for my life, and everything would fall into place someday, as long as I continued to do what He wanted me to do.

God's favor and grace just continued to fall upon me, but my home life seemed to be falling apart. Stormie and I were nowhere near as close as we had been, and I could feel the animosity every time we were in the same room. Even when I would try to take her out for a nice night on the town, she never seemed to truly enjoy it. I could always tell that she was trying to act as if she was, only because of the effort I was putting forth, and she didn't want me to feel bad, but I saw straight through it.

I spoke to Pastor Ervin privately about what was going on at home, and he told me that God wanted to elevate me, but my wife needed to be on board. He also told me what I already knew, which was, God has a plan for all of us, and works through us in different ways. Everything happens for a reason, and there was a reason that Stormie and I had found each other. I just needed to continue to pray that God would do His will in both of our lives and things would work out just as they should. During that same conversation, Pastor Ervin told me that he had been led by the Spirit to ask that I take some time every Sunday to minister to the congregation before he started service.

I felt extremely honored and overwhelmed at the same time. I had never actually ministered to the congregation, although I did teach Bible School. In my mind I was thinking that it couldn't be too different.

Pastor Ervin must've noticed the unsure look on my face and said, "Don't worry. You're anointed, my brother. God will put on your heart whatever people need to hear. It won't be coming from you. It will be coming directly from Him, and everything He says is right, whether people agree or not. God is your only true audience, so always remember that."

I nodded my head, agreeing with Pastor Ervin. When I got home and told Stormie the good news, she just stared at me as she took a sip of her wine and walked away. I knew that I had tried my hardest to understand my wife and get her on the same page, or at least the same chapter, or even the same book as me, but there was nothing else I could do. I had done my part, and I had to let God do the rest. I loved Stormie and couldn't see myself without her, but I loved God more and I had to be obedient by doing His will for my life. If I had said anything like that to Stormie, she would've flipped all the way out, and I knew it. After telling Stormie what I considered good news, and received undesired feedback, I went into the den, shut the door, and called my mom. She was ecstatic.

"I told you that you were special, Ezekiel. Just follow God's lead and keep being obedient."

Don't get me wrong, I was extremely pleased with my mom's response, however, I just wished that my wife could've felt the same way.

Chapter Twenty-Four

After a couple of years of working under Pastor Ervin, to the point that I had become Associate Pastor, I decided to become the pastor of my own church. I felt that it was time, and Pastor Ervin had been a great influence and role model in my life. I didn't know how to tell him because I knew he enjoyed having me there with him. When I decided that's what I wanted to do, it took me a couple of weeks to even go to him and tell him what was on my heart. Finally, God obviously got tired of me beating around the bush and told me that this was what He wanted, and Pastor Ervin would understand.

I finally called Pastor Ervin, asking to meet with him for dinner.

"Sounds good!" he said," sounding excited as he always did. He then said, "Let's make it a double date and invite the ladies to come."

I hadn't even told Stormie about my plans because I didn't feel like having an argument, or her telling me that this wasn't the life that she had planned to have with me. A lot of things she would say were very hurtful and discouraging, but I continued to stand strong, believing God would fix it.

Hesitantly, I said, "Ok, yeah, sounds like a plan."

When I told Stormie we had a dinner date with the pastor and his wife, First Lady Joy, she wasn't ecstatic, and I didn't expect her to be.

"Why are you always trying to run my life and make plans for me? How do you know I didn't have plans?" she yelled as she stomped up the stairs to the bedroom.

"I just thought it would be nice for us to get together, and for you and Joy to have some time to get to really know each other. The two of you may have some things in common," I said as I followed her up the stairs."

As she reached the top of the stairs, she turned around and said, "What in the world would I possibly have in common with the wife of a pastor?"

With that one question that Stormie had asked, my heart dropped because unbeknownst to her, she would also soon be the wife of a pastor. As a matter of fact, she was already the wife of an associate pastor, which she'd seemed to have forgotten.

She continued, "Joy and I live in two totally different worlds. She lives a life of walking on eggshells, and I'll never be that woman! I'll never walk on eggshells for anyone! Even if God existed, and he himself came and stood right in front of me right now, I would tell him exactly how I felt about Him! He left me to struggle through life and did nothing. Who does that to a child, especially if He supposedly has the power to do anything?"

She continued towards our bedroom as I continued to follow her as she spoke such offensive things into the universe about our creator.

When we made it to the room and she sat on the bed, I stood there shocked at what Stormie had said. I was expecting her to be upset, but not to go to the lengths that she did to downplay God for who He was and what He could do. I knew this had to be a test. Did I really have what it took to be a pastor, especially when it was my own wife questioning God and disrespecting His good name?

Something suddenly came over me. I could feel the Holy Spirit moving throughout my entire body, and I was silently praying that God would give me the right words to say.

I stood in front of Stormie and held both of her hands. She tried to pull away, but I continued to hold on and gaze into her eyes.

I then said, "Storm, I know it's hard for you to believe and trust in God because of the things you've gone through, but just think about it. You're still here, and it's not just by coincidence. You could've been killed in several of the situations that you've encountered, but God is who brought you through because you have an assignment, as we all do. God has a calling on my life, and since you're a part of my life, there's a reason He wants you to be there for this journey. You're not done yet. There's still so much for the both of us to do.

God is real and He has been there for us through everything and will continue to be there for us. Even through the hard times you went through, He was always there with you, even though it may have not seemed like it, and He got you through it. We are married, Stormie. I put God in the center of this marriage, and in this house, we will serve the Lord! There is no other option. God has given you so many opportunities, and everything you've accomplished, and all that you have, you didn't do it on your own. He did it. So, with that being said, you need to try to at least get to know God and give Him a chance to be a part of your life because He's a big part of mine and always will be. I don't want this marriage to fail, but I also don't see how it can last if you don't believe that God provides for, and protects you every day of your life."

"I hear everything you're saying, Zeke, but I also believe I can be your wife without us having the same faith."

I was confused because I didn't know of any faith that Stormie had. She just lived life thinking that she was somehow thrown on this earth to live however she pleased, and one day she'd die and go nowhere. She didn't believe in eternal life or any of that, and I knew that should've been a red flag from the beginning, but I was naïve enough to think that I would be able to change her. I still felt that she could change, but it wouldn't have anything to do with me. It would have to do with the desire in her own heart to want to change.

I was just tired of going back and forth with her, so I plainly asked, "Do you want to go to dinner with the Drew and Joy, or not?"

She rolled her eyes and said, "Yeah, I'll go, but I am going to be myself."

"Stormie, that's fine. I fell in love with you being yourself. You're a strong woman and I love that about you. I don't want to change you. I just want you to be open-minded. You can still be yourself, and be open-minded to different things, you know."

"You know I'm stubborn," she said, with a slight grin.

I grabbed and hugged my wife, and said, "You know I know that better than anyone, but can you please just put a little bit of that aside for me and go out with me for a nice night of good food and good conversation?"

Stormie agreed, but I still wasn't sure how the night was going to go, especially after I would announce what I felt God's plan was for my life, in which I intended on pursuing.

As I watched Stormie get dressed, perfecting her look as she always did, I began to have thoughts to go through my mind, causing me to doubt my decision. I never liked to question God, but I wondered why I would have such a calling on my life, but a wife who didn't even believe in Him. I was taught that God loved marriage, and I was also taught that God didn't make mistakes, so I was really confused as to how God wanted me to handle the situation in which I was in. What I did know was that I had to be obedient to Him, accept my calling, and complete my assignment. Where did that leave my beautiful Stormie?

At that moment, I heard God tell me to just trust Him and stop worrying. Things would happen just as they should, but I must cast all my fears, worries, and cares on Him.

[10] "So do not fear, for I am with you; do not be dismayed, for I am your God. I will strengthen you and help you; I will uphold you with my righteous right hand." – Isaiah 41:10 NIV

I always finished getting dressed before Stormie because she had to make sure every hair was in place, every eyelash was perfectly curled, that her makeup was flawless, and that her clothing accentuated her shape just the way she wanted them to. I sat in the living room on the sofa as I waited for her, but when she came down the stairs, it was well worth the wait. One thing that no one could ever deny was that Stormie was definitely gorgeous.

"You ready?" she asked as she stepped off of the last step, showing off her beautiful smile.

Her red lipstick stood out from the black cocktail dress that fit her shape perfectly. Her smile always reminded me of the progress we made from back in our college days when all I could get from her was an evil glare or frown. Back then, I knew she would be a challenge, and I was up for it, but never would I have imagined all of the challenges I'd gone through with her already. Back then I said she would be the woman I married, and I didn't give up, and now that we were married, I definitely didn't plan to give up.

"Earth to Zeke!" Stormie said, while I was staring at her, reminiscing.

"Yeah, I'm ready," I said, smiling.

I grabbed her hand and said, "You look amazing."

"Thank you. You don't look too bad yourself."

On the way to the French restaurant where we were meeting the Ervins, I felt very uneasy, but I knew I was doing the right thing. I felt peace in my heart about it, but I didn't want to hurt Stormie or anyone else.

"Why are you so quiet?" Stormie asked.

"No particular reason. Maybe I'm just a little nervous. You know, there's always a little pressure when you meet with a pastor."

Stormie looked at me and rolled her eyes.

"That's what I mean," she said. "There should be no pressure. You should be able to be yourself, and not have to overthink. You know you're a good person, so what's the problem? He's no better than you."

"I know that, but you're a little more outspoken than me. It's easier for you to carry on conversation, even though sometimes you can be very blunt."

"Yes, I can be blunt, but that's the way you have to be sometimes for people to know that you know who you are, and that you're not playing with them. You have to demand your respect, and that's what I do. Take me or leave me. People will run over you if you don't represent yourself as being confident in who you are. You shouldn't even be nervous about this, though. You see Drew all the time, and he's known you since you were a kid. I don't understand what you're worried about. What did you say? This is going to be a night of good food and good conversation, right?"

I looked over at Stormie as we sat at a red light, and said, "Yes, Ma'am. That's what I said, and that's what I hope it is."

She then cut her eyes at me.

"What was that for?" I asked.

"You know I don't like you calling me ma'am. You make me feel like an old woman. I'm trying to stay young as long as I can."

I squeezed Stormie's thigh and said, "Girl, you know I'm going to still love you with wrinkles, gray hair, no teeth, and all!"

I laughed, but Stormie didn't seem very amused by my joke. I cleared my throat and proceeded on driving to our destination. When we got to the restaurant, I saw Pastor Ervin's black Mercedes parked close to the door, and I was able to find a parking space nearby. I parked, got out the car and went and opened the passenger door for my queen. I grabbed one of her hands and helped her out, and we walked arm in arm into the restaurant as the hostess opened the door for us.

We immediately saw Pastor Ervin and his wife waving their hands in the air, trying to get our attention. They were already sitting at a table, waiting on us to get there. As we walked over, they stood up, and we greeted each other with hugs. Stormie and I sat down across from the Ervins. The waitress quickly came over and asked what we would like to drink. Pastor Ervin and Joy already had their drinks, which Stormie assumed was wine.

With that being said, Stormie said, "I would love some of that white wine that Joy is drinking! This is going to be a better night than I thought!", she laughed.

The waitress waited for Stormie to stop laughing, and said, "I'm sorry Ma'am, but she has Sparkling White grape juice, and the gentleman has regular Sparkling grape juice, but I can get you wine if you'd like wine."

Stormie looked at me as I looked down at the table, pretending to look through the menu. When I looked up, Pastor Ervin and Joy had a confused and awkward look on their face. They were never the types to judge and condemn people for things that they did, but the embarrassed look on Stormie's face made everyone else feel a little uncomfortable.

Stormie gathered her composure, smiled, and said, "If no one else is having wine, no wine for me either. I'm trying to cut back anyway, so I'll have a Coke."

Joy said, "Girl, if you want some wine, get some wine. We're not here to judge you. We like for everyone to be comfortable around us."

Joy was very down to earth, and was always very friendly. That was why I wished Stormie would've spent some girl time with her, even though she was older than us. She was still very youthful, and I thought that she would've been a great role model for Stormie, and maybe some of her Godliness would rub off on her. Anytime I would bring it up to Stormie, she made it clear that she had absolutely no desire to hang out with a woman who was old enough to be her mother.

I wanted to get what I really wanted to talk about off of my chest because I knew if I hadn't, I wouldn't be able to enjoy the rest of the night. I still may have not been able to enjoy the rest of the night if Stormie reacted the way that I had imagined her to.

Either way, it needed to come out, and tonight would be the night.

I started off the conversation by saying, "I'm so glad we could all get together tonight. It's so important to have positive role models in your life who support you one hundred percent. It makes it easier to share things going on in your life, and things going on in your mind, knowing you'll get an honest response, no matter what it is. That is really why I wanted all of us to come out to dinner tonight. I thought it would just be me and Pastor, but I'm glad that he suggested that you women come, too. I think it's equally important for you all to be here and give your thoughts and opinions as well."

I looked over at Stormie and she looked confused. She had no idea that I had a big announcement, and neither did anyone else.

"So what is it that you'd like to talk to us about?" Pastor Ervin asked curiously?

Hesitantly, I said, "Well, it's really been on my heart that it's time for me to start my own ministry. I think I've been trained up by the best mentor ever, and it's time for me to soar."

Looking straight across the table at Pastor Ervin, I saw him smiling ear to ear.

"I already knew it!" he said. "God has been putting that in my ear for a while now, but I was just waiting for you to listen and let God lead you in His timing. I do support you one hundred percent, and we're here to help you in any way we can! Isn't that right, Joy?" he said, as he and Joy smiled at each other.

"Absolutely! This is amazing!" Joy said.

I looked at Stormie, and said, "Babe, what do you think?"

Without looking at me, Stormie took a few deep breaths and said, "What do I think? Oh, that's important now, huh?" Loudly, she then said, "I think you should've consulted with your wife before making such a big decision!"

She then slid her chair out, causing it to shriek loudly against the wooden floor, jumped up and quickly walked towards the women's restroom.

Pastor Ervin and Joy looked at me with worry on their faces.

Pastor Ervin asked, "You didn't discuss this with your wife before you brought it to us?"

I took a deep breath and said, "Unfortunately not."

Speaking in concern, he asked, "Why not, Ezekiel? She's your partner, your teammate . . ."

"I know I should've spoken with her about it, but there's a lot you two don't know regarding Stormie. She doesn't support me and my journey, she doesn't believe in God, and she doesn't want to have a conversation about God. I knew that this may have been the cause of the demise of my marriage. God comes first, and if she can't respect my relationship with God, I don't know what's going to happen. I've been praying for years for things to change. I thought maybe with the two of you here, it might've gone better, but obviously not."

"We had no idea," Joy said, sounding concerned.

"No, we didn't. I think you're doing what you're meant to do, but we need your wife on board. We really need to pray on this because your wife needs to be able to stand next to you in complete support of you as you preach the word of God. We need to pray for her deliverance. The good thing is you've gotten her to church, which means, the Word is in her. She's just fighting it, but as you know, all things work for good for those who love the Lord, so we have to be in agreement that this is going to work out. Even when things seem to be getting worse, you have to believe that they are going to get better," Pastor Ervin said.

"I'll go check on her," Joy said, as Pastor Ervin stood up and pulled out her chair.

"Be careful," I said. "She can be vicious."

"So can I," Joy said with a smile and wink.

As she walked away, Pastor Ervin tapped his fingers on the table as he gazed at me.

I tapped my feet nervously as I tried to speculate what was going through his mind.

"Ezekiel, I know it's hard talking to Stormie about these things when she's not on the same page as you, but when you're married, you have to have those difficult and uncomfortable conversations. You have to let her know what's going on, especially before telling others. Trust me, I'm proud of you and the decisions you're making by allowing God to lead you, but you have to keep Stormie in the loop. If not, she'll despise you. She'll feel unimportant and undervalued, and that's not what you want. If she gets to that point, it's going to be even harder for her to understand you, and accept what you've been called to do."

"I know, Pastor, and I try to do things the right way, but she makes it so hard. Sometimes she makes me feel like I have to choose between her and God. Did I make a mistake in marrying her?" I asked Pastor Ervin, desperate for an answer.

"Ezekiel, the position you are in right now is extremely difficult, but you took vows in front of God, and you have to do your best to make your marriage work. God does not make mistakes, so ask Him for guidance. Let Him order your steps and ask Him to help you to do His will in your life. I'm telling you things you already know. This is a unique situation, but nothing is too hard for God. Just trust Him, but don't shut out your wife. The first lady is an important component of the church, and I remember your dad telling me that he knew you would be a great man, and your wife would be a great woman. Your dad was also a very anointed man, so I took nothing that he said to me lightly. We don't know God's plan, but we know He has one, and we also know it's perfect."

Right at that moment, Joy and Stormie came walking towards us. Joy had a smile on her face, which she did most of the time. Stormie also had a smile on her face, but it was one of those smiles just to appease someone else. I had known her long enough to know the difference between her genuine smile and her smile that she would put on just so people would leave her alone. Whatever Joy had said to her hadn't made her feel any better, although Joy probably thought she had helped the situation. I knew that I would hear about it as soon as we got in the car on the way home, and it wasn't going to be pleasant.

After having a quieter than expected dinner, Stormie and I hugged the Ervins, and we then went our separate ways. As soon as Stormie and I got in the car, I didn't even give her a chance to say anything before I apologized.

Before starting up the car, I said, "Storm, I'm so sorry. I shouldn't have kept you in the dark about the plan of starting up a church of my own. That should've definitely been a conversation between the two of us before announcing it to anyone else. I'm deeply apologetic. I love you so much."

As I spoke, Stormie seemed to become more and more annoyed. She sucked her teeth and folded her arms before she began to speak.

She slowly turned towards me and said, "You love me? You sure have a crazy way of showing it! I try my best to be the woman that you want me to be, but that still doesn't seem to be enough. I have my beliefs and you have yours. I've changed many things about myself since we've been together, but I'm not willing to change my beliefs just to say that I have the same beliefs as my husband. I'm my own person and will continue to be my own person. This dream of yours you have is your dream, so who am I to tell you to not to follow your dream? Just like who are you to tell me that I have to believe in what you believe in?"

What Stormie had just said hit a nerve and I couldn't just let it go. My beliefs and values meant a lot to me, and for my wife to just downplay them both really bothered me. She not only downplayed my beliefs and values, but she had also downplayed the meaning and importance of marriage. We were supposed to be one, and she spoke as if we had two separate lives. I understood that I was wrong for not involving Stormie in my decision, but she didn't seem to feel as though she felt that there was anything wrong with what she was saying.

"Stormie, do you hear yourself? Follow my dream? This is not a dream. It's my calling. It's what God has called me to do. There's a big difference. A dream is something that you want to do, and it's not always what God wants you to do. A calling is what God wants you to do. It may be something you never imagined yourself doing, just like this. You may not even want to do it, and it's your decision as to whether or not you answer that call. Some people don't answer their calling and they truly miss out on something great. I'm choosing to be obedient and answer my calling."

I said what I had to say and then I started the car so we could head home.

"So, I guess you're done," she said, as I pulled out of the restaurant's parking lot.

"You know what? No, I'm not done. You treat this marriage as if we're still just dating and basically have our own lives. We are one, Storm. We're not going to always like what the other is doing, or the ideas that we have, but we have to find some compromise somewhere in order for this to work. My spirituality is very important to me, and not once have you tried to give it a chance."

"But . . ."

Stormie was about to interrupt me, but I already knew what she was about to say, so I interjected.

"I know. But you go to church, right? Yeah, I already know, but are you really there when you're sitting there in the pew? You sit there on social media while the pastor is preaching his sermon. You even do it when I'm in the pulpit, so how can you say you're giving it a chance? Anyone can sit in a church, but what are you taking from it and practicing once you leave? I've never said anything because I don't like to argue, but it's very disrespectful."

Stormie took a deep breath and said, "I don't know who you are right now, but you're not the Zeke that I met in college who fell madly in love with me before he even knew anything about me."

"I know I'm not. I'm Ezekiel, and I'm evolving. I wish my wife would evolve with me."

Stormie was speechless, which wasn't very often, but I could tell that she was beginning to realize just how important God was to me and there was nothing she could do or say to change that.

After that night, I decided to hand the situation over to God and stop trying to change things that I couldn't. I began working on finding a building for my church, which I decided to name "The

Path of Righteousness Worship Center". After about six months of
intensely searching, I finally found something perfect for the time
being until my congregation grew. Stormie didn't talk much about
the entire process and chose to not even be a part of it. However,
my mom did step up and helped me pick out the building. She was
there whenever I needed her support. She would often ask about
Stormie, and how this was going to work out with being the
pastor of a church with a wife who had no desire to be a first lady.
My answer would always be the same. I was just being obedient
and trusting God. What hurt me most was that my mom made it
clear to me that she didn't feel in her spirit that she should leave
Pastor Ervin's church just yet. She believed in me and my gift,
however, she had to follow her spirit. I always taught people that
they should listen to their spirit, so I couldn't be upset with my
mother, but I did know that the main reason she didn't want to
leave Pastor Ervin's church to become a member of her own son's
church was because of her son's wife, Stormie.

[7] **"Then you will experience God's peace, which exceeds anything
we can understand. His peace will guard your hearts and minds
as you live in Christ Jesus." – Philippians 4:7 NLT**

Chapter Twenty-Five

Within the next year, I opened my own church and every year that went by, my congregation grew larger and larger. I had the crazy idea in my head that eventually I would rub off on Stormie and she would suddenly be this woman of God that I dreamt for her to be, but that wasn't happening. It seemed as if the closer I got to God, the more Stormie distanced herself from me. We would still have good days, but it had come to the point where we had more bad days than good. Some days she would make a full day's worth of plans without me, but I just took it as her needing her space. She seemed happy again, which made me believe she was still going out doing the same things she had been doing for years, but I had stopped questioning her a long time ago. I was truly tested and had to learn to find my joy in God. If I hadn't, I would've been miserable.

Although I didn't have the best first lady by my side, my congregation grew to the point of needing a larger building, so almost five years after being in my first building, I went through that process all over again of securing a larger building, once again, without the help of my wife. That Saturday before my first Sunday in my new building was when God revealed to me what I needed to see.

As I was leaving my new church that Saturday evening after praying through the building before the next morning's service, and debating back and forth with God about what my sermon should be the next morning, I was driving and saw someone that looked just like Stormie crossing the street, but she wasn't alone. It was dark outside, so I thought maybe it wasn't her, but the closer I got, I realized that it was, and she was with another man. A man that I had never seen a day in my life. I kept going, without making a scene. She never even saw me. While I sat at a red-light, I looked in my rear-view mirror and noticed them walking into a restaurant that Stormie and I once frequented very often. Although I was hurt, I also felt peace in my heart. I knew I had been doing everything that I possibly could have to make our marriage work, so I had no regrets. As a matter of fact, I was still willing to give it a chance because I understood that we all made mistakes, and I still loved Stormie even after what I'd seen. Love just doesn't go away like that, so I had decided to give Stormie a chance to come clean in her own time. I figured if she had any type of conscience, she wouldn't be able to live with herself without coming out with the truth. I also didn't want to automatically jump to conclusions. Stormie was an accountant, and the man she was with could've easily been one of her clients.

That evening, I made it home before Stormie. I showered, then prayed for the Spirit of Discernment to help me to discern the truth from what was untrue. God showed me exactly what the truth was, including revealing that this wasn't Stormie's first time stepping out with this unknown man. I couldn't understand why God allowed me to go through so much with Stormie over the years when it would all just come down to this, but even though I couldn't understand it, I also wouldn't question it.

I finally heard Stormie come through the door as I laid in bed watching television. She walked in the bedroom with this glow about herself. Maybe it was a glow that she'd been having, and I just hadn't been paying close enough attention. She had a genuine smile on her face when she asked me how my day had been.

"It was good," I said. I went by the new church to pray, and I must say, God revealed a lot to me."

Stormie's smile immediately turned into a look of irritation as she subtly rolled her eyes.

"How was your day?" I asked, anxious to see what her answer would be.

"It was actually really good. I've been pretty busy with a lot of new clients."

"I see. You were in the office pretty late. I was surprised you went in at all on a Saturday," I said.

"Yeah, I had a lot of paperwork to take care of. I didn't want to leave it on my desk until Monday. I knew there would be an entirely new pile waiting on me."

"So, I guess you didn't get a chance to eat either since you were so busy," I said.

As she sat on the edge of the bed and slipped off her heels, she said, "No. I just grabbed a bag of apple chips and a bottled water from the vending machine."

"Hmmm," I said, getting more and more frustrated with our conversation.

Stormie turned around and looked at me and said, "What does that mean?"

"Nothing. You must still be hungry. You want to order something? Or we can go out really quick and grab something."

She quickly refused my offer and said, "No, I'll be ok. I haven't had much of an appetite today. You know how you have those days that you're just so busy, food is the last thing on your mind?"

"Yep, I know all about it."

She walked over to my side of the bed and gave me a kiss. I immediately smelled wine on her breath.

"You had wine today?" I asked.

"Huh?" she said, looking startled.

"I smell wine on your breath. When did you have time to have wine?"

"Fidgeting, she said, "Um, you remember my co-worker, Victoria, right? We went and had a glass on our lunchbreak today."

"But you didn't eat anything?"

I knew the more questions I asked, she would become more and more angry and defensive. That's how I could always tell when she was being dishonest.

"No, I didn't eat! Do I have to eat in order to have myself a glass of wine to relax? It was a long stressful day, and I needed something to take the edge off in the middle of the day."

"Not at all," I replied. "Just don't get too worked up over things going on at work."

I was now completely sure that the person Stormie was with was no client, and if he was, whatever they were doing wasn't innocent because if it had been, she would've told me. I decided to stop questioning her and just wait on God to lead me before making any hasty decisions.

Stormie seemed relieved after the questionnaire session had ended. She got undressed, got in bed, and then said, "You don't seem very nervous about tomorrow in the new church."

"God has given me all I need. There's nothing to be nervous about, although, my message may make some people reevaluate some things in their lives."

God had definitely made it very clear to me as to what I needed to preach on the following morning, and He did it by presenting it to me through my own personal life. I was praying that Stormie would pay close attention to my sermon the next day. I was sure that God had probably also given it to me for some other members of the church, but I was one-hundred percent positive that Stormie was meant to hear it. I told Stormie goodnight and that I loved her, as I did every night, and turned off my lamp. I knew the next day was going to be an interesting one.

After my sermon on adultery the next morning, Stormie walked around with a chip on her shoulder. We went out for

Sunday dinner as we always did, even though we weren't in the best place. She could barely even carry a conversation with me, or look me in the eyes as she sat across the table from me at the restaurant. I just knew that she would feel so convicted that she would end up telling me the truth before the end of the evening. I just didn't want to have to force it out of her because that could've caused the issue to become bigger than what it had to be. Don't get me wrong. The situation was serious, but it was also sensitive, and I tried to treat it as such. I wasn't the type to automatically put all of the blame on someone else. It could've been something that I also did to help push Stormie in the direction in which she went, but there was still never any excuse for adultery.

I tried to start up a conversation by saying, "So how did you like the new church?"

As she seemed to play with her food with her fork, without looking up, she said, "It's nice. I didn't expect any less."

It was the first time Stormie had seen the church since she never wanted to be any more involved than she had to be in that part of my life, which should've been a part of our lives that we could enjoy and celebrate together. She didn't see it that way because she felt like anything that had to do with God and my ministry was put before her and she resented me for it. I had tried to explain to her over and over again that all of this was about us. God was doing it for not only me, but for the both of us, and it could've been so much greater and powerful if she would've just trusted God and trusted me. I wanted to be able to enjoy this journey with her, and I would've loved to see the woman she could've been and should've been in Christ if she would've just allowed Him in, but she was not having it. She reminded me of a child whose parents asked her to do something, but chose to be rebellious and not do it just to prove a point.

"Is there anything else you want to talk about because it seemed like you had a lot on your mind at the end of service today," I said.

"Nope. Nothing at all," she replied.

"Ok, well, can you tell me what you're feeling? I'm confused as to where our relationship is right now. I want to be closer to you, but it seems like you're drifting further and further away from me. You act like you're angry at me most of the time. If I'm doing something wrong, tell me, and I promise I'll try to fix it, Storm. You know that. You know I love you and will do whatever we need to do to make this work."

Stormie looked up at me with a blank look on her face and said, "We'll talk about this later. This isn't the time nor place."

Stormie turned my own words around on me. That was exactly what I'd told her at the end of church service when it seemed that she was trying to start an argument.

"Ok. I can respect that, but as soon as we get home, we need to talk," I replied.

"Ok," she replied.

I looked at her, trying to figure out what was going through her mind, because there definitely seemed to be a lot.

She had never really shut down the way she seemed as though she had in that moment, so all I could say in response to her "ok" was, "ok."

We finished eating, and from there, it was a long ride home.

Chapter Twenty-Six

When we finally got home after the long, uncomfortable ride, I began probing Stormie more and more. I just wanted her to tell me the truth. I knew we could never get to a resolution without her being honest about what was going on. The more I probed, the more anxious and irritated she seemed to become. She kept going from room to room, and I continued to follow her wherever she went. She finally realized I wasn't going to give up, so she stopped in our bedroom and sat at the edge of the bed.

"Look, Zeke. There is nothing bothering me. At least nothing more than what has bothered me over the past seventeen years of knowing you."

"That's why we need to talk, Storm. We don't need to continue going on like this. I remember how we used to feel about each other, and I still feel the same. I think I love you even more than I used to, even though it doesn't seem like you love me the same."

Stormie looked down at her phone as she held it in her hand.

"Can you please put your phone down while we talk?" I asked politely.

"I'm waiting for a phone call," she replied.

"Well, this conversation right here in front of your face is important, Storm."

"And this phone call that I'm waiting for is just as important," Stormie replied, shrugging her shoulders, and rolling her eyes, as she did when we were college students.

She continued, "That is part of the problem. You always think that what you have going on is more important than anything anyone else has going on. You didn't even ask who I'm expecting a phone call from, or what it's about because all you care about is yourself!" she said as she stood up.

"Stormie, you know that's not true. You are the most important person to me after God. I always care about how you feel, what you think, what you're going through, how you feel about me, and burdens you may be carrying . . . I can go on and on. I pray for you and our marriage all day, every day. Can you say the same?"

Stormie stood there with her arms folded as she stared up at the ceiling.

"Exactly what I thought. How could you possibly pray for us when you feel as though you have no one to pray to?" I said.

Her phone then rang, and she quickly grabbed it off of the bed where she'd left it when she stood up.

"Hello?" she answered with a smile on her face, sounding totally different than the way she sounded whenever she spoke to me.

She began walking out of the room as she cut her eyes at me. My first thought was to follow her and listen to the rest of her conversation, but I knew that wasn't going to resolve anything. I had a feeling she was probably talking to the same person that I'd seen her with, but I felt like I didn't want to believe it. I didn't want to accept the truth, even though it was right in front of my face. I was in complete denial. Something that I could never understand when others were experiencing it, but now that I was going through it, I could completely understand how people could indeed seem so blind to the truth.

A few minutes later, Stormie peeked around the corner into the bedroom and said, "Hey, just letting you know I'm going to be having company in a little while."

"Ok," I said, sounding as if I really didn't have an opinion in the matter. I didn't know what else to do, so I right at that moment, I got on my knees and prayed that God would work through my mind, body, and soul. I needed Him to give me the patience to deal with Stormie because I had been dealing with her and her antics for a long time, and honestly, my faith never wavered, but my patience was running thin. I asked God to cover me and Stormie with His blood, and for His presence to fill our home. I wanted Him to comfort me. I felt lonely, even though Stormie lived with me. I wasn't receiving what I needed from her, and I tried resting in God, and waiting for Him to fix whatever problems we had, even if part of the problem was me. I didn't believe in divorce. I felt like whatever problems we had could be fixed without even allowing divorce to cross our minds.

After praying, I got out of my church clothes into something more comfortable. I had decided to just leave the issue alone for the day, relax, and watch a little television. I knew Stormie would be busy hanging out with her girls in the entertainment room anyway.

I turned on the television, and laid back in our bed with one of my arms behind my head, while I scrolled the channels with my other hand. Not much later, I heard the doorbell ring. Stormie's friends were normally pretty loud whenever they came over and there were always at least three of them. I didn't hear any voices, so I turned down the television, thinking, maybe Stormie hadn't opened the door. I gave it a few more minutes, and after still hearing nothing, I became worried. I got up out of the bed and walked down the hall towards the stairs with my shorts and t-shirt on.

As I got towards the stairs, I could faintly hear Stormie's voice, but no one else. It almost sounded as though she was whispering.

I crept down the stairs and walked around the corner towards the entertainment room. When I finally did enter the entertainment room, I walked into something that I obviously wasn't expecting.

I looked at Stormie's face, waiting for an explanation. She took a deep breath and looked as if she was at a loss for words.

Finally she said, "I have rehearsed this a million times in my head, but when it's happening for real, it feels completely different."

"Storm, what are you talking about?" I said, looking back, staring at the man I'd seen her with, face to face. I couldn't believe she had the audacity to have this man in my house. If I had been any other man, and not a pastor, things would've gone left very quickly. I was thankful that I had just finished praying, and I knew this was just another test that would end up making me stronger in one way or another.

Without asking, the tall light skinned brother with the bald head that I'd seen going into the restaurant with my wife hand in hand the night before, decided to speak. The revelation that God had given me was staring me right in the face. Stormie had been cheating on me, and it hadn't just begun.

The man said, "Look Man, this may look messed up, but Stormie wanted to give you the respect of expressing her feelings to you, and telling you what she really wants. She requested that I be present since I'm that person that she's now in love with."

Stormie stood there looking clueless. She looked as though she had no remorse, nor did she look as if there was anything wrong with what she was doing. I didn't even know who she was anymore. My blood was boiling.

I got as close to the man as I could without actually kissing him.

"She is my wife!" I said with the most fierce, forceful voice that I had. "This has nothing to do with anyone else except for me and her, so you need to leave! Get out of my house!" I yelled.

Stormie ran over and said, "Brandon, you don't have to leave," and grabbed his hand.

She then looked at me and said, "Zeke, I'm sorry. I just don't love you anymore. You're not the type of man for me. You never were. I regret wasting so many of my good years with you when I could've been with someone like Brandon. You and I both know that I was never the first lady type," she said, with the audacity to laugh.

"Stormie, you were lost! I helped you find yourself. We loved each other and I still love you. I'm willing to do whatever it takes to make this work. You're making a mistake, and you know it!"

"Zeke, I'm leaving you. There is nothing you can do to change my mind."

"Damn. I didn't think this would be so intense," Brandon said with a grin.

He was a snake, and Stormie being Stormie couldn't see past the swag and flattery.

I folded my arms and looked at Stormie without any tears in my eyes, although I did hurt inside. One thing I did know as a believer was that pain, nor storms, lasted forever.

"Do what you have to do to make you happy, Stormie, but if you're looking for happiness in him, you are going to be extremely disappointed. Only God can make you happy and you refuse to let Him in. I accepted your flaws and loved you unconditionally, but you could never see past mine, or try to compromise about anything and have even the slightest amount of peace with it."

"Compromise?!" Stormie yelled, getting so far in my face that I could feel her saliva splatter across every inch of it. "You never compromised! You made me become this person who I never was meant to be! I was just fine before I met you! I knew who I was, what made me happy, and I didn't have any complaints. With you, I feel like I'm just existing. I'm bored! I'm not living! I don't even know why I would've given someone like you a chance! I can't think of one woman who could deal with a man like you!"

"Storm, I'm going to ask you something, and then you can go. Since you just said you knew who you were and what made you happy, were you happy being an alcoholic and drug addict? Where do you think you would be if you hadn't met me?"

Stormie became quiet for a moment and looked over at Brandon, whose eyes were bucked after what I'd just said. I assumed he didn't know that part of Stormie's past that I'd just revealed.

She then raised both fists at me, and said, "I hate you!"

"Stormie, just leave. I can't keep a woman that doesn't want to be kept, but I'll continue to love and pray for you."

Stormie seemed to become even more upset when I didn't beg her to stay, and began swinging on me. I grabbed both of her wrists, trying to calm her down. Brandon stood there, doing nothing, looking as if he was trying to figure out what he'd gotten himself into, and was confused about whether he really wanted any parts of it.

"Man just let her go!" he said, not realizing how Stormie could get if I released her while she was in that state. When she got upset about anything, nothing else existed and it was almost like she was a totally different person.

"No, and if you knew what was best for her, you wouldn't have even said that!" I replied.

I didn't want to let Stormie go until she fully calmed down. She was crying, breathing hard, and I still felt how tense her muscles were, which told me, she was still ready to swing if I'd let her go.

"Stormie, calm down. I'm giving you your freedom. Go find what you're missing. There's no need to fight because I'm not going to fight you on this. I already knew what was going on. I saw you last night with him, and God allowed me to be at peace with it."

Stormie seemed to be calming down.

"Can I let you go without you swinging on me?"

She didn't say anything, but I slowly released her any way. She quickly grabbed her phone and called the police, telling them that her husband was assaulting her.

After she hung up, she said, "Now you're going to jail, Pastor!"

"Stormie, really? What do you want from me? Please tell me because I'm so confused right now. I thought you just wanted to go and live your life, so go!"

"Yeah, I did until you put your hands on me! You saw it, Babe, didn't you?" she asked Brandon.

Brandon looked stressed as he sat on the sofa, wiping the beads of sweat from his forehead.

When the police came knocking at the door, I opened it and let them in.

It was two black cops, who I actually knew. Being a pastor, I knew a lot of people in the area by officiating weddings, providing counseling, visiting different churches, and many of them were members of my church. I had never been in a situation quite like this one, but I can say it was embarrassing. Especially the fact that my wife was sitting underneath another man on my couch, crying as he wrapped his arms around her.

"Pastor Zeke, is everything ok?" one of the officers, Officer Grant, who happened to be a member of my church asked, while peeking around me, noticing Stormie and the situation that was going on over there.

"Yeah, this was really not necessary. Just a marital disagreement. You know how that goes. No marriage is perfect. Not even mine."

Stormie stood up and ran over to the officers and said, "He's acting like everything is ok, but I told him I wanted to leave and he grabbed me and started shaking me! Look at the bruises on my wrists!"

"Pastor, is that what happened? She does have bruises."

"She was trying to hit me, so I grabbed her wrists to restrain her. It was in self-defense."

The officers came further into the house and asked Brandon who he was.

Before he could answer, Stormie said, "He's my man! That's why Zeke is so mad. I'm leaving him for someone who he could never compare to!"

Officer Grant said, "Look, there are a lot of emotions here, and they're going to be fresh for a while. Ma'am, if you were going to leave, I can stay while you pack up some of your things, and then when you're both calm, maybe you can talk to each other with some sense and make some decisions."

I interjected. "You know what Officer Grant, I'll leave. Give me a second so I can get a few things."

"You sure?" he asked.

"Positive."

"Good! Because I didn't feel like packing things up tonight anyway, but you better believe I'll be ready in a couple of days, and don't be blowing up my phone, Zeke! This is my house as much as it's yours!"

I had so much on my mind to say, but silence is golden. I never thought things would end this way, and then, maybe it wasn't the end. Maybe it was something we had to go through to get to where we needed to be. I went upstairs and packed a week's worth of clothes because I didn't know how long this episode was going to last. When I came back down the stairs, the cops were still standing there, and Stormie gave me the evilest glare I had ever seen her give anyone.

"Ok. You ready?" Officer Grant asked, as the other officer walked outside.

"Yeah, but I do have one request."

"What's that, Pastor?"

"Can I request that this other man gets out of my house?" I said loudly.

"He ain't going nowhere!" Stormie yelled.

Officer Grant took a deep breath and said, "Let's talk outside."

When we got outside, Officer Grant said, "I hate seeing you go through this, but I know you'll get through it."

"Most definitely," I replied. "God has my back at all times."

"Unfortunately, because the house belongs to both of you, I can't request that she puts her "guest" out. I wish I could because this is very ugly. I'm sorry."

"I understand. You're just doing your job," I said.

"You need anything, Pastor?"

"No, I'm ok. I'm just going to go get a room and try to calm down. This is a lot to take in."

"I understand, but I know you, and I know you know God, and you'll be just fine. I'll be praying for the both of you."

Officer Grant gave me a hug, and he went and got into his squad car, in which he hadn't turned the flashing lights on in respect of me and Stormie. He didn't want to cause too much attention at the pastor and first lady's house. I appreciated that.

I got into my car and just sat there for a moment. I looked through the picture window of my house and could see Stormie and Brandon sitting closely on the sofa, and it could've been my imagination, but it looked like they were laughing. There was a lesson to learn in all of this and I wished that I had known what it was. One day, the reason may have been revealed to me, and then again, God has his reasons for everything, and sometimes we never know those reasons. If we do ever find out, it could be years later. All I could do was be patient, take things day by day, and allow God to order my steps.

Chapter Twenty-Seven

As I drove out of the driveway of the home Stormie and I shared, so many things crossed my mind. I had never been a fighter, but I couldn't believe I was allowing another man to stay in the house with my wife, while the police sent me away to stay at a hotel. My flesh wanted to do something totally different, but I had a calling on my life, and that was to be a role model for others, and not to beat anyone beyond recognition. I know that's probably what many men would've done, but that wasn't me. My job was to be more like God. I wanted to think like Him, speak like Him, and act like Him, and I knew I would've never caught God beating someone's butt. There was a process to this entire situation and that would have to be a conversation between me and God.

While driving to my destination, I remained in deep thought. I was so deep in thought that I almost missed the woman that I almost hit as she tried to cross the street while a ton of traffic headed in her direction. It was almost like she was trying to commit suicide. As I hit the brakes on my car, it came to a screeching halt. I immediately turned on my emergency lights, and quickly jumped out to make sure the woman was ok. The other cars also stopped as they approached us and realized what was going on.

This woman, whoever she was, was in bad shape. She was wearing a short, slinky dress, and high heels. She could barely even stand, and I could smell the alcohol seeping through her pores. I was having a bad day, but she seemed like she was having an even worse day. If I hadn't stopped, It might've become even worse.

I wrapped one of her arms around my neck as I walked her over to the passenger side of my car. Her wild, curly hair flopped all over the place. So much that I could barely even see her face. I opened the door, put her in, and strapped her into the seatbelt. She looked at me and smiled, still not knowing what was going on.

She pushed a few of the jet-black tendrils that had fallen into her face, and said, "I know you."

"No, you've had a little too much to drink. You think you know me. I'm just trying to get you home safely, so where is home?"

"A few blocks from here," she said, with her speech slurring. "My id is in my purse. I have to pay you."

"Pay me for what?" I asked.

Naively, she said, "Aren't you an Uber driver?"

"No, I'm not. I'm just helping out. Now, where's your purse?"

The beautiful light complected woman with the gorgeous smile smiled at me again and shrugged her shoulders.

"I'll be right back. Don't go anywhere," I said.

I waited for traffic to pass and backtracked across the street from where the woman had come from. After walking half a block, I saw a bar and decided to take my chances by walking in to see if I could find what I was looking for.

"Pastor Zeke?" I heard a man say as soon as I walked in.

I turned around to find that it was one of my members.

"It's not what it looks like."

"And this isn't what it looks like, either," my member said, laughing, as he sat at the bar with a glass of brown liquor sitting in front of him.

I gestured for the bartender to come over as she served one of her patrons.

When the tall blonde woman walked over, she said, "I've never seen you around here. How can I help you handsome? You need directions?"

I took a deep breath and said, "No, I don't need directions. I think I just ran into one of your drunk patrons and she may have left her purse here."

"Oh, you must be talking about Miracle. She leaves her purse here quite often."

The bartender looked over at one of the booths and said, "Yep, there it is sitting right in the seat of that booth over there." She pointed in the direction of where the mystery woman, Miracle, had been sitting.

Before going to grab the purse, I looked at the bartender's name badge and said, "Jessica . . . "

"Call me Jessie," she replied, before allowing me to finish.

"Jessie, isn't it illegal to let people get that drunk? Aren't you supposed to cut them off at some point?"

Jessie rolled her eyes at me and said, "Can you please go get what you came for and leave? I have customers to serve."

She walked off smiling, towards one of the men sitting at the bar, smiling, as I went and grabbed Miracle's purse.

As I was leaving out of the bar, my member who greeted me when I first entered said, "See you, Sunday, Pastor!"

I ran all the way back to my car with Miracle's purse on my shoulder and got back into the driver's seat. When I made it back, she was passed out in the front seat where I'd left her.

I gently shook her and said, "Miracle."

She moved a little bit, and quietly said, "What do you want? Just take me home. Didn't I pay you already?"

I was trying not to go into her purse without her permission, but I knew there was no way I was going to get her to sober up enough to do it herself. I had no choice, so I opened her purse and took out her wallet. This was beginning to feel like déjà vu of the time when I found Stormie drunk and passed out at that Frat party in college. At least I was able to find Miracle's ID with her address because I definitely couldn't walk into a hotel with a passed out woman thrown over my shoulder, but I would've had to do whatever I had to do to make sure she was safe. Miracle actually lived only about five minutes from where we were, which explained why she was probably walking. When I pulled up in front of her house, I wondered what her occupation was because she had a very nice home and a white Porsche that was basically brand new, but how could a person possibly keep up a lifestyle like that if they were, in fact, drunk the majority of the time?

I knew it wasn't my business, so I got out of the car and went and opened Miracle's door. She still didn't move. I unfastened her seatbelt, and gently grabbed her out of the car. She was very small framed, but her dead weight made her heavier than she probably was. She was probably only 5 feet 4 inches tall and around one hundred fifteen pounds. Her driver's license said she was thirty-four, but she looked more like twenty-five. I carried her to her front door. There were no other cars, besides the Porsche, parked outside, and it looked pretty dark inside. I struggled as I held her, attempting not to drop her, as I dug into her purse once more, in search of her house keys.

When I finally found her keys, there were at least ten keys on the ring, and I kept having to try each one until I finally found the magical one that turned the lock. I pushed the door open and felt around the walls for a light switch. After I finally found one, I walked through the foyer into the living room. I then laid Miracle on the sofa, removed her shoes, and went into the kitchen and found a bottled water in the fridge. I laid the water next to her in case she woke up and needed it. I then rummaged around for a pen and piece of paper, and stumbled upon an office. Whatever Miracle did, by the looks of her office she was very tidy and organized.

I sat in the black leather desk chair and wrote a note so she wouldn't be completely confused when she finally came to.

It read, *"Hi, Miracle. My name is Pastor ~~Zeke~~ Ezekiel. You walked right in front of my car last night, and I'm so glad that no one was hurt. I was able to retrieve your purse from the local bar to find out where you lived, which is how I was able to get you home safely, and I pray that you stay safe from this point on. I hope you don't mind me bringing you into your home, but I really didn't have any other choice. If you have any questions, please don't hesitate to call. I'm leaving my card with my information in case you need to use it. God bless you.*
Sincerely,
Ezekiel"

Since I'd been with Stormie, the name Zeke had become more common to me and everyone else around me, instead of my government name, Ezekiel. My mom hated the fact that I didn't go by the name she'd given me because she believed from the time that I was born that it had a lot of significance and strength behind it. That was one of the reasons she never really cared for Stormie because she felt that she took part of who I was away from me by calling me Zeke. No one ever called me that until I met Stormie, who refused to call me Ezekiel. For some reason, I felt the need to introduce myself to Miracle as the name my mother had given me.

Chapter Twenty-Eight

A fter being kicked out of my own house, and after the strange, unexpected interaction with Miracle, I went and found a hotel to stay at until who knew when. This was one of those moments I felt I needed my mother because she always knew how to encourage me when I needed it. Stormie had formed such a wedge between me and my mother that I felt ashamed to even go to her with what I was dealing with. She always felt that Stormie wasn't the one for me, but I felt differently. I felt that God placed everyone in our lives for a reason, and once you were married to someone, problems in a marriage could be fixed as long as someone wasn't getting beat on, or adultery wasn't a problem. Well, evidently, adultery was a serious problem in our marriage, and I honestly tried to ignore it because I loved Stormie that much. In my crazy method of thinking, I thought that she would grow tired of it and realize that she had everything she needed at home. The thing was, I had never seen it right in front of my face, and I'm not going to lie, it did hurt, but God had been preparing me for it, and giving me peace.

The next step would be to see where Stormie's mind was, and where she stood in the situation. I felt she made it quite clear when she let me leave and allowed another man to stay in our home. I didn't want to assume anything, especially when emotions were flying all over the place. I felt like we just needed to talk one on one without any distractions. I decided to give her at least a few days, thinking she would call me before those days were up, but she never did. I felt like calling her numerous times, but I didn't because I wanted to give her time to sort things out in her mind. I didn't need to sort things out. I knew what I wanted. I wanted my family, and Stormie was my family, and had been for a long time. We'd had some bad times, but we'd also had some very good ones. I had been around long enough and performed enough marriage counseling sessions to know that no marriage was perfect, and expecting perfection was just a recipe for disaster.

During our time apart, I did receive a phone call that I wasn't expecting.

"Hello," the soft, timid voice of a woman said as soon I answered the phone while I was going through some paperwork at my engineering firm.

"Hello, is someone there?" I said.

"Thank you," the woman said with both shame and genuine appreciation in her voice.

I then knew exactly who I was talking to.

"Miracle, is that you?"

Before responding, she hesitated, and said, "Yes. I'm sorry that I'm just now calling. I should've called the very next day, but after realizing you were a pastor, I had no idea what to say because I didn't quite know what you thought of me."

I stood up and began pacing the floor of my office.

"Miracle, listen to me. I don't judge anyone. We all have our ups and downs. None of us are perfect, and we're all sinners. God is your only judge, and He still loves you unconditionally."

"I appreciate that, Pastor Ezekiel. I've been going through some hard times for a long time."

"You can just call me Ezekiel, and if you don't mind talking about it, what are some of the things you're dealing with? Everything we talk about is confidential."

I had dealt with many different types of people, and many didn't want to open up and talk to anyone about their problems, but it just seemed like Miracle was crying out for help. I felt as though I had already earned her trust, even though we didn't know much about one another.

"I don't talk to anyone about this, but I've been a recovering alcoholic several times in my life. So many times that I've just really given up on even trying to recover. I feel like this is who I am, and I'm not quite sure why God chose this life for me."

"Well, Miracle. I wish I could answer that for you, and I'm sure there are so many other people wondering the same thing about their lives, but God puts us in different places and different situations for very specific reasons, so we just have to trust in that. From the looks of your home, it looks like God has still been blessing you. He's going to look out for His children. He was definitely looking out for you the other night."

Miracle said, "Honestly, I don't remember much about the other night. I don't remember much about many nights these days, but I always manage to make it home safely, and act as if nothing happened the next day.

"That's because you're a functioning alcoholic, and God is giving you chance after chance. If He wasn't, you wouldn't be here right now. There are programs that can help you overcome your habit. They can help you figure out the root of your problem."

"I've tried them all," she said, with tears in her voice.

"How about God? Have you tried His program?"

She took a deep breath, and said, "To be honest, I haven't. I used to go to church with my parents when I was younger, but they died in an accident when I was twelve. I then lived with my grandmother, and she died about a year later from the heartache of losing her only child, my mother. I ended up having to live in a foster home until I was eighteen, and then I was able to move into the house that I live in now, which I inherited from my grandmother."

Listening to her story, I wanted to begin praying for her right then and there, but I didn't. I didn't know how she'd respond, but I knew I had to pray for her as soon as we ended our call. A lot of times we don't really know that so many people in this world have gone through so many things that have caused trauma in their lives, but through God, we have to beat those demons, and show Satan that we can still live great lives. We can't let the past control us, no matter how hard it is to let go.

"I'm so sorry to hear that you had to go through all of that, Miracle. What do you do to keep yourself busy? To keep your mind away from those things? I noticed you had an office, and no, I wasn't snooping around your house," I laughed. "I was just getting you a bottled water before I left you lying on the sofa."

I heard Miracle giggle, and that made my heart smile because I felt it in my spirit that she hadn't laughed in a long time.

"I work from home as an underwriting manager for a mortgage company, so I spend the majority of every morning and afternoon couped up in the house, and then I go out and try to forget about the past. Sometimes I think I forget both the past and the present, especially by the vague, or maybe I should say, the non-existent memory I have of the other night."

Just as I had figured, she didn't remember anything from that night besides walking down the sidewalk leaving the bar. She was very grateful that I came to her rescue because, in her words, "It could've been anyone, and that anyone could've been the wrong one."

She was right. Anyone could've picked her up and took advantage of her. I'm just glad that God put her in my path. It just could've been a little more subtly, but we know that God does have a sense of humor.

She said that she'd graduated from college twelve years prior with a bachelor's degree in business management. She didn't have any kids and only took care of herself, but did want a family someday. She said her family was her life, and when she lost them, she felt like she lost everything. I wanted to know more about her parent's accident, but I didn't want to get too deep into her business, so I didn't even ask. I knew those subjects could be quite sensitive.

Being a pastor, I felt the need to ask, "How's your relationship with God, now?"

She sighed, and said, "I don't have much of one, but I know I need to do better. I'm very aware that if I developed a closer relationship with God, much of what I'm going through would be a lot easier to deal with."

[12] "For the word of God is alive and powerful. It is sharper than the sharpest two-edged sword, cutting between soul and spirit, between joint and marrow. It exposes our innermost thoughts and desires." – Hebrews 4:12 NLT

I was impressed. At least Miracle was able to admit that she did need a relationship with God. Since she said that, I felt comfortable inviting her to church service. She said she couldn't make any promises, but she would try.

"I'll take that," I said. "I really hope to see you there one of these Sundays. In the meantime, you take care of yourself."

"I will, Pastor . . . I mean Ezekiel."

"Good," I said, feeling like I had gotten somewhere with her, and I had a lot of faith that she would be just fine.

"Before you go, what's your last name, Miracle?"

"Cummins."

"Miracle Cummins, huh?" Well, Miss Miracle Cummins, I feel like your miracle is comin'."

Miracle laughed again. It wasn't just a little giggle this time. She was laughing from her gut, and that's what I liked to hear.

"I know I'm not that funny," I said. "Most people, especially my mom, only laugh at my jokes to make me feel good," I said, laughing.

Trying to talk through her laughter, she said, "The joke was kind of bad, but that's what made it funny. She then got silent for a moment, and said, "But I truly believe my miracle is coming. Thank you so much for the talk."

"You're most welcome."

Chapter Twenty-Nine

A fter getting off of the phone with Miracle, I contemplated whether or not I should call Stormie, or just go by the house. Calling would've probably been the best thing to do, but I had given her enough time to sort things out in her mind, which was way more than I had to do, and after all, the house belonged to both of us. I felt like she should've had no question in her mind whether or not she loved me and still wanted to be with me if that's what she wanted. In my opinion, there was nothing to think about, and if she had to think about it, then I already knew the answer. After everything that had occurred, I was still willing to work things out. Some may have called me stupid, but I loved my wife, and unless God told me it was time to let go, I was going to keep trying.

After I left work, I headed home, instead of back to the hotel. I knew Stormie should've been home from work if she hadn't made any other stops. I left work a little later than usual, so even if she had to make a few stops, she still should've been home. When I pulled up to the house, I saw a light on through the crescent shaped picture window in the living room. She always parked in the garage, so I figured she was home. I sat in the driveway in the car for a few minutes trying to prepare for whichever side of Stormie I was going to be dealing with that particular day. I had no idea how things were going to go, but I just hoped that we could speak to each other like adults, be honest with each other, and tell each other what we really wanted from this marriage.

I finally decided to get out of the car, and when I got to the front door and put my key in to unlock it, the knob began turning from the other side. I pulled my key back out, and suddenly, Stormie opened the door.

She folded her arms and said, "I don't recall calling you and telling you to stop by."

"Stormie, I'm your husband and this is my house, too. I don't have to wait for you to give me permission. I've given you plenty of time to calm down and sort through your thoughts. Now I think we need to talk."

The next thing I knew, Brandon came to the door and put his arm around Stormie's waist.

"Baby, is everything, ok?" he asked.

While staring me directly in the eyes, Stormie said, "Yeah, I was just about to tell Zeke that he needed to make plans to get the rest of his things so he doesn't have to come back."

My jaw almost hit the ground.

"Stormie! Are you serious right now? Is this how you really want it? After everything we've gone through?"

"I absolutely know this is how I want it. I've been pretty sure about it for a while now, but just didn't know how to say it. I finally realized that there's really no polite way to say it. I don't love you anymore, Zeke."

I couldn't believe what Stormie was saying, but I could feel my blood boiling again, worse than the first night when all of this drama began, and I knew that it was best that I got some more of my things while I was there and find time to go back another day while she and her friend wasn't there. This entire ordeal was unbelievable, and I never would've imagined our relationship being in this state.

While still standing on the porch, I told Stormie I was going to come in and get some more things, and I'd get the rest while she was gone so she didn't have to be around me for too long.

"Sounds great," she said, as she opened the door wide enough for me to come inside.

As soon as I got my foot halfway through the door, I began to smell weed. The further I walked in, the stronger the odor became. I looked around and saw bottles of liquor lined up along the island, and glasses that were half filled sitting on the table next to the living room sofa. This was what she wanted. She wanted someone to sit up and drink and get high with her all day like the old days. She didn't want to grow up and leave her past behind her for a better life. To her, drinking and smoking was a better life. That was only because it kept her from thinking about the past. The thing she had been running from all of her life. Obviously, Brandon hadn't taken me seriously when I said that she'd struggled with addiction, and it looked like she was right back on her way to those old habits that she'd worked so hard to break.

"Stormie, can I please talk to you alone before I get my things?"

"Talk about what?" she asked defensively.

"Can I please just have five minutes?"

She took a deep breath and said, "Brandon, can you give us a few minutes, Bae?"

"Whatever he has to say to you, he can say in front of me. I'm your man, right?" Brandon said, as he began walking up on me.

I then began walking up on him and said, "I don't know what you are to her, but she's a married woman, and I'm her husband. However you're feeling right now, doesn't mean a thing to me. This is between me and Stormie."

Brandon balled up his fists and began swinging on me. I tried blocking his punches, but he was too quick and ended up knocking me to the floor. I began wheezing from the asthma that hadn't flared up in years. I never carried an inhaler anymore because I never had any issues with it. I began taking long deep breaths to try to fill my lungs back up with air.

Stormie walked over to me, and I was assuming she was coming to help me up, but no.

She said, "You are so weak! You call yourself a man of God, but real men of your supposed God are supposedly strong! You're actually the weakest man I know and that's exactly why I don't want you anymore! As long as I've known you, you've let other people change you. You're not this big shot pastor that you portray to be. You know deep down in your heart that's not who you are. I know who you are, but people who don't even matter made you into this person I don't know. That's why things are the way they are now!"

Once I was finally caught my breath and was able to stand, I stood in front of Stormie, face to face, and said, "People didn't change me. God did. He can still do the same for you."

I then headed towards the stairs to get some of my things from the bedroom.

What I said to her must've really struck a nerve because she began screaming, "I don't need to change. I'm perfect just the way I am. You just don't know how many men would love to be with a woman like me, but you messed that up, Zeke! No one wants you, and never will! Good luck with your lonely, miserable life because that's all you'll ever have!"

I continued to walk up the stairs as she continued to carelessly say hurtful things, but the truth was, she wasn't even sure what she was doing. She wanted to hurt me because she was hurting. The things that came out of my wife's mouth did hurt, but I couldn't let my emotions control me.

I made it to the bedroom and pulled a couple of pieces of my luggage out of the closet. As I went to lay them on the bed, I noticed the bed wasn't made. That may not have meant much to many, but it meant a lot to me because Stormie could never stand the bed to not be made. As soon as we'd get out of it, she would make it, and it would remain that way until it was time to go back to bed. I also saw men's clothing lying on my side of the bed on the floor, and they didn't belong to me.

I went through the closet and my drawers and put as many of my things into the luggage that would fit. I didn't know when the next time would be that I would be back, but after this particular day, I was in no hurry to enter that house ever again. At that moment, I actually would've preferred to leave everything and start all over again. Again, I couldn't let my emotions control me. I knew God saw all. He was with me, and He'd be sure to take care of me.

After getting back downstairs with my two pieces of luggage, Stormie and Brandon watched from the sofa as I headed to the front door.

When I opened the front door, Stormie stood up and said, "When will you be back to get the rest of your stuff?"

I turned and looked at her and said, "Soon. Why, are you in a hurry?"

"Brandon doesn't want to be here with all of your stuff here!"

"Stormie, you do realize this isn't as easy as just telling me to leave and you do whatever you want to do with this house, right? I do also own this house, and frankly I could care less how Brandon feels."

"Whatever, Zeke! Just leave!"

I stepped out and shut the door behind me. Stormie was acting as if she hated me, and I had no idea why she was treating me that way. I knew that Stormie had a side to her that most would've never wanted to meet, but I never thought I would've had to deal with that side of her on this level. I began to think maybe our marriage had really run its course. All I could do was put it in God's hands.

<u>Chapter Thirty</u>

After leaving Stormie's and my house that evening with just a couple of pieces of luggage, I went back to my hotel room and did what I had been forced to do. Normally, I didn't get my mom involved in any disagreements between me and Stormie, but in this instance, it was much more than a disagreement, and I was going to need my mother's help and full support with this one.

"Hey, Baby! It seems like it's been forever since I've talked to you!" my mom said as soon as she answered.

"Ma, it's only been a week."

"Well, it still seems like forever, and every time I talk to you, you sound more and more like your father!" she said with joy in her voice.

I chuckled, because it made me feel so good whenever she said that anything about me reminded her of my dad. I felt like anything that she said comparing me with my dad was a huge compliment.

"How is everything? I'm happy to hear from you, but you don't sound like yourself," she continued.

"It's not good, Ma."

Her voice immediately changed to one of concern as if she could feel what I was going through without even knowing what it was.

"What's wrong, Son? You know you can talk to me about anything."

"You know I don't like to worry you, and the only reason I'm bringing this to you right now is because I'm really going to need somewhere to live for a little while."

"What happened, Ezekiel? What did that Stormie do?"

"She doesn't want me there anymore. She said the harshest things to me, and on top of that, she has another man there with her."

My mom was silent for a moment, and then said, "So she's been cheating on you?"

"Yes. I've had an idea for a while, but I found out for sure about a week ago when I saw them going into one of our favorite restaurants."

"Oh, Ezekiel. I'm so sorry. You do not deserve this. You were created for so much greater than this, but I already know, you will not let this break you."

"No, Ma, I'm not. It's just going to make me stronger. I feel like I've done all I can do. It's in God's hands now. I can't make anyone change, and I certainly can't make anyone love me."

"You're right about that! You already know I would've had a few choice words for her back in the day, but God!"

"I know, Ma. This is not worth you losing your religion over. Nothing is. I'll be ok."

"Yes, you will, and I'm here for you. Whatever you need, just ask, and don't be in a hurry to find a place. Get everything else taken care of before you even think of renting or purchasing a new home. That would be way too much stress. Take all the time you need."

"Thank you, Ma. You already know how much I appreciate you. You've always been there when I needed you the most."

"And you have been there for me during the moments when you didn't even realize how much I needed you. I love you so much, Ezekiel."

"I love you, too, Ma. I'll talk to you later."

The very next day, I took a day off of work and hired some movers so that I could get the rest of my things out of the house while Stormie and hopefully no one else was there. I didn't plan on taking much. Only the things that specifically belonged to me. I had a pool table in the basement that I was definitely taking, some of my family photo albums from before Stormie was in the picture, and a ton of clothes, being mostly suites and dress shoes. I left all of the furniture, besides everything in my home office. Stormie and I both had our separate offices, and I had all of my things extremely organized in my desk drawers and file cabinets. I just really wanted to start over when I did get a place of my own. I preferred to not have anything in the new place that I would someday call home that would have the tendency of constantly reminding me of Stormie. When the movers were done, I walked through the house one last time, making sure there wasn't anything extremely important that I was forgetting. I then got into my car and had the movers to follow me to the storage unit that I'd rented that morning to drop everything off.

I was still in disbelief. I never thought I would be going through something like this, although it probably shouldn't have come as a surprise to me. I just always liked to think positively about things. If I hadn't, to be honest, things probably wouldn't have lasted as long as they had.

After dropping everything off at the storage unit, I stopped over by a diner nearby to have lunch. I sat alone at one of the booths, thinking to myself, that most of my outings would probably be this way from now on.

"Hello, Sir! Have you had a chance to look at the menu?"

I looked up at the waitress, who was an albino. She had a beautiful spirit about her. Her smile alone could brighten someone's day because it definitely had brightened mine.

I didn't have much of an appetite, but knew I needed to eat. I hadn't eaten much in the past week.

"Hi, how are you today?" I asked he waitress.

"I'm great! I probably should've asked you how you were doing first. How are you?" she asked, with a look of embarrassment.

"No, you're just fine. Thank you for coming over with such a welcoming attitude. You don't get that much anymore."

"I'm sorry to hear that," she replied, genuinely.

"I don't mean to hold you up. I just wanted to tell you that you're doing great at what you do, and to answer your question, I'm doing pretty good myself. Thanks for asking."

She nodded her head and said, "Thank you so much for that."

"You are very welcome. With that being said, I'll take a bowl of your cheddar broccoli soup and a large Coke."

"Will that be all?"

"Yes, that's all."

"Ok. I'll get that right in for you. Let me know if you need anything in the meantime. My name is Joy."

"I sure will, Joy. That name fits you perfectly," I replied.

"My mom says the same thing," she said, smiling, as she walked away to put my order in.

As I sat at the table, taking care of some business on my phone, I heard a voice at the cash register that sounded a little familiar. I turned around, but could only see a thin woman that stood a little under five and a half feet tall, with a head full of wild curly hair from the back. When I saw that hair, I knew it had to be Miracle.

"*What a coincidence,*" I thought, as I shook my head and laughed to myself.

"Miracle?" I said, hoping to get her attention.

After grabbing her to-go bag from the cashier, she turned around in my direction and squinted.

"Ezekiel?" she said as she began walking my way.

When she arrived at my table I stood up and gave her a friendly hug.

"How are you?" she asked, as she seemingly looked me up and down, but it could've been my imagination. I did feel a little self-conscious because I wasn't at my best. It had been a busy morning, and I definitely didn't want to put on any of my best attire to move.

"I'm good. I just decided to stop by for some lunch in the middle of trying to get some things done today."

"Yeah, me too," she replied. "I'm actually so surprised that I even recognized you since the one and only time I did see you was when I was . . . you know."

"I wasn't sure if you'd recognize me either since you didn't remember anything else, but I'm glad you did."

The waitress then came over with my drink.

"Your soup will be right up, Sir. They just made a fresh batch!" she said.

"Thank you so much, Joy."

As she walked away, Miracle said, "The soup, huh? Don't tell me you got the cheddar broccoli."

I laughed, and said, "Yes, I did. How did you know?"

She held up her bag and said, "That's the only thing I come here for. I love it."

She then looked at me with a strange look and said, "I don't have much work to do at home right now. Do you mind if I sit and have lunch with you? I don't know if that's inappropriate for a pastor. I see you have a wedding ring on, and I definitely wouldn't want to disrespect your wife, but I promise I don't have any ill-intentions. I already have enough problems."

"No, it's fine, if you don't mind sitting with someone who looks like they just woke up and walked out of the house."

Miracle laughed as she sat down, and said, "You look fine. You can't wear suits and ties all the time, can you?"

"I guess you're right. I've been moving this morning, so I'm sure you can probably understand that."

With a look of surprise while taking her soup out of the bag, she said, "You're moving?"

"Yeah, long story."

"If you want to talk about it, I'm a good listener."

"I'm sure, but I'd prefer not to talk about it. At least not today. You actually helped me take my mind off of a lot of things that I have going on."

"I can respect that," Miracle replied, and just at that moment, the waitress came with my soup.

"Both of you enjoy!" she said, and walked over to check on the table next to us.

As soon as Miracle was about to take a spoonful of her soup, I asked, "You don't mind me blessing the food for the both of us, do you?"

Miracle looked embarrassed and said, "No, I don't mind. I'm so sorry. I'm just not used to praying over my food. To be honest, I don't do much praying at all, as you've probably already assumed."

"I don't assume anything, and don't be ashamed to say that you need to work on some things. We all do. When you start praying, the more you do it, the more it will become a natural and regular part of your life. We all have to start somewhere, and you can start right now."

I prayed over our food, and when I was done, I heard Miracle softly say, "Amen".

Miracle and I enjoyed or lunch, while having random, however, enjoyable conversation. We avoided anything that might've triggered any negative emotions. We remained in a positive zone the entire time, which was a little different for me. I didn't even want to compare her to Stormie because she was my wife, and I felt a little bad for just sitting, having lunch with another woman, but I had to say, Miracle was a breath of fresh air, regardless of the things she had gone through, and was still going through.

While eating, I suddenly remembered that the night I picked up Miracle, she said she knew me. I didn't think much of it that night because when people are intoxicated, they say a lot of things, and I probably could've looked like anyone to her. I still asked her if she remembered saying that, and she said she didn't, but she did feel like there was something familiar about my eyes. She said I probably just reminded her of someone that she'd known from the past, which was probably the case, because I knew that I didn't know her before that night.

After finishing lunch, Miracle and I went our separate ways. I went to my mom's house to drop off and put away the clothes that I'd packed up in the back of my SUV.

My mom gave me a hug as soon as she opened the front door, and acted as if she didn't want to let me go.

"Ma, not to be rude, but can I please go in to set some of this stuff down?" I said, as I struggled trying not to drop everything that I was holding. I had tried to grab as much as I could so I wouldn't have so many trips back and forth to my vehicle.

"Oh, I'm so sorry!" she said, laughing, as she released me. "Let me take some of that," she said, trying to grab some of the clothes from me.

"I got it, Ma."

"Boy, you are just like your dad. You can accept help sometimes, you know?"

"I know, Ma. I'm accepting help right now by moving in with you until I get on my feet, aren't I?"

I could always tell when my mom had something she wanted to say, but was trying to think of the best way of saying it, and this was one of those moments.

She finally said, "Yeah, you're accepting my help, but I want you to accept it without feeling ashamed. You never have to feel ashamed when you need a little help. I can tell that you feel defeated and this isn't one of your proudest moments, but we all go through storms, and the sun does come back out. Even then, another storm will eventually come, but that one won't last either. It's called life. You're going to be just fine."

I needed that at that exact moment. That was the thing about having a mother like mine. She knew exactly what I needed when

I needed it. It was like, when she said everything was going to be ok, you really knew it was going to be ok. Even having the relationship that I had with God, and how much faith I had that all things worked out for good, sometimes I had those moments when I did need my mom.

"Thanks, Ma. I really appreciate you," I said.

"I know," she said with a smile.

I finished bringing in everything and decided to take a break before putting everything away. My mom had left my room exactly as it was when I was living there. I laid down in my full-sized bed, which, I must say, felt very different from a king-sized bed, but I was grateful, regardless. I lied on my back with my hands behind my head, reminiscing about all of the good times in that house. I particularly thought about all of the talks my dad gave me as we both sat on that same bed. I was very grateful that I able to come back to a home with so many wonderful memories. My mom had thought about selling the house several times, but I think she enjoyed having those memories as well. For some people, it would've been too hard trying to stay in the same home after their spouse died, but my mom was always a strong woman, and I knew she'd had her rough days, especially in the beginning, but I believed that being able to have beautiful memories in every room of the house that she shared with the love of her life, after she got past the grieving stage, meant a lot to her. She was ecstatic to have me home, and I was blessed to have someone who appreciated and loved me enough to welcome me back with open arms.

Chapter Thirty-One

The time had come. It was the first Sunday that I would be preaching without my first lady sitting in the front pew. Even when I knew that she didn't want to be there, which was the majority of the time, I still felt better that she was there. I had already made up in my mind that if anyone asked about her, I would just be very vague, letting them know she was ok. My mom had already given me a talk, telling me that it was no one's business what was going on in my house, so I shouldn't feel forced to tell anyone anything. Especially when things weren't set in stone.

11 **"A fool uttereth all his mind: but a wise man keepeth it in till afterwards." – Proverbs 29:11 KJV**

Although I had told my mom that it was ok for her to go to Pastor Ervin's church and she wasn't obligated to come to mine just because I was living with her, she still felt like she needed to be there. I think deep down, she just thought that I probably needed the support. I had prayed very hard the night before, and I felt very confident that everything would be fine. God spoke words of comfort to me, and told me that I had to go through some things that were going to be painful, but it was in my best interest, and very necessary for me to get to where I needed to be. I knew God's plan was perfect, and I wouldn't dare question it.

As I preached my sermon, titled, "How are you treating your enemies?" I looked out in the crowd a few times expecting to see Stormie, but God continued to help bring me back to reality by reminding me that I had an assignment, and I couldn't continue to be distracted while trying to bring others to His kingdom. Yes, I had issues going on, but God had told me to cast all of my burdens on Him. I had even lost my train of thought for a moment, which I never did. I looked out at my members and almost gave in to my emotions. I looked at my mom sitting in the second row, and she nodded her head. At that moment, God brought me right back to where I'd left off.

I kept looking at the time, and it seemed to be going so slow. I felt as if it was my first sermon ever preached, and felt very unsure of myself. It was still early, and I was praying that no one would be able to tell that something was wrong. I didn't think that this would be so hard, but it was. I continued to preach, just praying that the Holy Spirit would continue to speak through me.

As I finished reading Luke 6:27-28, which are the verses in which Jesus says, "But to you who are willing to listen, I say, love your enemies! Do good to those who hate you. Bless those who curse you. Pray for those who hurt you," I looked up and saw Miracle walking down the aisle, looking for a place to sit. It seemed to become completely quiet in the house of the Lord until Miracle sat down, and I immediately continued with where I was going with my message.

Every so often, I would glance at Miracle in the crowd, and I noticed how attentive she was, looking as if she was extremely interested in every word I said. To be honest, I didn't even expect her to come. I threw the invitation out there, which I always did. Some would make it, but most didn't. The important thing was that I was helping as many as I could, in whatever way that I could.

At the end of my sermon, I came down from the podium and greeted the members of my congregation, one by one. It felt different not having Stormie by my side, and a few people did ask if she was ok. I just told them that she was fine, and thanked them for their concern. My mom was way towards the end of the line, and I knew that was because she didn't want to feel rushed to give me a hug and keep the line moving. Right behind her, I saw Miracle. I looked towards them at the back of the line and smiled. Miracle was a little taller than my mom, so my mom was able to immediately tell that I was smiling at someone else besides her, so she looked back, staring Miracle up and down. I saw her smile at Miracle, and then started a conversation with her until they reached the front of the line. My mom never cared who she talked to, and seemed to make friends wherever she went.

"Hey, Ma!" I said as she approached me. I immediately opened my arms wide and hugged her tight.

"Hey, Baby. Today's sermon was fantastic, which I never doubted."

I looked over at Miracle, and my mom followed my eyes. Miracle stood there looking timid, as if she didn't know what to say.

"Hey, Miracle! Glad you could make it!"

Looking surprised, my mom said, "Oh, you know Miracle?"

"Yes, and you act as if you do, too, Ma."

"No, I just met her in line. She told me this was her first time visiting. I told her to make herself at home because she'll never want to go anywhere else, but she never mentioned that the two of you already knew each other," she said, looking at both me and Miracle, trying hard to draw her own conclusions through our facial expressions and body language.

"Yes, your mom is very sweet! I see where you get your great personality," Miracle said.

"I can't take all the credit. Ezekiel is a wonderful man just like his dad! I'm so proud!"

"I know you are, and I would love to meet his dad. Is he here?"

My mom and I looked at each other, trying hard to keep a smile on our faces.

My mom finally said, "No, he's no longer here. He's in a better place. That place where we should all be trying to get. We know that he's looking down on us, and at this very moment, he's probably smiling ear to ear."

Miracle put her hand up to her mouth and said, "I'm so sorry! I didn't know," being extremely apologetic.

"It's ok," I said. "There's no way you could've known."

"Hey, Pastor Zeke," I heard someone say from a distance.

When I looked into the crowd of parishioners who were still hanging around, I saw Officer Grant walking towards me.

When he finally approached, I gave him a brotherly hug, and said, "Hey, how are you?"

"I'm great. I just wanted to see how things were with you."

"Everything's great," I said, and winked, letting Officer Grant know it wasn't the time or place for that conversation.

"Ok, great. I'll be seeing you later, Pastor Zeke." He then waved at my mom and said, "Take care Mrs. Whitfield."

"Thank you, Sweetheart," my mother said with a smile, before mumbling under her breath, "Now he knows better than that."

"It's ok, Ma."

Miracle was still standing in the midst of everything going on, and said, "I'm confused. Is it Pastor Zeke, or Pastor Ezekiel?"

"Well, either one is fine. People actually call me both."

My mother, of course, interjected, and said, "All of his life until he got married, everyone called him Ezekiel. I made that a requirement when I named him because it has such a significant meaning, and with a strong name as such, you should never shorten it."

I looked at Miracle and said, "Please feel welcomed to call me Zeke."

She smiled and said, "No, I actually like Ezekiel. . . Or maybe I should clarify and say, I like name 'Ezekiel'."

I laughed, and said, "I knew what you meant."

My mom cut her eyes at me, which meant there were a million things going through her mind that she would probably be questioning me about later on. Beginning her questionnaire sooner than later, she quickly tried to get deeper into my Kool-Aid.

She asked Miracle, "So how did you find out about this church out of all of the churches in this city?"

"Ezekiel invited me!" she quickly and excitedly replied.

Drawing out her words in suspicion, she said, "Oh, ok. Well it sounds like we need to put together a dinner for all of us, and the two of you can tell me how you met."

"Mrs. Whitfield . . ." Miracle began before being interrupted by my mom.

"You can call me Faith."

I was shocked because my mom always made sure that Stormie called her Mrs. Whitfield. Even after we were married.

"Beautiful name, Faith. What I was going to say was it's nothing like that. We just ran into each other, and he invited me to church. We're not dating or anything, and I also think I heard you say he's married."

My mom said, "We can talk about all of that. I'm sure Ezekiel has your number, so we'll get back with you on a day and time for that dinner, ok, Doll?"

Realizing my mom wasn't going to take no for an answer, Miracle said, "Ok. Sure."

My mom kissed me on the cheek and hugged Miracle, telling her it was nice to finally meet her. That caught me completely off guard because she made it seem as if I had been talking to her about Miracle, which I hadn't.

I gave her a strange look and she just grinned, and said, "Ok, Baby, see you at home later. I have a few stops to make."

"Bye, Ma. Be careful," I said as I watched her walk towards the exit.

"So you and your wife live with your mom?" Miracle asked, looking around.

"You can stop looking. My wife isn't here today."

"Do you think she's going to mind me coming over for dinner? I'm practically a complete stranger."

"It'll be fine. I promise," I replied.

"Ok, well I better go. I have some work to catch up on this evening, and I want to get started early."

"Ok, I'll talk to you soon," I said as I gave her a hug.

As she walked away, I watched the curls in her hair bounce with every step that she took. I knew I shouldn't have been looking at her in that way, but I had to admit, my flesh was weak. I would've blamed it on vulnerability, but her beauty, conversation, interest in what I had to say, intelligence, and great style were all very attractive. I knew that I wouldn't be able to talk, and spend much time with her because I needed to keep everything completely professional. I was still a married man. My mom had made this harder than what it needed to be. She had never been so quick to invite a woman over, or anyone for that matter who she didn't know much about, but my mother had a great sense of discernment, so I assumed she felt it in her heart that maybe Miracle needed a good support system.

Chapter Thirty-Two

"**H**ey, Ma, I'm home," I said as I walked through the door, finally making it home from the church.

As I walked through the house, I could smell that my mom had already started dinner. I found her in the kitchen chopping up onions.

I gave her a kiss on the cheek and said, "Whatcha cookin'?"

"Just some fried chicken, greens, macaroni and cheese, candied yams, and some of my famous hot-water cornbread."

"Ma! Why are you cooking all of this food? It's just me and you, and you surely don't have to do all of this for me. You're going to make me have to spend even more time in the gym."

As she pulled the greens out of the fridge, getting ready to soak them, she said, "Now you know I have to make sure my baby eats good. You've been missing out over there with Stormie. Did she ever cook for you?"

"Yeah, she did every so often, but we went out a lot or just ordered in. It was no big deal."

I noticed the amount of greens my mom had pulled out, and I said, "Who's going to eat all of that? Do you have a friend coming over?"

"No, I don't, but I think you should," she said, grinning.

"Ma, absolutely not! I'm married!"

"Yes, you are married to a woman who is not thinking about you, and had the audacity to move on without even telling you. This is just an innocent dinner with a friend and your mom. I'm sure Stormie is doing a lot more than that. Miracle just seems like a sweet young lady. She also seems a little timid, and in need of a little direction. I can't wait to hear how the two of you met."

I mumbled under my breath, "I think you can definitely wait."

"What was that, Son?" she asked while she cleaned and picked the greens.

"Nothing, Ma."

"Ok, so what are you waiting for? Call her and invite her over. Tell her to be here around six."

I took a deep breath and went up to my room to get into something more comfortable. I thought about how my mom felt about Stormie from the very beginning. She disliked everything about her. The things that she saw, I couldn't see because I was too in love. She knew that Stormie had introduced me to the life of drugs and alcohol, and now here came Miracle, in and out of rehab for alcohol addiction. Not saying that I was looking to get into a relationship with Miracle, but I just didn't want my mom to be disappointed once again by me allowing someone like Miracle into our lives, even as just a friend.

After I finished changing clothes, I sat at the end of my bed, holding my cellphone, still contemplating on whether or not this was a good idea. I really didn't see the harm in it, but I didn't want to lead her to think that it was anything other than a friendly dinner that my mom had chosen to invite her to. With all of that going through my head, I took a deep breath, searched for her number in my contacts, and made the call.

The phone rang and rang until the voicemail picked up, which stated it was full.

"Well, maybe she'll see that I called and call back," I said to myself.

I went back downstairs with my mom and as soon as I entered the kitchen, she said, "Well?"

"Well what?" I replied.

"Boy, don't make me smack you with this spoon!" my mom said playfully as she held up her favorite wooden spoon that she'd probably had since before I was born.

I laughed and said, "I called, but she didn't answer, and I couldn't even leave a message because her voicemail was full. She did say she had a lot of work to catch up on this evening, so maybe she's just busy. We can do this another day."

My mom squinted her eyes at me and put her hands on her hips, and said, "I may not feel like cooking this big ole meal another day! So, Ezekiel, did you really call her?"

I threw my arms up and said, "Yeah, Ma. I promise I did. I wouldn't lie to you."

"Ok. Well, I guess the only other thing you can do is stop by there," she said, nonchalantly, as she mixed up the noodles and cheese, preparing to put it in the oven.

"Wait! Stop by where?"

"Her house. Where else? You have her address, right?"

I looked at her strangely, not knowing how she knew that information without me telling her.

"Son? Are you listening to me? You do have it, don't you?" she asked, nodding her head as if she was answering for me.

"Yeah, but how do you know that?"

"Ezekiel, I am your mother! Do you really think that I don't know you?"

"It wasn't like that, though. I didn't ask her for her address."

My mom licked some of the cheese from her finger, and said, "I'm sure you didn't, but you have it, so go. I'll see you in a little while."

I took a deep breath, and my mom revealed that smile that neither me, my dad, nor probably anyone else in the world could have possibly resisted.

I put on my shoes and said, "I'll be back soon."

"Ok. I'll see the two of you in a little bit. Be careful!" she yelled, as I walked out the door.

As I drove, heading to Miracle's house, I couldn't believe what I was doing. My mom hadn't put a gun up to my head, making me go to Miracle's house, but something inside of me was telling me I was doing the right thing.

I called Miracle two more times before I even got to her house. I didn't want to intrude on anything. I honestly didn't know what she may have had going on, but I was beginning to feel a little stalkerish. When I finally pulled up to her house, I saw only the white Porsche, which I had seen the night I'd driven her home, parked in the driveway. With that being said, it didn't look as if I may have been walking in on anything romantic. I just hoped she wouldn't lose it by me just showing up at her house.

As I walked to the door, I became extremely nervous because I didn't know how to expect for her to react. If it had been me on the other end, it might've been a little scary. I was praying she wouldn't feel that way. I didn't want to make her feel uncomfortable in any way, but I had never known my mom to steer me wrong. As I reached the top of her steps to her porch, I rang her doorbell and stood there for about a minute. I put my ear up to the door and didn't hear anything. I then grabbed my phone out of my pocket and tried calling again. What was strange was that I was able to hear her phone ringing inside of her house, but she still didn't answer, which caused me to worry. I rang the doorbell one more time, giving her a chance to get to the door just in case she needed time to get decent.

All of her shades were drawn, so I couldn't see any movement at all. I turned her doorknob and the door popped open. I really didn't want to just go inside without being invited. This would've been the second time, but I felt I had no choice . . . again.

"Miracle, are you here?" I said, hoping she would answer.

"It's me, Ezekiel. I'm just worried about you."

Still no answer from Miracle. As I walked through the house, nothing looked out of place on the main floor. I did see her cell phone lying on the kitchen counter, which could've been the reason she didn't hear it. I slowly headed up the stairs, not wanting to startle Miracle in case I ran into her. Once I got up the stairs, I walked down the hall and went into the first room I saw. I found Miracle lying there on her back with her arms sprawled across the bed, looking as if she had been in a fight and had gotten knocked out. Her laptop was lying next to her on the bed and there were papers that looked like they had been thrown all over the room. It looked like she might've started working on what she needed to get done, but was negatively triggered by something.

I put my ear near her face and could hear her breathing, and as I did that, I saw two empty bottles of alcohol lying on the side of the bed. I immediately began shaking Miracle's limp body.

"Miracle! Miracle, wake up!" I yelled, becoming more and more nervous.

I was now realizing just how serious Miracle's alcohol addiction was. I could see her finally coming to, and as soon as she opened her eyes and looked at me, she sat up, quickly hung her head over the bed, and vomited all over the floor. I quickly grabbed the trash can that sat in the corner of the room and put it next to the bed on the floor. I comforted her by gently rubbing her back as she continued to expel the poison from her body. It went on for about another ten minutes, and I was praying over her the entire time. I didn't want to have to call for an ambulance, or take her in for alcohol poisoning.

After the vomiting stopped, I hurriedly went and got her a glass of water, and when I came back, she was crying hysterically.

As I handed her the glass, I said, "Miracle, why are you crying?"

Sniffling, and struggling to get her words out, she said, "I'm so embarrassed. I've only known you for a few days and you've had to basically save my life twice because of the habit that I'll never be able to kick."

"Miracle, there's no reason for you to be embarrassed, and don't you say you'll never be able to kick this habit. Don't you know that life and death are in the power of the tongue? I decree right now that you will kick this habit in the butt in the name of Jesus. You already have the victory! Are you in agreement with me?"

Miracle nodded her head and took a sip of water.

"I need to hear you say it. Are you in agreement with me?" I repeated.

"Yes," she said with the little bit of strength that she had left.

"Ok. Well, it is already done," I said, with all of the faith inside of me.

21 "Death and life are in the power of the tongue: and they that love it shall eat the fruit thereof." – Proverbs 18:21 KJV

I knew Miracle could overcome this, but she had to believe she could, and she needed a good support system, which it seemed like she didn't have. She seemed to be alone. No parents, grandparents, or siblings. She hadn't mentioned any other family during the conversation we'd had a few days before. I wanted to help Miracle because I wanted great things for her. I could tell she was a good person. She just needed to know that there were people who cared about her. She needed to know that she wasn't alone.

"Finish your water. I'll go get you some more. I don't want you to get dehydrated."

She looked at me as if she hadn't experienced anyone showing so much care for her in a long time. When I came back, she had finished the water, and I handed her another glass. I also had a cool towel, and held it against her forehead.

"Miracle, we have to get this under control. I know we don't know each other well, but I don't want to see anything bad happen to you. I'd feel like I could've done something and didn't."

As she attempted to stand up, she stumbled, and said, "I'm not going back to rehab. It doesn't help. All they do is condemn me. I drink because it takes away the memories, not because it's just something I like to do."

"Sometimes it's best to talk about the things you're trying to forget so that you can fully heal. You can't even begin to heal if you're just suppressing those emotions. Do you want to talk about it?"

"No!" Miracle said aggressively.

"Ok. That's fine. Just know that I'm here if you do ever want to talk, but right now I would like for you to go with me back to my mom's house. I think you need to be around other people right now. I was actually trying to invite you to Sunday dinner with some coercion from my mom. We both would really like for you to join us. I know you're probably not feeling well enough to eat a whole lot, but you need something on your stomach. I'll drive you and bring you back home."

Miracle looked down at the mess she'd made on the floor.

"Don't worry about that. I'll get that cleaned up for you. Just tell me where the cleaning products are, and I got you. Go ahead and take a shower and take however long you need to get yourself together, and I'll be waiting."

Miracle told me where to find everything in the kitchen.

Before I walked out of her room to get them, she quietly said, "Ezekiel."

I turned around as I was exiting the doorway, and said, "Yes?"

"Thank you," she replied.

I smiled and said, "There's no need to thank me. This is part of the job description that God gave me."

While Miracle was in the shower, my mom called. I almost didn't answer, but I knew she'd worry and keep calling if I hadn't.

"Hey, Ma," I said.

"Ezekiel, was she home?"

"Yeah, she's here," I said, speaking as low as I could.

"What do you mean? You're still there?"

"Yeah, there was a situation."

"What kind of situation, and why do you sound like you're whispering?" she said, sounding as if she was getting more and more concerned by the second.

"There are some things you don't know about Miracle. She's had a rough childhood and some problems with alcohol. Let's just say I walked in right in time, and I owe it to you for making me come over here."

"Why didn't you tell me?" my mom asked.

"I know how you felt about Stormie, and I didn't want you to judge Miracle based on that."

"Ezekiel, now you know I don't judge anyone. I can just feel a person's spirit, and I know when it's not right. I knew Stormie's spirit wasn't right, but Miracle is different. I wouldn't have asked you to invite her over if I didn't feel how beautiful her spirit was. None of us are perfect and we all have fought our demons. Bring that girl over here. She needs some support."

"She's getting herself together right now and then we'll be there, but please don't tell her that I told you anything. Let her tell you if she wants you to know. I don't want to lose her trust already. We just met and I want her to know that she can confide in me."

"You have my word, Son."

"Thanks, Ma. I love you."

"I love you, too, my Ezekiel."

Chapter Thirty-Three

Miracle fidgeted in her seat the entire way to my mom's house. I tried to tell her that she had nothing to worry about, but she still felt like she wasn't herself. She would normally give herself more time to sober up, and she just didn't want to come across the wrong way. I cared not tell her that I'd partially told my mom what I'd walk in on. I kind of felt like telling her so that she could be comforted by the fact that my mom was more concerned with her and her well-being than trying to be judgmental towards her.

"Stop worrying," I said to Miracle, trying to calm her nerves a little bit.

"I can't," she said, sounding defeated. "I still feel like I smell like alcohol, my stomach is queasy, and I don't want to offend your mom by not really having an appetite. On top of that, I feel like I look a hot mess."

"Miracle, trust me. You don't smell like alcohol, and my mom isn't going to care if you don't eat a lot of your food. She's just going to make sure you leave with a plate to take home," I said laughing. I then hesitated before I said, "And I hope you don't take this the wrong way, but you look beautiful. You always do."

I looked over at her and she shyly turned her head towards the passenger side window. When we finally pulled up at my mom's house, Miracle began to panic.

"What's wrong now?" I asked.

"This is not right at all! I forgot about your wife. I can't go in there! What are you going to tell your wife? I'm sure she's here. Why would you bring me here as a married man? A pastor at that! What kind of game are you and your mom playing? I won't have any parts of it!"

I kept trying to interrupt Miracle as she hysterically asked question after question. I really wasn't ready to have the conversation with her about my wife, but I knew I would have to, especially if I didn't want her to think poorly of me.

When she finally stopped talking, she began breathing heavily.

"Miracle, listen. My wife is not here, and there are reasons for that. Unfortunate reasons. I just haven't had a chance to tell you. To be honest, I haven't talked to anyone about it, except my mom. I'll just start by saying we are separated right now, and not trying to put the blame on anyone, but it wasn't what I wanted."

"I'm so sorry. I shouldn't have assumed anything. I apologize for the things I said. Me of all people should never assume that other people don't go through things."

Miracle looked at me with pure sincerity and said, "I really hope things work out for you."

"Thank you. I appreciate that," I said, feeling the comfort in her words. "Now, let's get in this house before my mom comes out here and drags us in herself," I said laughing after the serious moment I'd just had with Miracle.

I got out and opened the passenger door for Miracle and we headed to the door. Before even opening the front door, I could smell the wonderful aroma of the meal my mom had prepared. It reminded me of the good ole days when my dad was around. My mom would make meals like that at least a few times a week.

Miracle and I walked in, and she immediately said, "Oh my goodness it smells so good! I may have an appetite after all!"

As my mom came down the hall, with joy in her voice she said, "Is that my baby and his guest? I hope y'all are ready to eat because I have been slaving over this stove all day!"

"Hi, Mrs. Whitfield. Dinner smells delicious!" Miracle said as soon as she saw my mom.

My mom immediately grabbed Miracle and hugged her. As she held her tight, she said, "I told you to call me Faith."

"Oh, yeah, I'm sorry. I'm just not used to calling my elders by their first name."

"I understand. That lets me know that you were raised to have good manners and that's a wonderful thing."

My mom then hugged me and said, "The two of you can go wash your hands and have a seat at the table. I was just finishing up putting everything on the table, buffet style. You know how we do!" my mom said, smiling and nudging me with her elbow.

I showed Miracle to the bathroom, and I ran upstairs to wash my hands in the other bathroom. By the time I made it back down, Miracle and my mom were already at the table, talking, laughing, and filling up their plates.

"Y'all started without me, I see!"

"You took too long!" Miracle said, laughing.

"We did wait for you to come bless the food, though!" my mom said, nodding, letting me know to get the show on the road.

I sat at the head of the table, which was where my dad used to sit, and my mom reached for my hand before I began the prayer. I then looked over at Miracle and reached my other hand towards her. She quickly grabbed it and bowed her head.

I began, "Heavenly Father, thank you for this meal in which we're about to receive. Thank you for causing it to be strength and nourishment for our bodies, and for blessing us with my mom and her skills in the kitchen. We also thank you for blessing us with our very special guest, Miracle, this evening, and to be able to share our love and comfort amongst one another. Last, but not least, we thank you for allowing us to be able to enjoy many more of these delectable meals in the future with the honor of being in your presence. In Jesus' mighty name, I pray, Amen."

My mom and Miracle said, "Amen" simultaneously.

Miracle took a deep breath as she looked over all of the options, and said, "Wow, I haven't had a meal like this in so long."

"You don't cook?" my mom asked, curiously.

The entire time, I'm thinking, *"Here we go."*

"I have to be honest and say that I don't cook often, but I do cook very well. I just don't like cooking only for myself. One day, I hope to have a family that I can share the skills that my mom and grandma passed along to me before they passed away."

Sounding as if she experienced a sense of relief as she filled her plate with greens, mac and cheese, candied yams, and fried chicken, my mom replied, "I'm sure you will."

As we enjoyed dinner and had great conversation, I noticed that Miracle had eaten two full plates. I wasn't trying to put her on the spot, but I guess I had.

"I thought you didn't have much of an appetite, Miracle," I said, grinning.

Miracle began blushing, and said, "I thought I didn't either, but it miraculously came back when I saw all this delicious food! You really did a great job, Faith."

"Thank you, Miracle. You are so sweet."

Miracle looked like she was about to say something, and she suddenly cleared her throat.

"Is there something you want to say, Miracle?" my mom asked, looking concerned.

"Well, I like to be honest with people, and there's no exception with you. Ezekiel already knows, but I have a really bad drinking problem. I'm actually a functioning alcoholic and have tried everything to quit. I've been going back and forth about telling you the entire time we've been sitting at the table. I just don't want to be judged, and didn't want to ruin this fantastic dinner. I've been through a lot, and that's still no excuse, but I just don't like people to look at me a certain way because I suffer from an addiction."

"Miracle, I wouldn't judge you. I like to help people. Judging them is not going to help them, but some people don't want other's help, so I just step back and let them deal with what they're dealing with on their own. Isn't that right, Ezekiel?"

"That's right, Ma. Miracle, you're not the only one who has dealt with a bout of addiction. So did I."

Miracle's eyes became big as saucers. "You? What were you addicted to, if you don't mind me asking?"

"Cocaine, heroin, alcohol . . . Basically anything that would give me that feeling of intoxication to the point of feeling invincible and like I was floating on clouds."

"I left him alone, but I never stopped praying for him and his wife," my mom added.

"Your wife was an addict, too?" Miracle asked, sounding extremely surprised.

"Yes. We met in college, and she got me hooked. We were both out there, but I know it was my mom's prayers that pulled me back out of that lifestyle."

"Miracle, you said you've tried everything. Have you tried praying about it? And I'm not talking about a few times. I mean consistently," my mom asked.

Miracle fidgeted a little before answering, and said, "I've prayed, and I do pray, but I have to honestly say, I'm not consistent."

"What triggers you to drink?" my mom asked.

I was hoping she wasn't digging too deep and making Miracle feel uncomfortable, but my mom had a way of talking to people, and most of the time, they seemed comfortable talking to her.

"Most of the time, it's when I'm alone, day after day, with no one to talk to or just hang out with. The loneliness gets to me. I have no family, and really no friends. It gets me down a lot, so in order to forget that I'm so lonely, and to be able to function normally in the world, I drink. As you probably already imagine, I drink every day. The times I've been in rehab, once I got out, I've been able to stay clean for thirty days at the most, and the loneliness starts to hit me again."

"What if you had people to keep you company? Not people in a rehab facility. I'm talking about actual people who you can enjoy real life with to keep you from being so lonely and resorting to the alcohol."

I sat back in my seat and folded my arms. I looked at my mom with confusion all over my face, waiting to see where she was going with this conversation.

"I think you lost me, Faith," Miracle said, looking just as confused as I did.

"I mean, why don't you come stay with me. I know you don't know me very well, but you didn't know those people in the rehab centers either. We can do things together, like cooking, shopping, watching movies, and maybe even bring out some of those old board games that we used to play when Ezekiel was a kid. We'd do those things outside of your working hours, of course. Ezekiel already shared with me that you work from home."

"Faith, that is really sweet of you, and it really sounds great, but I couldn't impose on you like that. You don't even know me."

"You won't be imposing on me, and I know enough about you. Shoot, I'm lonely, too! Having some company around here might do me some good, even though my precious son is here with me for now. I don't know how long that may last. I know he likes his privacy. Who wants to be living with their mother at his age?" she laughed.

"So are you kicking me out now," I asked my mom jokingly.

"Of course not. I told you that you can stay as long as you need to, and I mean that. There's enough space here for all of us to enjoy."

"Well . . ." Miracle said.

"You don't have to decide now. I just feel in my heart that an arrangement like that would help you tremendously. Your being in your home all alone without someone to talk to, and liquor probably in every room . . . No judgement . . . will never let you get over this and become the best possible version of yourself. You're already a wonderful person. I can tell. Just imagine the things you could do without this addiction weighing you down."

There was complete silence at the table. I was not expecting this conversation at all, and I definitely knew Miracle wasn't. My mom didn't know about Miracle's addiction until tonight, so I completely trusted and believed that she was being led by the Spirit and doing what God told her to do. The ball was now in Miracle's court.

After the moment of silence that seemed to last at least five uncomfortable minutes, Miracle said, "Ok."

"Ok, what?" my mom asked.

"Ok, I'll do it. Both of you seem like good people, and I believe you genuinely have my best interest at heart. For you to invite a complete stranger into your home to live with you until who knows when lets me know that you truly care about people. You believe in me, and that's what I need right now."

[13] "I can do all things through Christ which strengtheneth me." – Philippians 4:13 KJV

My mom got up and stood behind Miracle's chair and gave her a hug around the neck.

"I am so glad you're agreeing to this. You won't regret it. We're going to have ourselves a good time."

Miracle helped my mom clean up the table and wash the dishes before I took her back home.

When they got done and we got ready to leave, my mom said, "Ok, so you'll be here tomorrow afternoon when your shift ends, right?"

"Yep. I'll see you then, and thanks again. I really appreciate this and feel good about it."

My mom hugged Miracle like she was her own daughter, and said, "I'm glad you do. I feel good about it, too."

On the way back to Miracle's house, I saw a joy in her eyes that I had yet to see. I believed that she was really looking forward to spending time with my mom, and I was sure my mom would make her feel as comfortable as possible.

Just to be on the safe side and make sure Miracle wasn't just trying to appease my mom, I asked, "Miracle, are you sure this is what you want to do?"

She looked over at me and said, "I'm positive. Why? Do you not think it's a good idea? Do you not want me to?"

"I feel like it is a good idea, and I put a lot of trust in my mom because she has never ever steered me wrong. I just want to make sure it's what you want to do, and you don't feel like you're being forced, or just don't want to hurt my mom's feelings."

"Ezekiel, trust me when I say, I never do anything I don't want to do. If I didn't want to come to church today, I wouldn't have come. I'm good. Don't worry about me."

"Ok," I said, as I smiled, and we continued on our way back to Miracle's house.

Miracle

Chapter Thirty-Four

After spending the previous evening with Ezekiel and Faith, I did a lot of thinking about my life. I had basically gone into seclusion from the world, outside of my best friends, Tequila, Hennessy, and Vodka. As you can see, I didn't discriminate, and it seemed that they always gave me what I wanted, and that was a peaceful mind. I hadn't really thought about the fact that the peace that I would seem to find in them was only temporary, which was why I had to continue indulging in them once that temporary peace wore off.

Ezekiel and his mom were the only people that I'd had a real conversation with in a very long time, and it felt good. Their spirits felt so sweet and comforting. I needed that comforting feeling in my life. Just knowing that I'd have genuine people there for me whenever I needed them gave me a sense of security, and made me feel like I could really potentially kick my habit.

As I worked, during my last day living in my home for a while, I would take random breaks throughout the day, packing up some of my necessities. I found myself repeatedly going to my liquor cabinet, opening it with intentions of taking every bottle out and pouring them down the kitchen drain. Each time, I just stared in awe of the amount of liquor one person could have stored away, and then would close the cabinet. I was finally facing the reality of how much of a problem I truly had. I had been using the trauma of losing my parents as an excuse for way too long, and I had never talked to anyone in full detail about them besides my grandmother, who'd also passed. I'd have to eventually stop using that as an excuse because all that did was help convince myself that I had a valid reason for doing the things that I did.

Just as I was almost done packing up my work equipment that I would most definitely need while I was away, my doorbell rang.

When I got to the door, I peeked through one of the side glass panels and saw that it was Ezekiel. He had told me that he would come by to help load up my car, and that I could put some things in his car If I needed to.

I opened the door and said, "Hey, Ezekiel!" as I gave him a hug.

"Hey, Miracle. How's everything going?"

I looked around and said, "Well, I think I'm about done, but I need help with something."

Looking confused, Ezekiel said, "I told you to just let me know if you needed help with anything."

"Ok, follow me," I said, gesturing for Ezekiel to follow me towards the hallway leading to the kitchen.

We stopped at the liquor cabinet, and when I opened it, Ezekiel's jaw almost hit the floor.

"Is this all yours?"

Before I could say anything, Ezekiel continued, and said, "I know that was a dumb question, and please don't think I'm being judgmental at all. I just wasn't expecting this."

"I would never think that you're being judgmental," I said. "I'm actually really embarrassed."

"Don't be embarrassed. Just let me know what you want me to do, and I'll do it," Ezekiel replied.

"Well, I've been trying all day to pull all of this crap out and get rid of it, but I can't bring myself to do it. I know it's a mind thing, but it's been getting the best of me."

"Let me ask you this, Miracle. Do you plan on coming back to all of this after working extremely hard to leave it behind?"

"Of course, not. I don't plan to."

Ezekiel said, "Well, if it's gone, you would have to go and re-up on your supply, and if you do that, obviously it was all in vain, and I don't see you as a person who does anything in vain."

I took a deep breath and said, "You're right. It's time for me to move forward. There's nothing in the past that I need to go back to."

I began grabbing a couple of bottles out of the cabinet at a time, and Ezekiel began doing the same. We poured each one out into the kitchen sink, and the crazy thing was, I felt a boost of strength go through my body each time a bottle was emptied. I actually felt like I was taking my life back this time around.

After we finished, Ezekiel asked, "How do you feel?"

"I actually feel like a weight has been lifted off of my shoulders, but ask me tomorrow," I laughed.

"Well, just expect great things. We're going to agree that you won't even desire to have a drink."

"I'm in agreement with you, Sir."

Ezekiel put his fist up and we gave each other a dap. Ezekiel was the coolest, most down to earth pastor I'd ever met. I still didn't know what had happened between him and his wife, but unless he was putting on a façade for me, she had let go of a good one.

"You don't have much luggage," Ezekiel said, as he looked down at the bags I'd packed.

"Well, I work from home, and I don't need all the fancy things that are in my closet. Most days I just wear leggings and a t-shirt. I just like to be comfortable. Don't get me wrong, I do have some things to wear to just go outside and have a good, innocent time with your mom. If I need anything else, I can always stop by and get it. Your mom sounds like she's been waiting to have someone to do some exciting, fun things with for a while now," I laughed.

"Yeah, my mom is a lot of fun. She and my dad used to have a lot of fun together. People just liked being around them. She's been missing that for a long time."

"Well, I'll take good care of her while she takes care of me."

"I'm sure. I can see the two of you getting along very well."

As we carried my things outside, Ezekiel grabbed one of my white shoe boxes, and said, "This is pretty light. Are there any shoes in there?" he asked, as he vigorously shook the box.

"No, but be careful. There are some very important documents in there."

"I don't like to be responsible for very important anything, so here you go," Ezekiel said, handing me the box as he laughed, showing his bright white smile.

Before I locked up my house, Ezekiel grabbed the two large trash bags full of empty liquor bottles. Before he got into his car so that I could trail him home, he threw them in my recycling container.

He then walked over with me to my car, opened the door, made sure I was safely inside, and said, "See you at home!"

"That sounds so crazy," I said giggling.

I wondered what my mom and dad would've thought about all of this. Hopefully they would've been proud of the decision I was making. As I trailed Ezekiel to his mom's house, I began thinking deeply about why things happen when they do, and why certain people are put into our lives at certain times. I would've never imagined in a million years that I would've been doing what I was about to do, but I guess as a kid, I never thought that I'd be an alcoholic either. God always has a plan for us, and I was curious as to what He had concocted for me and my life. Whatever it was had to have been great because He had definitely connected me with some awesome individuals. Ezekiel and Faith.

Chapter Thirty-Five

As Ezekiel and I pulled up in front of his mom's house, he put his arm outside the window and waved for me to park in the driveway. He parked on the side of me, and we both got out.

Are you sure this is ok?" I asked.

Looking confused, Ezekiel said, "Is what ok?"

"Parking in the driveway. I can park on the street. It's no problem."

"No, you're good," Ezekiel said. "My mom wouldn't have it any other way!"

Just as he said that, Faith came to the front door and said, "Finally! I was wondering what was taking so long! I thought I was about to have to come and look for y'all!"

I gave Faith a hug, and said, "No, we just had to get rid of some things."

Looking pleased, Faith said, "Ohhhh. I know what that means. Good for you."

"I just have to thank you again for this," I said.

"For what?"

"For caring. I haven't had anyone to genuinely care about me in a long time. I appreciate it and I'll probably say, 'thank you' a thousand more times before the end of all of this."

"You don't have to say 'thank you' anymore. I'm just doing what God put in my spirit to do. You are only one of my many assignments. I'm not going anywhere anytime soon, so I know I'll have plenty more, and who knows . . . I just may be one of your assignments!"

"Faith, I doubt that. You have such a beautiful spirit already. I can't think of one way that I could possibly help make you any better than what you already are."

Faith began blushing and said, "You are so sweet! See, I might need some of that to rub off on me. I can be a little rough around the edges sometimes, but I have calmed down over the years."

"Yes, she has!" Ezekiel interjected, as he came in carrying two handfuls of luggage.

"Now, you weren't supposed to agree, Son!" Faith giggled.

Faith had a couple of rooms for me to choose from. They were both very nice and spacious. A lot more than what I was expecting. I was very low maintenance and didn't need much. Both rooms had a walk in closet and bathroom. I ended up choosing the room furthest down the hall away from Faith and Ezekiel's rooms, which were right across the hall from each other. I didn't want to disturb them in case I needed to leave the room in the middle of the night for a glass of water or something.

As soon as I finished putting my things away, Faith knocked on my new bedroom door.

"Miracle, I have the leftovers all heated up if you're ready to have dinner."

"I'll be down in a minute. Thanks!"

I took a moment to look around the room to make sure everything was in place and then headed down the hallway. I had never seen so many pictures hanging on walls. There were lots of pictures of Ezekiel as a baby and young boy. He hadn't changed much at all. I then noticed a picture of him, his mom, and who must've been his dad. They all looked so happy. Ezekiel resembled his dad a lot. I figured that's why his dad looked so familiar to me when I saw him in the picture. I wished that I had been able to meet him. Just by knowing Ezekiel and Faith, I knew his dad had to have been awesome.

"It smells good down here!" I said, as I stepped down off of the final step.

Ezekiel was already sitting at the table eating.

"Sorry, we thought you might not be coming. I already said the prayer," Ezekiel said.

"No, I was just admiring all of the pictures on the walls. They made my heart happy. You have a beautiful family. I wish I could've known Mr. Whitfield," I said, as I sat and fixed my plate.

"Trust me. He would've loved you!" Faith said.

"She's not lying," Ezekiel chimed in before stuffing his mouth with a forkful of collard greens.

"That's so nice of you all to say," I said, as I bowed my head and said a silent prayer.

When I lifted my head back up, Faith and Ezekiel simultaneously said, "Amen."

One thing I could count on with Ezekiel and Faith was a good conversation. She talked about her teaching career and how it didn't pay a lot, but she loved being around the kids. Ezekiel talked about the life of an electrical engineer, which didn't sound very interesting to me, but that's why we're all different and are interested in different things. He didn't seem the least bit excited about the mortgage field either. After discussing careers, Faith brought up Kyle, who I had already gathered was Ezekiel's childhood best friend.

"Have you spoken with Kyle lately?" Faith asked Ezekiel.

"I talk to him every so often. You know he's in love again, so whenever that happens, I don't hear from him often."

Faith laughed and said, "Who is she this time?"

"Madison," Ezekiel replied.

"Madison again?!" Faith exclaimed.

"It seems like no matter how many women he dates, he always ends up back with Madison after all these years. That should tell him something. I think Madison is the one for him, but who am I to tell someone who their person is when I was wrong about mine?" Ezekiel said, sounding disappointed.

"I tried to tell you, but anyway, Miracle, Kyle was . . . well, still is Ezekiel's best friend. They went to college together in California and everything."

"That's so exciting! I wish I'd had the opportunity to go away to school. I just went to a community college."

Ezekiel quickly said, "Don't downplay what you did. After all you went through, you made a life for yourself, and going off to school can be a little overrated, especially for nerds like me."

"Nerd?" I said, surprisingly.

"Yeah, nerd. How can I say this. Ummm, I didn't have the most swag in the world. That was Kyle. We kind of balanced each other out for the most part. I kept him out of a lot of trouble, but he saved me a couple of times, too."

"Yeah, that's where Ezekiel met his wife, and Kyle just couldn't seem to save him from her!" Faith said, shaking her head.

"Ma!"

Faith took a sip of her water and said, "Sorry, but it is what it is."

That topic seemed to feel a little uncomfortable, so I said, "Well, the food seemed even more delicious today than yesterday. I'll be honored if you let me fix you guys something tomorrow."

Faith said, "That sounds nice, but you have to work."

"That's the nice thing about working from home. I can multi-task. It'll be fine. Maybe I can make one of my famous lasagnas."

"Perfect," Faith said. "And speaking of working from home, I wouldn't want you to have to be cooped up in that room with your work all day. Do you need some office space?"

"Not really. I have my laptop that I typically sit at my desk with, but I can really work with it anywhere."

"Ok. If you need anything, let me or Ezekiel know. He'll be at work in the morning, but I'll be here."

"Thank you, Faith. I'm going to head to bed. It has seemed like a long day, and I probably need to go to sleep before my body realizes it's not getting any of its usual beverages tonight."

Faith stood up and gave me a hug. As she was holding me, she said, "Everything is going to be ok. Trust me. God got you!"

Ezekiel then stood up and hugged me. "If you need anything, just holler. We'll be right down the hall. You might hear me super early in the morning, praying, so don't mind me. I have to bust down the demons before they have a chance to put their plans into play."

"That's right! My baby is a praying man. I named him Ezekiel because it means 'strength of God'. This is one strong man right here. I couldn't imagine my life without him."

Ezekiel said, "You won't even have to worry about that, Ma."

Before heading to my room, I tried to help Faith with the dishes, and she insisted that I just get some rest. I just felt bad living under someone else's roof and not helping out as much as possible. They had made things so comfortable for me.

I went to my room, showered, and lied in bed watching television until I dozed off. Not too long after that, Faith and Ezekiel were in my room trying to restrain me from both sides of the bed. I could feel tears pouring from my eyes, and hear myself screaming, but I couldn't stop it.

"Miracle! It's just us. Calm down," Ezekiel said.

"It's ok. We're here. You're ok," I heard Faith's sweet voice say.

I finally calmed down, and my breathing began to slow down. Ezekiel slowly sat me up in the bed and asked if I was ok.

I looked at them both as they looked at me with extremely concerned looks on their faces.

"I'm so sorry. This is one of the reasons I drank. I try to keep the memories away. The alcohol suppresses those memories, especially during my sleep. Other than that, I have nightmares."

"Have you tried anything else to help you relax and get a good night's sleep?" Faith asked.

"No, I haven't."

"I'll be right back," she said.

While Faith was gone, Ezekiel sat on the edge of the bed and said, "Whatever you experienced must have been very traumatic. I know you don't want to talk about it, just like I don't like to talk about when I lost my dad, but whenever you're ready, let me know. We may be able to help each other."

"Thank you, Ezekiel, but I just want to move forward."

Faith then walked in with a glass of water and a pill in her hand.

"Ezekiel, don't pressure her to talk about it. When she's ready, if she's ever ready, she will. She may not ever want to, and that's fine, too," Faith said.

"Understood," Ezekiel replied.

"Here you go, Baby," Faith said as she handed me the pill.

"What is it?"

"It's just a supplement that I take to relax my mind. Magnesium Glycinate. It works miracles."

"I definitely need that right about now," I said as I put the pill in my mouth and washed it down with water.

"I'm so sorry. I didn't mean to wake you guys."

"It's ok. I'll bring some more of those that you can keep in here with you. Let's see how the rest of the night goes, and if it works, try taking one every night before bed. Just remember, we're here for you, and will never judge you. Also, never think of yourself as a burden."

As the weeks went by, I can say that my desire to have a drink became less and less, and although I did experience a lot of discomfort, my withdrawal symptoms weren't as severe as I feared they'd be. I also didn't have many other nights where I woke up in a panic from a nightmare that I'd had like the first night of staying at Faith's house. I was beginning to feel more and more at peace without needing something to temporarily erase my memories. Most of that credit went to Faith. She was always able to plan something to keep my mind occupied when I wasn't working. Sometimes it would just be me and her, and other times, when Ezekiel wasn't busy, he would tag along.

Faith and I became almost inseparable. She reminded me of what it was like to have a mother. She treated me no differently than she would've probably treated her own daughter if she'd had one. We would pray together, cook together, go on shopping dates, to the movies, to dinner, bowling, and she even got me to go golfing with her, which I never saw myself doing. Most of the things we did, she hadn't done in years because they were things that she and her husband did together, and it had been hard, even after all of those years for her to go back to doing them.

We talked about everything except our traumas. She didn't ask about my parents, and I didn't ask about her husband. I figured if the time would come for us to talk about those things, we would know it without any doubts, and feel comfortable doing so. I knew that I was going to have to eventually release it, but I felt as though I was just getting back on track and didn't feel that I had yet become strong enough to talk about it without regressing back to my old ways. I never wanted Faith and Ezekiel to feel as though all of the effort that they had been, and were still putting into me was in vain, and I vowed to myself that they would never have to worry about that. I had been blessed. God had sent angels into my life, and I appreciated it more than anyone could've ever imagined.

Ezekiel

Chapter Thirty-Six

Five months had passed since I'd last been in the home that I shared with Stormie, and of course, I still thought about her and even missed her, but I never believed that God made mistakes, and there was nothing different about this situation. I trusted Him and trusted the plans and the path that He had made specifically for my life. Knowing God and who I was in Him helped to alleviate a lot of the pain that I could've experienced during the entire ordeal. I didn't understand how people could get through things, such as, a divorce without having a relationship with God. I'm not going to say it was easy, even with God by my side, but I knew that it could've been a whole lot worse.

I even believed that God bringing Miracle into our lives at the time that He had was no mistake. Whenever I would begin to feel a little down, especially during my workday, as soon as I would walk into my mom's house and see Miracle laughing and smiling with my mom, it was like a breath of fresh air. I felt nothing but joy and happiness come from her spirit. Even though she had gone through some things in life, as we all had, she had made the best of it. She didn't know how much I appreciated her, and how much of a difference she had made in some of my worst days.

One Saturday morning, I got up and Miracle was in the kitchen cooking breakfast in her light pink robe and pink, fluffy house shoes. Most women would try to doll themselves up when they knew a man was in the house, but not Miracle. She was real. However she woke up, that's how she came downstairs in the morning. No make-up with her curly hair all over her head. Even a blind man could see that she was a very attractive woman, but the effort that she was putting into bettering herself from the inside made her even more attractive.

"Good morning! It smells great down here," I said.

"Why thank you!" Miracle replied. She then turned away from the stove and looked at me.

"You're up and dressed early for a Saturday," she said.

"Yeah, I have a meeting with my attorney. He's going on vacation for a few days and there are some things he wanted to get out of the way regarding my divorce so there won't be any delays."

"Oh, ok. That makes sense," Miracle said, looking as if she wanted to say something else.

As she turned back around, tending to the delicious smelling food on the stove, I said, "Is something wrong?"

Miracle turned back around, took a deep breath, and folded her arms.

"It's just that you never say anything about her. Neither you nor your mom will even say her name out loud. I've been here a while now and still don't know her name. I just don't like to say anything because I know I'm just a guest here and don't want to overstep my boundaries."

I realized that what Miracle had said was the truth. I didn't like talking about Stormie because of the fact that what she had taken me through had been so painful. I knew that keeping things inside wasn't healthy, but to be honest, I didn't even like saying her name. The only person I really talked to about her was my attorney, and that was because I had to. As far as my congregation knew, one Sunday, she just didn't show up anymore. No one asked any questions, and I was ok with that because I wasn't quite sure as to how I would've answered. That fear was something that I would have to work on. I was sure that there had been chitter chatter and gossip about what happened between me and Stormie, but whatever was being said, never came from me. I was sure that when the time had finally come when I felt that I needed to address it, God would give me exactly the right words.

"Stormie," I said, as I stood there in front of Miracle.

Looking and sounding confused, she said, "Stormie?"

I was puzzled as to why Miracle seemed so bothered by what I'd said.

"Is everything, ok?" I asked.

Hesitantly, she asked, "Her maiden name wouldn't happen to be Summers, would it?"

Becoming even more curious, I said, "Yeah, how do you know that?"

Miracle began nervously moving around the kitchen as she attempted to get the plates to set the table. She had the stove on as she walked away from it, and I quickly turned it off.

"Miracle, please tell me what's going on."

Miracle still wouldn't say anything. She just continued to frantically set the table.

I finally grabbed her and said, "Miracle, sit down for a minute. I need for you to talk to me. Did Stormie do something to you?"

Miracle took a deep breath and said, "My mom and dad fostered her for a short time."

I looked at Miracle strangely because Stormie had told me how cruel her foster parents had been to her. Even how some of the foster dads had molested her.

Before I knew it, without asking any other questions, I'd jumped to conclusions and angrily asked Miracle, "What did your dad do to her?"

Tears immediately began streaming down Miracle's face and she shouted, "Don't you ever say anything about my dad! You didn't know him! You aren't the only one who had wonderful parents! My mom or dad would've never done anything to Stormie. They wanted to give her a great life, but she didn't know how to accept pure, genuine kindness! She turned it into some sort of perversion. She was already too damaged to accept the type of love my family was willing to give her!"

I immediately regretted what I had said without knowing the full story.

"I'm so sorry, Miracle," I said as I hugged her.

"What is going on down here?" my mom said, as she quickly came walking down the stairs.

Miracle was still crying in my arms, and my mom was staring at me with her arms folded, and with her eyes, she silently asked me what I had done to Miracle.

She began gently rubbing Miracle on the back, comforting and reassuring her that everything was going to be ok.

"Ma, can you get her some Kleenex?" I said.

She nodded her head and told Miracle she'd be right back.

By the time she got back with the entire box of Kleenex, Miracle had calmed down. My mom handed her the box, and as Miracle wiped her tears, she apologized to us.

"Miracle, you do not need to apologize," I said. "That was my fault."

My mom sat at the table and said, "Can someone tell me what's going on?"

Miracle and I looked at each other and she nodded her head. I told my mom about the conversation Miracle and I had before she had broken down. Miracle then continued to tell us both about her experience with Stormie.

"My mom and dad were foster parents for many kids while I was growing up. They had begun before I was even born because my mom was told that she would never be able to have children. They both loved kids so much that they just loved having them around. All ages. It didn't matter to them. My mom miraculously became pregnant with me. The doctors never knew how it happened, but I'm here. That's how I got my name. They still continued to foster kids, and when I was twelve, Stormie came along. She was a year older than me. When she first arrived, she seemed angry inside. I would hear the caseworkers talking to my parents about all she had gone through, but they were up for the challenge. She had been molested by several of her foster dads. Some of the moms even knew and did nothing, but my parents were great to her," she said, as she looked straight at me, making sure that she made that very clear.

She continued, "They treated her like their own, just as they did every child. I think she had begun to think kindness meant that she had to have sex with the men. She liked my mom, but she became very clingy and attached to my dad. We all noticed the way she would look at him and seemed to always try to impress him. Whenever my dad and I would spend time together, or have a special daddy/daughter moment, she would become noticeably jealous. She was never mean to me, but I would always have this strange feeling in my stomach when she was around. When I got older, I realized that was my intuition. I knew deep down something wasn't right.

One night, we were all in bed, except my dad. He would stay downstairs in the den a lot of nights until late, reading a book, or watching television. He didn't like disturbing my mom because she was a light sleeper. This particular night, he fell asleep. Stormie and I shared a bedroom. I heard her when she got out of bed and crept out of the room. I figured she was going to the bathroom, but it took a while for her to come back. I quietly got out of the bed and tiptoed out of my room down the hall. I walked past the bathroom and Stormie wasn't in there, so I decided to check downstairs.

As I tried to walk down the stairs without making them creek, I heard my dad yell, "What the hell are you doing, Stormie?"

I then quickly ran down the rest of the stairs and my mom came right behind me.

When we made it to the den, Stormie was standing there naked, with her nightgown lying on the floor.

"What's going on?" my mom yelled.

Stormie grabbed her gown off of the floor and tried to quickly put it on.

"Why don't you have clothes on, Stormie?" my mom asked.

That's when all the lies began.

"Gavin loves me! He told me to meet him down here. I just wanted to show him that I love him, too!"

My dad said, "Stormie, stop lying! You came down here while I was asleep. You're nothing but a child! I would never!" He stood up, grabbed me and my mom, and told Stormie, "You have to go!"

A lightbulb suddenly went off in my head when Miracle said her Dad's name. I remembered the time when Stormie had told me about the couple, Gavin and Mena. She told me that I had made her feel rejected like Gavin had. She told me a little bit about them, but not much. Things were starting to make sense, except the fact that Stormie had told me their daughter's name was Coco.

"Who is Coco?" I asked.

Miracle lowered her brows and asked, "Where did you hear that name?"

"Stormie told me about your parents years ago, but she just told me that your dad didn't want her around and they sent her back to the orphanage. She told me that their daughter's name was Coco."

"That was me. My parents called me that for as long as I could remember, as a term of endearment, but after they died, I just became Miracle again. Hearing people call me Coco always reminded me too much of them."

"I'm sorry," I said, regretting bringing it up.

"It's ok. You didn't know," Miracle replied. She then continued with the story.

"I had never seen my parents so angry. They were more so hurt that she would do something like that after treating her just like a daughter. The next morning, my parents immediately called Stormie's caseworker and told her what happened. They requested that Stormie be removed from our home asap. My mom personally packed up her stuff and she was picked up that same day. That was the last we saw of Stormie, and my parents weren't sure if they would ever foster again. They died before they were ever able to make that decision."

"Wow, Miracle. I am so sorry you and your parents had to endure that. That girl really has some problems, but I had no idea of how deep they were," my mom said.

"I'm sorry, too, Miracle. The more I find out about Stormie, the more I wonder why we crossed paths and how I managed to fall in love with her," I said.

My mom said, "Ezekiel, you have to trust and believe that the two of you crossed paths for a reason. There's no telling where she might've ended up if she hadn't met you. She was part of your assignment. We can't question God's motives, but you already know that. Everything I'm telling you right now is nothing you don't already know."

"Your mom is right, Ezekiel. I'm sure there were quite a few things you learned in your marriage through the good times and the bad times. Don't let that period of time be in vain. We live and we learn, and we have to go through things in order to get through things. Once we get through those things, we can finally be in the place that God has prepared us for."

"Someone has definitely been listening to my sermons!" I laughed.

I was extremely proud of Miracle and her positivity. I could definitely say that morning started off quite emotional for Miracle, me, and my mom, but it put a lot of things into perspective. My divorce hadn't been finalized because we had been going back and forth through our lawyers. We refused to be in each other's presence throughout the entire process, however, we couldn't agree on a decision regarding the house. We had both put money into it, but I felt that since she had been the one that had been unfaithful, I should've been able to keep the house, or we should've been able to sell it and both get half of the proceeds. Stormie felt as if she was entitled to keep the house since she was still living there and paying the mortgage. I kept fighting her on that, but after hearing Miracle's story, I left the house that day, went to my attorney's office and told him to give it to her. He asked me was I sure, and I told him I was positive. It was time for me to completely let go. I didn't need that house or any of the memories it held. I needed a fresh start with a new home to make beautiful, new memories whenever it was time.

My attorney had me to sign a few things and said everything would be processed asap. He also said as long as Stormie agreed with everything, and he couldn't see why she wouldn't, the divorce would be finalized within a couple of weeks. As angry as I had been with how things turned out, the thought of being divorced from Stormie was bittersweet. I loved Stormie unconditionally. She was my first love and would always be that. When we first separated, I felt like I would never love again, but now, I knew someday I would, and I just prayed to God that whoever she was would be the one that I was meant to spend the rest of my life with.

Chapter Thirty-Seven

A couple of months passed, and my life was finally feeling like it was getting back on track. Just as my attorney had said, my divorce was finalized right after I said Stormie could have the house. We were able to quickly and painlessly get my name removed, and after all of that was settled, I felt as if so much had been lifted off of me. I had been feeling like I couldn't move on, and honestly felt guilty for even thinking about moving on with my life because I was still legally married. With everything Stormie had put me through, I still had this crazy idea that I still owed her something. I really hadn't gotten the closure that I needed, but after seeing all of the paperwork signed, things became very surreal. Even though my divorce was final, officially closing that chapter of my book, it still had taken a couple of months for me to completely accept it. Until then, I hadn't told a soul.

After I was finally able to talk about it without it hurting so bad, I told my mom. By talking about it, I had finally gained the courage to speak with my congregation about Stormie and I not being equally yoked, and unable to reconcile our differences. They looked as if they didn't know whether to rejoice or feel sorry for me. I knew most of them wanted to rejoice, but they knew that would've probably been a bit inappropriate. They didn't know the full circumstances behind our divorce, and I didn't want to get too personal with it. I knew that I had built a great foundation and relationship with my congregation to the point that they completely trusted me and my decisions, so what I had told them was enough for them not to question my judgment on my own situation. I was so relieved that they had that type of respect for me, and I planned to keep it, but, of course, there was that one person out of the entire congregation who just had to let it be publicly known that she hadn't cared much for Stormie. Sister Simmons.

"I knew it! I knew it!" she yelled out, looking around at the rest of the congregation after my announcement. "I told y'all something wasn't right with that woman!"

The rest of the congregation glared at her, wanting to tell her to just shut up and that this wasn't the time. A few of them shook their heads at her, and when she finally recognized that no one else was participating in the blatant disrespect of Stormie, she realized that she was being extremely inconsiderate.

Looking embarrassed, she said, "Sorry," underneath her breath.

The rest of Sunday service resumed as normal without any other disruptions or anymore talk about my divorce.

After Miracle found out with the rest of the congregation that my divorce was final, to my surprise, she insisted on taking me out to dinner and wouldn't take no for an answer. I didn't feel right about it, but no matter how much I tried to find something wrong with it, I couldn't. I had even talked to my mom about it, and she was even confused as to why I felt as if there was something wrong with it. She gave me some great advice, and that was to talk to God about it. She was right. She said there were some strongholds that needed to be lifted and only God could help me break them.

"Listen to me, Ezekiel. You don't owe Stormie anything. You gave her the best life that you could've possibly given her, and you tolerated things that most men wouldn't have. Stop letting her control you. I know you feel guilty about the divorce, but she was unfaithful. You were even still willing to work it out, but she wasn't, so there is nothing you should feel guilty about. You did everything that you possibly could have done to save your marriage. That's not what she wanted," my mom said, making things seem so clear.

She was so right. I was still allowing Stormie to control me. I was bound by our emotional, mental, and physical ties and I needed to cut them loose.

"I agree with you completely, Ma. It's easier said than done, but I know God will heal my heart."

I had already told Miracle that I would take her up on her offer, even though I wasn't completely sure about it. After talking to my mom, I felt a lot more confident about my decision. She made me realize that it was ok to move forward. My faithfulness and obedience to God was very important to me, so I always tried my best to make sure He wasn't disappointed in me. When Miracle and I were both living with my mom, there had been moments when I thought about Miracle in other ways outside of just being friends, but as soon as those thoughts would cross my mind, I would correct my thinking and repent.

Miracle was no longer living with my mom, but she might as well had been because most days when she finished up her work at home, she would show up at my mom's to spend some time with her. I loved the bond that they had formed. It was the bond that I always wished my mom and Stormie would've had. Even if my mom had eased up on Stormie, I still didn't think that Stormie would've ever desired to form a bond with her, and my mom knew it before I ever figured it out.

After talking to my mom, I called Miracle to make sure we were still on for the night.

"Hey, Ezekiel!" Miracle said in her sweet voice when she answered the phone.

"Hey, you. I was just making sure we were still on."

"Of course, unless you plan on standing me up. You didn't sound very enthusiastic when I asked you to go to dinner with me."

"I know. There were some things going on in my mind that I had to take control of."

"I understand. You good now?" she asked.

"Definitely."

"Good," she said, giggling.

"I'll be there at seven to pick you up," I said.

"I'll be waiting."

When I hung up the phone, I sat there on the sofa, grinning from ear to ear. I don't think that I had smiled that big in years.

"It's so nice to see you happy," my mom said, startling me.

I frantically looked over and saw her standing in the doorway.

"How long have you been standing there?" I asked, feeling a little embarrassed.

"Oh, just long enough to know that you're really good at hiding how you really feel."

"What do you mean by that?"

The whole time you and Miracle were living here together, I saw no signs at all that you were the least bit interested in her, but that smile when you just hung up the phone with her was priceless. You can't fake a smile like that."

"Ma, now you know I have to do things by the good book! I have people looking up to me. I can't stray from my beliefs."

"And that's why I love you so much, Son. Go and have a good time. Miracle is a good woman, and your dad would approve."

"You act like we're getting married or something. It's just dinner as friends."

"That's how it always starts off," she said, winking at me.

I shook my head at my mom as I stood up and towered over her.

She wrapped her arms around me like I was her personal big teddy bear, and said, "Ok, I'll leave you alone. Go ahead and get dapper for your date."

"Dapper? Is that what you used to call, Dad?" I laughed.

"As a matter of fact, I did. Your dad was the most dapper man I've ever known, and you're following right in his footsteps! I'm proud of you, Ezekiel," she said as she walked away with her eyes filled with tears.

My mom always got a little emotional when we talked about my dad. Even the smallest memory would make at least one tear fall from her eyes.

When I got to Miracle's house to pick her up, I almost blew the horn to let her know I was there, but then I could hear my dad say, "Son, don't you dare blow that horn. Go to the door like the gentleman that you are."

I got out of the car and walked to the front porch. Before I could ring the doorbell, Miracle opened the door. I obviously wasn't expecting the vision that was before me because my heart felt like it had skipped a beat, and my mouth was stuck wide open. I knew Miracle was a beautiful woman, but this particular night, she was drop-dead gorgeous. She had removed the distraction of her hair from her face by pinning up her lovely curls, allowing her beauty to be fully seen and admired. She wore just a little make-up. Just enough to accentuate her beauty. The black dress she wore fit her perfectly. It was very classy, just as she was.

"Excuse me if I'm gawking, but you look absolutely amazing!" I said, in complete awe of her.

Miracle smiled and said, "You look pretty dapper yourself!"

Laughing, I said, "Wait, have you been talking to my mother? I thought she was the only one who used 'dapper'."

"Well, I did live with her for a little while, so I can't deny that she may have rubbed off on me a bit, but I can't have you feeling like you're talking to your mother, so scratch that. You look very handsome, Pastor," she said with a smile.

She didn't know it, but I loved when she called me Pastor. Maybe it was the little twang she had when she said it. She would drop the "or" at the end and add an "a", making it sound more like Passta. I loved it.

That night, we went to an Italian restaurant, ate good, and had great conversation. Although it was our first official date, it didn't seem like it. We were both very comfortable around each other and didn't have to start from the basics of learning those initial things about one another. One thing that we had not yet experienced was a first kiss, but we did that night. That was our first date of many more to come. We not only went on dates. We would also call each other and pray together, go for walks together, workout together, and she also became very involved in whatever we had going on at the church. All of the members loved her, and she loved them. It all just seemed too good to be true, and many times, I had to stop myself from thinking that way because I didn't want to sabotage something so beautiful. I didn't know what the future held for me and Miracle, but I continued to pray for God to order our steps and keep us both on the right path. Whatever His will was, that's what I wanted for my life.

Chapter Thirty-Eight

Six months into dating Miracle and being completely celibate, I felt like I knew enough about her to know beyond a shadow of a doubt that she was the woman that I wanted to spend the rest of my life with. Since we'd begun dating, I had been praying for God to not allow me to make any rash decisions without first presenting them to Him, and waiting for Him to answer. I talked to God about Miracle all of the time, thanking Him for placing her into my life at the right time. I felt as though Miracle and I already had a great foundation to start with. Our faith in God was strong, and we both made it a priority to put Him first in our relationship. There was nothing left to confirm that what I was about to do was definitely the right thing to do. I knew that God had created Miracle just for me.

"Ma, where are you?" I yelled, as soon as I opened the front door and rushed into the house.

She came running into the kitchen, and said, "What is it? What's wrong?"

Smiling, I said, "I can't live without Miracle, and I won't allow her to get away."

With a smirk on her face, as if she knew where this was going, she raised her eyebrows and asked, "Ezekiel, what exactly does that mean?"

She needed confirmation that what she was thinking was exactly what I meant, so that she could react the way that I already knew she would.

I eagerly pulled the small black box out of the bag that I was tightly holding on to.

As soon as my mom saw the box, she put her hands up to her mouth and began jumping up and down.

"Oh my God, Ezekiel! I knew it! Let me see it!" she said, snatching the box out of my hand.

"Calm down, Ma! You're more excited than I am!" I said, laughing.

As she opened the box, her eyes lit up. "Ezekiel, this is gorgeous! She's going to love it!"

"But is she going to say yes?" I asked my mom, sounding extremely doubtful.

"Of course she will! She loves you, and the two of you are perfect together! I'm so happy!" she replied, as she closed the box that held the engagement ring that I'd carefully picked for a very special woman.

"So, when do you plan on giving it to her?" my mom asked, inquisitively.

"I don't know. I want it to be very special. Something she'll never forget. I know she's pretty simple, but I want her to be clear as to how much she means to me."

My mom grabbed my hand and said, "Son, trust me when I say she already knows how much she means to you and the feelings are mutual. Whatever you decide to do is just going to be icing on the cake. I just ask one thing of you."

I squinted my eyes, not knowing what my mom was going to say next.

"What's that?"

"Please just let me be there! I have to see this live and in person! I don't want to see any videos of it unless it's later on down the line when we show my grandkids."

"Grandkids, Ma?"

"I know! Just messing with you! We have to get the married part done first, and then we can talk about grandkids," my mom said, giggling.

It was so good to see my mom so happy for me. I was already confident in my decision, but whenever my mom was with me on something, that made things even better.

She began tapping the tip of her index finger against her lips, and I could tell she was thinking hard. I knew she wanted this moment to be just as special as I did.

"So, basically you want something simple, but special. I got you, Son!"

"What do you have in mind?" I asked, excited to hear what she'd come up with so quickly.

"How about a picnic in Central Park? It's beautiful out there this time of year."

"That sounds nice. I think she'll like that."

"She'll love it! I'll get everything set up. You don't have to worry about anything. Just be there with the ring and the woman of your dreams!"

I trusted my mom. She always knew exactly what to do and she had never let me down, so I let her do whatever it was she had in mind without any questions. I went into my room and sat at the foot of my bed, talking to God, and preparing my mind for what was next. I was feeling pretty nervous, but I could feel God comforting me, letting me know that everything was going to be ok. I didn't understand how anyone got through life without God being a major part of it. God was definitely an essential part of my life. I called on Him before every decision I ever made, no matter how big or small.

A few days later, Miracle and I went to Central Park. She had no idea of what was about to happen. All she knew was that we were going to have a relaxing day in the park, enjoying one another. I was afraid I might've blown everything because I was sweating bullets. I wasn't even this nervous when I asked Stormie to marry me. As we walked around, admiring the beauty and tranquility around us, my mom called.

"Hey, Ma," I said, trying to sound surprised. I was waiting for her call to give me instructions on where to go, since she had volunteered to set everything up.

"You have a horse and carriage ride scheduled. They're expecting the two of you, and they'll drop you off exactly where you need to be for the picnic."

"Ok. Miracle and I will be by when we leave Central Park," I said to my mom, trying to sound convincing.

After I hung up the phone, Miracle said, "Is everything alright?"

"Oh, yeah. You know how that kitchen drain clogs up from time to time. It happened again."

"Well, we can go now," Miracle said, sounding concerned.

"No. She'll be ok until we get there. How about we go on a horse and carriage ride?"

"That sounds romantic!" Miracle said, looking at me smiling.

When we got to the area where the horses and carriages were, a man in a black suit and top hat walked up to us.

"You must be Mr. Whitfield," the coachman said.

Yes, I am, and this is my . . . lady, Miracle," I said, as I grabbed her hand and squeezed it tight.

"Beautiful couple! I have your horse and carriage ready right over there," he said, leading us to the beautiful white horse.

He first helped Miracle into the carriage, and I got in after her. I could tell she was already enjoying herself.

The coachman got on the horse, and before giving it the signal to go, he looked back at us and said, "I'll take you around the park to do a little sightseeing. There's quite a bit going on this afternoon. After I take you around, I'll drop you off at your next destination. Just holler if you need anything."

"Thank you," we both said.

"Enjoy the ride, lovebirds," he said, right before we felt the carriage begin to move.

As we rode through the park, everyone smiled and waved at us. Miracle laid her head on my shoulder, and I kissed her on the forehead as I intertwined my fingers with hers.

Out of the blue, she said, "I'm your lady, huh?"

I laughed and said, "I do like to think that you are. Am I wrong?"

Miracle looked up at me with her beautiful eyes and said, "No. I like to think that you're my man. I just don't think we've ever introduced each other as such."

"I think it's because we never have to. People look at us and immediately know what it is."

Miracle laughed and said, "I guess you're right."

I felt the carriage stop and saw the coachman jump down off of the horse.

He then came and opened the door to the carriage and said, "We're here!"

He helped Miracle out, and I got out right after her. She was looking around in amazement. It was definitely a beautiful sight to see. My mom had outdone herself.

"You two enjoy the rest of your afternoon!" the coachman said, as he hopped back onto the saddle and went on his way.

Miracle's mouth was still wide open.

"It's so beautiful here!" she said.

"Not as beautiful as you," I said, as I took her hand and walked her along the path that was covered with pink rose petals, leading us to the area that was set up especially for our private picnic. There were also rose petals that surrounded the oversized blanket that had been laid out for us directly underneath a large Cherry Blossom tree. On top of the blanket, there was a wine table set up with a bottle of Sparkling White Grape Juice and two glasses.

"I can't believe you planned all of this, Ezekiel," Miracle said with tears in her eyes.

"Are you ok?" I asked, confused as to why she was about to cry.

"Yes, I'm fine. I'm just so happy. I've never had anyone do anything like this for me. It's so thoughtful and I appreciate you so much. You really know how to make a girl feel special."

Every day, I realized how different Miracle was from Stormie. I never tried to compare the two because there was truly no comparison, but I couldn't help but notice the differences and appreciate them. Stormie wasn't emotional at all. No matter how many nice things I did for her, she had never gotten to the point of shedding a tear. I would get a thank you, but she still never seemed to be impressed, so I was truly grateful for the reaction that I got from Miracle.

I hugged Miracle tight before we sat down to enjoy more of each other's company. As we began to sit down, I heard music coming from somewhere. Unbeknownst to Miracle, most of this was all a surprise to me as well. Miracle and I both looked around, trying to see where the music was coming from. Suddenly, I saw my praise and worship leader, Kelly, who was one of the best singers I'd ever heard, walking towards us singing Chrisette Michele's song, "A Couple of Forevers".

I looked over at Miracle and her tears had already begun to fall. She looked at me and mouthed the words, "I love you."

"I love you, too," I replied.

After Kelly was done singing, she nodded and smiled at both of us. As she walked away, my mom appeared.

"Faith? What are you doing here? Do you need Ezekiel to go fix the drain?"

My mom began laughing as Miracle looked around confused. While she was in a state of confusion, I was able to catch her off guard and grab her hand. I then stood her up in front of me.

"What's going on, Ezekiel? What else do you have planned?" she asked.

As I held both of her hands, I said, "Miracle, you are such a special woman. In fact, you're my miracle. I never thought I'd be able to love another woman, but the love I have for you cannot be matched. I know we haven't known each other very long, but I feel like I've known you all of my life, and I know that meeting you wasn't by accident. That night when I ran into you was perfect timing. God's perfect timing, and my entire life changed after that night. I thank you for being you, and for loving me for me."

As I poured my heart out to Miracle, my eyes filled with tears of joy as I looked into her eyes. My mom watched with a smile on her face as she tried to hold back her tears. Suddenly, it looked as if people had come from every direction to see me either become the happiest or most disappointed man alive.

It was then time for me to take my chance, so that was exactly what I did.

I pulled the ring out of my pocket, got down on one knee, and said, "Miracle, I can't imagine my life without you. I don't know how I've done it this far because you are definitely the missing piece to my puzzle. We have both placed God at the head of our lives, and with that, we already have begun building a strong foundation. I just want to continue to build on that foundation with you, Miracle. Will you make me the happiest man alive and be my wife?"

It was completely silent for what seemed to be forever to a man who was down on bended knee waiting to hear what the destiny of his future held.

"Ezekiel, I love you so much. It's scary sometimes because I haven't loved anyone like this in a very long time, but I'm willing to overcome that fear and become the wife of the man that God has set aside just for me."

I stayed down on my knee for a moment, not realizing Miracle had accepted my proposal. Everyone standing around began clapping, and I realized what Miracle had just said. I quickly stood up, lifted her off the ground and twirled her around. As soon as I put her back down, I put the ring on her finger and gave her a big kiss.

My mom came over, hugged us both, and said, "I love my babies! This was so beautiful!"

"Thanks to you, Ma. I appreciate everything you did to make this moment simple, yet special."

Many of those who had stopped to watch just one of our special moments of many more were also in tears. This day had gone exactly how I wanted it to, and I owed it to my mom. I wouldn't have traded her for the world. She always had my back and my best interest at heart.

After the hard part was over, my mom had servers to come over with the meal she had prepped for our picnic. For the rest of the afternoon, into the evening, the three of us enjoyed food, sparkling grape juice, and a lot of laughter. Things could not have been more perfect.

Chapter Thirty-Nine

Miracle and I got married only three months after the proposal, and it was the happiest day of my life. I could honestly say that Miracle showed me love in a way that I had never experienced it. Just the small, kind gestures, such as, blowing me kisses and winking at me from the other side of the room, getting up out of bed extra early just to prepare a lunch for me to take to work, or massaging my temples as I laid my head in her lap after a stressful day at work, made me feel undoubtedly appreciated and loved. It felt even greater on my end to be able to share the abundance of love that I had inside of me with someone who had mutual feelings, and appreciated the effort that I put into making her feel like the most beautiful woman in the world. Miracle was most definitely a rare jewel that I would forever love and care for with everything that I had in me. I didn't know how I hadn't met Miracle long before I did, but I was trusting that God had been busy preparing us for one another for the absolute perfect time.

As hard as it had been to talk about the death of my dad with everyone, Miracle was my wife, and even though she never forced it, I knew she deserved to know all about my dad, so one day I decided to tell her everything. As I told her the story about him saving a young girl, tears flowed heavily from her eyes and her body quivered as if I was telling her about someone that she was close to. In essence, I guess she had lost someone. Her father-in law that she never got to meet. She was speechless when I finished telling her the story of how my mom and I had lost such an important part of our family, and she could do nothing but hug me. I thought that maybe that would've given her the courage to tell me about her parents, but evidently, she still wasn't ready. After seeing how she had reacted over my dad, I couldn't even imagine how she would've been able to manage her emotions if she'd tried to tell me how she had lost both of her parents, so I decided not to bring it up.

Miracle and I found a home that we both loved and would be able to raise a family in, so I finally moved out of my mom's house, and Miracle kept hers since she had inherited it from her grandmother. There were so many special memories in that home, and she wasn't quite sure as to what she wanted to do with it yet.

Since we had both been the only biological children in our families, we both wanted a big family. We knew what it was like not having siblings and agreed that we'd want our children to have brothers and sisters. Kyle was like a brother to me, but I always wondered what it would've been like to have a blood brother around my age always hanging around. It sometimes got lonely, although my parents tried their best to keep me entertained and away from the wrong crowd. I had to admit, they had done a pretty good job at it. I didn't know how Kyle had snuck in there, but I was glad that he had.

Life was so good, it sometimes seemed unreal. I had never been a negative person, and had always looked to find something positive about every person I met, and the bright side of every situation. I have to admit that things seemed so perfect, which I wasn't used to from my previous relationship, that I felt like there was always something in the back of my mind causing me to expect the worst. I had to pay close attention to my thoughts and keep them under control, making sure that I didn't allow them to sabotage the great things that God had blessed me with.

Miracle literally fit perfectly in every aspect of my life. My church congregation absolutely adored her, and she genuinely loved them and did whatever she could to help them. She was involved with everything, not just because she was the first lady and felt obligated to do certain things, but because she enjoyed being the first lady and doing the things that she did for the members. She was there for every choir rehearsal, she taught Bible study, and oversaw Sunday School. The church's financial books had been a mess for a long time because I didn't have a bookkeeper to manage things, but Miracle stepped up to the plate, organizing everything and keeping things in order.

Five months of marriage flew by, and Miracle and I hadn't had even the smallest argument or disagreement. I knew it was still early, and I couldn't have even imagined what our first disagreement would've been about, or how silly it would've probably been, but I didn't have to try to imagine for long. It happened, and it came with a vengeance. Out of all of the things it could have possibly been, I definitely wasn't expecting this.

One Saturday afternoon, while Miracle was gone out to lunch and shopping with my mom, I decided to go through a box that I'd thrown a bunch of random stuff into when we moved into our home. One thing I hated was packing and unpacking, but this particular day, I didn't have anything else to do, and I honestly got tired of seeing that huge box sitting in our closet just taking up space. When I opened the box, I took a deep breath and began pulling everything out. I had forgotten about all of the ties I'd packed up in that box, and probably didn't miss them because I had so many more. I grabbed some extra hangers from the back of the closet where Miracle hung her handbags, to drape them over. When I grabbed just one hanger, all of Miracle's bags began to fall. I took another deep breath, asking myself why I had even started this project.

As I began picking Miracle's things up off the floor, on the shelf behind where her handbags were hanging, I noticed the small white box that I had seen before, in which Miracle had told me to be very careful with because it held some very important documents. Being curious, I forgot all about what I was doing and grabbed the box off of the shelf and went and sat on the bed. When I opened it, indeed, there were some documents that looked very important. When I realized they were the death certificates of Miracle's parent, I immediately felt bad for going through her things. Although I had opened up to Miracle about my dad's death, she still hadn't talked to me about how her parent's died, which did concern me a little bit because I sometimes felt it might've been a trauma she hadn't completely dealt with. I just didn't want it to negatively impact her or our relationship later on down the line. I didn't want to force her to talk about it, but I did feel that it would've been good for her. I just kept hoping that she would someday come around. Someday was coming sooner than I'd thought, but it wouldn't be because Miracle was ready and had made the decision to talk to me about it. I always said I wouldn't force it on her, but it ended up being forced upon her anyway.

As I was about to close the box to put it back where I found it, I noticed the death certificate that was on top had "Mena Cummins" on it. Mena was Miracle's mom, and the death certificate showed that the manner of death was homicide, and the cause of death was thermal burns.

Looking and sounding confused, I said, "What?!?!"

I had absolutely no idea that her mom was murdered.

"No wonder she's so traumatized," I quietly said to myself.

I then looked at her dad, Gavin's, death certificate and it stated the same thing.

"What in the world happened to you two?" I said, as if they were sitting right there with me.

I became even more curious and began rummaging through the rest of the papers. I ran across an old newspaper article that had to have taken up the entire front page. The headline read, "New York City Fire Chief Dies After Saving Girl from Violent Home Blaze. Arson Suspected."

As I read the article, my heart began beating so hard and fast that I thought it was going to jump right out of my chest. I suddenly felt a huge lump in my throat, and my eyes began to fill up with tears. I couldn't believe what I was reading, but I really couldn't believe that I had married the person responsible for my dad's death. He died trying to save her. I remembered that night so clearly. I watched the television as that girl, who I now knew was Miracle, ran back into that home, and my dad, being the man that he was, just had to go in after her. If she had never run back in, my dad might've still been alive. I felt so much anger building up inside of me. All of the love that I felt for Miracle seemed to quickly turn into hate. My mind was all over the place.

I stood up and began yelling, "God, why?!?! What type of cruel joke is this? How could you allow me to marry the person who murdered my dad?!?!"

I quickly paced our bedroom floor. I had never felt the type of emotions that I was feeling, and I had no idea what to do with them, so I balled up my fist and punched a hole in the wall.

While in the middle of my crazed eruption, Miracle ran into the room and shouted, "Ezekiel! Calm down! What's wrong with you?"

As she tried to grab me, I pulled away and looked at her with resentment in my eyes.

"How can you possibly tell me to calm down after I just found this?!?!" I yelled as I threw everything that I'd just found at her.

She just stood there in shock as tears began streaming down her face.

"So, you don't have anything to say? Did you know he was my dad? Did you realize that my dad sacrificed his life for you? Did you start the fire? He left me and my mom for you! He was our everything and you took him away!"

I plopped down on the bed and put my hands up to my face as blood ran down from my knuckles. After sitting there for a couple of minutes with my face still covered with my hands, I felt Miracle gently sit next to me.

She began speaking softly, and I could hear her voice trembling. I didn't know whether it was from fear, or the thought of having to face her deception.

"Ezekiel, I'm so sorry. I did know who your dad was after you told me what happened to him, but I didn't have it in my heart to tell you that I was the little girl. I love you so much, and I've never had a man to love me and treat me like you do. I didn't want to mess things up between us and I knew they would never be the same after you found out the truth. I knew that you would forever blame me for your dad's death, and resent me. I don't know if I could blame you, but what I do know is that I wouldn't change what I did. I was trying to save my parents. I ran out in a panic, thinking they were already out of the house. When I looked around and didn't see them, I panicked again, and at that point, I would've done anything to save them. I wish that your dad wouldn't have come in after me, but he did because he was a wonderful man, and I see where you get it from. Please don't let this come between us, Ezekiel."

I sat quietly without saying a word, and Miracle sat patiently, waiting to hear what I was going to say next. I tried to comprehend my feelings and gather my thoughts, but I felt as though I was failing at both. The emotions that I was feeling seemed to be incomprehensible. I know it sounds crazy, but I felt as though I had defied my father because I'd fallen in love and married Miracle. Then I thought about my mom. I'd let her down again by falling for the wrong woman, and I knew that when she found out, she'd really be crushed because she genuinely loved Miracle. There was so much hurt behind this that there was no question in my mind about what I had to do.

I looked at Miracle, with blood-shot eyes and tears streaming down my face and said, "We can't be together. This runs too deep, and I would never get over it. I'll despise you for the rest of my life and I can't put myself in that position. I loved you, but what you kept from me is inexcusable. I'll forgive you for myself, but you aren't the woman I thought you were."

Miracle began crying uncontrollable and tried to hug me, but I pushed her away.

"Do not touch me, Miracle. I can't be around you at all right now. I want you to leave."

Miracle still wouldn't give up. She stood in front of me and said, "But Ezekiel, I love you! The person that's to blame is whoever started that fire. It wasn't me. We're meant to be together! You of all people know that all things work together for good to them that love God. Can't you see this was ordained by God? I'm sorry that your dad died. Maybe it was God's will that he saved me so that you could find me and save me again."

Listening to her continuing to speak and throwing God, his reasoning, and Bible verses at me seemed to make me even angrier.

"Leave, Miracle!" I yelled.

She then ran out of the room, and soon after, I heard the front door slam. I sat there on the bed and cuffed my face in my hands. I didn't know what to do next. I thought, *"God, is this my punishment for not trying harder to save my marriage with Stormie, and divorcing her?"* I definitely didn't know how to tell my mom what I'd found out. I didn't plan to until it was my very last option. I would've done anything to save her from having to go through that hurt all over again.

Chapter Forty

An entire month had gone by of me sleeping alone and thinking about Miracle and our situation every single day. The thinking that I did during that time was more so focused on convincing myself that I was right, and had every right to react and feel the way that I did. Miracle called me all day, every day, for the first week. She stopped by one day and emptied the closet of her things. After I'd realized she had come into the house while I wasn't home, I changed the locks. I tried to get rid of everything that reminded me of her, so I took down all of our pictures and put them into a box. No matter how hard I tried not to think about her, I still did. I knew deep down that no matter what Miracle had done, the way that I was treating her wasn't right. I prayed every day that I would be able to accept what happened and forgive Miracle. I preached on forgiveness all of the time, but I definitely wasn't practicing it. I felt as if God had left me alone to figure this one out on my own, but I knew better than that. I knew He was there listening every time I spoke to Him, and I also knew that He saw every move that I made, and knew every thought that went through my mind. I didn't know what to do next, and I needed God to answer me asap.

Sometimes I thought maybe He was answering me, but I just didn't want to hear what He was saying. I knew that we, even as believers, would call on God to help us through certain situations, but when He would tell us what to do, or show us the way, we wouldn't listen because it wasn't what we wanted to do. In other words, it wasn't at all what we wanted to hear, and many times we can be selfish. Everything has to be about us and what we want. Just like we sometimes have those "yes" friends who tell us whatever we want to hear, but then we have the ones that are real with us, who will try to bring us back to reality by telling us the truth, which actually ends up being everything we don't want to hear. Many people choose to go with the friends that say whatever they want them to say, even though they're not helping them to become better or adding any type of value to their life.

As believers, we should never base our decisions and actions on what we want and how we feel, but what God wants for us. I had my mind made up, and how I felt was how I felt. I chose to react based on my emotions, which is a big no-no. In those moments that bring about lots of painful emotions, we have to keep in mind that emotions are temporary, so we should never make decisions during those moments. It's easier said than done, and I was definitely learning that. Those things that I'd taught others, I couldn't bring myself to follow. All I could think about was the fact that Miracle had been a major factor of the most hurtful part of my life.

Everyone around me, including my mom and congregation, noticed that Miracle had been MIA. Of course rumors swarmed around the church, which I refused to acknowledge. I knew I would have to address it sooner or later before everyone drew their own conclusions. Honestly, I was afraid that this might've caused me to lose my ministry, although my congregation had been understanding the first time around. I'd had two failed marriages, and I knew that if I had been one of the members of my church, I would have been looking at myself sideways, wondering if I was qualified enough to have anyone under my leadership.

My mom kept asking what happened, and I kept putting her off, telling her that I didn't want to talk about it yet. She said that she had been calling Miracle, but she wouldn't answer. I already knew that she probably wouldn't answer because she saw how much this hurt me, so she could've only imagined how much it would've hurt my mom. Miracle had stopped trying to contact me, and I when she did, I seemed to be very unbothered by it. I no longer had to feel guilty every time I saw her name come across the screen and immediately sent her calls to voicemail.

One afternoon, after I'd ended my workday, I stopped by the supermarket to get a few things for the house. Miracle and I would go to my mom's house a lot, and vice versa, so that we could eat together, but these days I was avoiding conversation with my mom, so I would cook small meals for myself. After I'd picked up all of my items, and as I pushed my cart towards one of the checkout lines, I suddenly heard a familiar voice say, "What's up, Stranger?"

I looked back, and to my surprise, it was Stormie walking towards me, carrying a shopping basket. I hadn't run into her not one time after we'd separated, which made it seem strange that now, when I was going through my situation with my wife, I just so happened to run into her.

I was really caught off guard because I never really thought about how I'd react if I did happen to see her again.

"Hey, Storm . . . I mean, Stormie."

Stormie smiled and folded her arms as she looked me up and down. "It's ok if you call me Storm, Zeke. I loved when you called me that. You look really good. How have you been?"

I was so confused in that moment, mainly because Stormie was being so cordial. There was no yelling and acting rude and indignant, which I had experienced the last time we'd seen each other.

"Earth to Zeke," Stormie said, noticing that I seemed to be dazed.

I came to and cleared my throat. "Ezekiel," I said.

Looking confused, Stormie said, "Huh?"

"Please don't call me Zeke. I only go by Ezekiel."

Stormie stood quietly for a moment, and then hesitantly said, "Ok . . . Ezekiel."

Stormie was still the physically beautiful woman I knew, but I had the unfortunate privilege of knowing how ugly she was on the inside. Although she pretty much looked the same after an entire year, something was different about her. She was naturally curvy, however, she appeared to be a lot slimmer. I knew it couldn't have possibly been from the stress of the divorce because she didn't seem stressed about her choices at all. I didn't have much to say to her, however, she tried to carry on a conversation.

"So, I heard you got remarried," she said.

"Yeah, I did," I replied.

She looked at me as if she was waiting for me to spill all of my business to her.

"Ok, that's it? You're not going to tell me her name or anything?"

"I don't think that concerns you," I said, as I thought about the fact that Stormie had lived with Miracle and her parents for a short time.

"Okayyyy . . . This is pretty awkward, Zeke . . . I mean Ezekiel. Why are you acting this way?"

"No, Stormie. Why are you acting this way? A little over a year ago, you treated me like I was trash . . . like you hated me, and now I run into you, and you want to act as if none of it happened. How do you think I should be acting? As if I'm happy to see you? Honestly, I never had to see you ever again!"

Stormie looked around to see if people were watching, and then put her index finger up to her lips trying to shush me.

"Ezekiel, people are looking."

"And when have you cared about being embarrassed or embarrassing?" I asked, as I became more and more irritated.

"I've changed a lot over the past year. I'm not perfect, but I know I hurt you, and I'm sorry," Stormie said, sounding genuine.

I felt as if I was being punked. I never imagined the day that Stormie would be apologizing to me, but it honestly didn't mean a thing. I had forgiven her and let her go. I didn't know what she was expecting, or if she had ulterior motives, but just like she said she had changed, so had I. I was no longer the man that she could just walk all over. She was my ex-wife, and that's what she would always be. She was a part of my past, and that's where she needed to stay.

"Stormie, I accept your apology, and I forgave you a long time ago."

"So, that's it?"

"What do you mean, that's it? What else do you want? Where is Brandon?"

I suddenly saw extreme sadness in her eyes, and that sadness was communicated through her voice when she said, "He left me."

The saddest part about that moment was that I actually felt bad for her. I didn't know why, after the way she had treated me, but I did.

I grabbed her and gave her a hug, and whispered in her ear, "Whatever happened, it's going to be ok, Storm. You'll get through this."

"Thank you, Zeke."

As I held Stormie, comforting her after her breakup with the man she cheated on me with, her gentle embrace and the smell of her sweet perfume brought back a lot of memories. The good ones. That was not a place I wanted or needed to go back to, so I quickly released her as I told her that I had to go and that I'd be praying for her. I then headed to the checkout line. As I stood in line, I looked back, and Stormie was still standing in the same spot in the aisle where we'd been talking. I felt bad for leaving her in the state of mind that she was in, but I'd done all that I could do for her. Not to sound selfish, but I was already dealing with a lot going on in my own life and didn't need any other distractions. I was sure that Stormie didn't feel bad for me when she told me that she didn't love me anymore, and that was what I used to help justify that I had just done the right thing.

Chapter Forty-One

After getting home with my groceries, I began preparing my dinner, and while it was in the oven, I took a long, hot shower. I kept thinking about how vulnerable Stormie had seemed in the supermarket. I had never seen her that way in all of the years of knowing her. Even if she was vulnerable, she kept her walls up and never let anyone know when she felt weak. I felt like something else may have been going on, but I knew it wasn't my responsibility to help fix whatever it was. I would pray for her like I told her I would, but that was the most I could do.

After I got out of the shower, I threw on some pajamas, and went to check on the chicken I'd put in the oven. As soon as I closed the oven to let it cook a little longer, the doorbell rang.

"Just a second," I said, as I walked to the door.

When I opened it, I was in complete and utter disbelief.

"Zeke, I need you," Stormie said, as she stood outside my door with desperation written all over her face.

"What are you doing here, Stormie, and how did you know where I live?"

Before she could answer, I said, "Wait, did you follow me today?"

"No, I didn't follow you. I've known where you lived for quite some time now. If you really want to know something about someone, it's easy to find out with all of the technology we have."

"Ok, so now what?"

"Can I please come in, Zeke?"

"Stormie, you know I'm married."

"Zeke, look. I told you that I've been knowing where you lived for a while now. I've been trying to get up the courage to come ring your doorbell for the past few weeks. I've watched you come and go, and I haven't seen a woman, so I know that you're either divorced or separated. I didn't even see a ring on your finger, so I'm assuming you're divorced."

"Wait! You've been stalking me? Stormie, do you really think you can just run back to me because you and Brandon didn't work out? You destroyed us. It's over."

A tear ran down Stormie's face, and she said, "You're serious. You really don't care about me anymore."

"I care about you, and I wish you the best, but I can't deal with this right now."

Stormie grabbed my arm and said, "Please. Can we just sit down and talk?"

Just then, the timer on the oven started beeping.

"Wait here," I said, as I quickly walked to the kitchen.

When I got to the kitchen, I opened the oven and looked at the chicken. It was perfect. I put on my oven mitt, and as I was pulling it out of the oven, I almost dropped it when I heard Stormie's voice.

"That sure does smell good," she said, as she stood on the other side of the island.

I sat the hot baking dish on the stove and said, "Stormie, you have to go."

Grinning, she said, "Why? Your wife will be home soon?"

"Get out!" I yelled.

"I'm just kidding. I'm sorry. Seriously, though, who taught you to cook? We always ate take-out when we were married."

"Yeah, because you didn't know how to cook. Is that why Brandon left you?"

That sad look that I had seen when we were in the supermarket came over Stormie again, and she softly said, "No. That's not why he left."

I then regretted making that comment, and in an attempt to forget that I had made it, I said, "My mom and wife taught me to cook."

"You mean your ex-wife?" she quickly replied.

Aggressively, I replied, "No. My wife. Despite what you think you know, I am still married."

Stormie, looking disappointed, nodded her head and sat on one of the barstools at the island. As I made mashed potatoes to go with the chicken and asparagus, Stormie sat there quietly, and all I could do was think about how quickly she had gotten so comfortable in my house. When everything was done, I first fixed Stormie a plate without her asking, and sat it in front of her.

She looked at me strangely, so I asked, "You hungry?"

"Yes. Thanks," she said. "I really appreciate it."

"No problem," I said as I fixed my own plate. I kept looking back at Stormie as she sat there staring at me.

Finally, I said, "Is something wrong?"

"What do you mean?"

"Why aren't you eating?" I asked.

"I was waiting for you. You are going to pray over the food, right?"

At that moment, I knew Stormie was playing games with me. Even when we were married, she didn't wait on me to pray over the food. She would start eating while I prayed over mine.

I stood right in front of her, folded my arms, and said, "Stormie, I don't know if you're trying to impress me, or deceive me into wanting to be with you, but you have to remember that I know you, Sweetheart. I've known you for a long time, and you don't care anything about a prayer."

"I told you that I'm not the same. You can't see yet that I've changed?"

"The only thing that I can see has changed about you is your weight. What have you been doing, working out?"

"Is it that noticeable?" Stormie asked.

"I guess so since it was one of the first things that I noticed. When I first met you, your beautiful curves were like a goddess. I'll never forget that. It just seems strange for you to no longer have those curves that you've had since I've known you."

I sat my plate down and sat down next to Stormie.

I noticed her smiling, so I asked, "What are you smiling about?"

"So, you do still have eyes for me."

I shook my head and said, "I knew the old Stormie was still in there."

I then prayed over our food.

While we ate, we talked about some of the enjoyable times we had when we were nothing but kids. She roasted me about how lame I was and how she wasn't trying to give me the time of day. It was funny now, but it wasn't so funny back then. I put my all into getting her to notice me and practically begged for some of her time. Now, when I looked back at it, I was pretty lame for that, but I thought I knew what I wanted.

"Don't you still think there was a reason for us being together, Zeke?"

"There's a reason for everything. Sometimes it's only meant for a season of our lives to teach us and prepare us for things or people we'll experience later in life," I replied.

"Well, you taught me how a man should treat a woman, and being with a man that ended up not knowing how to treat me made me really appreciate you and your patience."

I wasn't expecting what Stormie had said, but I appreciated it. It made me feel like something good had come out of our toxic situation, but I really didn't know how to respond, so I just said, "I'm really glad that you now know what you want in a man, so you can now more easily weed out the ones that you know aren't a good fit for you, and ask God to help you in the process. That's considered growth in my book."

I was waiting on Stormie to rebuttal the comment that I'd snuck in about God helping her, but it never came.

Stormie sighed, and said, "Yeah, but I really don't need to weed out anyone. I already know who's a good fit for me. I just needed to get myself together and figure some things out."

I knew exactly where Stormie was going, and I wasn't about to entertain any of it.

"So, what did you learn from being with me?" she asked.

Before I knew it, I said, "I learned what I definitely don't want in a woman, and that I can't keep a woman that doesn't want to be kept. I also learned that no matter how much I'd like for a woman to see their value and know who they are meant to be, I can't make them see it. Only God can."

Stormie sat there nodding her head, and hesitated before she said, "Wow. That hurt."

"Well, it hurt when you told me that you didn't love me anymore, it hurt when you brought another man into our home, it hurt when you belittled me in front of that other man, and it hurt when I still had hope that you would come back to me, and I never got a phone call."

"You were still willing to take me back after everything I'd done?" Stormie asked, sounding completely surprised.

Stormie stood up and grabbed my hands, gently tugging, gesturing for me to stand up. I stood up and she wrapped her arms around my neck.

She looked me right in the eyes and said, "I'm so, so sorry. I know I can't say it enough, but I want you to know I mean it. I don't want there to be any animosity between us."

"There's no animosity. Like I told you earlier, I forgave you back then. I got over it and moved on. That was all I could do. You'll forever be my first love, but there's no longer any possibility of there being anything else between us."

Stormie pressed her forehead against mine and began crying.

"I'm sorry if I led you on in any type of way, tonight. I didn't mean to. This was probably a bad idea," I said.
Just then, I heard footsteps, and then heard Miracle's voice.

"Ezekiel, the door was unlocked so I came in . . ."

When Miracle walked into the kitchen and saw me hugging Stormie, her mouth almost hit the floor. Tears immediately began streaming down her face.

I quickly released Stormie and said, "Miracle, this is not what it looks like!"

"Coco? Stormie said, sounding like she was in shock. "You have to be kidding me! This is who you replaced me with? She's not half the woman I am!"

Miracle focused her attention on Stormie, and said, "Stormie? Really Ezekiel? After everything she put you through, you go right back?"

Still trying to explain myself, I said, "Miracle, listen to me, please! It's not what it looks like at all! I promise!"

It was so crazy to me that even with all of the anger that I had towards Miracle, it was still so important for me to reassure her that what she thought was going on, wasn't. That let me know that the hatred that I thought I had towards her really didn't exist. If it had, I would've had no problem pretending as if something really was going on between me and Stormie. I would've never wanted to hurt Miracle like that.

"It looks like I've been praying for us every single day, and trying to give you time to deal with things the way you needed to deal with them, but you had other plans. I was coming here to see if you were ready to talk about things, and you're sitting here having a nice dinner with your ex-wife while your wife is alone all day, every day, trying to think of ways to bring us back together," Miracle said, in the most livid voice I'd ever heard her use.

Stormie began laughing and said, "You are still the overdramatic little girl that I knew. Girl, Zeke does not want you. Do you see me? Just think about it. Why would he want you?"

"Stormie, stop it!" I said.

"I'm done, Ezekiel. I took accountability for not being completely honest with you, but what I did doesn't even come close to this! Do not try to contact me! You'll be hearing from my lawyer."

"Miracle, wait!" I said, as I tried to catch her before she jumped in her car and sped off.

I tried to catch my breath as I walked back into the house. Stormie was standing against the wall, smiling.

"I can't believe out of all the women in the world, you married Coco! You think I was messed up? Her entire family had issues, especially her daddy!"

"Stormie, don't talk to me about people who aren't here to defend themselves. As a matter of fact, grab your things and leave."

"Oh, sounds like she didn't tell you about her daddy, Gavin. He molested me and then turned her entire family against me."

"She told me everything, and that wasn't the way it happened."

As she grabbed her purse, she said, "Well then, she lied to you."

"I should have never let you stay! You're evil, Stormie. You haven't changed at all. You just do what you feel you have to do to try to get what you want, but I'm not going for it."

I grabbed Stormie's hand and led her to the front door. I opened it and said, "Goodbye, Stormie. I'll be praying for you because you definitely need it."

Stormie grabbed me by the arm and said, "Zeke, she doesn't want you, and you don't really want her. You just don't want to look bad. That's the way you've always been. Always worried about how people perceive you. Always trying to do right. Well, let me let you in on a little secret. You don't win by always doing right, and you know that. You and I also both know that you don't always do right. Like right now. There's no point in you trying to fix things now. You've already sinned."

Letting Stormie get in my head, angrily I said, "Nothing happened between us, Stormie. I just felt sorry for you and was being nice."

"If that's what you want to believe, Zeke. I don't need anyone to have pity on me. I've gotten through life just fine without anyone feeling sorry for me, but we both know something did happen. I learned a little bit while being with you. You immediately looked at me with lustful eyes when you saw me at the supermarket, so you've already sinned, Baby. Isn't that what Matthew 5:28 says?"

"So you're one of those non-believers who still wants to use the Word of God to your advantage. Just get out! I can't even look at you anymore."

Stormie rolled her eyes and proceeded to walk to her car. Before she got in, she turned around and sarcastically said, "But really, Coco? You could've done better."

I slammed the door, went into the family room, and plopped down into my recliner. I put one of the throw pillows over my face and began punching it with all of the anger and frustration I had inside of me. I wasn't just angry with Stormie. I was angry with myself for allowing this to happen. Even though I was still upset about Miracle not telling me about my dad, I still had to take accountability and fix the mess that I had caused today that I was sure had caused her a lot of pain. I knew that I'd told Miracle that I didn't want to be with her anymore, but the look in her eyes tonight when she said that she was done, hurt me to the core, which led me to believe that I wasn't ready to lose her. I didn't know what to do. I knew she was probably staying at her old house, which she hadn't rented out yet, as planned, but I had too much pride to just go and try to have a talk with her. I didn't want to call her, because if she did answer, I knew we wouldn't be able to effectively communicate without a bunch of yelling, crying, and talking over one another. I did the very best thing that I could've possibly done in that moment. I prayed, and asked God to order my steps and to give me the right words to say whenever I did get the opportunity to talk to Miracle.

Chapter Forty-Two

had fallen asleep on the sofa, and it seemed like as soon as the sun rose and began shining through my large picture window, my doorbell rang. I looked at the time, and it was only seven-thirty. I wasn't expecting anyone, so several thoughts started running through my mind. There was a strong possibility that it was Stormie coming back to give her plan another chance to succeed, or it could've been Miracle, wanting to talk about what had happened. The only way I was going to find out was by opening the door for whoever it was. I jumped up off of the sofa and wiped my hand across my face, that I hadn't even gotten a chance to wash, as I walked to the door. When I opened the door, I looked down and saw my mom, and she didn't look happy.

Without saying a word, she pushed me out the way, and headed towards the living room. I had known my mom long enough to know that meant to get my butt in there. When I walked into the living room, my mom was standing in the middle of the floor, with a pouted mouth, and her eyes glaring at me.

"What's wrong, Ma?"

"Really, Ezekiel? You leave the best thing in your life for Stormie?"

Immediately realizing things had gotten misconstrued, I said, "What? Nooo, that's not what happened at all!"

Before I could explain myself, my mom asked, "So, was Stormie here last night?"

"Yes, but . . ."

"Were you holding her?"

"Yeah, but . . ."

"Did you have dinner with her?"

Before I responded, I realized how badly this really did look. Sometimes when we do things, they don't seem as bad as they are until someone else expounds on the situation, describing the details, out loud. Regardless of how Miracle had hurt me, there was no excuse for allowing Stormie to get so close.

"Well?" my mom said, waiting on me to answer.

Of the events I took a deep breath and said, "Yes, I did all of the above, and there is absolutely no excuse for it. I took the bait, but that's all that happened before Miracle got here. I didn't invite Stormie over. I didn't even give her my address. She just showed up. She made me feel sorry for her, and I let her come in. I just happened to be in the middle of cooking myself some dinner."

My mom shook her head and said, "Ezekiel, I know you know better than that. After all you went through with Stormie, and on top of that, the things that Miracle told us about her, you should've made sure to stay as far away from her as possible."

"Believe me, that was my intention, but I don't know what happened. There was something that tugged on my heart."

"What?!?! Are you really thinking that there's something still there?"

"No, nothing like that. It just felt like something was wrong. Like she really needed someone."

"My poor son with that huge heart like your daddy's. I can't fault you for that, but you have to be really careful in this life."

"I know."

"Well, this all just happened, so obviously Stormie wasn't the cause of you and Miracle initially separating, so are you ready to talk about it? Miracle said if you hadn't told me yet, then she didn't want to go into it without the two of you being on common ground."

I sat down, and my mom sat down next to me.

She put her hand on my shoulder and said, "What is it, Son? She wasn't unfaithful, was she?"

I could tell in her face that it hurt her to even say that, and she was hoping that wasn't the case.

"No, Ma. I found out some things that opened up some old wounds.

Nervously, my mom said, "What is it?"

"I found a box in our closet with the information about how her parents died."

My mom slowly held her head down and sighed.

"Ma? You ok?"

She took a deep breath and hesitantly said, "I was hoping this didn't happen, or at least when it did, it would be at a point in your marriage that you would be able to handle it in a way that it wouldn't negatively affect your marriage."

Angrily, I stood up and said, "So this whole time you knew? So you and Miracle just kept this from me? When did she tell you?"

"Boy, sit down!"

I did as I was told, trying to control my emotions, and waiting to hear my mom explain herself.

"Miracle didn't tell me, and she has no idea that I know who she is. I never mentioned it because I didn't want it to interfere with what was preordained by God. I recognized her name from the police report when I first met her. It was supposed to be undisclosed because she was underage at the time, but you know, I knew a lot of people within both the fire department and the police department."

My mom didn't look sad about this at all. I didn't understand that. She loved my dad so much that it didn't seem right for her to be ok with being around the person who he died, saving. The thing that was even more strange to me was that my mom loved spending time with her. She loved Miracle just as much as I did.

"How do you not resent her?" I asked.

"Ezekiel, your dad loved what he did. He loved people, and he loved saving them and doing whatever else he could do for them. Miracle has been a carrying a lot. Both of her parents died in that fire and she survived. In addition to that, someone else died trying to save her. Just imagine all of the sadness and guilt that she has lived with as a child and as an adult, until she met us. Do you think that was a coincidence?"

I couldn't even answer. My mom was making a lot of sense, but it still hurt. Miracle was with my dad during his final moments. I wondered what he was feeling or what he was saying, if anything. Was he thinking about me and my mom, or worried whether or not he would come home to us that night?

"Miracle is a beautiful person inside and out, and I know that God led her to us. More specifically, He led her to you. Without talking to her, I knew that she had a beautiful spirit. They held her at the police station after that fire and tried to charge her. I knew she couldn't have done what they said she did. They tried their best to convince me that she had started that fire, so that I could be angry with her and blame her for your dad's death. They had no other leads, and wanted to pin it on her just because she was the only survivor. I told them that they would regret it if they continued to pursue her as a suspect."

"So what happened?" I asked.

"Let's just say when I spoke those powerful words to the police chief, I had no idea what was going to happen, but I had faith and prayed that they would leave that girl alone and let her live her life because it was already going to be hard enough. That's exactly what they did. They never found the culprit, and the only evidence they had were three empty gas cans that were left on the side of the house."

A tear ran down my face, and I quickly wiped it away.

"It's ok to be sad, cry, yell, scream, whatever you need to do. Yes, it is an unfortunate situation, and I wish your dad could still be here, but fortunately, God gave us someone else just as wonderful."

I was still speechless. I wanted to feel betrayed by both Miracle and my mom, but I couldn't. I also wasn't sure that things could just go back to the way they were with me and Miracle.

My mom stood up and said, "It looks like you need some time by yourself to think, and I hope some of the things that I've said helps in your thinking process, and in giving you some peace and clarity. Just remember, Miracle loves you, and so do I."

She kissed me on the forehead and showed herself to the door. I heard the door shut, and I broke down in a million tears. I had never felt so torn in my life. This was the type of pain that no matter how hard you tried, it wasn't going to go away without calling on God. I got on my knees in the middle of my living room floor and threw my hands in the air, surrendering everything that I had inside of me to God. I wanted whatever it was that He wanted for me. I wanted to stop trying to do things on my own, and I knew that God knew the desires of my heart. I prayed and pleaded with God to help me through what I was going through. I had been through so many things throughout my life, and He'd brought me through each and every time. Yes, I had to experience a lot of pain, but I'd never succumbed to it because God had given me His strength. Whatever was meant to happen was going to happen regardless, and I would prevail.

After over an hour of talking to God, crying out to Him, repenting, and begging for Him to speak to me and lead me onto the right path, I sat quietly with my eyes closed, waiting on Him. While I waited, I heard my dad's voice say, "Standing by your side, you're going to have a great woman to accomplish all those great things with you."

It sounded exactly how it did when he had said it to me when I was only ten years old, and I had never forgotten. It sounded so real that I could've sworn he was in the room with me.

"But who is this woman, because every time I think I've found her, I end up feeling misled. I just don't know anymore," I said out loud, wanting God to answer me.

While my eyes were still closed, I suddenly felt a presence. I'd felt it many times before when I would pray, but this time, it was a little different. Although things in my life had been extremely hectic, I suddenly felt a peace come over me. I suddenly felt like I was kneeling atop a cloud with nothing else underneath me, but I still felt safe and protected. My body felt light as a feather, and I knew that God was there, holding and comforting me. I finally opened my eyes, and I saw a vision. I saw my dad fighting through the smoke and flames until he found Miracle. He was coughing profusely, but he never gave up. It was as if I could see his thoughts, and my mom and I were on his mind the entire time, but he had to save the girl. He couldn't let this girl who hadn't even had a chance to live her life yet, die. She had so much more life to live. He felt that if he didn't make it, he had completed his assignment.

When he finally found her, the smoke was also overtaking her. He lifted her up and as he hopped over the flames and struggled to breathe, he managed to ask her what her name was.

She was also struggling to breathe, but she managed to say, "Miracle."

He replied, "My name is Ezra, Miracle, and after this, you are going to be a great miracle to someone."

The vision ended there. I couldn't believe what I'd just seen, but I believed it was real.

Just then, I heard a voice that clearly said, "Receive your miracle."

That was my confirmation.

Chapter Forty-Three

Although I had already assumed where Miracle was, my mom confirmed that was where she was, since Miracle wouldn't answer any of my calls. When I pulled up to her house, I saw her car outside. I didn't know how she was going to react, but I had to at least make things right on my end, even if she never wanted to talk to me again. I knew what it had looked like the night before, and I couldn't blame her for how she felt.

I got out of the car, feeling nervous, due to not knowing how Miracle would respond to me. Miracle had never come across as an irrational person, but under the circumstances, and with them involving Stormie, I really didn't know what to expect. I rang Miracle's doorbell, then nervously cleared my throat and put my hands in my pockets. I stood there patiently, waiting for Miracle to answer. After about a minute, right before I was about to ring the doorbell again, I heard the knob turn.

Miracle appeared, only slightly opening the door, and she said, "What do you want, Ezekiel?" sounding irritated.

"Will you please just let me in? We need to talk."

"Oh, now you want me to talk when you want to talk, but when I felt that we needed to talk, you didn't want to have anything to do with me. Now how is that fair?"

"I know, Miracle, and I'm sorry. Please just let me in."

She just stared at me through the small crack, with disappointment written all over her face. Feeling defeated, I slowly turned around and began walking back towards my car. Suddenly, I heard the door creak, so I turned around and saw that the door was fully pushed open.

I didn't see Miracle, so I still knocked, peeked in, and said, "Miracle, is it ok if I come in?"

Sounding as if she was in another room, she sarcastically said, "The door is open, isn't it?"

"That it is," I quietly said, as I stepped in and shut the door.

Miracle came from the kitchen with a cup of coffee in her hand, wearing a robe and a towel wrapped around her hair.

"Have a seat," she said, not looking very excited to see me.

I put my arms out and said, "Can I at least have a hug first?"

"I think we should talk first," she replied, sounding like she meant business.

I nodded my head, and said, "I can respect that," as I walked over to the sofa and sat down.

I looked around and said, "Your place looks nice. It looks like you've changed some stuff around," I said, trying to lighten the mood.

"Yeah, you seem to find a lot of things to do with your time when people you love make themselves inaccessible to you."

Miracle didn't say another word as she sat down in the chair across from me.

After a few minutes of dead silence, she took a sip of her coffee and said, "Ok, Ezekiel. Tell me what you could possibly have to say to me after last night."

I took a deep breath, realizing that this wasn't going to be easy, and I really needed to let Miracle know just how much I loved her, after I'd completely shown her otherwise.

"I just want to first apologize for how I treated you when I found out that my dad died saving you. I was just caught off guard. It took a long time for me to get past the pain of losing my dad, and it was like that pain suddenly came back and erupted into anger. My emotions took control so quickly that I didn't even have time to see your perspective, or even really hear what you were trying to say. I know how caring my dad was, and there was no way he was going to watch you run back into that house and not save you, or die trying."

I took a deep breath and tilted my head back to keep the tears that had formed in my eyes from running down my face.

"The more I think about it, and the more I pray, I realize more and more that this was definitely predestined by God and I'm not going to let anyone, or anything come in between us."

"Ezekiel, I really do accept your apology, but you have hurt me so much. I can completely understand you being upset with me about not telling you that I knew who your dad was, but the things you said to me were completely unacceptable. Yes, I could've definitely been honest and told you the truth, but I knew how much your dad meant to you and I was honestly just trying to save you from this pain. No matter how we handle this situation, it's not going to change what happened all those years ago."

I held my head down and said, "I know."

"I came to the house last night so that we could talk things out, but the last thing I expected to see was you there with Stormie. So many things went through my mind at that moment. I could barely even sleep last night because I was sitting back wondering if you had been in contact with her all along, and if you had just been waiting for a reason to leave me for her."

Miracle could no longer hide her true emotions and began to cry.

I quickly jumped up off of the sofa so that I could console my wife. I lifted her up out of the chair and held her tight. I never wanted to let her go. I knew exactly how special she was, and I would never allow anything to make me question that again.

"Miracle, I love you, and you never have to worry about me wanting to be with Stormie or anyone else."

As Miracle sobbed with her head on my chest, I told her how I'd seen Stormie in the supermarket that day, and she just showed up at the house later on. I assured her that there was nothing at all going on between me and Stormie. I didn't want Miracle to have any reason whatsoever to not trust me, but even after I told her what happened, she continued to cry, which made me think that she didn't believe me.

"Miracle, look at me," I said, as I gently raised her chin with the tips of my fingers. As she looked at me with tears in her eyes, I said, "You don't have to worry about a thing. I know what I have in you, and I would be crazy to mess this up. You are everything I've ever wanted in a woman. My dad would always tell me that I would have a great woman by my side, and I know for a fact that woman is you."

Miracle said, "I only knew your dad for a few minutes, but it was long enough to know that he was a wonderful man. In the midst of him trying to get us both out of that house alive, he tried to comfort me and keep me calm. He asked me my name and then told me his. Then he said that I was going to be a great miracle to someone. I had no idea that it would be his son. Now I wonder if he did somehow know that it would be you."

I wrapped my arms around Miracle even tighter than before because the words that had just come out of her mouth were confirmation that the vision that I'd had was true. The Lord truly worked in mysterious ways.

I kissed Miracle on the forehead and said, "Pack up your stuff, Baby. We're going home."

Chapter Forty-Four

Allll was well in the Whitfield household. I was so happy to have my wife back with me, although we were never truly apart in spirit. After everything was out in the open, especially all of the trauma that we had experienced that we didn't want or like to talk about, I realized that those traumas were some of the reasons that Miracle and I were brought together. We could talk to each other about anything, and it was so comforting. We understood each other like no other, and we complemented each other like no one else could have. It was a beautiful thing to know beyond a shadow of a doubt that when God created me, He knew that He would also create Miracle just for me.

Sometimes we can become disappointed and give up on love because the person that we believed to be our soulmates turned out to be someone that we never really even knew. We tend to see someone and instantly feel an attraction and gravitate towards them, but we don't realize that it's our flesh doing the thinking for us. Sometimes we allow people to fill voids within us that were never meant to be filled by that person. They were meant to be filled by God. We end up shutting the door on God's will for our lives, and that's how we end up in situations with people that wasn't ordained by God. Sadly, it happens every day, even to people who are already in marriages that were ordained by God. A husband or wife may have a void that they can't fill, causing them to be unhappy. They end up thinking that they're unhappy with their spouse, but that really isn't the case at all. The problem is that they haven't allowed God to fill that void and to be in the center of their marriage, so they want their spouse to fill it. When they can't, in many cases, they go to someone else, thinking that they can. Sometimes it seems like that other person fills that void for a little while, and the grass seems so much greener, but then they feel empty once again, and the grass begins to turn to hay.

Miracle and I put all of our faith in God. We weren't perfect, but we were perfect for each other, and we were willing to accept each other's imperfections. It was different for me to be with a woman and not feel like I had to walk on eggshells in fear that I would say something that would cause an argument. If either Miracle or I had an issue or concern with one another, because we sometimes definitely did, we were able to talk things out instead of raising our voices, cursing each other out, or walking away in anger. No marriage is perfect, and that was what I tried to keep in mind while trying to save my marriage to Stormie, but both parties have to be willing to work on things and sometimes make sacrifices. Miracle and I were a team, and God was the captain. We knew that as long as we kept God first, we could get through anything victoriously, and what we were about to experience, we were definitely going to need God's grace and mercy.

About six months after Miracle had moved back in, one morning as soon as I got to work, Miracle called me, and as soon as I heard the tone in her voice, I knew it was serious. I actually knew it was serious as soon as I saw her calling because she was normally exceptionally busy working in the morning, and I wouldn't hear from her until the afternoon, whenever she would decide to take a break.

"Hey, Babe," I said as soon as I picked up the phone.

I heard Miracle take a deep breath into the phone, and I instantly became worried.

"Miracle, are you ok?"

"Yes, I'm fine," she hesitated. "I'm actually sitting here in the living room with Stormie."

"What?" I said, immediately becoming both upset and worried at the same time. I was upset because Stormie had no business being at my house, and worried because I knew about Stormie's past and how her mind could work. I was afraid that something could trigger her to become dangerous.

"I'm on my way!" I said, as I began to pack up my things.

"Calm down, Ezekiel. Everything is ok, but I do need to talk to you so we can figure this out together."

I then heard Stormie in the background, attempting to yell, but her voice didn't sound the same.

"This is my ex-husband's house! I had him first, so you don't have a say-so in anything! He loves me!" she said.

"Miracle, what's going on. I'm coming home."

I then heard Miracle say, "Stormie, sit right there. I'll be right back."

"I know you will! Tell my husband I need to see him!" Stormie said.

"Ezekiel, Stormie is not well," Miracle said, after walking out of the room.

"Well we already know this. Just tell her to leave, or call the police if you have to."

"You don't understand, Ezekiel. She's really ill. You should see her. She doesn't look like herself at all."

"Miracle, listen, she has caused enough chaos in both of our lives. We can't allow her to come in and try to destroy what we have. Just tell her she has to go."

Miracle became silent.

"Miracle? You there?"

"I can't do that, Ezekiel. You're really not hearing what I'm saying to you right now. I'll call you back."

"Miracle, wait!"

Miracle had already hung up, and I quickly headed for the door. My wife needed me, and I was going to be there no matter what. When I pulled up to our house, I saw Stormie's Audi parked out front. I pulled into the driveway and quickly jumped out of the car and ran to the door.

"Miracle!" I said, as I stormed through the door.

Miracle came from around the corner and said, "You didn't have to come home. I'm ok."

"Well I'm not ok with her being here," I said as I attempted to walk towards the living room.

Miracle kept jumping in front of me, trying to talk as I was trying to make my way to Stormie.

Finally, Miracle realized she wasn't strong enough to hold me back, so she said, "Ezekiel, stop!"

I immediately stopped in my tracks.

"Listen, you cannot go in there angry. Take a moment and gain your composure. You'll understand in a minute. Just calm down. It's going to be ok. I promise."

I couldn't understand how Miracle was being so calm, but that was just one way in which we were a team. Sometimes one of us had to be the voice of reason. Sometimes it was me and sometimes it was her.

Miracle grabbed my hand and when we walked into the living room, I couldn't believe my eyes. Stormie no longer looked like the woman that I once knew. It hadn't been that long since I'd last seen her, but so much had changed in so little time. Stormie was sitting on the sofa staring at the wall. Her once beautiful brown skin had a grayish undertone, her almond shaped eyes were now sunken with dark circles around them as if she hadn't slept in months, and her beautiful, long, thick hair, was now thin and stringy. Stormie couldn't have weighed more than ninety pounds, and she had never been thin as long as I'd known her. I had noticed the last time I'd seen her that she had lost weight, but I thought that maybe she had just been a little stressed. This weight loss was more than stress. Something wasn't right.

"Oh, you finally decided to arrive, Husband," she said.

I looked at Miracle, and she gestured for me to talk to her.

I had no clue what to say, and I didn't want to say the wrong thing, so I said, "Hey, Stormie, what's going on?"

"Oh, the other woman didn't fill you in?"

I couldn't stand there and allow Stormie to disrespect my wife, no matter what was going on with her.

"She's my wife, Stormie, so you need to address her as such."

"Whatever," Stormie said, disregarding what I'd said. "Anyway, I'm a little sick, and you and I both know that when we said our vows, you said 'through sickness and health', so this is the moment that you need to stand by what you said, Zeke."

"Stormie, we're not married anymore. If you need us to help you find the proper care you need, we can do that."

Stormie sat there silently and began shaking her head. "I knew you never really loved me. Look at me, Zeke! If you ever loved me, you wouldn't even be able to stand seeing me like this. Don't you think I know how to find proper care? Doctors and nurses have been caring for me for a while now, but they say there's nothing else that they can do. They want to put me in hospice. I have no one, Zeke, and I need you. When Brandon found out that I had ovarian cancer, you know what he said? He told me that he was looking for a lifelong partner that he could start a family and have children with, and that I wouldn't be around long enough to do any of that. He told me that you had dodged a bullet."

Stormie began to cry. I sat next to her on the sofa and hugged her. As I hugged her, all I could feel were her bones. It felt as if I held her too tight, her fragile body would break.

"I don't want to die alone," she said as I held her.

I looked at Miracle, and she looked as if she was about to cry. I was stuck in between a rock and hard place. I knew what the right thing was to do, but I didn't want to do it. I couldn't even let the words come out of my mouth, but my teammate could, and she did.

"Stormie, how about we have hospice set up here? I work from home, so I'll be here with you even when the nurses aren't."

My wife was exceptional. Just like that she was able to put the past behind her and offer to take care of her enemy. The world would've been a better place if there had been more people out there like Miracle.

"I don't need you, nor did I ask you to do me any favors," Stormie said, unpleasantly.

I was taken aback by the way Stormie spoke to Miracle when she ultimately needed her help. It was very apparent that Stormie had a lot of hatred and resentment towards Miracle that had not been addressed.

Sweetly, Miracle said, "Sweetie, you asked my husband, so therefore you asked me because we are one."

I could tell by the expression on Stormie's face that she was confused and didn't know how to respond to Miracle's kind demeanor.

"So, Stormie, would you like to take us up on our offer, or do you have something else in mind?" Miracle continued.

Stormie really didn't have any other choice besides going into a hospice facility, or going home alone without any assistance.

"I just want to lie down. Where's my room?" Stormie said, sounding agitated.

Miracle gestured for me to show Stormie the guest room.

When I opened the bedroom door, I told her to make herself at home, and asked if she needed for us to go get some things from her house.

"I keep everything in the same places that I used to at the house. Nothing much has changed since you left . . . Except that you weren't there," Stormie said, with a sense of sadness and remorse in her voice.

"Clothes, shoes, toothbrush . . . I'm sure you know what I need. I probably won't need much to last me very long."

When Stormie said those words, reality set in that Stormie really wasn't going to be around much longer.

"Don't talk like that, Stormie," I replied.

"But it's the truth. I've lived my life and now it's coming to an end. I never thought it would end like this. The person I mistreated the most is the person that I had to run back to."

I felt myself becoming emotional, so I told Stormie to get comfortable and get some rest. After I walked out and shut the door, I turned around, leaned by back against the door and took a deep breath. While standing there, I could hear Stormie on the other side of the door crying. No matter how she had treated me in the past, I could do nothing but have sympathy for her.

Miracle came down the hall and said, "Is everything ok?"

Before I could answer, she heard Stormie crying and saw the tears in my eyes that had not yet fallen.

She hugged me and said, "I know, Babe. It's going to be ok."

After regaining my composure, I called my mom. I wasn't excited to tell her what was going on, but I needed her help. I was going over to Stormie's house to pick up some things, but I needed Miracle to come along because she would better know what Stormie needed than I would, so I needed my mom to stay with Stormie while we were gone.

"Hey, Baby," my mom said cheerfully as soon as she answered the phone.

Dreadfully, I said, "Hey, Ma."

My mom's cheerfulness immediately turned into concern.

"What's wrong, Ezekiel?"

"We have a situation."

"Now what? I don't know how many more situations I can handle with you two," she said, teasing.

"It's Stormie. She's . . ."

"Wreaking havoc again?" my mom interrupted. "She's going to do whatever she can to break the two of you up, but you can't let her win. You probably need to get a restraining order against her because this . . ."

"Ma, it's nothing like that." I said, stopping my mom midsentence.

"Well, what else could it be?"

"Ma, Stormie is extremely ill. She has Ovarian Cancer and the doctors have referred her to Hospice, but she refuses to go. She said she doesn't want to die alone."

"Not trying to sound heartless, Baby, but what does that have to do with you?"

"Ma, I felt the same way. I feel bad for her, but I don't think this is a good idea."

"What are you talking about? What isn't a good idea?" my mom asked curiously.

"Miracle offered to set up Hospice here at the house."

"What??? That girl is something else. After all that Stormie has done, she still wants to help her. That's a hell of a woman!" my mom said, sounding impressed. "So what are you going to do, Son?"

"If that's what Miracle's spirit is telling her to do, who am I to tell her not to obey God? My biggest concern is how Stormie has already been speaking to her. She talks to her as if she and I are still married and Miracle's the other woman. For her to be in the condition she's in and need our help, she's pretty rude."

"Well, I believe Miracle can hold her own, and if it gets too bad, I'm sure she'll do what she has to do."

"I'm sure she can," I said, feeling reassured.

"So what's next?" my mom asked, sensing I needed to ask her something.

"Well, since that's out the way, I wanted to ask if you could come by and stay here with Stormie while Miracle and I go over to her house and pick up some things."

My mom took a deep breath, and said, "Now that may not be a good idea!" She then laughed and said, "Of course I can, but let me pray first."

"That's fair," I said, knowing my mom well enough to know that she was very serious, and she definitely needed to pray before dealing with Stormie.

Faith

Chapter Forty-Five

When I got to Ezekiel and Miracle's house to watch over Stormie, I really didn't know what to expect. Ezekiel had made it sound like the situation was pretty bad, and I knew it had to have been bad for Miracle to allow Stormie back into her home. Ezekiel told me that Stormie was in the guest room sleeping when I got there, so I decided to not even enter the room if I didn't have to. I sat in the living room and pulled out a book I'd brought with me to read. While reading, I must've dozed off, but I was suddenly awakened by a somewhat familiar voice.

"Zeke! Where are you, Husband?"

I quickly jumped up when I realized that it was Stormie calling for Ezekiel. I slowly opened the door to the guestroom and peeked in. The room was dark, but I could see Stormie trying to figure out who had cracked the door open.

"Zeke, is that you?" she said, still unsure.

I turned the light on, and said, "No, Stormie, it's me, your lovely ex-mother in law."

Stormie looked very surprised, and in fact, did look very ill. Stormie was always a beautiful girl on the outside. I couldn't take that from her, but she was always so ugly on the inside. As soon as I stepped into the room, I could feel a dark presence. It shook me for a moment, but I knew that the Lord was covering me. Stormie was terribly emaciated, and I could understand how Miracle couldn't turn her away.

I could tell she wasn't expecting me at all, but seemed as if she had been waiting a long time to get some things off of her chest.

"I wouldn't consider you very lovely, but you are in fact my mother in law."

"Ex mother in law," I stressed. "Sometimes people who aren't very lovely themselves, can't identify with or don't notice the lovelies of this world when they're right in their face."

Frustrated, Stormie said, "Why are you here?"

"Why are you the way that you are?" I asked Stormie, sincerely not understanding how someone could be as evil and vindictive as she was.

"How am I? Please tell me," Stormie said, forcefully.

"I know you've had some rough times in your life, but we all have. If we get through those rough times, we should be able to better appreciate the good times. You've had so many great opportunities in your life. You went to a great college, met a great, God-fearing man, got your degree, got married, got a good job, a nice house, and a nice car. In the midst of all of that, yes, you and Ezekiel went through some difficult things, but you had a man that was willing to go through those things with you and grow from them. He's not perfect, as none of us are, but he would've never given up on your marriage if you hadn't. You just couldn't appreciate all that you had, and you treated someone who loved you more than you probably could've ever been loved by anyone else like a piece of trash. Now he lets you into his house with his wife to take care of you, and you're still disrespectful while lying there not knowing how long you have left to be on this earth, or where you're going when you leave here."

Confidently, Stormie said, "I know exactly where I'm going when I leave here. I'm going where everyone else goes, and that's nowhere. When our lives are over, they're just over. You all kill me, thinking there's something so beautiful waiting on the other side when we die. If that was the case, why would God put us here to suffer instead of letting us experience "Heaven" in the first place?"

I was so disappointed to hear Stormie speak the way that she was speaking about God and Heaven. I would've thought that being in the situation that she was in, she would've had some type of epiphany, realizing that God is real. I was obviously wrong, so I just knew that I had to do some heavy duty praying that God would speak to her and show her His face before it was too late. I had learned long ago that religion was very touchy, and I couldn't force anyone to believe what I believed. If I did, in most cases that would push them further away from the truth, so I learned to just plant seeds. I felt that I had done that with Stormie by making her face who she truly was as a person. Sometimes people are in denial and don't truly see how the way that they are and the things that they do affect not only others, but also themselves.

"Stormie, I know you're going to believe what you're going to believe, but just remember that people around here do actually love and care about you. Believe it or not, it's not because of the "great things you've done" or the way you've treated them."

Stormie actually looked as if she was pondering on some of the things I'd said, so I took that opportunity to say, "So, what was it that you needed with Ezekiel? He's not here right now. There's only me, and I'll be happy to get whatever you need."

"Did he call my doctor yet to set up hospice?" she asked, humbly.

"I don't think so, but if you give me the doctor's number, I can do that for you."

Stormie slowly got up out of the bed with her oversized jeans barely holding on. She went into her purse and grabbed a folded up sheet of paper. I walked over to get it from her, but first I attempted to give her a hug. As soon as I got too close, she immediately backed up as if something was prohibiting her to even touch me. That's when I felt that dark presence become even stronger, and I knew that Stormie had several demons that she needed to be delivered from. I took the paper from Stormie and told her that I would get it taken care of.

As soon as I left out of the room from with Stormie, I no longer felt the presence that I was feeling, which was a relief. I immediately began praying for Stormie, as well as Ezekiel and Miracle, and I prayed throughout the entire house, commanding all demonic forces to vacate the premises. The last thing Ezekiel and Miracle needed was for Stormie's demons to think that they had an invitation to wreak havoc in their home.

Miracle

Chapter Forty-Six

When we pulled up to Stormie's house, I began feeling a little uneasy, knowing that this was the home that Ezekiel shared with her. I was just hoping that I wouldn't see anything to upset me, or that the memories wouldn't negatively affect Ezekiel.

"You ready?" Ezekiel looked over at me in the passenger seat, and said before we got out.

I nodded, and said, "Yep, as ready as I'm going to be. Hopefully this doesn't take long."

"It shouldn't. I know where everything is."

I knew I shouldn't have been bothered by Ezekiel's response, but for some reason I was. I began questioning myself, wondering if I was insecure and threatened by Stormie, even in the condition that she was in, and if I was doing the right thing. I began thinking maybe I should've just let her go to a Hospice facility, or fend for herself, but that just wasn't in my DNA.

When we walked into Stormie's home, I immediately noticed the scent in the air. It was Ezekiel's favorite plug-in scent that he always bought for our house, so I was sure Stormie felt right at home while at our home. I sighed and continued to follow behind Ezekiel up the stairs to the bedroom.

"She was right. Everything is exactly how it was when I left," he said.

At this point, in my head I was thinking, *Will he just shut up?*

"Does she hang most of her clothes up?" I hesitantly asked Ezekiel as I walked towards the walk-in closet.

"Yeah, all of her clothes should be in there."

"Ok, I'll grab some things out of there."

When I walked into the closet, I was amazed at the amount of clothes and shoes Stormie had. I would've never been able to find anything to wear if all of what she had was mine because I would've been too overwhelmed by it all. I know people say that you can never have too many clothes, but in my opinion, Stormie had way too many clothes. I could've thought of a whole lot of charities to donate a lot of her stuff to.

While in her closet, I found a couple of suitcases to pack her things in. After I was done, I rolled the suitcases out of the closet and found Ezekiel going through Stormie's lingerie drawer, pulling out panties and bras.

"I could've gotten those," I said, slightly rolling my eyes.

Ezekiel said, "I know. I was just trying to help." He held up one of her bras, which was a lot bigger than mine, and said, "I don't know if she can even fit any of these anymore."

Trying to keep my cool, I said, "Well, she probably can't fit a lot of this stuff anymore. You saw the pants she had on. She was wearing a belt, and they were still falling down."

"Yeah. Poor Stormie. I would've never wished any of this on her," he said, sympathetically.

I walked over to Stormie's nightstand that was next to her bed and picked up a beautiful picture frame with a picture inside. It was actually a picture of her and Ezekiel. They looked like they have may been on an island, and they genuinely looked happy with the biggest, brightest smiles on their faces.

Ezekiel walked up behind me and wrapped his arms around my waist.

"That was the first vacation we were able to take after graduating from college and becoming established in our careers. We called it a late honeymoon," he said.

"You two look happy and perfect for one another."

"We were happy, but obviously weren't perfect for one another. I'm both happy and perfect with you," he said, before kissing me on the cheek.

He made my heart smile again because being in Stormie's house had definitely done something to me. I felt like a dark cloud had come hovering over me as soon as I'd stepped in the door. I didn't understand why Stormie would still have a picture up of the two of them, especially right next to her bed unless she felt as though she still had a chance with Ezekiel. Maybe she did regret all that she had done to Ezekiel and the guilt had eaten her up inside to the point of illness.

"I think we have everything. You ready to go?" Ezekiel said.

As I looked around the room, I said, "Yeah. If she needs anything else, we can always come back."

I then noticed the journal sitting next to the picture of Stormie and Ezekiel. I had missed it before because I was so focused on the picture. I thought it might've been something important to her, so I grabbed it before we left.

When we arrived back at our house, Faith's car was still parked in the driveway, so that was a good sign that Stormie hadn't run her off with her horrible attitude.

"I see your mom was up to, and met the challenge!" I said, giggling, as Ezekiel and I grabbed Stormie's things out of the car.

"Ezekiel laughed and said, "My mom can handle anything that comes her way. The two of you are the strongest women that I've ever encountered, and I love that about both of you."

"You're so sweet, Baby," I said, as I rubbed my hand across Ezekiel's back.

As we walked up to the door, Faith opened it.

"How did things go, Faith?" I asked, curiously.

"Oh, they went," she said laughing.

I already knew what that meant. Obviously, things between Stormie and Faith had gone the same way that they had gone between me and Stormie. Faith told us that she had taken care of setting up Hospice and the nurse would be coming to get everything set up the very next day. When Ezekiel and I went into the room with Stormie to put her things away, she looked at him and smiled, but that smile quickly dissipated when she looked at me. I didn't understand why she had so much animosity towards me when I had never done anything to her. She treated me as if I had stolen her husband, when she was the one who had let him go. I definitely hadn't done anything to her while we were kids. I treated her like a sister, just like my parents had treated her like their own daughter. She messed that up by coming on to my dad and accusing him of molesting her. I wanted so badly to ask her why she had done that, but I was sure that she probably didn't know. I knew she had gone through a lot as a child before coming to our house. I also knew that I had no idea of how deep that trauma was, but I did know trauma could cause a person to do things that they wouldn't have normally done, so I decided to let it go. It had happened and nothing was going to change the fact that it happened.

"Thank you so much, Zeke. I appreciate all of this," Stormie said, without addressing me at all.

Before Ezekiel could check her, Faith was right on cue, saying, "Stormie, you need to be thanking Miracle as well. This isn't only Ezekiel's home, therefore, it wasn't only his decision to help you in this unfortunate situation."

Stormie glanced at me, but still said nothing.

Faith folded her arms and cleared her throat as she looked at Ezekiel.

"Stormie, my mom is right. I didn't know if this would be such a good idea, but Miracle refused to have it any other way."

Stormie still didn't say a word, and I wasn't expecting her to. I was doing my part and that's all that mattered to me.

I pulled Stormie's journal out of my purse and handed it to her.

"Here you go," I said. "I saw this and thought you might need it. For me, writing is sometimes a good form of therapy."

Stormie immediately became defensive and said, "Are you saying that I need therapy?"

"Stormie, no matter what you may think, I don't hate you, and I'm not coming for you in any way. I just want to help you. Therapy isn't always sitting in front of someone telling them all of your problems. Therapy can be a range of things. Like I said, I like to write. When I read back over what I've written, it sometimes gives me clarity about things that I'm concerned with."

"Whatever, Coco! You never really liked me. If you did, you would've defended me when I revealed what your daddy had been doing to me. Instead, you let everyone think I was crazy and let them send me away instead of sending your daddy to jail like he deserved!"

Stormie had struck a nerve, and she knew it. She wanted to see me lose my cool, and she was willing to say or do whatever she had to in order to make that happen. That would've satisfied her deep craving that she had at that moment, but I refused to let her take me there. I decided to call her out on her lies so that she would know that the things she was saying would never hold any value, or have any truth to them, no matter how much she tried to make herself and others believe them.

"Stormie, I don't know why after all of these years, you continue to keep up these lies. My family was always good to you, and my dad would have never done the things that you said he did, which is exactly why you were the one that was sent away. No one believed you then, and no one believes you now. I won't let you continue to defame my dad or anyone else in my family."

"Daughters always defend their daddies. I understand . . . Then again, maybe not since I never had a daddy to defend," she said. She paused, and then continued by saying, "One thing I do know is karma is something else. By the way, what ever happened to ole' Gavin?"

I couldn't take anymore. I quickly walked out of the room before I gave Stormie the satisfaction of falling right into her trap. Faith and Ezekiel walked out right behind me.

Faith compassionately said, "Miracle, do not let her get to you. She's very miserable right now. She sees you In the position that she feels she should be in, and is angry at herself because she gave it up. Now she feels that she'll never even have the opportunity to win back her spot, so she wants to make you as miserable as she can for as long as she can. Listen, I'll do whatever you need me to do to help you through this. I know you're passionate about helping her as much as you can, but I also know she's making it very difficult.

"We're both here, Miracle," Ezekiel said.

The three of us huddled in a group hug, and that day, I vowed to make Stormie's transition as peaceful as possible, and to not allow myself to take anything she said personal, because like Faith had said, she was angry at herself, not me.

The next day, the Hospice nurse came in to set everything up. She explained the process to all of us, including Stormie. When the nurse mentioned that the doctor determined that Stormie would live for about another month, Stormie's eyes filled with tears, but she worked hard to hold them back. At that moment, I saw right through her. I saw a scared woman who had been running all of her life, unsure of what she was looking for. She had been dealt a bad hand to start off with, and refused to believe in, and call on God. . . the only one that could've changed things for her, and put her on the right path. I still believed that God was able. He was a miracle worker, and could still change Stormie. She just needed to let Him into her heart. I prayed every day that she would.

Faith

Chapter Forty-Seven

Every day, I went over to Ezekiel and Miracle's house to help with Stormie while Miracle tried to get some work done. Sometimes I just went by to keep Miracle company. I watched her day in and day out, catering to Stormie, while also enduring Stormie's verbal and mental abuse. She fixed her meals, prayed by her bedside as she slept, and made sure she was always as comfortable as possible. The nurse had said that Stormie had only about a month left to live, but three months in, Stormie was still holding on. Although she was slowing down more and more, she was still able to move around on her own. I would check in on her from time to time when she'd be alone in her room, and surprisingly, she would be writing in her journal that Miracle had brought her from her house. I couldn't even lie. I was very curious as to what kinds of hateful things she was writing in it.

Eventually, Stormie got to the point where she could no longer shower or bathe herself. It was so hard to watch her suffer so much, but I watched in admiration of Miracle as she stuck with what she said she was going to do. I could tell that it hurt Miracle to see Stormie going through what she was, and it was affecting her energy level. Both she and Ezekiel seemed to always be tired because Stormie had begun waking up throughout the night, crying out in agonizing pain. It was like having a newborn baby. I offered to come over later in the evenings and spend the night so that I could get up when Stormie would wake up from the pain. Miracle and Ezekiel didn't hesitate to take me up on my offer. They needed some relief, and I was happy to give it to them.

One evening I got to their house for one of my many sleepovers, and Ezekiel let me in.

"Hey, Son. Where's Miracle?"

"She's in the room with Stormie, cleaning her up," he said, looking and sounding exhausted.

"You look tired. Go get some rest," I said softly, and gave him a hug before he headed up the stairs to his bedroom.

I crept around the corner to Stormie's room. The door was cracked, and I could hear talking. I stood by the door without making my presence known.

"I don't know why you're still so nice to me when I've been so mean to you," Stormie said to Miracle, sounding extremely weak.

As Miracle washed her down as she laid in the bed, Miracle said, "Stormie, I know all of the things you've said and done was not you. What's the point in me treating you the way you've treated me and others? That's what Satan wants me to do. That demon that has attached itself to you causes you to be the way that you are, but I'm not going to let that demon keep me from doing God's will. We all care about you, Stormie. If we didn't, we would have given up on you by now."

Stormie closed her eyes and began sobbing.

"Stormie, don't cry," Miracle said, as she stopped what she was doing and leaned over to gently hug Stormie.

Surprisingly, Stormie didn't push her away. It was as if that hug was something she needed. Stormie slowly raised her arms and wrapped them tightly around Miracle.

"You were the sister I never had, and Gavin and Mena were the parents that I always dreamed of having. I could've had a good life with all of you and I made a mess of it. Now look at me. I've done so much and now I don't have time to fix it."

"Stormie, you've never done too much for God to forgive. You are still here, which means God is giving you time to make things right. Not with us, but with him," Miracle replied.

"How do I do that?" Stormie asked.

"Repent of all of your sins and accept God's forgiveness. God loves you unconditionally, Stormie. The love that you've been looking for all of your life, God could've provided that to you if you would've let Him."

Miracle grabbed some tissue off of the dresser and wiped Stormie's eyes for her.

"I've denied God all this time. How do I just expect Him to listen to me now?"

"Listen, Stormie. He will always open His arms to us. We are his children, and just like most Earthly parents, He wants what's best for us. Jesus died on the cross for our sins, and every day that we wake up is a chance for us to do His will and make Him proud. Ezekiel and I have forgiven you, so why do you think that God wouldn't?"

"I guess because I don't know Him the way that I should."

"Do you want to start knowing Him now? I need you to be honest when you answer that question."

"Yes, I do," Stormie said without hesitation.

As I stood there watching Miracle leading one of God's children back to Him, I was in tears.

Ezekiel came out of nowhere, startling me.

"Ma, what's going on? Why are you crying? Is Stormie . . ."

"Shhh," I said, gesturing for him to be quiet.

He looked through the crack and began watching his wife be the beautiful person that she was.

"Do you believe that Jesus is Lord, and that He died and rose from the dead to save mankind?"

"Yes, but does it really matter what I believe now? What if God thinks that I only believe now because I'm on my deathbed?" Stormie said, sounding concerned about her destiny.

"God knows your heart, Stormie. He knows everything about you, so if you truly believe, and I believe that you do, He knows that, ok?"

"Ok."

Miracle held Stormie's hand and said, "Close your eyes and repeat after me, saying and believing every word with your entire heart," Miracle said.

Stormie nodded in agreement, with tears still streaming down her face.

Miracle prayed, and Stormie repeated, "Heavenly Father, I come boldly to your throne in the mighty name of Jesus. I thank you for allowing us to feel your presence in this room right now, Lord. Your Word says in the book of Acts 2:21, 'Whosoever shall call on the name of the Lord shall be saved.' I'm calling on you right now, praying and asking Jesus to come into my heart and be Lord over my life. I choose to turn away from my sins and everything that's not of you and your will for my life. I give myself to you, and I receive your forgiveness. Please, Lord, take your rightful place in my life as my Personal Savior and Lord. Lord, reign in my heart, cover me with your blood, and fill me with your love. Live in me, Lord, helping me to become more like you. According to Romans 10:9-10, 'If thou shalt confess with thy mouth the Lord Jesus, and shalt believe in thine heart that God hath raised him from the dead, thou shalt be saved.' I do that right now, in the mighty name of Jesus. I confess that Jesus is Lord, and I believe in my heart that God raised Him from the dead. I thank you for hearing my prayers and for restoring me right now. Thank you, God, for loving me unconditionally. In Jesus' unmatchable name, I pray, Amen."

Stormie repeated every single word after Miracle with as much conviction in her voice that she could've possibly had under the circumstances.

They both then opened their eyes, and Miracle looked around the room with a confused looked on her face. Ezekiel and I then began looking around trying to figure out what she was looking for.

She then said, "Did you feel that?"

"Feel what?" Stormie asked, as she also began looking around.

"It's nothing. I just felt a cool breeze. It was probably just the AC coming on. Now back to you. How do you feel?"

"Is that all?" Stormie asked.

"What you just did is major. You just made the biggest decision of your life. As long as you truly believed those words, you are saved. You are a part of God's kingdom and there's nothing anyone can do to take that from you."

Stormie smiled and said, "I'm so sorry, Coco . . . I mean, Miracle."

Miracle smiled back at her as she held her hand and said, "It's ok, you can call me Coco. I kind of missed being called that, and I know you're sorry. I forgave you a long time ago."

"You forgave me for the things that you know of. There are things that you don't know."

"Well, I forgive you for all of it," Miracle said.

"Thank you . . . Coco."

"You're welcome, Stormie. I think we've done enough here tonight. Do you need anything before I head to bed?"

"No. I'm fine. I actually feel a lot better."

"Good," Miracle said, as she walked towards the door.

"Hey, Coco."

Miracle turned around and said, "Yes, Stormie?"

"Tell Zeke . . . I mean Ezekiel and Faith that I said I'm sorry, too."

"You can tell them in the morning," Miracle said, as she turned back around, smiling.

I could see the joy all over Miracle's face that came from accomplishing one of God's purposes for her life. When she walked out of that room, she was surprised to see us.

"How long have you two been out here?" she asked.

"Long enough to know that God is very proud of you," I said, smiling from ear to ear.

"Yes, indeed. I love you, Baby," Ezekiel said, grabbing and hugging his wife.

We all went to bed with the joy of the Lord all over us.

Chapter Forty-Eight

The next morning, the sun shined brightly throughout the entire house. Stormie must've had a good night's sleep because she hadn't woken up screaming in excruciating pain all night. I was happy for her because I knew she needed a night of complete rest, and so did everyone else in the house. When I got out of bed to get ready to go back to my own home, I looked out of the window and saw the Hospice nurse walking up to the door to obviously check on Stormie. I threw on my robe and walked out of the room to wake Ezekiel and Miracle, but their bedroom door was already open, and neither of them were inside. I walked downstairs and heard talking, and it sounded like someone was crying. I followed the voices, which led to Stormie's room. When I entered and saw everyone standing around the bed, my heart sank.

"She's gone, Faith," Miracle said, wiping the tears from her eyes.

I put my hands up to my mouth, unable to comprehend that Stormie had left us. She had lasted so much longer than the doctors had said she would, that I wasn't expecting her to leave so soon.

I looked at Ezekiel, and I could tell he was trying his best to stay strong as the nurse finished checking Stormie's vitals to confirm what we weren't quite ready to accept.

"I'm so sorry for your loss. I'll go call the funeral home so that they can come pick her up," the nurse said before leaving the room.

As soon as the nurse left the room, a gorgeous, violet, black, and teal butterfly flew through the open window, into the guestroom. It then landed on the headboard right above where Stormie's lifeless bodied lied. We all took that as a sign that Stormie had made it to her desired eternal home.

"Wow. I never thought this would hurt so bad," Ezekiel said, as he quickly wiped the tear that had caught him off guard.

"It's ok to feel that way. You loved her, and you were probably one of the best things that ever happened to her," Miracle said, trying to console Ezekiel.

"Thank you for being there for her, Babe. She truly needed you."

Ezekiel looked at me and said, "You too, Ma. We were a great team. Stormie's last days were better because of us. I truly know she's in a better place now."

After Ezekiel said that Stormie was in a better place, I began thinking about God's timing. Stormie lived for 6 more months after the doctors told her one month. That in itself was proof that God has the final say. He made sure that Stormie was given enough time to come back to Him, and she did just that. God gives us plenty of opportunities to do right by Him, and it's up to us to use those opportunities whenever they present themselves. Sometimes it takes us being at the mercy of others to realize that the person that we've been towards them hasn't been the person that we were truly destined to be. That realization in itself can sometimes give us the desire to want to change. We can truly appreciate people when they've shown us unconditional love even when we haven't reciprocated it. God has a way of making us look in the mirror at ourselves instead of constantly blaming others and situations for the way that we are. We may not have control over what others do, or the situations that we find ourselves in, but we can control how we respond to people and those situations. We can never let the trauma around us become the trauma within us.

Ezekiel and Miracle organized a beautiful Homegoing service for Stormie at their church. Many of Ezekiel's friends and classmates, including Kyle and his wife, Madison, who he'd finally married, showed up to the service. Most of Ezekiel's entire congregation was also there to show their respects and send their condolences. After everything was all said and done, we all mourned in our own way. Stormie and I had our differences, but I still learned to love her, no matter how hard I tried not to. I knew that it was no one but God who placed that love in my heart for her, and I realized later on just why I needed him to, and that if He hadn't, I may have carried unforgiveness for her in my heart for the rest of my life. The day that I realized that was an extremely emotional day for not only myself, but also for Miracle and Ezekiel.

As I was helping Miracle clean out the guest room that Stormie had used in her final days, I noticed the journal that I had frequently seen her writing in, sitting on the nightstand next to the bed. I tried my best to ignore it, but my curiosity got the best of me. I first picked it up, assessing it without opening it. It was brown and made of leather material. I noticed that the edges were pretty worn, which let me know that she'd probably had it for some years. I really wasn't concerned with what she'd written in the past. I was only interested in knowing what was going through her mind as she knew her life was coming to an end. What was she thinking of us, or even herself? Did she truly have remorse about anything she'd done in the past or during the time she had spent here with us?

As I sat quietly on the edge of the bed, Miracle stopped what she was doing and looked over at me.

"Faith, are you ok?"

I raised up the journal and said, "I don't even know if I should open this. Would she want us to invade her privacy even though she's gone, or do I really even want to know what's in there?"

Miracle sat next to me and said, "I understand your dilemma."

"So, what would you do?" I asked Miracle.

"Well, I think of it like this. If she didn't want anyone to know what was in it, she would've gotten rid of it, knowing that she didn't have very long. Maybe she left it there, right out in the open for a reason."

"So, in other words, you would read it," I said.

Miracle giggled, and said, "Honestly, I probably wouldn't because whatever is in there is in the past, and I would fear that something in there would upset or sadden me. I want to remember Stormie's spirit as it was on that final night that I had the honor of spending with her."

"But Miracle, you just said she may have left it out for a reason. I saw her writing in it often while she was here. Maybe there's something she wants us, or at least you and Ezekiel, to read."

Miracle and I stared at each other for a moment, trying to make the best decision.

Miracle finally said, "Ok, but start from the back."

"I think that's a good idea," I said, smiling.

I opened the journal and flipped towards the back. As I was flipping, I noticed several pages that were filled up from top to bottom. The dates looked like they had begun a little over a year ago. Her very last entry was pretty long, and happened to be written the same night that she'd died.

"Do you want to read," I asked Miracle.

"No, you go ahead."

As I began to read, Ezekiel walked in the room.

"What's going on here?" he asked.

Hoping that Ezekiel didn't feel as though we were making the wrong decision, I looked at him and said, "Well, Stormie left her journal sitting right here on the nightstand, and Miracle and I felt as if there may have been some things that she wanted us to read, so that's what we're doing."

"Are you sure you should be doing that?"

"Well, we're not going to read the whole thing. We don't need to know all of her business, but maybe she wrote some things in here while she was living with you all that she wanted to communicate with you, but didn't know how."

Ezekiel just stood there for a moment, looking back and forth at me and Miracle.

"You could be right, but what if she wanted to keep those things to herself?"

I replied, "Now you and I both know that if Stormie didn't want anyone to ever get ahold of this, she would've ripped each page into a million pieces and burned them before she left here."

He giggled and said, "You're probably right about that."

He then sat next to Miracle as I began reading her final journal entry.

It read:

"If you're reading this, then more than likely I'm dead and gone because you'd know better than going through my stuff while I was still living. (smile) Hopefully I've done enough at the end of my life of only thirty-five years to make it into that better place that so many of you talk about. I didn't believe in God or any of that eternal life stuff for basically my entire life, but when you're at the mercy of others, and can't do much else except think, you tend to think about a lot of things. I've had a lot of time on my hands to ponder on the things that I've done in my life, and the reason that I did them. I used to blame others for the way that I was, but in these past few months I've realized that I had choices, and at the end of the day, I made the decisions that I did because I wanted to. Yes, my past and upbringing did have an effect on me, however, I didn't have to allow it to control me, but I did. I missed out on having a great life of genuinely enjoying wonderful people because I wanted them to be as miserable as I was.

I'm happy that in my final days I had people around me who showed me love, and I hope that they know that I loved them, too, no matter how badly I treated them in the past. I'm also happy that those people are able to read this because there are some things that I've been needing to release that I've been carrying for a very long time. The guilt of all of it has been eating me alive, and is probably what ended up killing me. Neither here nor there, I've done a whole lot of other things that probably had something to do with me leaving this life so soon, but one the of most unforgiveable and disgraceful things that I've done is one in which deeply hurt a lot of people. At the time, I didn't care. It actually made me feel good because I felt as if people could feel the type of pain that I had felt all of my life, but the people that I hurt didn't deserve it. They were great people who actually treated me better than I had ever been treated in my life, and would've probably done anything for me.

Miracle, when your family took me in, I had mixed emotions. I was ecstatic that such a lovely family had chosen me, but was also afraid because I'd been placed with families before that I thought were perfect, and I ended up being molested, and physically, mentally, and emotionally abused. I always felt as if something was wrong with me, and I would constantly try to figure it out. I just couldn't understand why people would treat me the way that they did. I finally had a realization that if I did exactly what people wanted me to do, especially the men, things weren't so bad. I even began to feel loved and comforted by them.

With all of that being said, by the time I reached your home, it was instilled in me that I was supposed to cater to men. If I did this, they would love and care about me. The problem was, your dad, Gavin, wasn't like the other men. He was actually a good man. Not a child molester like the others, but I didn't understand that. My mind had already been polluted with things that no child should've ever had to think about and be consumed with. That night when I tried to seduce your dad and he rejected me, I felt so much anger and pain inside of me. I was confused all over again. What I had come to understand didn't work this time. 'Why doesn't he want me? I did everything that I was supposed to do,' I thought.

Besides my mom pawning me off for drugs when I was only four years old, your parents sending me away was the worst thing that ever happened to me. It was my fault, but I was only a kid and didn't realize that it was my fault for a very long time. Instead of blaming my mom, I blamed them for years for the way that my life ended up. When I think about it now, my life still wasn't that bad. I went to college, met a great man, graduated, and got married, but there were things that still didn't allow me to be genuinely happy.

Anyway, back to that night. When your dad rejected me and I was sent away to a group home, nothing was on my mind except for vengeance. I had to get him and your mom back. I didn't want to hurt you, but honestly, I really didn't care if you did happen to get hurt in the process. I laid in my bed every single night in that group home, and instead of sleeping, I thought out a perfect plan to get rid of Gavin and Mena, just like they got rid of me.

One day, I decided that it was time that I began executing my plan. I had remembered that your dad kept three gas cans in the garage, so this particular day, after being dropped off at school, which was only a couple of blocks from your house, I snuck away and hung out around your house until everyone had left for work and school. I remembered the garage passcode, which hadn't been changed, so I went in, grabbed one of the gas cans and went to a local gas station and filled it up with the money that I'd stolen from one of our social workers. I took the can to the woods near your house and covered it with branches and whatever else I could find. I did this every day for the next couple of days until I had three full cans of gas.

I had the advantage of knowing your family's schedule and daily routines since I'd lived with you all. One night, after I knew you and your family would be in a deep sleep, I snuck out of the group home, only taking with me my lucky lighter, which was the only thing I had left of my mother's. I was able to sneak into your garage, undetected, with the gas cans. I took them into the house and poured gasoline all over, both upstairs and downstairs. I was sure to pour a sufficient amount outside of your parent's bedroom door, which was shut. I remember looking down the hall at your bedroom. The door was cracked so I walked down the hall and peeked in at you. You looked so peaceful, and I knew that I was about to destroy your life forever in one way or another. Whether you survived or not, I knew that either way, the outcome would be satisfactory to me. The evil inside of me was overpowering, and it seemed like nothing could stop me.

I had forgotten one important detail. How would I ignite the gasoline without burning myself? My heart began racing, thinking about if someone woke up and found me inside the house. I quickly ran downstairs and found a piece of paper sitting on the kitchen table. I ran back upstairs with it, stood in front of your parent's door, and lit it with my lighter. I then threw it down. I immediately began to panic because I hadn't imagined the fire to ignite and grow so quickly. I didn't have time to do anything else except to collect the gas cans, run out the house, and close the garage. I threw the empty gas cans on the side of the house, and before I ran into the woods, I could see the flames glowing through the windows.

I stayed in the woods to make sure the job was complete. The fire department arrived pretty quickly, which made me angry at the time, but now I wish they would've arrived even sooner and been able to save your family. They didn't deserve what they went through one bit.

Zeke . . . I mean, Ezekiel and Faith, I'm so sorry that your family also became involved in my wickedness. I stuck around and saw your loved one, Ezra, enter Miracle's home to try to save her. I'm glad that he did, but I wish that he would've survived. Ezekiel, when I met you, I had true feeling for you, but after I found out who your dad was, it was hard for me to love you because I couldn't get past the guilt of being the cause of his death. The entire time we were together, when I saw you, I would see him. I was punished mentally every single day. I don't expect anyone to feel sorry for me, but I just wanted to let all of this out before I was gone so that all of those questions you may have had could be answered, and there could be true closure.

*So many innocent people were hurt because of my actions,
and I felt nothing. How could someone be that way? I may never
understand it, and I'm sure you all may not understand it,
however, I do want you to know that I'm sincerely sorry for all of
it, and whatever is coming to me, I deserve it. Thank you for caring
for me and loving me, and I just ask that you all don't hate me. I
may have caused pain to you all in life and in death, but you now
have the opportunity to continue to live and enjoy all of the
beautiful things that God has brought together.*

    Sincerely,

    Stormie"

When I finished reading, I was at a loss for words. I was in
complete shock, and I was sure Ezekiel and Miracle were also. I
closed the journal and sat there, staring at the wall while Miracle
and Ezekiel held each other, crying uncontrollable.

Stormie had been the cause of my husband, who was my best
friend, being taken from me prematurely. She had been the cause
of a thirteen year old boy losing his dad before he could learn all
of the things his dad had been prepared to teach him. She had
been the cause of a twelve year old girl tragically losing both of
her parents, leaving her to feel lost in the world without them,
and eventually turning to alcohol for comfort. One thirteen year
old girl caused so much pain, but I felt that the justice system had
failed her. No one except Stormie knew the extent of her pain,
but I could imagine that it was unbearable. That was still no
excuse for the things that she had done, which she humbly
admitted.

So often, we find it hard to forgive people when they've hurt
us so much, but sometimes we have to take that pain and ponder
on it, realizing the strength that it gave us, and the lessons that
we learned from it. I was always a firm believer in everything
happening for a reason, whether good or bad. Life isn't always
going to be great with beautiful things happening around us. It's
full of trials, tribulations, and tests. We are tested every day, and
from every test comes a testimony. This entire situation involving
Stormie went on for over twenty years and we had no idea.

Finding out the things that we did after she'd died was a test of how we would respond to that information. Life doesn't always seem to be fair. Most people would've probably wished that Stormie had still been alive so that they could've killed her themselves, but what would that have accomplished? Some people would've chosen to never forgive her, but forgiveness is for ourselves, not the people that we need to forgive. There were a multitude of reactions and responses that we could've had, but the necessary thing to do was to forgive Stormie, and that's what we did.

There was nothing that we could do to change a thing. What had happened, happened, and we got through it. In addition to getting through it, two families were brought together through what we had once looked at as a tragedy. It was God's will that Ezekiel and Miracle were brought together, and as crazy as it sounds, Stormie was the one that helped make that happen. She created a connection between them which I knew existed, but I would've never imagined that she was the missing link. Some events in our lives can seem to be the worst things that could possibly happen in our lives, but great things can come from those horrible things. It may not happen today, tomorrow, next week, next year, or even twenty years from now, but it will happen. Do you know why?

"And we know that all things work together for good to them that love God, to them who are the called according to his purpose."

Romans 8:28

The End

The MIRACLE

After

The STORM

Qiana Rae

Beautiflaw Books

www.ingramcontent.com/pod-product-compliance
Lightning Source LLC
Chambersburg PA
CBHW050903250626
47155CB00001B/86